THE KAZOLA CHRONICLES

TWO

MARKED BY TRUTH

KATHRYN MARIE

MARKED BY TRUTH

For information contact:

Kathryn Namenyi

55 Spencer St

PO Box 342

Lynn, MA 01905

authorkathrynmarie.com

Cover design by Saint Jupiter

Map Design by Vanessa Garland

Developmental Edits by Cassidy Clarke

Copy Edits and Proofread by Karen Sanders Editing

ISBN: 9781734832365

First Edition: October 2023

10 9 8 7 6 5 4 3 2 1

Author Note:

Thank you so much for picking up my book! Before you begin, I just wanted to make you aware of a few things. This book contains scenes and talk of PTSD, depression, anxiety, panic attacks, sexual assault/rape, suicide, grief, kidnapping, physical and mental torture, starvation, strained family relationships, grooming, spousal loss and mild language. This book will also contain spicy, on page sex scenes.

Dedication

To Ellen.
The incredible mother who always encouraged me to reach for my dreams. Thanks for supporting me and being my cheerleader when I needed it most.
Love you, Mama!

THE ISLE OF KAZULA
XOBLAR
ROTHERLII
BELDWAR
FOLANOCH
DALCHUS
TERLANTRIK
OCHRAT
CAELFALL
LUSPAN
RYSTIN
ORILON
CRELANTI
ILFRA
KILERTHE
ADRO
SEATHRA
EROSTE
ARKALEY
RAVAGH
VAPALLES
ACCRITON

<u>GLOSSARY</u>

<u>Amalgam Blade</u>-(uh-mal-gm blayd) The primary weapon of the Onyx Guard

<u>Blackthorn</u>-(blak-thorn) An illegal drug primarily used by Shrivikas

<u>Blood Consort</u>-(bluhd kan-sort) A person meant to assist a Shrivika or an Ibridowyn to properly feed and stay strong

<u>Faction</u>-(fak-shn) A military unit in the Onyx Guard

<u>Fuiliwood</u>-(fwee-lee-wood) The strongest tree in Kazola

<u>Futeacha</u>-(foo-teh-chaa) Old Kazalonian swear: means tainted blood

<u>Hierarchy</u>-(hai-ur-aar-kee) The Leadership team of an Onyx Guard Faction

<u>High Faction</u>-(hai Fak-shn) The ruling government of the Isle of Kazola

<u>Ibridowyn</u>-(ih-brih-doh-when) Genetically modified soldier created from either a Varg Anwyn or a Shrivika

<u>Iona Silver</u>-(ai-ow-nuh sil-vr) The purest silver in Kazola

Kazola-(ka-zoh-la) Means Peace-Bearer in the language of the God and Goddess

Keturi-(kah-tur-ee) The top four leaders of an Onyx Guard Faction

Lectracycle-(lee-tra sai-kl) Primary form of transportation for the Onyx Guard

Ogdala Dagger-(ahg-dah-la da-gr) The ceremonial dagger of the Onyx Guard

Onyx Guard-(aa-nuhks gaard) Special ops section of the military. made up exclusively of Ibridowyns

Shrivika-(shriv-ick-ah) Vampire. child of the God Firenielle

Tsio a Chisain-(si-o ah chee-sahn) Old Kazalonian for Protect the Peace

Varg Anwyn-(varg awn-win) Wolf shifter. child of the Goddess Lunestia

Wolfsbane-(wulfs-bayn) An illegal drug primarily used by Varg Anwyns

Faction outline

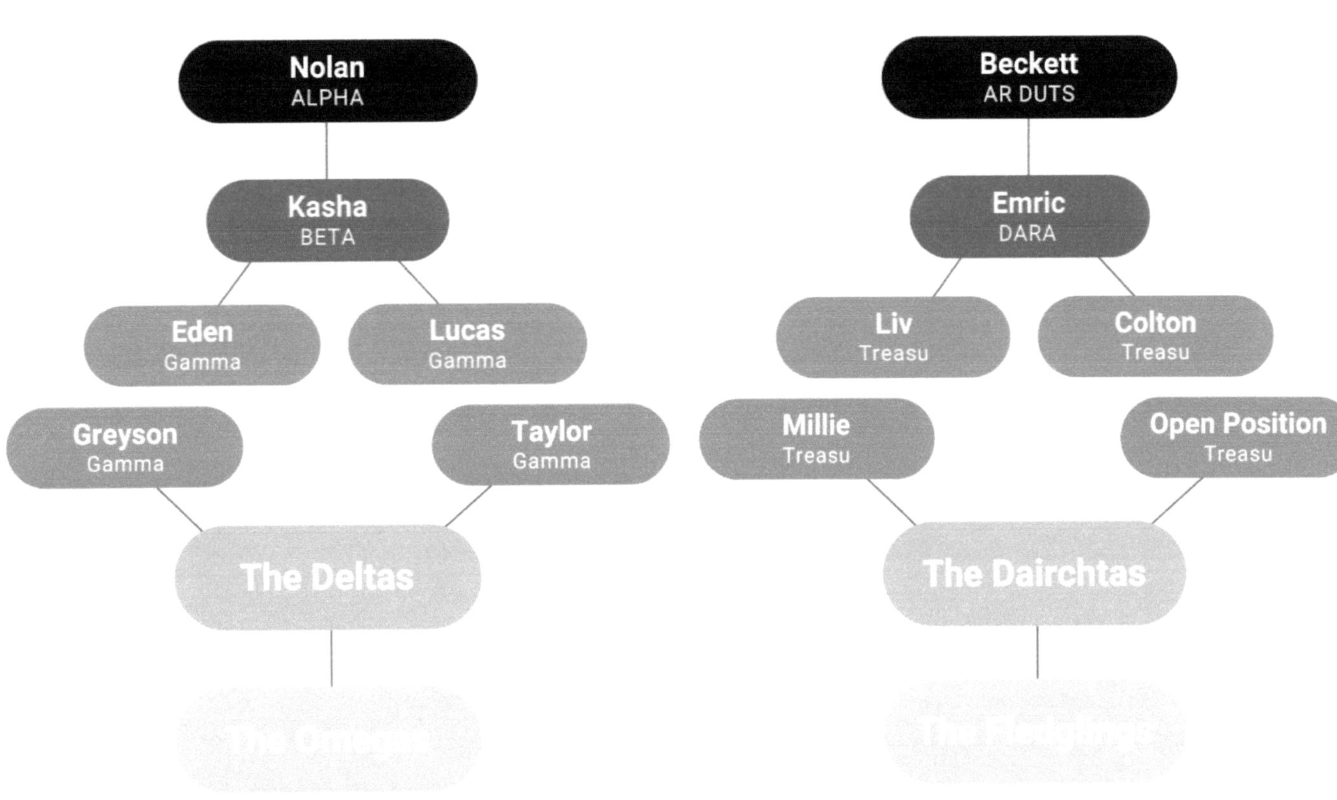

CHAPTER 1

The silence between us was deafening.

It took a lot to render our group completely quiet, but Vanessa's confessions had done just that. It had taken over an hour, but finally, she had told me most of the truth. At least, the truth about Elliot. She had conveniently left out her part in all his plans.

A revolution. A cult. A coup.

There were so many things you could call the militia Elliot had been slowly building over the past ten years under the guise of being a singular serial killer. He sent us on a wild chase for years, keeping our focus preoccupied while he created an army. An army we knew nothing about and could attack at any moment.

This was an utter disaster.

The entire Hierarchy sat around our large conference table, no one speaking a word, trying to comprehend exactly what we were up against. Some cradled their head in their hands, others stared off into space, hoping an answer would appear before them. I rocked back and forth, the dirt and grime from the warehouse Elliot had kidnapped me to only hours ago still clinging to my clothes and sweat-slicked body. So much had happened, and somehow, this… monster decided he wanted me to be a part of it.

But what was my part? That was the question I was already searching desperately to answer.

"Will someone please say something!" I finally said, unable to stand the silence any longer in fear of suffocating within it.

"I don't think I understood you." Eden was the first to come out of her daze, wrapping her sweater tighter around herself.

"Elliot isn't a serial killer." I rolled my eyes, not surprised I had to explain it once again. "Well, he isn't just that. He's been using it as a front to form an army against the High Faction. He preaches that they're corrupted and that he's the answer to all of the issues that plague our country."

"So, what? He wants to rule over Kazola?" Taylor asked. "Like a dictatorship?"

"He preaches it as more of a monarchy." I shook my head. "According to Vanessa, at least, so who knows if that's the case?"

"It's easy to prey on people's fears and promise them one thing to then change it when you gain power," Liv whispered, rubbing her hand across her lovely ebony face.

"How many followers does he have?" Greyson asked, the only one smart enough to have been taking notes this entire time, even though his face seemed a bit paler than usual.

"No idea." I shook my head. "She didn't know that."

"Did she know anything about his plans on when to attack?"

"She said he was playing the long game and that by the time we caught up to him, the government would already be lost." I fell back in my chair. "Of course, I still wasn't able to get out of her how long ago she left his little group, so for all we know, this information is very outdated."

"*Futeacha*," Nolan swore under his breath, my spine tingling at the first thing he had said the entire time.

"We need to get more information out of her," Lucas said, his fingers tracing patterns on the table. "More about his rhetoric and the tactics he's using to lure people into his group."

"I don't think she knows anything more." I shrugged, believing my words. She had seemed exhausted by the end of our talk.

"She must have been high up in his world if she's been on the run for a time," Lucas argues. "She must know something."

"We don't know that," Beckett said. "He probably kills anyone who tries to escape. It's how he has been able to keep this a secret for so long. No one gets out alive."

"Goddess above," I whispered. "Those are who all the murder victims are. People who tried to get out."

"Would answer why there was no victim pattern for us to track," Emric added, fiddling with his slim, wired-rimmed glasses.

My head began to ache, my eyes throbbing. For weeks, I had wanted answers to so many of these questions. Any ideas on why and how Elliot did what he did. But these… these answers were far more than I could ever have fathomed. This wasn't just a case, this was a fight none of us expected. The threat of civil war hung in the air, tinged with fear, anger, and pain. What would our future hold if he let his forces free? Even worse, what would our future be if he won?

What would my future be if he finally got a hold of me?

My stomach churned at the thought because he *had* gotten me. Stolen from the Blood Moon Tavern right in front of all of my Faction as we celebrated what we thought was a break in the case. He had me in his clutches and he could have disappeared with me easily. So, why did he let me go?

He said I was ready to learn the truth, but really, I felt wholly unprepared to discover what this man was willing to do to Kazola. What did he expect me to learn? Obviously something, as he had hinted at as much before he left me to be found.

"What does this have to do with you, though?" Nolan asked, his voice a few octaves deeper than usual, his jaw tensely set.

"She didn't know." I shook my head, heart dropping. "She said my part to play must have been conceived after she left."

"Convenient," he mumbled, his eyes expertly avoiding mine.

I swallowed a hard lump in my throat at that. Was he mad at me? That I had yet to give him an answer to his beautiful confession only a few hours previous.

I shook my head. That would have to wait until later.

"Whatever Kas's place in his messed-up plan, we need to report this." Beckett leaned forward, running his long fingers through his white-blond hair, tousling it into his eyes. "The High Faction needs to be notified tonight so they can send a mass report out to the rest of the Factions. Everyone needs to be on high alert."

My pulse rushed at the mere mention of our government. The High Faction oversaw all of Kazola, governing in equality across all three of the natural races: The Humans, the Shrivikas, and the Varg Anwyns. They kept us safe. They kept the peace.

Yet, I still distrusted them for everything they had done to me the past year. Was that why Elliot wanted me? He thought I was an easy target? How would he have even found out about my issues with them?

"Who needs to be there?" I asked, the words sticking to my mouth, but I forced them out.

"Beckett and I should." Nolan sat forward, finally unclenching his fists. "It needs to be a quick and concise report. The fewer people on the call, the better."

I nodded. "What will you tell them about my place in all of this?"

Silence fell once again, everyone avoiding my gaze.

"We can't ignore it." I shook my head. "Question is, should we tell them now or when we get more details about how I'm connected?"

"There's no reason to report something without concrete proof," Beckett said, staring at me with the kind gaze I had come accustomed to over the years. Forever a physician. "We'll tell them that Elliot's identity has been discovered due to you being taken and recovered and that Vanessa confessed to knowledge of a potential uprising that we need to prepare for. We will explain that we will continue investigating that and will report as things are discovered. No need to go deeper than that."

"All right." I sagged in my chair. It was the right move, but even still, the idea of them knowing I had been weakened and kidnapped bit at the inside of my chest. Would I ever be able to escape the stain of my past, or would I submit to its taint for the rest of my career as an Onyx Guard?

I supposed only time would tell.

CHAPTER 2

After taking a quick shower at Lucas and Taylor's house, I knew there was one more place I had to go before this night could end.

With everything that had happened, everything I learned, I still could not forget the beautiful words whispered to me during a dance. Words that set my heart aflame and gave me new hope for my future. I wasn't about to let them go. In the midst of all the chaos, I needed to find happiness anywhere I could. I had a feeling it would be in short supply in the coming weeks.

I walked across the way to Nolan's house, the soft glow of lights filtering through the curtained windows. He had come back here after his call to the High Faction with Beckett, probably trying to figure out the tangled mess of information we had all learned that night. But that wasn't why I was going. I walked up with purpose, not missing a beat as I knocked, my heart flipping the moment I heard him yell, "Come in."

I cautiously opened the door, peeking around it to find him

sitting in the living room. He was lounging on the soft gray couch, his legs propped on the table in front of him. His head was supported by the back of the couch, and a glass containing a generous serving of whiskey dangled from his hand.

"Hello," I said, closing the door and moving a few steps forward.

He sat up straight. "Hey. Are you okay?"

"Yeah, I, uh…" I shook my head, unsure how to answer that question. "Honestly, I'm probably still in shock."

"Is there anything I can do?" He leaned forward, placing his glass on the table in front of him.

"I wanted to, um… talk about what happened before I disappeared." My fingers twisted together behind my back, my stomach doing too many flips.

"I should probably apologize, huh?" He smirked up at me.

I froze. "For what?" Was he about to take back all the beautiful things he said to me earlier? He had said he wanted a romantic relationship, to discover what was growing between us. Did he regret it after what Elliot had done?

"Looks like I'll be sticking around longer than expected." He laughed, but it wasn't his normal chortle with a wicked gleam in his eyes. His lips strained against his smile, his whole body tense.

I sighed, walking towards him and sitting down on the couch. He angled to the left, so we faced each other. "We need you here. You don't need to apologize for that."

"I appreciate that." He nodded, his face solemn.

"But that wasn't what I was talking about." I took a deep breath, rubbing my sweaty palms along my thighs. "I think we need to talk about what you confessed to me tonight. You deserve an answer."

"Look, I know a lot happened tonight…" he started.

But I couldn't let him finish. "Yes, but that doesn't negate what you said to me."

"Do you want it to?" he whispered.

"What?" I sat up straighter, my skin prickling. "No! Unless you want to take them back…"

My stomach churned at the thought. *Please, for the love of the Goddess, don't let that be the truth.*

"Your dedication to the Guard is one of the many things I admire about you." He leaned his elbow on the back of the couch, cradling his head in his hand. "After what we discovered tonight, I wouldn't be upset if you thought this was too much of a distraction."

Words escaped me for a few seconds, confusion swirling in my heart and mind. He was right, this would be a distraction. This wasn't something casual or fun; we were already too far gone for that. If we were to start something, it would be to pursue a potential future. There was nothing else I could imagine with him. With that came the expectation that I would put him first. Not all the time, but sometimes. We would need to make what we had a priority. We would need to work for it.

Could I afford to do that when a rebellious man was determined to pull me into his clutches?

But a part of me just didn't seem to care. I thought back to before everything blew up, to when it was just him and me dancing in the Blood Moon Tavern, wrapped in each other's arms, forgetting about the world around us. I knew then what I was going to say. Even before he admitted it, I had been thinking about it. I wasn't ready to watch him walk away, so how could I do that now? Especially when I would need strength to make it through this next phase of the investigation. Nolan always seemed to be what I needed to discover exactly where my strength lay.

"You would be a distraction at times." I looked up at him. "But you want Elliot caught just as much as I do. We wouldn't let it get to a place where we would risk that. If we worked together."

His lips turned upward. "That is true."

"That hadn't crossed my mind when I came here," I admitted, not exactly sure why. A part of me wanted to admit it, I guess.

"Then what did?"

"Um, I just…" I shook my head, already regretting that odd decision of mine. "It's hard for me to say."

"Talk to me. Please." His face softened, eyes pleading with me.

He had been one of the few people I had recently felt comfortable opening up to, and he had never let me down. So, if this was to work, I had to tell the truth once again.

"I'm scared." I shook my head, and his hand reached out to grasp my knee. "I haven't wanted… romance since before everything with Logan. I don't know who I am in a relationship anymore."

"I haven't dated anyone since Cleo," he said, a whisper of past pain glinting in his gaze over his fiancée. "You aren't alone in your vulnerability. But that doesn't mean we shouldn't try."

My heart shuddered at his words, both the confession and the truth to his statement. I was concerned that I wouldn't be enough for him, or that I would be too much to handle. Who knew what would happen when I started to be romantic? It was a new phase for this reborn self of mine, and I already knew there was a lot to discover about who I was. In the end, though, what mattered was that I didn't let that fear stop me from pursuing happiness.

Nolan wasn't; he was moving forward.

We were both a bit bruised and shaken, struggling to imagine a future we never planned for. Yet, with each other, maybe we could find the life we deserved.

All that was needed was a leap of faith.

"You're right." I sat up straighter, my pulse settling. "We shouldn't stop ourselves from doing what feels right."

"You want this? Me?" He shifted forward, our legs touching.

I pulled in a shaking breath. "Yes. Do you still want me?"

He reached forward, cupping my cheek. "More than anything."

I couldn't help but smile, my hand reaching up to grasp his wrist, my heart pounding. He leaned forward, touching our foreheads together, and I wrapped myself in the spicy cinnamon citrus comfort that was Nolan. He gently rubbed circles on my cheek, his eyes staring into my own for a few peace-filled moments that settled something within me. Another fear moved past.

"Thank you," I whispered.

"For what?"

"For not giving up on me." I smiled at him. Instead of saying anything else, he closed the distance between us, his free hand moving to the back of my neck to pull my lips to his. He tantalized me, slowly teasing mine apart with the tip of his tongue, gently and thoroughly making me melt into his embrace. It was a promise sealed, a perfect way to begin this new journey together.

It was a kiss I would have happily drowned in for eternity.

CHAPTER 3

A pounding woke me the next morning, a groan escaping my lips at the furious banging. I sat upright, my muscles a bit sore and my mouth dried out from what I could assume was the after-effects of consuming Elliot's anesthetic. I had come home late the night before, and Lea was still up cleaning the house.

She had been struggling to sleep ever since she had been tangled in a hostage situation; one that my team and I ultimately intervened in. At first, she had been staying late at work, making up excuses that she was catching up from the time she missed when on leave post-attack. Then, when she couldn't use that as an excuse anymore, she took up completing as many projects as possible throughout the house. We had new curtains, she fixed the slightly shaking banister, and she was in the process of repainting the common area.

My guess was she hadn't slept long and was back to one of her many projects, the banging increasing in volume the longer time dragged on.

That was it. She couldn't avoid my concern any longer, no matter how many times she told me she was all right. This was far from it. I should know; I was familiar with trauma all too well.

I trudged out of bed, ripping my door open. "Adelaide, I'm gonna—"

"Kasha, what the—" Lea groaned, opening her door at the same time, her dark curly brown hair messily piled on top of her head in a bun.

We blinked at each other, sleep still dazing us as the pounding continued. Since it was no one in the house, it meant there was only one other place it could be emanating from.

The front door.

"Oh, whoever that is better be here for a good reason," I grumbled, grabbing one of my well-worn sweaters that I had slung over my piano bench and shoving it over my head before stomping down the stairs. "Or else they're dead to me!"

"They must have a death wish if they thought it was prudent to come here before you get coffee," Lea mumbled, her footsteps slow and heavy behind me.

I reached the door, flinging it open, ready to tell the person behind it off, but unfortunately, they beat me to it.

"You were kidnapped!?" Ollie, my older brother, screamed in my face as he pushed his way into my house.

I guess the High Faction sent out a report already.

"Good morning." I yawned, rubbing my eyes.

"I'm sorry, what did he just say?" Lea squealed, still standing a few steps up on the staircase.

I growled at Ollie, his eyes flashing golden, just as mine did.

His tall, lithe frame was filled with tension, his fingers flexing by his sides, claws starting to poke out of the tips of his nails. I rolled my eyes. He may have been the laidback, goofy one in our family, but he was still a Varg. Even he couldn't calm his wolf when something he loved was in danger. It was in our ingrained nature to protect—exactly what Lunestia created us for.

Most of the time, I loved it. However, this early in the morning and without caffeine, it was grating on my nerves a bit.

"I'm fine," I told them both, moving into the common room off to the left of the front door. "I was found within the hour. It was nothing."

"Kidnapping? Kidnapping?" Lea shook her head, hazel-green eyes wide. "Were you going to tell me about this?"

"Eventually." I gave her a softened look. "I already talked it to death last night with my team. I wasn't in the mood to talk about it more. Still not." I turned to Ollie, my lips pursed.

"Too bad," he said, crossing his arms. "You can't just brush this off. So, you're going to tell me what in the name of the Goddess is going on, or I'm barricading you in your bedroom until you do."

I stifled a groan. It may have seemed like an over-dramatic threat, however, it wouldn't have been the first time he had done that to me. The joys of being the youngest sister with two brothers ready to prank me at their leisure.

I took a deep, cleansing breath, reminding myself that, if I was in his shoes, I would have done the same thing. And, of course, I did want to tell him. He was my big brother, after all.

"Lea, could you give us a moment?" I sighed, knowing this wasn't a conversation a civilian should hear.

"Are you sure you're all right?" she whispered, taking a step forward, her hands shaking. "Promise?"

I smiled at her, pulling her into a hug. "I promise."

She relaxed in my embrace, giving me a tight squeeze before pulling away. "I'll go start some coffee." She stifled a yawn, turning towards the kitchen and disappearing.

"Come on." I tilted my head towards the stairs, and Ollie headed right up and into my bedroom.

When I closed the door, he pulled me into a hug, his arms warm and protective around me. "Moonlight, what is going on?"

My heart prickled; he rarely called me that nickname.

"I don't know everything quite yet." I sighed, pulling out of his embrace to sit down on the edge of my bed. He sat next to me. "All I do know is Elliot wants me for something to do with this revolution he's planning."

"He didn't tell you what?"

"He's too smart for that." I shook my head. "If he had told me anything, he wouldn't have let my team find me."

Ollie's face went white at my word choice. Elliot could have kept me in his clutches but chose to let me go. The why still evaded me, and it was a question I was determined to answer as soon as possible.

"Did he give you an indication of what he wants with you?" Ollie squeezed my hand in his. "Anything that you could read between the lines with?"

I looked down towards my lap, recalling every little thing he had said to me. Most of it had been boastful, his ego getting off on the manipulation he had so perfectly enacted on me and the entire

Faction. He relished in it, taking in every moment. However, at the end, just as he was about to leave, he said something…

"He called me something in Old Kazalonian last night." I looked up at Ollie, remembering when he had translated the phrase Elliot's cult used. "Do you know what *Rogthna* means?"

His face pinched inward. "No, I'm sorry. You'll have to talk to an actual linguist for that one."

My shoulders sagged. "I figured."

"I hate this, Kas." Ollie shook his head. "I knew it had to be something bad when Father called Caleb and me at the same time."

"He called you directly?" My skin crawled at the idea. Like me, Ollie barely spoke to the other half of our family.

Ollie nodded grimly. "Woke Caleb and me up from a dead sleep at two in the morning. I was rushing out my door before he even finished telling us all the details."

"How…um…" I couldn't finish the sentence, but I wanted to know.

"Father was his typical, all-business self." Ollie rolled his eyes. "Caleb… I couldn't get a read on him through the Comms connection, but he looked concerned. Stunned even."

I snorted at that. I shouldn't have been surprised that my oldest brother had been concerned for my well-being. It was what siblings typically did. But Caleb and I were no longer typical siblings anymore. He had made sure of that when his best friend attacked me and he chose friendship over his baby sister. I didn't trust him anymore. Not with my life or my heart.

I tried my best to pretend it didn't break my heart constantly. I tried my best to ignore the tattoo on my left bicep that held the weight of what our bond used to mean: Born by Blood. Bound by Loyalty. An oath lost in the midst of all the chaos.

I shook my head; Caleb was the last family member I should have been giving so much thought to when I had much more important things to think about.

"Don't tell Nana about this." I poked him in the arm. "We don't need her worrying about something we have no answers to yet."

"Well, technically, I can't tell anyone." He frowned, shaking his head. "All of these details have been deemed highly confidential. The High Faction doesn't want any of this getting out to the general public before we know how dangerous Elliot is. Mass panic across the country will not help us at all."

"Yeah, that makes sense." I wiped my hands across my face.

"What are you going to do?" Ollie asked, leaning forward to catch my gaze. His eyes were full of worry and concern, his head most likely filled with a dozen scenarios of what could potentially happen to me and Kazola.

I took a deep breath, the weight of what I was about to say settling on my shoulders. "If only I knew."

CHAPTER 4

It had been only a few days, and already I was tired from the investigation.

We had been doing everything we could to find a link between Elliot and this unknown uprising he was organizing. We looked over all past cases, trying to look at it from a new angle and see why each of these victims would try to join and how they found their way there. We sent Deltas and Dairchtas out into towns around Seathra undercover, trying to hear any news or discourse that may bring us an inkling of what was happening. We questioned the owner and employees of the Blood Moon to see if anyone suspected anything from their time working with Benji. Or, really, Elliot.

So far, nothing.

At least when we thought he was just a serial killer, we had a direction we could work towards. We had investigated killers before; we knew the steps to take to hunt him down. This, however, was new territory. Insurrection and war were not things we had direct experience in. We were soldiers. We had been trained as if it was imminent any day now, however, we never expected it to actually happen.

Even soldiers dread war.

But we were soldiers, and we would defend Kazola at any cost under the oaths we took entering the guard.

Tsio a Chisain. Protect the Peace.

I would until my dying breath if necessary. Still, it didn't make this whole investigation any easier. In fact, it made it even more stressful.

***

Nolan and I were alone in one of the workout rooms on the second floor of the training building. The room housed some weights, a workout bench, a hanging punching bag, and a small sparring mat. We had started by stretching with each other and doing a little light sparring before splitting off to do our own thing, the presence of each other all we needed.

I had split off to lift some weights, wanting to build back a bit of strength I was still rebuilding after losing a few months of training from when I was hospitalized. Although my abilities as a Varg Anwyn-born wolf and an Alchemist-made Ibridowyn gave me natural strength, I still enjoyed honing it and keeping it up to the par of the Beta I was. So, I spent the last hour working my chest and triceps, while Nolan punched out his frustrations on the bag.

However, by the increased impact and grunting coming from that side of the room, I thought it was having the opposite effect.

Unfortunately, the same could have been said about me. The longer I worked my muscles, the more I felt underprepared for what was brewing on the horizon for Kazola. It was not enough of a distraction to pull me away from the churning in my stomach and the constant questions rushing through my mind.

I needed to relax, and it was obvious Nolan did too. And I knew exactly what helped him relax.

Flirting.

I sat up from the bench, dramatically wiping my forehead with a sigh to get his attention. His gaze flicked over to me just in time to watch as I reached my fingers down to the hem of my tank top and pulled it over my head, leaving me in my training bandeau, the straps pressing tightly against my shoulders.

His guttural growl rang out from across the room. A coy smile spread on my lips as I watched his eyes shift from intoxicating forest green to their gorgeous wolf gold.

He smirked at me, eyes taunting as he did the same, removing the short-sleeved shirt to reveal his well-defined torso. The black tattoos that ran up his arms glistened under the harsh light from the sheen of sweat coating them. He was playing too, his delicious scent of cinnamon citrus mixing with the musky sweat. My wolf growled inside me, rumbling deep in my belly, begging me to rush him. But instead, I held control, raking my eyes slowly up and down his body as he did the same to me. We were in a silent battle of wills and seduction, and it looked like neither of us was willing to back down.

Good. That was exactly what I wanted. And obviously, so did he.

"Can you come spot me?" I asked, my gaze never leaving his as he abandoned the bag and crossed the room in as few steps as possible.

He stood at the head of the bench, looking down at me as I looked up at him. I gripped the two weights, one in each hand, resting them on the side of my chest before pushing upward, my pectoral muscles flexing under the pressure. Although he kept his hands held out in case he needed to spot me, I could see the concentration set on his face and the way his eyes would slide away from my hands for a second before returning. He was struggling to focus, his attention keener to travel up and down my flexing abs and chest.

Looked like I needed to kick it up a notch and test his attention.

I pretended to falter, the weights trembling slightly in my grasp as I pushed upward. His distracted gaze caused him to hesitate before reaching out to help, his fingers getting caught under mine. He grunted in pain, helping to shift the weights back properly in my hands before pulling away, shaking his fingers out.

"Aww, too weak to even spot me, Nol." I winked, pushing the weights up again, my pectoral muscles starting to burn. "What a shame. But I suppose I shouldn't be too surprised. I am stronger than you."

"I'd be careful there, Beta." He smirked, his glowing eyes staring down at me with wickedness. "Don't forget, I did beat you during our sparring match a few weeks ago."

I dropped the weights to the side, propping myself up on my forearms. "Because I threw the match."

"Are you saying you would have won if you hadn't?" He cocked his eyebrow at me.

"That's exactly what I'm saying." I bit my bottom lip, watching a multitude of thoughts cross his face.

He circled around, bending over and bracing his arms on the bench, our faces only inches apart. He stared at me for a few moments, my thoughts getting lost within his gaze. Before I could even breathe, he ripped me up from the bench, twirling me around and slamming me against the wall, his body pressed firmly against mine. "Is this what you hoped for? Huh?"

"Maybe." I giggled, leaning forward to try to capture his lips, but his hold on me made it difficult.

He leaned forward himself, the tip of his nose grazing up my jaw as he pulled in a deep breath. "Then why don't you just take what you want?"

"I'm not sure what you mean." I raised my eyebrow at him, another growl rumbling in his chest, my stomach clenching.

"Teasing me. Taunting me." His hands roamed downward, gripping my hips and pulling them against his. "Are you saying you don't want me to kiss you?"

"Are you saying *you* don't?"

He chuckled. "Not what I'm saying at all."

"Then do it," I challenged. Tension crackled between us, his tongue darting out to lick his lips. I watched every micro movement he made, hoping he would make good use of it.

There were so many other things he could have used that tongue for.

In an instant, we crashed together, lips moving in fierce possession, tongues darting out to taste and play. Seconds passed, my body savoring every moment of having someone near me again. For so long, I had been terrified that my body would fear everyone, forcing me to cower away from the idea of being intimate. But with Nolan, with his body so close and his lips so tantalizing, I couldn't stop myself from craving and desiring more.

My hands roamed, fingertips sliding down his back, tracing the corded muscles that rippled under my touch, a shudder running through him. His hands explored me in turn, slowly moving up my exposed, sweaty stomach so his thumb could gently push under the bottom of my bandeau and gently rub circles under my breasts. I moaned, silently begging that he would move farther upwards. Yet, he seemed completely content to continue his teasing of my sensitive flesh without giving me what I wanted. I growled, his lips smirking against mine.

"Something wrong?" He laughed against my skin, the tip of his tongue tracing the edges of my lips.

I growled again, but he soon distracted me, his lips tracing my jaw, tongue lapping along as he tasted every inch of me. He groaned against me as if savoring the most delectable wine he'd ever tasted. He was slow and methodical, making sure every little bit of my face belonged to him as he kissed, licked, and nipped his way downward. My body tensed as he reached my chin, his sharp teeth biting just a bit harder, releasing a moan from my lips.

I was lost to this man already.

I pressed farther against the wall, letting my body relax in his embrace to savor every part of him, desire-fueled heat pooling in my lower body, begging me for more. Once he had covered every inch of my jaw, he moved farther down, lips pressing firm kisses down my neck before stopping to give extra attention to the sensitive spot where my neck met my shoulders. And as his lips trailed over that area, his teeth gently grazing on my pulse point, there was only one thought that overtook me.

A sharp, forcefully possessive bite. A cruel, devious smile relishing my pain and fear.

Danger. Escape. Fight.

My body reacted before my mind could even catch up, shoving Nolan off me, his feet stumbling backward. I snarled, legs shaking, my breath heaving as if I had just been running for miles.

Protect. Fight. Get out.

It was all I could think, the adrenaline coursing through me, preparing me for a battle I had yet to understand.

"Kas?" Nolan stared at me with wide eyes. "What's wrong?"

"I—" I shook my head, trying to clear it of the tornado of panic that filled me up to the brim. "I don't know."

"What—" He took a step forward.

"Stop!" I raised my arms. "Stay away!"

"Sweetheart." His voice softened as he took a few steps back, giving me a bit more distance. "I'm not going to touch you again."

"Promise?" My words shook, my arms falling to my sides, clawing at the wall behind me.

"I promise," he said, sincerity fueling every syllable.

It was all I needed to let a bit of tension out of my shoulders, my body sliding down the wall to crouch on the floor. I tangled my fingers in my hair, trying to understand what just happened, but fog had already started to roll into my mind, attempting to hide the fact that I had just panicked over something. It didn't want me to know, it just wanted to protect me from it.

I knew this would happen.

Nolan crouched but kept his distance. "What can I do?"

"I don't know," I whispered, before screaming and slamming my fists on the ground. "For the love of the Goddess, I don't know!"

"Kasha, just—" Nolan was probably about to tell me to breathe, but he was interrupted, the door to our room swinging open, pulling our attention.

"Am I… uh… interrupting?" Taylor looked between us, his posture rigid.

"Yes!" we both barked, my fingertips going numb.

"I'm sorry, but it's urgent." He took a few steps in, looking at me with concern. "Mylo is at the gate. He's demanding to see Eden."

"What?" That was all I needed to snap out of my fog. "Stay here."

I pushed past the two men, rushing out the door with only one thought: Find out why Mylo had the worst timing in existence.

CHAPTER 5

I rushed out of the building, pulling a warm wool sweater over my head to protect me from the new winter chill. With each step I took, my gold eyes blazed brighter, my sharp instincts and drive propelling me forward.

This criminal was coming to us. He was at our gate, willingly, for the first time since I joined this Faction. My skin prickled, my body tense with every passing thought and terrible idea I had about his motivations. I could guess, but the only way to know the truth was to confront him. So, that was what I would do. As I passed through the circle of Hierarchy townhouses, I wasn't surprised to find Liv rushing out the door of her and Beckett's house, Lucas standing in the doorway watching her march away from him.

"You too?" Liv looked me up and down, the two of us keeping the same quickened pace up the drive towards the front and only entrance to the Compound.

I nodded. "What do you think he wants?"

"When it comes to Mylo? It can't be anything good."

My heart shuddered at the notion, knowing that Liv only spoke the truth. We both knew one thing for sure, though. He wouldn't get anywhere near Eden unless we deemed it necessary. When Mylo had first taken power as head of the most notorious crime family in Seathra, he had tried his best to manipulate his way back into her life. Eden had let her hurt heart hope it was for the right reasons, even though the rest of us could see the manipulation behind it; sweet talking his Onyx Guard sister to try to expand his business with us in his pocket.

He had no idea that Eden was more loyal to the family who loved her, not the ones who only loved what she could give them.

After that mistake, she knew she couldn't be trusted to face him alone. We promised to protect her. To keep Mylo at arm's length unless it was absolutely necessary. It was moments like these that I knew I was exactly where I belonged, with the people I was meant to walk life with.

It took a few minutes for us to make it to the gate, the checker-patterned iron rods closed tightly, the Delta and Dairchtas on guard standing rigid in front of it. There he was, arms crossed against his chest, dressed once again in an all-black suit, making his olive skin tone stand out and contrast with the blond hair that was perfectly styled. The scowl on his face, though, was unexpected. He tended to be the charm-your-enemies-with-a-smile kind of criminal.

He sneered as he saw Liv and me approach. "You are not who I asked for."

I stared at him through the gate, crossing my arms and giving him the most unamused look I had in my arsenal. "Too bad. We're who you get. What do you want?"

"To see my sister."

Liv hissed. "She's not here."

He leaned forward, wrapping his fingers around the gate tightly. "I don't believe you."

"She's a busy woman, protecting Kazola from people like you." I shrugged, taking a step towards him. "So, you get us, or we'll have the guards here physically drag you away from our Compound. Now. What. Do. You. Want?"

He huffed, his bright bottle-green eyes flashing gold for a moment. "I have information for you lot. Information that I suspect you'd be keen to have in your possession."

"Oh, yeah?" Liv said, her frown telling us she believed anything but that statement. "And why do you think we care about anything you have to share?"

"Because your Beta and Alpha came sniffing around about it a few weeks ago." He smiled, smug glee written all over his face.

My spine straightened, tingles zipping up it. "About the missing people? And the new drug traders?"

"Yes." Mylo nodded.

"What is it, then?"

"Ah, ah, ah." He shook his finger in front of us as if scolding a misbehaving child. My blood boiled at the demeaning gesture, but I swallowed my words. I needed to know what he had to say now, especially if it helped get Benji, no Elliot, captured. "You get answers only when my sister is there to hear them from my lips. Not a moment before."

I turned to Liv, closing the two of us off from Mylo. Still, as a Varg, he had sensitive hearing, and this wasn't the time to risk him hearing us talk. Luckily, a perk of becoming an Ibridowyn meant being able to mind speak between us.

"He's lying." Liv shook her head, tugging me back a step. *"He's using our investigation as a way to get back into her life."*

"Maybe." I peered back over at him, his face hard as stone, staring at us as we had our private conversation. We kept the Guards at the gate closed out as well, the ability flexible to allow only those you permitted to enter your mind.

"You believe him?" Liv's eyes widened.

"I don't know." My gut churned, trying to get my attention. Something about the way he stared at us, cool and in control, just as he had been taught as the leader of such a prestigious criminal family. Yet, I saw something different this time lurking just beyond it. The same look I saw when I last went to the Black Howl. He was scared and trying desperately to hide it. That was what made me wonder… could he be here to help?

"Why come here, then?" I asked. *"He could have sent her a note or something, luring her to his turf. Seems like the more logical thing to do if he's going to try to manipulate her. To come here, alone, where she is surrounded by people to protect her? Doesn't seem the best choice."*

"Appearing vulnerable in hopes she lowers her guard?" Liv suggested, my mind trying to go through the probability of that being a viable theory.

"If you two are done staring lovingly into each other's eyes." Mylo's voice cut through our conversation, of course, not knowing that we could communicate without talking. "I should also mention that this important information includes an update about Lila."

"Ugh." Liv groaned at the mention of Eden's other sibling. "You couldn't have led with that?"

He smirked. "I like to keep a little mystery with you ladies."

Liv and I side-eyed each other, but we didn't have to speak a word to know what we had to do next. "We will go to Eden," I said. "We will ask her if she wants to hear what you have to say, but it will be her choice and no one else's."

"Very well." He straightened himself, adjusting his knee-length wool jacket.

"Escort Mr. Brelachi to interrogation room three," I instructed two of the guards. "Don't let him out of your sight until we meet you there."

I gave him one last disdainful stare before turning on my heels. This was certainly going to be an eventful afternoon.

★★★

Eden had agreed to meet with him.

Yet, that didn't mean she was going alone. Liv and I were right behind her, Grayson by her side. She held steady, standing in front of the door to the room Mylo was being held in, her breath a bit staggered and her olive skin a bit paler than usual. She had taken the time to dress in full gear, her blood-red hair braided to pull her sharp features back.

She looked like she was ready for a battle in a war she had been fighting for far too long.

"Remember," I gripped her shoulder, "you can leave whenever you want. You control the room, no one else."

I knew the pain of facing those who had hurt you, who had tried to take away your power. I would never want someone I cared about to go through that ever again. She was in charge in that room.

"You can do this, Edy," Greyson said, his husky voice helping to loosen some of the tension in her shoulders.

"Let's see what my dear brother has to say." She straightened herself, eyes fueled with fire as she pushed her way inside, no hesitation in any of her movements. I smirked; that was the Eden I knew and loved. No one would bring her down.

We had made the plan on the way over, all of us knowing our places. Eden went right for the table in the center of the room, dropping into the only chair situated across from Mylo. Liv and I stayed on the perimeter, taking our places on either side of the table, leaning against the wall to give them space but see both of their faces during the conversation. Greyson stayed by the door, just in case Mylo tried anything and we needed to keep him secured.

My pulse thumped against my throat, my palms sweating. I wanted these answers, craved anything that would get me closer to figuring out why Elliot had set his sights on me. I had to put my trust in Eden now. She would be the one to see this part of the investigation through.

I knew my trust was well placed.

"What do you want?" Eden asked, leaning back in the chair, slightly slumped and arms crossed against her chest. Defensive yet casual, showing no emotion. She knew exactly how to rile him, how to control his responses without him even noticing the micro-manipulations that helped us get the answers we needed.

"Well, that is an incredibly rude way to welcome me to your place of work." Mylo placed his hand over his chest, feigning shock. "No welcoming hug? No quick catch-up to let your big brother know you've been well these past few months since we last saw each other?"

"That would make you think you're here as a welcomed guest and not the suspect that you are." She smirked at him. "So, I'll ask again… what do you want?"

"Many things, including my sister to look at me with a little less disgust in her eyes." He leaned forward. "Do you hate me that much?"

"You don't want me to answer that question," she said. "So, answer mine instead."

"Sister…"

"She asked you a question," Greyson mumbled from his perch by the door. "Are you really this much of an idiot?"

"Ah, if it isn't my baby sister's imposing shadow." He cocked his head, eyes gleaming as they stared at Greyson leaning against the wall. "Still enjoying following her everywhere?"

Greyson just shrugged, propping one foot against the wall behind him in a casual stance, as if he felt there was no threat in the room. Mylo's lip curled up at the subtle movements. Greyson just smirked, onyx-brown eyes glinting in amusement. I rolled my own. Greyson was a master at pissing people off without saying a damn word.

"Either speak, Mylo, or I'm leaving," Eden snapped, her words filled to the brim with venom. "I don't have the time for your silly games. Unlike you, I have important work to do."

"Very well, I see this is how it will be," he said slowly, his eyes steadily staring into Eden's. "Lila has returned."

My heart jumped, but I didn't move from my place as a silent watcher against the wall. What did this mean, though?

"When?" Eden asked, her face still coolly schooled, but I knew she was praising the Goddess for her sister's safe return from wherever she had disappeared to almost a month ago.

"About a week ago."

"Great job keeping me informed as you promised Kas you would." Eden raised an eyebrow, looking her brother up and down, the ire rolling off her in waves.

"A lot has happened since she got back." His face fell. "I was trying to figure out exactly what it was before letting you know. I wanted to make sure she was… okay."

"What's wrong with her?" Eden sat up a bit straighter, small fissures forming in her perfectly crafted armor.

"Physically, absolutely nothing. She is the picture of health."

"As much as she can be, you mean."

"No, I mean the picture of health," Mylo said. "That's why I was confused. She said she is clean from the 'bane, and everything about her proves that. She is outgoing, wakes up early, goes for a run, and hasn't been caught trying to steal or barter for a hit once. Trust me, my men have been following her every move since she returned."

"It's only been a week." Eden rolled her eyes. "She's done this before and fallen back into old habits."

"I would think the same thing if it wasn't for the… tales she keeps telling everyone."

"Stop being cryptic and explain." Eden ground through her teeth. My nerves sparked along my arms, Liv straightening from her post across from me.

"She says she was saved. That she discovered the truth." He shook his head in disbelief. "She talks about how she found the only detox center that can help others with a problem and that it's full of people who care more for Kazola than anyone on the High Faction. She claims that they are the real future we need."

My throat constricted, struggling to let air out. This was Elliot. I knew it was. I bit my tongue, clamping down without drawing blood. I promised Eden she would control the room and I meant it, but that didn't mean I wasn't tempted to lash my own questions out at him.

"So, why come and tell us?" Eden asked.

"Because she mentioned how her new drug dealer tried to kidnap her. These men saved her life and then brought her to the center to help her put her life back together." He looked over at me. "It just seemed a bit too perfect and was eerily familiar to the questions you asked me a few weeks ago."

I nodded, agreeing that it was all too perfect. To coincidental. Too calculated.

"This has Elliot written all over it," I said to all three of them, none of them giving away the fact that we were talking. *"We need to investigate this further."*

"I don't know how much more we'll get out of him for free," Eden

said, her eyes still staring ahead at her brother as if processing all the information he had just given. *"We should go see Lila ourselves."*

Greyson's eyes darted to her. *"Are you sure?"*

"Yes," Eden said. *"This is bigger than my family drama, and if Lila has a connection to the man threatening Kasha, then we need to get every detail about it."*

"Kas and I will go with you," Liv volunteered.

"Wouldn't have it any other way," she said, and I could almost hear the smirk in her words, even though it never graced her lips. *"Time to end this."*

"Thank you for letting me know." Eden stood up slowly, staring down at Mylo. "Some guards will be by shortly to escort you off the premises."

"It was good to see you, sister," he said, a smile stroking the edge of his lips.

"I can't say the same." She turned around and walked out the door Greyson held open for her before following right behind. Liv and I slowly trailed, Liv going through first, leaving me alone with Mylo. My hand clutched the door, but I hesitated, my chest squeezing.

"Thank you." I peeked over my shoulder at him.

"I didn't do it for you or your investigation." He looked right past me, eyes still trailing after Eden's disappearing figure.

CHAPTER 6

I was spending too much time in this dreadful bar already.

Finding myself back at the Black Howl within a month wasn't a habit I wanted to keep up. We parked our bikes off to the side, Liv and I quickly dismounting and heading for the door before we realized that Eden was still astride her own lectracycle.

I took a few steps towards her. "Are you sure?"

She pulled in a deep breath, a few strands of blood-red hair plastered to her forehead from the drizzling mist falling around us.

"I want answers." She swung her leg over, standing upright. "I just hope it isn't too crowded in there."

Before he was escorted out, Mylo had mentioned to us that Lila had taken up bartending, noticing she liked chatting with the patrons. It seemed to bother Mylo, probably because she was discussing the detox program that saved her life to potential dealers and buyers. Still, he said he had let her keep working, so we didn't question it.

We pushed inside, the dark, moody interior giving us a chilled welcome. Luckily, Eden got her wish; only one table was occupied by a group of men that looked to be a part of the Brelachi Pack. I made note of their scents and faces, making sure to keep an eye on them as we completed what we needed. I peeked over, noticing Liv doing the same, but Eden's gaze was somewhere else entirely. On the tall, lithe woman standing behind the long, black bar, polishing glassware.

Lila.

Although Eden dyed her hair and covered most of her arms and clavicle with tattoos, when I took the time to look, I couldn't deny the resemblance between the three siblings. With their bottle green eyes, angular faces, and olive skin tone, they were blood-related.

Lila had always been different, her addiction to wolfsbane changing her over the years. Yet, whatever transformation she had claimed to go through, her physical appearance certainly reflected it. Her bright blonde hair was shiny and long, much different from the brittle, thinning from before. Her skin was no longer sallow but full of color, and her eyes no longer held a deep rim of purple as if she never slept. She looked healthy, her laugh echoing off the wall as she bantered with the other bartender.

Lila halted, pulling in a deep breath before turning to the door, her eyes lighting up. "Eden!"

She rushed over, and without warning, pulled Eden into a hug. Everyone in the room stiffened, my throat closing as I watched Eden's stunned face try to process exactly what was happening. Lila wasn't just hugging her sister, she was hugging a Gamma in the Onyx Guard; an enemy no matter what blood ran through Eden's veins. Yet Lila didn't even seem to notice her pack's reaction, pulling away to grab Eden's hand and yank her towards the bar.

"Took you long enough to come and visit." Lila laughed, pushing Eden down into one of the high stools lining the bar. Liv and I exchanged wary glances before moving forward, sitting on either side of Eden.

"You were expecting me?"

"Of course, silly." Lila rolled her eyes, dropping three glasses of what smelled like very expensive whiskey in front of us. My stomach churned at the sight, my fingers instinctively pushing it away. Eden and Liv didn't reach for theirs either. "I was expecting all of you."

My heart thudded in my chest. Lila was different, and not just because of the drugs that were clearly out of her system. Even when she had kept sober for a time, she was quiet and reserved. She never seemed to fit in with the crowd, staying on the outskirts, even with her older brother at the head of the family. I had observed her a few times when investigations had pulled me there, and along with stories Eden had told me about their childhood, something seemed… wrong.

"Did Mylo tell you we were coming?" Eden asked, her fingers tapping on the polished wood.

"No." Lila smirked, her gaze flicking to me before returning to her sister. "So, how have you been, Little Sprite? The Guard treating you all right?"

Eden's jaw quivered at her childhood nickname. She had always loved to dance, like a wood sprite from fairytales. She hated being called that. Too many painful memories attached.

"Wonderfully, as always." Eden leaned forward. "Where were you, Lila? You had everyone worried, including me."

"I know, I'm sorry." She patted Eden's hand, pink kissing her cheeks. "I would have told all of you, but it was a whirlwind, and they said it was for my own protection. They took care of me, though, and it was exactly what I needed. Look how healthy I am now!"

She twirled around in front of us, the flurry of her knee-length sage skirt hitting the edges of the cabinets behind her.

"This is wrong. No one should bounce back from addiction in less than six weeks," Liv said, keeping her eyes trained on Lila.

"Where did they take you for your recovery?" Eden asked.

"Well, I can't tell you that." Lila sighed. "They said you wouldn't understand what they were doing quite yet and I needed to protect them. Family protects each other."

"Family?" Liv asked, her brows furrowed.

"They took care of me better than anyone in our actual family ever has," she said pointedly, ignoring the glares that were now directed at her. "You should understand that better than anyone, Little Sprite."

Eden's claws began to poke at the edges of her fingernails, the tips scratching along the bar top. I leaned over, squeezing her knee until the tension released from her body.

"If they are like your new family then why did you come back?" I asked, my stomach churning.

"Because Elliot needed me here," she said matter-of-factly, as if it was something we should have assumed all along.

My cheek twitched. "For what?"

"To keep an eye on things around Seathra and deliver a message." She bent down, rummaging under the bar before reemerging, a brown-wrapped parcel clutched in her hands. "He said it was imperative that you get this."

She pushed it towards me, the weight of Eden and Liv's stares branding against my side. I didn't touch it, just stared at it for a moment before looking back up at Lila. "So, you met him, then?"

"Just once, right before I was sent back to deliver it." She shrugged. "But I knew about him all along. He was the one who developed the program I went through. Everyone talked about him."

"What else does he want from me?" I couldn't stop the words from leaving my lips, even though I knew the probability of Lila knowing anything was fairly low. I needed to know. I needed the answers to why this psychopath had set his sights on me.

He needed me for something, and I would find out what it was.

"All I was told was to give this to you when you came to visit me." She pushed it closer. "He said to tell you your first answer is inside, so don't waste any time before opening it. And that is all I know."

I finally took it, pulling it into my grasp, the weight heavier than I expected. "We should get back. They'll be expecting us."

"Don't be strangers." Lila smiled. "I hope you visit again soon, Little Sprite."

"Yeah." Eden gave her a weary smile. "I'll try my best."

The three of us turned around, ignoring everyone else in the room who had obviously witnessed the entire encounter. We didn't care. The last thing they cared about was this package. All they wanted was for us to get out. I clutched it against my chest, my body numb as I prayed to the Goddess that the drive back to Compound wouldn't feel like an eternity.

CHAPTER 7

All of us stared at the package sitting in the center of the table as if we were waiting for it to sing to us.

"Can I please just open it?" I huffed, sick of waiting for someone to say anything.

"It could be dangerous." Nolan stared at me from across the table.

"With what? A bomb?"

"Potentially," Emric said, crossing his arms tightly against his chest. "I wouldn't put it past him."

"He has no motive to blow me up." I shook my head, leaning my hands on the conference table. "Especially since he had every opportunity to when he captured me the other day."

"It's not like a bomb could even kill us." Eden smirked, giving me a wink as support. "Lila said it was important, and we all know Elliot isn't one to do something randomly. This is a message, and the longer we wait to open it, the longer he has to keep walking the country."

Those who hadn't been at the Black Howl looked between each other with wary gazes, probably talking without the three of us involved since we were adamant this needed to be open. After the chilling interaction with Lila, we all wanted to know what was wrapped so neatly inside the plain package.

"Fine," Nolan huffed, walking around the table to stand next to me. "Just be careful."

"It's a package, Nol." I pulled it closer to me. "I'm not riding off into battle."

"Yet," he mumbled, but I left it alone.

My fingers slipped under the tightly taped edges, ripping into the rough brown packaging to reveal a plain white box. *How unoriginal.* I lifted the lid off, my body lurching at what looked like an oversized Comms unit in the box. Our units were palm-sized, easily slipped into a pocket so we could carry them anywhere. This one looked like four units had been fused together, the sleek, thin screen almost weightless as I held it in my hands.

"How do I—" I wondered how to turn it on, finding a button at the top and pushing it in hopes it was charged.

The moment I did, a face I had hoped to only ever see in a jail cell popped onto the screen.

My breath hitched at the sight of him. Gone was the flirtatious, easy-going bartender I had come to know over the past year and a half. In place of the tight cotton shirts and black slacks was a three-piece suit, perfectly tailored to his form, the textured mist gray of it contrasting well with the black of his button-up shirt and tie underneath. His hair was slicked back from his face, perfectly quaffed to match the clean shave of his face. He looked like a leader, a professional who should be sitting on the board of a wealthy business. Or on the High Faction.

And according to Vanessa, that was exactly what he hoped to do.

The entire team crowded around me, Nolan and Liv sitting on either side of me while the rest stood in a squished circle, cutting off most of the air. But I didn't care. I just stared at the giant Comms unit, waiting for something to happen.

"Hello, my beautiful *Rogthna*." Elliot's suave, crisp voice rang from the device.

"What do you want?" I asked, leaning forward to get closer as if I could reach through the screen, pull him through it, and punch him for drugging and kidnapping me before throwing him in a jail cell.

"It has already been too long since we last saw each other, but I know this time apart is what you need." He continued as if my question didn't matter.

"I don't think he can hear you," Beckett said, almost fascinated by it. "It's like it's… pre-documented onto the device."

"Shh," I chided, not wanting to miss a word seeing as I had no idea if I could stop or start the message.

"I'm sure by this point, Miss Vanessa and sweet Lila have told you a bit about what I plan to do to help Kazola be the best it can be." He smirked, leaning forward to rest his hand on the desk in front of him. Besides that, everything was plain. The walls, the chair he sat in. He wanted my focus solely on him. No distractions. "Just know that what I'm doing, many believe in. Many have seen the corruption of this country, of the way our esteemed government chooses to run us into the ground with each choice they make."

A chill ran up my spine. How many followers did he have?

"I think the best way for you to get an understanding of the revolution I want you to join is by visiting the next Seathra meeting I have scheduled for the end of the month," he said. "These meetings are for people who are interested in joining our cause. They can learn more about what hidden secrets the High Faction has been keeping from them, how I plan to change all of that for the better, and decide what kind of life they want to lead. It is the perfect place for you to learn more. Here are the coordinates and dates for you." A line flashed at the bottom of the screen, Liv already scrambling to get a pad and stilo to write down the details. The meeting was three weeks away.

"I hope you find all the answers you need there, *Rogthna*." His gaze raked up and down as if I was standing in front of him. "You are the future. Goddess blessed just as I am God blessed. Kazola needs us. Until next time, *Chu Fui na Deithe*."

And then the screen cut to black.

I angled my head towards Liv. "Did you get it all?"

"Yes." She let out a sigh of relief, sliding the paper to me.

"That's a small industrial space about forty-five minutes away," Lucas said. "I've been out there a few times for random theft cases."

"Does he actually expect me to go?" I leaned forward, perplexed by the whole encounter, if it could even be called that.

"He just gave up vital information about an illegal meeting against the High Faction." Beckett moved away, the rest of the group following suit to sit around the table. "Giving us a place where literal treasonous people will be meeting. How is that smart?"

"It's Elliot. There is a reason for this move." Nolan's eyes raked over the case board that still hung proudly on the far wall. "He has thought of every possibility and still sees it as a good option."

"Best option, I go, agree, and follow to his side." I roll my eyes at that. "But he isn't an idiot. He probably knows it will take a lot more than that to convince me."

"It sounds like he hopes this will be the first step. The one that creates doubt in your mind," Taylor said.

"Yeah, maybe." I shook my head. "Worst case, I use this information to put together a raid and arrest everyone there."

"Maybe that's what he wants too," Emric said, his brow creased, glasses slowly slipping down the bridge of his nose.

"What do you mean?" Nolan asked.

"He uses us to instill even more fear into these people. Think about it, if they are at these meetings at all, something is causing them to wonder if there is a better way than the High Faction. If we raided and began arresting, it could make us look like the bad guys they're making us out to be."

"That sounds like a tactic he would use." I leaned back in my chair.

I was the last person to say the High Faction was perfect. On the contrary, there were many things about them that needed to be reformed and changed. But this underhanded coup that Elliot wanted? This was not the way to go about it. Silent attacks were for cowards, for those who knew their plans were just as nefarious, if not worse than the current powers. My stomach clenched, knowing that his way was not the best, but with how much the High Faction was screwing up recently, I couldn't say I was surprised that people were listening to him.

He said I was Goddess blessed like him, but what did that mean? Did he believe that what he was doing was in service to our Deities? That the two of us had some kind of destiny meant to save the people of this Isle?

I had never heard of such a prophecy in Kazola's teachings, but to be fair, I hadn't studied past the storybook my parents used to read me growing up. I knew there was much more to our history than that. Maybe that was where the truth of his motives lay…

"So what?" Grayson said. "We just ignore this?"

"We can't go on a raid. We risk him using that action for his own benefit." I shook my head, making a mental note to go back to my lore theory later. There were more critical topics to discuss. "But we can still use this to our advantage."

"How so?"

"We can go undercover," I said. "We know the location. We can go and see what exactly he's trying to do and how many people are actually considering this."

"That's risky," Liv argued. "He's trying to get all types of people to join his cause, which means there are probably some criminals in there as well. If anyone recognizes us, we're done."

"What if we don't go to the one in Seathra?" Emric said, a smirk playing on his lips.

"What?" I asked, intrigued.

"They probably have these meetings set up all over Kazola to try and recruit people. We could go to one in a different territory.

One where we have a smaller probability of being recognized."

"A territory swap." I smiled, my heart racing at the prospect. "I love it."

"Honestly, it's something to consider getting every Faction in on," Lucas said.

"Even better," Nolan agreed, his face scrunching together. I knew he was making a mental list or notes of his own. I forced myself not to smile at how cute it was to me.

"We'll need to get the High Faction's approval for this," Beckett said. "I'm more than happy to go, but as per requirement, a Keturi along with one of their seconds will have to be present to make the case. However, I think with this, we need to have a member from the clan and the pack present. This isn't a small ask."

A silent question hung in the air, all eyes skirting to me, waiting for my reaction. I knew all of this, but it didn't stop my chest from tightening and my palms from sweating.

"I can go." Nolan leaned over, his gaze catching mine, filled with heated protection I knew he would unleash in a hurricane of wrath if I asked him to.

"No, I should be the one." I reached over to squeeze his hand in mine as a thank you for his kindness. "He's calling me out, no one else. The Faction should hear this plan from me."

Silence fell, but everyone knew I would not let them fight me on this. I needed to go, to stand in front of the High Faction and show them that not only was I still a capable soldier, but their actions had not stopped me from doing what was right. I needed this, not just for the case, but for myself.

Looked like I was going to visit my dear father.

CHAPTER 8

Beckett agreed to be the one to call the High Faction and set up a time for us to have an emergency audience with them. We would be leaving in two days for Crelanti.

There would be four of us going. Liv with Beckett as his second, and Eden taking the place as my Gamma second for the trip. In typical fashion, I would have taken Lucas or Taylor with me, but Eden had made an important argument as to why she should be the one.

"My family was involved," she had said during the planning for the presentation. "It was my sister who passed along the message and who has been within the inner circle of these people. If they have questions, I want to be the one to answer them directly."

How could I have argued with that? Taylor and Lucas were happy to step aside.

I had a lot to do between now and then, preparing to be away for an undisclosed amount of time depending on how the meeting went. But as I sat alone in my office, thinking over the past few days, I realized something that I had yet to give thought to. The panic attack with Nolan.

I swiveled my chair back and forth, leaning back to stare at the ceiling. He had been wonderful to not push me about it, probably just as engrossed in the Elliot case as I was. Still, my stomach knotted as I thought about it, remembering the utter fear that had shot through me at such a normal, intimate touch.

It was typical for us wolves to be tempted to bite our potential lovers with a Mark. I had never allowed myself to be Marked with any of my few past partners, but we had been tempted. They had done similar things as Nolan and never had I been scared. Even though I wished to ignore it, I knew why this was different. Technically, I had been Marked, wholly against my will by a man who had betrayed me.

Damn Logan to the depths for ruining this for me too.

Logically, I knew that Nolan was a tease and a flirt, but he would never hurt me or force me to do things I wasn't ready for. Looking back on it, I even knew he was nowhere near close to biting me. But in the moment, my logic disappeared, and all I wanted to do was fight, to get away from what my mind now perceived as dangerous.

I didn't want to lose this. I knew there was a high chance that sex would be different for me now. That things would change because of the rape. But to be scared of a Marking, something that I had wanted to do but was saving for the right person...

When I was Marked, I wanted it to be from someone I trusted implicitly, who I could see being my mate one day. It was cheesy and my friends picked fun at me for it, but it was something my mother had done. She always talked about how sharing that moment with Father for the first time was special, and it was easy for me to know that I wanted that same special moment.

Now, I may not ever have it, because of the actions of another.

"Ugh!" I grunted, kicking my desk in frustration. I needed answers; an understanding of what I could do to help heal this part of me.

But how?

I perked up in my seat, realizing that maybe there was a way to find an answer, even though a small voice in the back of my mind told me it was a bad idea.

I got up and rushed from my office, walking down the stairs until I made it to the lowest level—the cells. I don't know why I wanted to see or talk to her. I shouldn't have felt even a sense of right about it, but I couldn't stop. I wanted to know the truth about what was going on in my head. Although she was hiding things, although she betrayed me, she had helped me work things out in the past. It was a fact, and now, when I needed to figure out how to move forward, she seemed to be the only one I wanted to talk to.

I nodded to the guards on duty, grabbing the keys from them and wandering into the row of cells. She still lived here, in this place where we could keep an eye on her. Where we knew she couldn't divulge any details about me anymore.

I finally made it to her cell, leaning against the bars. A tray of food sat off to the side, the guards yet to pick it up. At least she was eating, the food mostly gone and the cup of blood next to it empty. The last thing we needed was a starved Shrivika throwing herself against the bars in blood starvation because she was too stubborn to eat.

"Hello, Kasha," she said, looking up from the book someone must have brought her. Her eyes were full of the same calm curiosity she always seemed to have in our old sessions. "Come for more questioning?"

I kept my features schooled, dangling my arms through the bars in a casual stance. "I came to talk to you."

"About anything in particular?"

"Actually, I need some professional knowledge." I cocked my head to the side. "If that's something you're still passionate about. Maybe your life as a psycho-physician was just a ploy."

"You said so yourself in our first interrogation." She closed her book, dropping her feet to the floor. "I've always wanted to help people. This situation was something no one could have predicted."

"You could have stopped it," I spat.

She sighed, dropping her head for a moment. "You don't understand all the facts."

"Because you won't tell us."

"I thought you said you wanted professional advice." Her eyes heated a bright red. "Is that true, or just a lie to try and get me to open up?"

"Fine," I gritted through my teeth, a pulse forming behind my eyes after yet again having this headache-inducing conversation. "In your history, what have you told past victims of sexual assault when they are struggling to… engage in sexual acts again."

Vanessa's shoulders loosened, her face softening. "I guess it would depend on what specifically they were struggling to try."

"Varg Anwyn Marking."

"I see." She nodded, standing up to pace a few steps closer. I didn't move, although my body begged to keep a distance. I took a deep breath, reminding myself that she was safely locked in the cell and couldn't get to me from there. "Well, first, I would let the patient know that they need to accept that this issue isn't something wrong with them. For victims of sexual assault, it is completely normal to have triggers with future sexual partners, especially the first when you are unaware of them yourself. You can't predict these things, no matter how hard you try sometimes."

Vanessa and I had never talked much about that night, never having time before we realized she was involved with Elliot. However, I had given her access to past records with my old physician, so she was aware of the attack and what had transpired since then.

"All right." My cheeks burned at the conversation, my stomach twisting. It was easy to blame myself, to think I was defective in some way, but the logical part of me knew she was right. I wasn't broken. It was just a new part of myself I needed to adapt to or readjust.

"What is important is that you are willing to get to the root of the problem, understand it, and then decide from there how to make it work for you."

I had to force myself not to outwardly groan at that, although I probably shouldn't have been surprised by the advice. "I'm sick of having to do all of the work after someone attacked *me*."

"It isn't fair, far from it, but it is the reality of what mental shifts happen after trauma," she said. "I would also suggest opening up to your partner about this. That is if there is a new partner to talk with."

"There is," I whispered. I peeked up, seeing a warm smile spreading on Vanessa's lips.

"Do you trust your new partner?" Vanessa asked, giving up the charade that we were talking about some hypothetical person.

"Yes," I said without hesitation. "More than I have any of my past partners."

"This isn't something that you can explore alone, which means ultimately, he will be involved with this part of your healing." She stood only a few feet away from me now, her face clearly visible in the dim lighting. "In the end, it will be up to you to work on the re-framing of your mental pathways. But exploring this, especially something so close to what your trauma was, you will want a partner who will be there to support you. To help you with whatever you need during this exploration journey and who will listen to what you need in both the moment and afterward."

I was terrified to talk to Nolan about this, my heart pounding in my ears. It was embarrassing and shameful for me to admit that what was supposed to be enjoyable could now be potentially ruined by my body's response betraying me.

But I knew she was right. I needed to find my way out of this, and the only way to do that was through. I needed to discover my triggers and then find a safe way to explore them. Luckily, I couldn't think of a better person to explore them with than Nolan. He had been there for me in past moments when I needed help. He had always been willing, patient, and kind. He would be the same way with this, especially when our combined future was involved.

No matter how much embarrassment heated my cheeks at just the idea of starting that conversation.

"Thank you." I nodded to Vanessa, taking a few steps back.

"You're welcome," she whispered. "I'm always here to talk when you need me."

I halted. "Unless it's about the truth?"

"You have been doing so good facing your trauma head-on, Kasha." She looked down. "I can't say the same for myself. I'm not ready to talk. I told you what Elliot is doing, and I will answer any technical questions about that. I will help you in any way I can, give you any information you want, as long as it involves Elliot and his people and what they're planning. But my story? That is something I have been running from for a long time. I need to heal myself before I can open up."

I didn't have a response to that, my mind and heart stunned. No matter how much I wanted to learn how she was connected to Elliot, convinced it could help our investigation, I understood her words. I sympathized with them. I knew she spoke the truth.

So instead, I just walked away.

CHAPTER 9

I t was my last night before I was to leave for the Capital.

After a flurry of two days preparing the presentation of our proposal along with packing and tying up any loose ends, it was now just time to wait for morning to come so I could hop on my cycle and drive off to Crelanti, the Capital Territory where the High Council sat in session.

Somehow, sensing that I would be anxious the night before, Nolan had invited me over to his house for the evening, wanting to cook me dinner before we were separated the following morning. My heart ached at the thought. We had only just started our romantic entanglement with each other, something that was wonderful to explore in between all the stress.

I sat at the counter, watching him move about the kitchen like a trained chef.

"How did you learn all of this?"

"Papa taught me." He smiled, rubbing the chicken down with some herbed butter concoction he had created.

"That's the one that was in the Guard, right?"

"Yeah, Leo." His face lit up at my remembering. "And my dad, Wyatt, is the furniture designer. Anyways, Papa used to use it as a bonding thing for the two of us. It just so happened I enjoyed it. Became stress relief for me. Like piano is for you."

"That's cute."

"Oh, I know." He winked at me. "I'm always cute."

"Cocky!" I leaned over, flicking leftover herbs that sat on his cutting board, the flakes of green flying across his apron.

"Rude!" He wiped himself off, shaking his head with laughter, my own joining in.

Moments like these were always precious, but I came into the evening knowing I needed to talk to him about something important. After thinking over Vanessa's advice from the day before, I knew I had to talk to Nolan before I left, or my anxiety might gnaw at me the entire time I was at the Capital. And I couldn't risk distraction.

So, with one final, deep breath, I looked at Nolan, his laughter stopping at what I could only assume was a concerning expression on my face. "What's wrong?"

"I wanted to talk to you about something." I rocked back and forth, my stomach churning at the thought of talking about this. I knew it was the right thing to do. I had come to learn that ignoring issues would never bring a solution. No matter how uncomfortable, you had to face it and work through it to find yourself in a place of contentment.

"What is it?" he asked, taking a sip of the ale he had poured himself.

"I wanted to talk about what happened in the training room before we were rudely interrupted."

He pulled a deep breath. "All right."

He looked at me, attention deep, waiting. Now or never. "First off, I wanted to say that I hope you know that I loved everything that happened. I don't regret it. I'd hate it if you believed that when it is absolutely untrue."

"That does make me feel a little better," he said, giving me a warm smile. "I never want you to regret anything we do together, sexual or otherwise."

"I appreciate that, I do. However, when you were touching me," I took in a shaky breath, sweat starting to form along my hairline, "something in me was sort of… set off when you got to a certain spot."

"You seemed to get scared when I was near your neck." His gaze traveled to my exposed throat, lingering on the sensitive spot that he had grazed his lips across.

"You got so close to where… he had taken from me." I shook my head, not exactly sure how to explain it. "Something about it, even though I knew you wouldn't hurt me, made me believe that you would. Made me want to fight my way out. I think Marking scares me," I admitted, my heart aching at the idea. "I think it's something that will take me time to accept for myself."

"That's understandable, sweetheart," he said, pulling a few vegetables from a bowl to chop. "I'm not mad at you for any of this, I hope you realize that. I would never be angry at you for something that was obviously a surprise for you and not completely in your control."

"Thank you." I smiled, watching as he went back to chopping. His words settled my heart a bit, but I still had a question nagging at my mind. "Did you want to Mark me?"

"The truth?"

"Always."

"I was tempted," he said, hesitating for a moment to focus his gaze on me. "I had you in my arms, somewhere I had wanted you for a long time, and I didn't want to let go. My wolf and I react intensely when you're near, and all I wanted to do was clamp down and make sure everyone knew that this strong, beautiful, courageous woman had chosen me."

My heart fluttered at his words, my stomach pooling with heat. "I see." I tried to keep a straight face, but I could feel a goofy smile pushing at the edges of my lips.

"However," he looked back down, focusing on the onion once again, "I never would have done it. Not without talking to you first."

"Thank you." I nodded, leaning forward on my arms. "I hope you realize that, logically, I believe and know that. It's just…"

"In the moment, it doesn't always compute?" I nodded solemnly. "I get it. It's a natural trauma trigger."

"You seem to know an awful lot about trauma." I tilted my head. He had been a perfect companion through the whole ordeal of walking through my healing journey, yet I had never actually thought about how he had become so knowledgeable on the subject.

"I went to a psycho-physician for a few years." He peeked up. "After Cleo passed. It was the right thing to do."

I chuckled. "Good for you for going willingly."

"Well, it took a little convincing from Dad and Papa." He turned around, dropping the chopped onions into a pot behind him.

"They sound like good fathers," I whispered, my fingers clutching my glass so I could take a sip and soothe my drying throat.

"They are." He smiled. "They can't wait to meet you."

I choked on my water. "You told them about me?"

"Of course." His eyes glinted with joy.

I shook my head, lightness spreading through my chest. Unfortunately, I couldn't say the same, but I had a feeling keeping this a secret for a little longer was best. As the only girl in the family, dating had always been an adventure for me. I wasn't sure if I was ready to subject Nolan to Ollie's extremely protective older brother side.

No, I think that's best kept tucked away for now.

"May I ask you something?" He kept his gaze trained downward as if our dinner was the most enthralling thing to be working on.

"Of course." My stomach flipped.

"Have you ever been Marked?" His voice was gentle.

"No," I shook my head, my fingers tracing a pattern on the countertop. "Not willingly, anyways."

His fingers tightened around the handle of the knife. "That will never count."

"It just never seemed right. Sounds silly, but it was one of the last things my mother taught me about before she died." I shrugged, my heart aching. There was so much she missed; so much more she was supposed to teach me growing up. "I suppose it just stuck with me that you don't Mark unless it feels right."

"That's not silly. It isn't something to be taken lightly." He went back to chopping his vegetables. "It's similar to sex. Everyone is ready at different times, and that's okay. There is no one set way to go about it."

My shoulders relaxed. Apparently, I had been nervous that he would find my admission odd. Overthinking as always. "Have you ever Marked someone? Or been Marked?" The answer was obvious, but I wanted to hear it from him.

"I have, to both." He worked at the stove, mixing and sauteing all the veggies in oil, the slightly charred aroma filling the air. "Just with Cleo, though. But we met young, so I never really had an opportunity to explore it with someone else."

"I figured." I shrugged.

He dropped the veggies into the pan with the meat before sliding it into the oven to roast. "Does that bother you?"

I took a deep breath, thinking over exactly what I wanted to say. I could see the worry creasing on his face with each second that passed. "No, of course not. I was expecting you to say that and I would never shame you for Marking someone that you wanted to. Did I have this fantasy in my head that the first guy I let Mark me would also be Marked for the first time? Yeah, I suppose, but I think that was more just societal expectation forming a basic idea in my head. What matters to me is what we will make of the moment. That's it."

"If you are ever ready, just know that I'm ready to have that conversation whenever you are."

"When." I winked at him. "Not if, when."

"Thank you for opening up to me about this." He walked around, gently picking up my hand and kissing it before gripping it against his chest. "It means the world to me that you trusted me."

"I won't be doing this alone," I said, remembering Vanessa's words but trying to forget that it was her who had given them to me. "Open communication will be what gets us to a place we both are comfortable."

He wrapped me in his arms, placing a kiss on my forehead. We stood there for a few moments, my pulse evening out as I found comfort in his warm embrace.

"Can I admit something to you now?" he whispered into my hair.

I pulled back slightly, resting my chin on his chest to look up at him. "Of course."

"I'm nervous about you taking this meeting with the High Faction." His grip on me tightened. "After what I witnessed when your father came to visit, all I want to do is keep you from ever having to experience such… pain ever again. And to now face the whole lot of them who betrayed you by dismissing your case? Goddess, Kasha. I just don't understand why you want to go."

"It's work. And with the way Elliot is involving me with his madness, it only seems right that I'm the one to face them."

"I get that, I do." He shook his head, pulling in a deep breath. "But it doesn't stop me from wondering what they could do or say to you while you're there. And I won't be there to support you just in case. It makes me feel…"

"Helpless?" I asked.

"Yeah." He sighed. "I suppose. I mean it when I say I want to be your partner in all things, and it just feels like this is something I should be there for."

My chest ached at his words. He was so worried about me all the time. Guilt mixed with the warming sensation filling me. He was determined to show that I could trust him, that we could make this work. Potentially as Mates, an idea that should probably have seemed scarier to me than it did. I adored him for it but also despised the fact that my own insecurities and trust issues were forcing such stress onto him. It wasn't fair.

I stood up, his arms still wrapped around me, but at least I wasn't completely dwarfed by his height. "Listen to me. I know you're there for me, always. When you're by my side or miles away. I trust you with that. But this is what Kazola needs from me right now. To go there."

He sighed, letting out some tension from his body and melting farther into our embrace. "I trust you and your instincts. If this is what you need to do, then I support you."

"Thank you," I said. "Besides, I'll have Beckett and the girls with me just in case. Plus, I promise to call in case anything too overwhelming happens."

"You promise?"

I placed my hand over his heart. "On my ability to shoot a bow, I promise."

"Well, then, I know you're certainly telling the truth." He laughed before cupping my face between his hands, leaning down to steal a warm, gentle kiss from my lips. "Thank you."

"Of course," I whispered into his chest. "I'm your partner too."

CHAPTER 10

The last of my things were strapped to the back of my lectracycle by mid-morning, parked outside Beckett and Liv's house as I waited for them to finish getting ready. A few minutes passed and they emerged, backpack strapped to Beckett's back and a coffee cup in his hand, and Liv right behind him carrying her bags.

"Morning, traveling companions!" I smiled at them, Beckett's eyes a bit bleary as if his coffee hadn't quite kicked in yet.

"Morning." He gave me a tired smile, downing the rest of his mug. "Ready for the long drive?"

"As I'll ever be." I shrugged.

Truth be told, I never minded long journeys on my lectracycle. It was so like running in wolf form, the rush giving me peace as I could just be with myself for once and not overthink. Hopefully, that stayed true with this ride, although I had a feeling that with our destination being so anxiety-provoking, it might not be the case.

Beckett ran back inside to probably ditch the cup while Liv headed to her cycle, turning around to strap one of her bags to the back. We had to pack more than necessary. Between not knowing how long we would be there, plus needing to bring our Formal Military attire, it was a lot. We could be headed home in less than a day or we could be stuck for weeks if the High Faction wanted to debate this. My stomach churned at the thought; we didn't have that kind of time. Hopefully, they would recognize that fact too.

"Just gonna leave without saying goodbye?" A voice came from behind me. I whipped around, a smile grazing my lips as Nolan approached, a bit sweaty and hair disheveled from a morning workout. Greyson was right beside him, while the familiar rumbling of an engine zipped down the way. Eden sharply pulled into the drive to park right next to me, her bags already strapped to the back.

"Morning," I whispered to Eden, patting her on the shoulder before I walked over to Nolan. I wrapped my arms around his torso, pulling in a deep breath of cinnamon and citrus. "Me? Never!"

"You've got this," he said, yet his grip tightened around me. "They'll see that this plan is the right path."

My stomach churned. "I hope so. I don't want…"

He interrupted me with a kiss on the lips. "No doubts. You are more than the lies they tried to feed you over the past year. Don't let them take away all that you have achieved."

"You're right." I nodded. I wasn't even there yet, and already I was letting them poison my own mind against myself. "I'll call tonight when I can."

He smoothed his hands against my cheeks, leaning down to kiss me one more time. "Show them just how strong you are, sweetheart."

★★★

The five-hour drive was not nearly long enough before we crossed the threshold into Ilfra, capital city of Crelanti, where the High Faction's Château resided. Whenever the High Faction was in session, which was most of the year besides a bit of time off during the summer months, they resided in or around the Château, so they could be accessed for any emergency or need.

Château didn't even begin to describe the monstrous building. The bright white brick reflected with the setting sun, a prism of colors echoing off the stone and against the slightly dampened drive from some daytime rain. It rose five stories above us, split into three main wings that made up almost a W shape. One wing was the professional wing, where the High Faction Chamber, their offices, and other board rooms and workspaces for their staff were held. The middle wing was completely made up of resident penthouses for the High Faction Members. Most of them resided on the property, although some with larger families preferred their own estates on the outskirts of the city. Finally, the guest wing, where people were constantly coming and going every single day.

Part of my life, I grew up in the Château. We moved in once Mother had passed and Caleb had joined the Guard. Four years of my life, but I never considered it home.

Our group was greeted right at the parking spaces we had been assigned for our cycles, a smiling assistant there to take us to our suite for the time being. We were assigned a three-bedroom space, with a common room for us to share. It was open and inviting, two misty gray couches and a matching chair set up in the center, well balanced with the steel blue walls. A table sat to the left of the sitting area, two covered trays and a pitcher of water waiting for us to have an early dinner.

The young man gave us a quick tour, letting us know that our meeting with the High Faction had been assigned for early afternoon the next day. My throat closed at the idea, my heart thumping. So much sooner than I was expecting, but at least they were taking the threat we were investigating seriously enough to give us precedence.

After finalizing our plans for the next day, we ate the dinner provided before we decided to share some blood to finish the feeding. Usually, we fed from stored bags of blood our assigned consorts provided, but unfortunately, they would not be able to travel safely such a distance. So, we had to feed directly from a source, taking over as each other's consort for now. Eden and I shared with each other, while Beckett and Liv went off to their room to share.

It was another reason why a Keturi member had to travel with a companion. We couldn't risk going into Blood Starvation, a bone-deep ache that drained a Shrivika or an Ibridowyn of their strength, making it just as important to us as food and water. It resulted in too many side effects such as irritation, lethargy, anxious tics, and even hallucinations. I never wanted to experience any of that for myself, that was for damn sure.

After we finished, we both decided to retire to our rooms for the rest of the night. I looked around my spacious bedroom, the opulence ridiculous for what was considered an official government building. The cream walls were carved out with gold-painted filigree patterns, the oversized bed big enough for four people, the sage quilt smoothed perfectly over the top and stacked with plenty of gold pillows to match. Even though an electrified chandelier hung from the ceiling, a white stone fireplace still took up half of the far left wall, the warming fire crackling within creating a cozy atmosphere for the wintry season beginning outside.

I sighed, dropping my bags beside the bed and pulling out a few items, including my uniform, to hang in the cherry wood armoire. I knew I should call Nolan before I fell asleep or he did, but there was one more face I needed to see, to help calm my tumbling stomach at the idea of seeing Father the next day.

"Hey, big bro." I smiled when the screen of my Comms lit up with his face.

"Hey, Little Shadow!" Ollie grinned back. Even on the small screen, I could tell he was in for the night, his informal burnt orange tank top pulling out some of the red undertones in his hair. "Where are you right now?" His face creased, focused more on the little bit of background he could see instead of me. One of the plagues of surrounding yourself with mostly military personnel. They noticed everything.

"The Château," I sighed, dropping down onto the plush bed, the gold-stitched canopy rattling above me. "I'm here with some of my team."

Ollie's cheeks reddened. "Why?"

"We have to present and gain approval for something." I gave him the quick version of the story. "Might want to watch out for a potential meeting in the coming weeks if this is passed."

"Noted." Ollie nodded. "So, you'll get to see Father while your there?"

"In session." A lump formed in my throat. "I haven't received any kind of missive about seeing each other outside of it."

"Does Caleb know you're there?" he asked.

"Not sure." I shrugged, but my mouth dried at the thought. "I didn't tell him, but Father might have."

"Screw them!" He waved his hand. "You have far more important matters to spearhead to be giving any brain power to them."

I laughed, a ripple of heat spreading up my neck. He was right, there were more important things to focus on instead of my Father and brother's drama. My Father may have been ashamed of me, but he was still a High Faction member, duty-bound to protect Kazola. He had raised us to be driven by logic and facts. To see every angle and learn everything we could before making an informed decision. We had a solid strategy in place to present to them, and Father wasn't one to let petty feelings get in the way.

Then, panic set in at the memory of the previous time I had stepped foot into the High Faction's Chamber.

"I'm scared." I swallowed. "The last time I was here…"

I couldn't finish the thought. The last time I had been there was to give my testimony against Logan to the entire Council. It had been one of the most vulnerable, fragile moments but I had pushed myself for what I thought was the right thing to do. Yet, it had been crushed by the very people I had to face the next day.

"You have every right to be scared, Kas." Ollie's voice pulled me out of the memory, helping to solidify me in the present. "But don't let your fear overtake your strength. Trust your gut. It hasn't steered you wrong before and it won't this time. I believe in you."

"Thanks." I gave him a weak smile. "I needed that."

"Don't worry." He winked. "You'll show them just how strong you are in spite of their terrible treatment towards you."

I chuckled. "Nolan said something similar before I left."

"Oh?" Ollie perked up. "Finally, the two of you are getting along just as I said you would."

"Yup," I said, my lips clamping down around the single word.

He had told me weeks ago, when I was still bitter and struggling over Nolan's assignment, that the two of us would enjoy working together. However, knowing Ollie, I had a feeling he didn't expect it to get to the place it had evolved to. I loved Ollie, but he tended to get overprotective when I started dating a man. With the stress of the meeting the next day and everything else revolving around Elliot, I wasn't in the mood to deal with his overreaction.

We continued for the next half an hour, catching each other up on life before hanging up so I could give Nolan the goodnight call I had promised. Of course, that one took even longer, the two of us talking for two hours about the most random things to continue learning about each other. It was the perfect distraction; something I desperately needed to hopefully be able to sleep.

When we finally said goodnight, I dropped the unit on the bedside table, staring out the window. I didn't know what the following day would bring, but I hoped to Lunestia that it was one step closer to figuring out why exactly Elliot had chosen me.

CHAPTER 11

It had been a long time since I'd worn my formal Onyx Guard uniform.

The outfit was head-to-toe black, the only way to represent a member of the Onyx Guard. The button-up shirt was layered with a sleeveless dress that reached a few inches above the knee. The top tapered at the waist before falling into the flared skirt. Opaque stockings and knee-high leather boots shined to perfection with a one-inch heel.

But the part of the outfit that stood out from the rest was the final layer—the Onyx Guard jacket. About an inch longer than the dress, it was made of cashmere and stitched with an intricate thread pattern that decorated the entire front of it from hem to collar. Like the symbol of the Onyx Guard, tree roots and branches twisted up my front, entangling with the moon phases that showed I was a Varg Anwyn Member. It was finished off with eight buttons up the front, each one a glittering onyx jewel.

My fingers tugged at the high collar of both the jacket and the shirt underneath. Everyone looked at me in this outfit and saw protection. But the last time I had been in it had been for Logan's trial. When I had laid my hurt and trauma out for the world, for justice, and had it squashed under the boots of those who turned against me. The memories tried their best to throttle me, making it difficult to sit still as we waited to be called into the Council Chamber.

I felt my friends' eyes trail every one of my movements. Beckett and Liv sat together off to the left of the Chamber, Eden standing right next to them in an outfit matching mine. People moved around me and my incessant pacing, some giving me odd looks, others ignoring me entirely as they skidded off to their destination.

"Kasha…" Beckett said, eyes narrowed at me.

"I'm fine." I shook my head. Honestly, I wasn't sure what I was. Too many things.

He leaned forward, twisting his hands together, Liv rubbing circles on his back. Like me, they wore their formal uniforms, Liv in a matching dress and Beckett in a pair of slacks, a button-up, and leather shoes. They had a similar version of my jacket, except the roots and branches were entangled with a twisted snake: the animalistic symbol of truth and lie.

After seconds or hours, the door opened, the aid who showed us to our room peeking out. "It's time. Are you ready?"

I straightened my jacket and, hopefully, my mind. Beckett and Liv stood, all three coming to me. I nodded to them before looking to the aid. "Yes, we are."

And with that, we walked into the one place I had never wanted to find myself again, my steps echoing off the expansive space as the doors slammed behind us.

The chamber was located under the tall dome of the Château, the white stone ceiling painted with a mural depicting the end of the Ancient Times. When the Isle was ravaged by infighting, Humans saw us as threats, no better than the wild things they were trying to hide from. It led to a division, war, and bloodshed that saddened the lovers who had created us in their image.

So Lunestia and Firenielle came to the Isle and they brought all of their children together and showed us what our future could be if we worked together as they planned. That was the day the first High Faction was established and, only six years later, the serum that created the Ibridowyn was discovered.

Underneath the beautiful dome sat the High Faction, all fifteen members. On a raised dais sat their u-shaped table, each side occupied by one of the branches: Human, Shrivika, and Varg Anwyn. Flanked by two Delegates on each side, in a slightly more ornate chair, sat the High Tribune for each branch. They were the ones who led each branch and who spoke on behalf of them when necessary.

I had no idea where to look as Beckett and I stepped up into the platform that we would present our case from, the circular lift rimmed with a twisted iron ledge that we could lean on and set any papers or materials we had. Liv and Eden stood one step below, flanking our sides with their stance hip-width apart and arms behind their backs. The pull to look to the left was strong, the eyes lingering from that side heavy with expectations of failure, I was sure.

The Varg Anwyn side. Too many people who had let me down sat there. My father, Cole, and, sitting at the farthest left of the table, Kyler, our previous Alpha before Logan. I stared ahead instead at the middle table filled with the Human branch.

Beckett cleared his throat, standing up straight and letting his silky voice boom into the room and towards the Faction. "High Tribunes and Delegates, thank you so much for taking time out of your busy schedule to see us on such short notice."

It took too much willpower on my part not to roll my eyes at the ego-coddling that was necessary when presenting to the High Faction.

"As all of you know, we have diligently been investigating the Elliot Wells case for a month and a half now." Beckett's confidence radiated around him, a beacon to be respected. It had always been a strength of his, which was why it was best for him to present the idea.

He went over what we had discovered and how we wanted to infiltrate more of these meetings to get a better understanding of what Elliot was preaching to get citizens to his cause.

"Thank you." Beckett gave a final nod before taking a step back, our shoulders touching in the small space we were confined in. Murmurs drifted to us, each branch quietly talking between them and digesting the information.

My skin prickled as I counted the seconds until something, anything, was said.

"And tell me," Cole drawled from the Varg Anwyn side, our High Tribune that was also Logan's uncle and someone who took a little too much pleasure in my downfall over the past year. "How exactly did you come across the information about the meeting in your territory?"

Beckett stiffened beside me, but I was the one who took the step forward with my shoulders pulled back and chin held high. I looked him right in the eyes when I said, "Elliot willingly gave the information to me via a piece of technology that we did not recognize, although it was similar to a Comms unit."

Cole's eyes narrowed at me. "And how did you come in possession of it?"

"My sister has found herself entangled with Elliot's people." Eden stepped forward, her shoulders pulled back, not backing down. "She was tasked with passing it on to Kasha."

"You mean the criminals that you call siblings?"

"Yes." Eden nodded, but I saw the clench of her jaw. Eden had a clean record and had earned her way to her position. We had planned to advocate for her to be Beta when we hoped I would be promoted to Alpha, but she always feared that her family ties would catch up to her one day.

Cole just nodded to her, turning back to stare at me. "And why, Beta Mallanis, would he give that information willingly to you?"

"Because when he revealed his identity, he made it clear that I was meant for something."

"When you were kidnapped?" Imogene, the High Tribune of the Shrivikas, asked.

"Yes." I nodded. "His hope is that I will learn something about him at the meeting. What, I do not know."

I couldn't help but let my gaze flick to Cole's right side, where my father sat. To see his reaction to the admission that a known killer and potential sociopath had become fixated on me.

His silver-gray eyes steeled against any idea of his thoughts, sharp jaw clenched and fingers tucked neatly in his lap. Nothing. Absolutely nothing.

"This idea of yours seems like a waste of resources." Cole twisted his lips into a sour grin. "We should just send in a unit to shut down the meeting and arrest anyone who has already joined this man's ranks."

"Please tell me, Cole, how a brutish method such as that would help what seems to be a very precarious situation?" a member of the Shrivika branch asked, her voice cold as ice. I turned; the name Evette scrawled on the nameplate that sat in front of her. A younger Delegate, if I remembered correctly.

"We cannot let traitorous civilians continue to walk the streets and poison the minds of others." He leaned forward, staring her down, but she didn't flinch under the weighted pressure. "We should even bring in the one who handed over the package."

I sensed Eden stiffening beside me.

Evette rolled her eyes. "That girl is the least of our problems. It sounds like the people going to these meetings already had doubts but have yet to be swayed."

"Undercover work isn't something that we take lightly, especially on a scale such as this." Mitchell, the human High Tribune, looked at us, his hazel eyes full of what looked like intrigue. "However, it is an ingenious idea of how to make it work with the smallest possibility of compromise."

"Are you actually humoring this idea?" Cole spat.

"Yes," Mitchell spat back, his face twisted in disbelief at Cole's venomous tone. "The threat is real. Taking down the one meeting could cause more harm than good and get us nowhere in the investigation."

"We would have prisoners that we could interrogate," Violet, one of the Human Delegates, pointed out.

"We have no guarantee that those at the particular meeting will be anywhere close to Elliot, his plans, and his strategies," Terrence, one of the Shrivika Delegates, argued.

"And since he offered this specific meeting to Kasha, there is a high probability that there won't be," Imogene argued. "Elliot wouldn't risk any of his higher-ranking officers or officials like that. It would be too obvious."

"You are asking the entirety of the Onyx Guard to risk themselves by going into these meetings. Even if only a few attend, if any of them are taken in the process…" Violet shook her head. "He is ruthless."

Jasmine, a Human Delegate, sat forward. "Ibridowyns can't die."

"He's killed one before," Father said, Cleo's name drifting in my mind. "A fact we still have no idea how he was able to, and the risk we would be asking the other guards to take is too great."

"They took an oath to protect Kazola and our peace." Mitchell shook his head. "This rebellion Elliot is creating threatens that peace. This is exactly what they were created for."

"This plan is half-baked at best, and you're all ready to jump right in, for what?" Cole laughed, his nose wrinkling in disgust.

"Maybe you should leave your ego at the door and listen to the facts and well-planned ideas that the Seathra Faction have presented us," Evette shot from across the room, a smirk settled on her full, red-painted lips. "Then you would understand why we want to follow through with it."

Cole's face reddened at the backhanded comment, the room stifling with a tension that tried to strangle me. I knew what the comment meant. I may not have known Evette well, but the more she spoke up, the more I noticed how vicious she could be.

I hid my smile at that little fact.

They kept debating back and forth between each other, to the point where it was hard to keep up with everyone's ideas. It seemed split down the middle, especially as more Delegates threw their opinions into the ring. My neck was stiff from constantly swinging back and forth by the time someone banged heavily on a table to silence the argument.

"It's obvious that this is a precarious situation that we have never had to deal with in the past," Imogene said. "So, a compromise to vote on. Instead of giving an order, we call a meeting of all the Factions, and they decide if they want to participate in the exchange. Those who do will be shuffled between them and will work with three members of the High Faction to bring the plan to fruition. Now, all for the plan, raise your hand."

I held my breath as I waited. Even though I hadn't been present for the vote on my case, I knew the outcome. Who knew what would happen, if my past was clouding too many people's judgments, or if our plan was just logical enough to sway them?

Slowly, hands raised into the air. Nine of them.

The majority had voted in favor.

I didn't know if I should celebrate or not. It wasn't our exact plan, but it was a compromise. One I could live with. Now, I just had to hope that some of the other Factions could be convinced. Already, I was listing them out in my head, trying to give a weight on which way I thought they would eventually vote.

"Since this is a time-sensitive situation and we don't want any unnecessary travel to hinder anything, I suggest we do a virtual meeting through the Comms system as soon as possible," Imogene said.

"Who will be the Delegates that everyone reports to?" I dared to ask.

Imogene looked at me, her face relaxing, before turning back to the High Faction. "Any volunteers?"

"I will." Evette was the first to raise her hand.

"I will as well," Mitchell said, giving me a curt nod.

The Vargs all sat a little too straight in their seats, gazes flickering to Cole.

"Well, High Tribune?" Imogene said to Cole. "Anyone from your side ready to fight for their country?"

"I will not force any of them to participate if they're not comfortable." He smirked back at her. My insides rolled. His arrogance was a thing of utter disgust.

"I'll do it." A voice came from that side, Cole's venomous stare fixed on the one who had betrayed him. My heart pounded at the sight of who had volunteered to help with our plan.

Kyler.

CHAPTER 12

My chest ached as we stepped out of the chamber, lungs screaming in thanks for the deep breath I finally took.

People bustled down the brightly lit hallway, the mid-day sunlight streaming in through the wall of windows that tracked along the expanse. We had been in there for a very long time, my shoulders knotted with self-inflicted tension.

I wasn't sure if I was pleased or disappointed. My mind was too fogged to even decide what to do next. That chamber had been a terrifying idea before I entered, but I conquered it.

Small steps. That was what mattered to me.

"So." Beckett sighed next to me, his fingers nimbly moving to the top of his coat to undo a few of the buttons. "That happened."

I began walking down the hall, my friends' footsteps echoing next to mine.

Liv turned to me. "Now we wait."

"Hey! Hold on!" A voice drifted down to us, our steps freezing. We all turned, my heart hammering in my chest at the sight of

Kyler hurriedly walking toward us.

Time slowed, sounds disintegrating around me. All I could focus on was the man coming towards me. He looked so different in his formal suit, the black slacks and jacket contrasting against the burgundy of his vest, complimenting his angular, copper face. His curly black hair was contained in a neatly tied ponytail at the base of his neck, the three piercings in each ear simple gold studs to match the gold rings on almost every finger.

So different from the man I once knew, constantly in ripped workout shirts to show off the two sleeves of tattoos, chains dangling from his ears and chest-length hair wild.

Kyler, the Alpha who had taken a chance on me and gave me my first Hierarchy position as his Gamma. Who had trained me, mentored me for the day I became Beta.

No, that Alpha was gone, replaced with a High Faction Delegate I barely recognized.

Inky thoughts overtook my mind, spewing the harbored hatred for him I for so long tried to keep contained, but no longer.

Betrayer. Liar. Backstabber.

The words filled my mind, rage brewing in my stomach, infecting my blood and mind. My eyes flashed, sharpening, my wolf ready to brawl in the middle of the bustling hallway if that was what it came down to. My claws pricked at my fingertips, digging into my leg as I scrunched the hem of my jacket in my fist.

"Screw him," Eden mumbled before grabbing my hand and yanking me away, our pace hurried. Liv and Beckett followed close behind.

I knew there were a lot of people that I would have to face in that chamber today. Some of them cut deeper than others, my father included. Yet, Kyler was different from the rest. He hadn't just betrayed me all those months ago, he had betrayed the Faction he once called his own. That was a wound all of us felt.

"Please, stop!" he yelled out to us.

My hand tightened around Eden's. I yanked back, bringing her to a stop, and Beckett barreled into my back with an *oomph*. He moved to stand next to me, eyebrows furrowed. *"Why are we stopping?"*

"Because I can't keep running." I took a deep breath, turning back around to watch Kyler close the last bit of distance between us. "What?"

He would not get faked submission or a docile soldier. He knew the real me, who I was before. Now it was time to introduce him to the person I had become. A person he had helped create.

He stopped in front of us, chest rising and falling a bit deeper from the chase he had given us. His dark brown eyes darted between the group, mouth slightly gaping as if he didn't know what to say.

"What do you want, Ky?" I asked once again, frost seeping from each word.

His shoulders sagged. "We just called recess. I wanted to commend you all on such a well-executed presentation."

Beckett scoffed, his towering build rigid next to me. "Glad to see the High Faction has completely indoctrinated you."

"What's that supposed to mean?" Kyler blanched, nose twitching.

"We don't take well to faked pleasantries and small talk." Liv sneered.

"We've developed an allergy to it." I crossed my arms, widening my stance. "So, what really brought you out here?"

"I—" He ran his hands over his vest, ironing away invisible wrinkles. "I just wanted to check in. It's been a while since we talked…"

"About ten months," I said, my heart aching.

Ten months ago, the last time I had walked these halls. The day of my testimony. The day Logan's case had officially been brought to trial.

I had left the final day of testimonies and evidence exhausted and depressed, but with at least a thread of hope that the High Faction would do the right thing. That was until three days later when my father showed up at our Compound and delivered the official ruling for Logan.

Not guilty.

The memory rippled through me, my now free wolf using it as fuel, scratching at me, begging to be let out. I mentally growled at her, forcing her to heel.

"I just wish it could go back to the way it was before," Kyler said, eyes pleading with me. "I never wanted it to be this way. I took this position to help the issues we all saw as Hierarchy members. You know that!"

"You aren't doing the best job at following through," Eden grumbled.

"It wasn't what I expected," he said, words slithering through his clenched teeth. "Everything takes a turn and it all got so complicated…"

"It's not complicated." I took a step towards him, the stiff fabric of my jacket tightening around my flexing arms. "It comes down to one question. Why did you vote against me?"

Kyler paled, his russet eyes glazing over with a mix of emotions I tried my best to forget.

When Beckett had convinced me to report Logan's assault, it was Kyler we reported it to. The youngest member of the High Faction. A person we believed we could trust.

And he had acted the part perfectly. Comforting me, threatening to kill Logan, jumping into action, and taking down every detail I fed him. He arranged the trial.

And then when the day came for the High Faction to vote on Logan's fate, he had voted in favor of dismissal.

Betrayer. Liar. Backstabber.

"There are things you didn't see, Kasha," He took a step forward, but I matched him with my own step back, keeping my distance. "None of you saw all the evidence presented. In the end, I just…"

"What evidence?" I asked. My skin prickled, remembering Caleb's blatant lie to me a few weeks ago. Something was being kept from me, and it sounded like it had been important to the case.

"I can't tell you," Kyler said, eyes darting every which way except to look at me. "Just know, it was… quite convincing."

I snarled at his perfectly rehearsed, well-trained response.

"You truly believe that Kasha lied?" Beckett stepped in front of me, going chest to chest to Kyler. "That she would make up some petty tale? For what?"

Kyler stilled. "I am not at liberty to discuss the particulars."

"Bullshit," Beckett spat, and my eyes widened at his crude words. He wasn't one to lose control, but it seemed his old leading partner was getting under his skin.

I grabbed his forearm, yanking him back to my side. "Then we have nothing more to discuss."

With my head held high, I turned my back on Kyler, walking away as if my heart didn't break all over again for what I had lost.

CHAPTER 13

The café we had walked to was close to the Château, a perfect balance of casual but simply decorated.

I had been using my free time trying to remember some of the ideals from Kazola's history and the Lore that was known around the Isle. But as I expected, I didn't know much past the children's stories most of us had grown up hearing. But I had a better idea of where I could go with this train of thought, as it was obvious Elliot felt it was somehow connected to the God and Goddess. The only question was in what twisted way was he thinking?

Sick of me sitting in my room all day, Eden and Liv had charged at me, announcing we were having a girls' night. They dressed me before dragging me out of the Château and into the city.

We were seated at a four-person table by the window, able to watch passers-by walking down the long street on their way home from whatever was keeping them out as the sun set across the horizon. The white-painted iron table lit up the space, the lavender walls reflecting the sunlight filtering through the gauzy white curtains that hung along the wide floor-to-ceiling windows. Since it was still early, just after five, we were one of a few tables occupied. The low hum of the servers milling about and other patrons chatting filled the empty air.

Liv and Eden ordered their drinks, with me once again asking for sparkling water, and we got a few different small plates to share between the three of us. I let out a soothing breath, happy to have a distraction that was just the three of us.

We had been close since I transferred to Seathra. Eden and I had started as Deltas around the same time, but Liv had been a Dairchta for a few years in Ochrat before she and Beckett had transferred to Seathra for his promotion to Treasu. We had started taking cases together when we could, hanging out in town, and growing close. Just as most of the relationships I had formed with my Faction, it had been simple and exactly what I had needed.

"So, what's up with you and Nolan?" Eden broke our silence.

I almost choked on my drink.

I really shouldn't have been surprised they had an ulterior motive for this dinner. Typical.

"What do you mean?" My stomach twisted a bit. I knew there was plenty going on, but truthfully, Nolan and I had barely had time to properly submit the paperwork to the High Faction stating we were starting a romantic relationship, something that was pretty normal in the Guard. My parents had met that way.

Still, because of the rush with the case and wanting to make sure we were all squared away with the proper professional channels, we hadn't made any formal announcements to our friends.

"Well, neither of you have spoken about it since we all witnessed a pretty passionate kiss in the middle of a disgusting warehouse," Liv teased, taking a sip of her martini.

"Oh, right, that." My cheeks reddened at the memory.

"We just want to know how you're doing," Liv said a bit more seriously. "We wanted to check in."

I sighed. "Thank you. It's been a whirlwind that I haven't completely caught up with yet."

"That's to be expected." She nodded.

"But," I took a deep breath before looking up at them, "he and I have decided to start courting each other."

"Eek!" Eden let out a squeal, her hands clapping quietly in front of her. "Finally!"

I gaped. "What do you mean, finally?"

"Well, I hate to break it to you, Kas, but the two of you weren't subtle."

I dropped my head into my hands, elbows braced on the table as I let out a groan. I figured we weren't, but still, hearing the confirmation from my friends made my insides squirm in embarrassment.

"Thanks." I looked down at my lap, my fingers tapping on the table. "I can't believe it's actually happening."

"What's that face for?" Eden pointed her finger at me.

"What face?" I tried to force a smile, but by their unamused looks, it wasn't working well.

"The one saying you're hesitant or hiding something," she said.

"Talk to us, Kas." Liv reached across the table, patting my hand. "What's wrong?"

"Do you think I'm moving too fast?" I peeked up through my

lashes, finally admitting the intrusive thought I had been trying to ignore. "That I'm moving on too quickly from everything I've been through?"

Of course, speaking it out loud for the first time meant it was the perfect moment for the server to drop our food off. He took his time arranging it and handing us each an empty plate, my stomach twisting tighter in knots as I waited for him to leave so I could talk to my friends.

Finally, Liv turned back to me, concern swirling in her chocolate brown eyes. "What do you mean?"

"What if people tell me I should wait longer?" I rambled. "Or that because it's only been a year, I must have been lying about Logan? What if they try and use this as an excuse to invalidate me again?"

My stomach was souring at the idea of food, the delectable mix of spices and buttery goodness turning rancid to me. It was a fear that had started to fester the day after I had accepted Nolan's courtship ask. It felt right and settled me in some ways, but I had spent the past year hearing and feeling the judgment of others follow me everywhere and over every little thing I chose for myself. It felt almost impossible to tune them out; they became so loud sometimes.

So, what would people think of this? I wished this wasn't the worry that plagued me, but I couldn't stop it from spiraling in my mind sometimes.

"First off, take a breath, Kas," Eden instructed. I pulled in a few cleansing breaths before she nodded. "Better."

"Now," Liv said. "Don't let people's expectations define what is right for you and your healing. You know what you need, and if you believe it's Nolan who will be the right support to help you take the next step in your healing journey, then you need to listen to that, not anyone else's ignorant opinions."

"I don't know if I can do that," I whispered.

"You really think people thought me joining the Guard was a smart idea?" She tilted her head. "After what happened to me?"

I sighed, remembering the tale. When she was twenty-five, her little sister and mother had been attacked and killed during a robbery gone wrong at her mother's custom jewelry store. It had devastated Liv, and worse, the man who had tried to rob her had gotten away and was never caught.

She and Beckett were newly engaged, and he was finishing up his physician training. All she had wanted was to join the Guard so she could save other families from the lack of closure and heartbreak. Beckett had understood, and after his training was completed the following year, they eloped and went right to a recruiter to start the process.

And now, here they were ten years later and thriving. Sometimes, things happen for a reason.

"When it comes to our healing, looking to others for validation on what is right can sometimes halt our growth." A solemn look softened her features, as if memories spun through her mind quickly. "I didn't let others' opinions about me change my needs. And you shouldn't either."

Every word she spoke made complete sense, subtly silencing the intrusive thought that I had been obsessing over recently.

"What do you think?" I turned to Eden.

"I agree with the married lady." She shrugged, finishing her ale. "She would be the one to take advice from."

"Not like you to keep an opinion to yourself," I teased.

"My opinion is that Nolan has looked at you like you're the most enamoring woman he ever met since the day he met you," Eden stated plainly. "I think it's obvious that the two of you are well-matched for each other. Support and challenge are what you need to thrive, and you can offer both to each other."

I had to hide the very wide smile that wanted to grow on my face. Butterfly wings fluttered deep in my stomach at the idea.

"He used to ask about you," Eden said. "In a way he hoped was subtle, but Grey and I knew he cared about you."

I snorted. "I used to hate that."

"Yeah, when you thought he was out to get you," Liv pointed out. I just shrugged.

"Are you happy?" Liv asked.

I blushed again. "Yes."

"Does he make your heart flutter?" Eden asked.

Now a giggle was busting through my lips. "Yes, all the time."

"Good." Eden nodded. "You deserve that. You both do."

To hear from two of the people closest to me that they saw the change for the better already settled the chaotic voices that had invaded my mind.

"Thank you." I smiled.

"Now," Liv leaned forward, pulling a few dumplings onto her plate, "on a scale of one to ten, how soft are those lips of his?"

We all laughed, my heart settling as we fell into silly conversation and delicious food. Exactly what I needed.

CHAPTER 14

Waiting was becoming obnoxious.

We were already on day four in Crelanti, and our group spent most of our time waiting in our suite, not wanting to venture out and risk seeing anyone that wasn't our biggest fan. We kept busy, having taken some paperwork with us. We checked in with the Faction to keep them updated. When we weren't working, I lost myself in the newest book in my favorite epic series about a cosseted princess who finds herself entangled with a cabal of outlaws from an enemy country.

Basically, we were trying to find anything to keep us occupied in the mind-numbing void that was waiting for the High Faction to schedule this meeting for the Faction Vote.

So, it came as quite a surprise to me on my third day to receive a dining invitation from one of the High Faction members. My heart hurt a little when I noticed it wasn't my father but Evette, one of the Shrivika branch members. The intrigue of the invitation certainly helped dull some of that pain.

I wasn't sure of the dress code, but I wasn't in the mood to wear my dress uniform. Instead, I pulled out a knee-length maroon leather skirt, a sleeveless silk black blouse, and a curve-enhancing black blazer. I finished it off with some black stockings and ankle boots. My Moonlight tattoo peeked out from my blouse, the last few letters and a poppy visible at the edge of my collarbone.

I smirked at myself in the mirror. It had been so long since I found an excuse, or even the energy, to wear one of these outfits. I used to put more effort into my clothes when I went out with my friends or on a date. I enjoyed the process. The little boost of energy I got as I moved through each step. But ever since the rape and life attempt, it never felt worth it. I never felt worth it.

My heart leapt when I realized that I was coming out of that. I was finding joy in the little things again.

I brushed out my hair, pinning it back so it stayed out of my face but still flowed freely down my back. I'd have to call Nolan when I returned. I was sure he'd appreciate this look of mine.

With one last appraisal of myself, I said a quick goodbye to Beckett, Liv, and Eden before hurrying down the hall, winding my way through the Château until I made it to the residential wing where all of the High Faction members' suites resided. I followed the directions on the invitation, knocking on the lapis blue door at the end of the second floor. It swung open immediately, a young housekeeper in a simple black dress welcoming me. She led me through the entryway and into the open sitting area.

"Welcome, Beta Mallanis. Thank you so much for joining me," Evette said from a cream velvet settee by one of the windows. She set down the book she was reading, picked up her glass of what looked like whiskey, and briskly walked toward me.

What shocked me was the little companion sitting on her shoulder; a red, orange, and green bird. It sat there contently, not a bit rattled when Evette moved towards me.

"Thank you for having me." I reached my hand out, shaking her offered one. "And please, call me Kasha."

The bird chirped in response, stunning me.

Evette just laughed. "Don't mind Mango. He likes to be vocal when new people come into the house."

"I can see that." I smiled, Mango approving with another chirp.

I knew Evette was a younger member of the High Faction, the most recent addition to the Shrivika branch. She was around Kyler's age, and the two had been added within the same year. I couldn't help but admire her after the other day. Everything about her demanded respect. Not just with the way she looked, with her curvy, hourglass form beautifully dressed in high-waisted silk black pants, a white corset-style top, and an oversized, knee-length blazer. It was how she held herself, with an air of respect and confidence that made people take notice. It drew me towards her, making me want to learn and listen.

"Very well," she said with a warm smile on her full lips. She gently coaxed Mango to perch on her fingertips before moving him to sit in a large cage full of different levels and climbing beams to play on. "Can I get you a drink before we head into the dining room? My chef was just putting the food out."

"Just sparkling water with lime if you have it," I said, following across the hall to the dining room. The black marble top table was big enough for at least a dozen people, perfect for entertaining, but just two seats were set: the head of the table and the one directly to the right. The pearl white plates, gold flatware, and crystal glasses contrasted well against the marble. A fire was crackling in the shell and stone fireplace, the gold chandelier hanging above dimmed low, perfect for the nighttime.

Apparently, I had dressed appropriately, even though it was just the two of us.

I took the seat to the right of Evette just as the young housekeeper placed my drink in front of me. She then went about setting a watercress, radicchio, and pomegranate salad in front of us, the light scents of orange and fennel seed complementing it well.

"Are you enjoying your time at the capital?" Evette asked, her brown eyes appraising me.

I sat up a bit straighter. "Yes… I suppose."

"I'm sure your Faction misses you." She took a bite of her salad, a hum of approval escaping.

My insides squirmed at the rigidness of the conversation. I hated small talk even before everything happened, but I had particularly come to hate it since then. When people learned that I had tried to take my own life, they tended to forget how to talk to me, leading to some of these very inane conversations that meant nothing. I had lost my tolerance for them. They made me feel weak and coddled, and I wouldn't let someone make me feel that way again.

It was time to learn how to get myself out of them.

"I don't mean to be an ungrateful guest, Delegate, but I am a bit confused about why you asked me here." My pulse pressed against my throat, but I kept eye contact, using the back of the chair as support to keep myself as straight as possible.

"Oh?" She raised an eyebrow.

"After watching you in Council yesterday, it was obvious you don't say things without thinking everything through. You like facts and details. You listen and learn before speaking." I ran through everything I noticed about her yesterday, remembering how she fought for our plan to be enacted. "You make your presence known and don't seem to back down, even from those who try to put you in your place."

"So?" she challenged. "What does that have to do with tonight?"

"In my experience, people with those traits rarely invite people over for small talk or a casual dinner." I took another bite, refusing to break eye contact as I chewed and swallowed before continuing. "They have motives for their actions. Whether they are altruistic or selfish motives I have yet to discern, but I know you invited me here for a reason."

Silence fell, her eyes raking over me, fingers clamped around her whiskey glass tightly as she swirled it. She didn't say a word, her dark, chiseled face giving away nothing. I tried my best to sit still, to not squirm under the scrutiny, sweat beginning to form along my hairline. *Breathe, just breathe.* It was all I could tell myself as I waited for her to say anything.

She finally smirked at me. "I shouldn't have expected anything less."

My stomach clenched. "What do you mean?"

"I knew you were as sharp as you seemed. Sharper, in fact." She took another bite. "You notice everything, don't you?"

"I try to." I took a few more bites, finishing off my salad before they took the plates away and replaced it with a juicy leg of lamb with bright green mint jelly and herbed baby carrots.

"You succeed," she said. "Very well. Let's get down to it. I brought you here because I felt it was only fair to officially introduce myself as one of your supporters from your trial."

I froze, my fork dangling from my fingers over my plate. "Excuse me?"

"I voted in favor of prosecution against Logan when you brought your case to us." Every word was laced with pride, her shoulders pulled back and a smile on her lips.

My heart clenched. "You did?"

"Those who wanted you to feel shamed and small made sure you did." Evette took a sip of her drink. "The easiest way to do that is to cut you off and hide any support you may have. That is exactly what they did."

"But they…"

"Made it seem like everyone voted in favor of dismissal?"

I swallowed a lump in my throat, nodding.

"Some were." She leaned back in her seat, pink warming her umber cheeks. "But not all. Not nearly as many as they wanted you to believe."

"How many?" I didn't even hesitate to ask. I could tell she was ready to give me answers, and I wasn't about to waste the opportunity.

"Out of the fifteen of us, ten voted for dismissal."

Which meant there were five who voted with me. A third of the High Faction believed me.

"Why are you telling me this?" I whispered, staring down at my lap, my fingers idly playing with the black cotton napkin laying on it.

"You deserve the truth," she said. "That, and I wanted you to see that people did believe you, even if others tried to silence your voice."

"It's something, I suppose." It was more than something, a warmth pooling in my chest at the new knowledge. Still, I didn't want to show her how relieved this made me.

"And, off the record, I think some who voted for dismissal believed you as well." She winked. "Let's just say, certain members know how to play the political game a little too well."

It was easy to read between the lines of her words. They were bribed, blackmailed, or coerced in some way. Just wonderful.

"I spoke to Delegate Kyler the other day." I tried my best to keep my words even and calm. "He mentioned some piece of evidence that compelled a lot of people to dismissal."

"Did he mention what it was?"

I shook my head. "Said it was classified."

"I understood why some were compelled by it." She shrugged. "Although something seemed off to me, which is why it didn't sway me or some of the other members of the High Faction. We all felt it was just too… well-maintained."

"Kyler didn't," I bit out, an acrid taste spreading over my palette.

"Kyler has the unfortunate pleasure of having Cole as his High Tribute. All the Vargs voted for dismissal."

"Not shocked by that," I muttered, the warm spices of the dish wafting towards me, my stomach growling in anticipation.

"Cole is one of the oldest members of the High Faction." Evette cut into her meal, and I followed suit. "There has been debate among the Shrivs and Humans that maybe he should have stepped down by now, but we know that will never happen until he's ready. We have no power to vote him out based on the laws of Kazola, and he is very content where he is."

"Oh, I know." I took a bite of the juicy meat, my mind wandering to thoughts of the arrogant, narcissistic man I had the unfortunate pleasure of knowing a bit too well from other connections throughout my life. Friend of my father, uncle to Caleb's best friend. And yet, somehow, we were all forced to put up with him.

I shook the thoughts away, focusing back on Evette. "Still, why tell me all of this? Why extend an invitation and show me favor? It can't be doing good things for your reputation as a Delegate."

"I'd rather lose my reputation as a Delegate than have to live with the shame that I compromised what I believe is best for Kazola," she stated with pride in her voice. "I brought you here to show you that you have allies outside of your Faction."

I side-eyed her, my brows crinkling inward. "Thank you, I think."

"You are not as isolated as they want you to think, Kasha." Evette looked at me, her gaze piercing. "With the way this whole Elliot case is going, I knew it was best to show you that."

"Why?"

"You have proven that he is so much more dangerous than any of us expected." She gently placed her flatware on her plate, dabbing her face with her napkin before leaning towards me. "Whether we like it or not, some kind of fight is coming. It may be a silent one or an all-out war, but either way, it is upon us. We need soldiers like you to lead us in this fight. Before that happens, you need to know that you will have support in this battle. You are not alone."

I didn't know how to respond, but the tingling along my arms gave me the impression that this was a moment I would not soon forget because it revealed another potential truth to me.

Someday soon, I would need to fight, and when I did, I would need the aid of others, or I might not survive.

CHAPTER 15

All the Factions had agreed to come to the meeting and hear the plan. Every single one.

It would take place over a large Comms meeting, where all of the Faction Keturis were on screen to discuss and would vote on what they wanted to do. We would be required to attend the meeting, even though it was our idea and everyone knew our vote. If questions or clarifications were needed, we would be there, and we were still required to put in an official vote.

Since it was already going to be difficult to get the entire High Faction on the screen, they had sent a technical team up to our suite that morning to set up a temporary Comms station so we could call into the meeting without having to be in the Chamber. It helped me breathe a little better knowing that it was only Beckett and me in the actual room when this whole vote went down. Liv and Eden had gone into the city for some shopping to give us some privacy.

"Ready?" Beckett sat down next to me, straightening the collar of his shirt. Once again, we were dressed in our formal uniforms.

"As I'll ever be." I sighed, playing with the ends of the braid I had twisted my hair into to help contain it. He gave me a curt nod before pushing the button in front of us, connecting to the meeting.

The screen lit up, more than half of the boxes already filled with images of different Factions who were tuning in to hear the latest updates. We were still waiting on three more by the looks of it, people chatting between themselves or catching up with others on the screen in awkward small talk we all had to endure instead of walking away like you could in person.

I caught sight of Ollie first, his bronzed brown hair slicked back and his team all sitting in a row with him. He winked at the video, and I couldn't help but smile because even in the sea of people who saw it, I knew it was for me and only me. I would have to check in with him tonight after the meeting. I had a feeling seeing all the people we would face today would be hard on him as well.

My gaze continued, settling on the box that contained my other brother, his dress uniform perfectly pressed, eyes cold and hard as he stared into the screen as if the meeting had already begun. I had been in his territory now for about five days and not once had he reached out. Granted, I hadn't made any effort to reach out to him, but that was the way I wanted it. Although it stung that he didn't try, I couldn't be too upset. If I didn't want to see him, I certainly knew he didn't want to see me. Especially since the disastrous last meeting at Nana Aggie's house that resulted in a fistfight between him and Ollie.

I shook my head and continued observing, my heart banging,

the feeling of being watched prickling the back of my neck. I couldn't help myself. Couldn't stop my gaze from flicking to the left of the screen to the Dalchus Faction Keturi. To his new Keturi.

Logan.

I clenched my jaw tight so it didn't quiver. He wasn't even looking at the screen, he and his team talking amongst themselves while they waited for the meeting to start. He let out a laugh, his dirty blond curls shaking against his forehead, casually leaning back in his chair as if he didn't have a care in the world.

As if he wasn't seeing the woman he raped for the first time since he came to the hospital to visit me after my suicide attempt.

He had no morals. He had no soul. I knew that for a fact.

I looked away, trying my best to calm down before the meeting started. I looked at the two people that I did trust. The people I missed. Nolan and Emric were also in their dress uniform, most of their forms hidden by the conference table in front of them. Just his presence on the screen made my heart stutter back to a typical pattern. I wished he was with me, but at least I had Beckett. I glanced over to him, an encouraging smile gracing his lips before a banging from the screen made us turn back to it.

"Thank you all for joining us," Mitchell said, pulling our attention to the meeting. Only because it was easiest to see him in the u-shape of the High Faction seating. "As you know from the briefing material we sent out, the threat of Elliot Wells has increased exponentially. With that, we are here to present an undercover mission to the entire Onyx Guard in hopes that it will help us gain clarity into what the threat is along with how big his numbers are. We ask that you stay quiet through the entire presentation."

Everyone murmured their understanding before the presentation began.

Imogene was the one to present the whole plan, probably because she was the one to come up with the compromise that was being presented. Yet, like Evette, she was also the type to command attention and respect. She stood in the center of the group, their video the largest box in the center with the ten other Faction boxes surrounding her. She was tall, most likely only a few inches shorter than Nolan if I had to guess. Her hip-hugging cobalt blue dress contrasted well with her alabaster skin, wavy white-blonde hair trimmed short and styled to stay out of her eyes and face. She stood tall, proud, and confident. She had earned her place as High Tribune of the Shrivikas, and I could tell she owned that fact with all her being.

She was a woman to look up to, my chest sparking with respect and awe as I listened to her perfectly presented argument.

When she finished, she closed her folder and strode back to her seat, revealing the rest of the High Faction back into view.

Mitchell cleared his throat, leaning forward. "Now that you have been presented with the option, we are going to allow you a few minutes to discuss between your teams before opening the floor for discussion. You know the rules. If you want to say something, you must light your block up red, and we will call on you."

Silence fell, the other Keturis crowding into each other, yet no lips moved, all of them keeping the conversations private in their mental connections.

"How do you think this will go?" I asked Beckett. Since we already knew the plan and our vote, we were watching the other Factions and their reactions. I could see half of them had been listening intently, leaning forward in their chairs or taking notes.

"If I had to guess, at least half are considering it." Beckett confirmed my suspicions.

I was already counting on Vapalles and Xoblar due to personal connections and saw interest in Adro, Ochrat, and Luspan. I couldn't get a read on Rystin's team, and Crelanti's team was a mystery to me, but I think that was more because I no longer knew how to read Caleb than anything else.

My gaze had completely ignored Logan's box.

Finally, people straightened back up, pulling their attention back to the meeting. The discussion was about to open up.

The first block to light up red made my heart race, my palms sweaty and the darkened thought banging on my mind to drown me.

"Yes, Dalchus Faction?" Mitchell called out.

"Of course, it's obvious that this is an important endeavor." Logan was the one to talk for his team, the arrogant confidence he always spoke with laced through every word. My throat closed in, my foot tapping under the table.

Breathe in. Breathe out. He's not here. He's a safe distance away.
He cannot get me here.

He continued, "I guess I was just curious which team had come up with this idea."

My fingernails bit into my palms, my fists sitting in my lap. Ours was the only Keturi that was separate on screen, making it obvious we had been the ones to come here.

But Logan had to call it out.

Mitchell paled, squirming in his seat. "The Seathra Faction."

"Oh, Beta Mallanis, was this your idea?" His eyes sparkled, a smirk on his lips. Unlike Nolan's which always had a wicked, teasing hint to it, Logan's was nothing short of evil. Smug, tempting evil that could lure you in before trapping you in his web of pain.

Air caught in my throat, closing in just like his hand when he had grasped me against the tree, cutting off my air supply. My tight clothes scratched against my back. Or was that the dry bark of a tree?

Goddess, just one word from him was setting me off.

Beckett slid his hand onto my knee, squeezing tightly, pulling me back to reality. I looked over at him, his eyes fixed on me, encouraging me.

I took a deep breath, turning back to the screen. "It was an effort of our entire Hierarchy, Alpha Brealin, but yes. I presented it along with Ar Dtus Willick."

My chest squeezed.

"You did great," Beckett encouraged. *"Strong."*

He knew exactly what I needed to hear.

"Ingenious." Logan smiled. "I should have known. I taught so many of you well during my time there."

My blood boiled. Was he really trying to take credit for our hard work?

"Funny, no one has mentioned you since I've been here." Nolan's face was carved from stone, eyes cold and detached as he addressed Logan.

That wiped the incredulous smirk off Logan's face. He sat up straight, mouth open ready for rebuttal but, once again, they were interrupted by a loud noise. When I saw Nolan next, I was going to give him the biggest kiss as a thank you for making such a baffled look appear on the face of a man who always exuded a confident shell.

"Let us get back to what is at hand." Mitchell banged the table, bringing the conventions back to what was important. Other Factions began weighing in, focusing on asking questions about the timeline and if we had a general idea of where we thought the focus should be for the undercover work. Most focused on the technical, but it was easy to notice that no one questioned the plan. They just wanted more details.

Finally, once it had quieted down, it was time to call the vote.

"If you are in favor, please light your screens green. If against, light it red."

Our screen and Nolan and Emric's were the first to light up with a rim of green around it. Slowly, others followed, until the entire screen was lit in the lime green glow; even Caleb's team.

Even Logan's.

I wasn't surprised. Voting no meant voting against what was obviously very personal to a lot of people and made it look like they did not care for the complete safety of Kazola, going against the oaths we took. Still, after Cole's fight against even presenting this to the Factions, I was surprised he didn't manipulate Logan into convincing his team to vote against.

Oh, well. At least the Onyx Guard still had their priorities straight.

Once the vote was over, Imogene took control of the meeting, launching into the next steps that needed to be taken- since this plan would begin immediately. I followed along as best I could, but it was my father's voice that pierced through it all.

"Since they're already here, I think it's best that the Seathra Faction switches with Crelanti." My spine straightened. Even with a screen full of other feeds, I felt his gaze lingering on me, focused on my reaction. I tried my best to keep my face neutral. "Unless there is a problem with that?"

I flicked my gaze over to Caleb's box, his jaw tightened and strained. What was our father up to? Yes, it was the logical decision, but why was *he* the one bringing it up? I was surprised he wanted me to stay, potentially tainting his perfect oldest son against him. I supposed he was confident in Caleb's loyalty to him or was hoping Caleb would convince me to apologize or admit I was wrong.

Yeah, like that would ever happen. The Goddess would have to physically come back to Kazola and force me.

But I wouldn't let my father see the snaking pain that worked its way up my neck and made my cheeks numb. I wouldn't let him see the weakness he had helped create in me. I wasn't the woman he thought I was. I was so much more.

So, before Beckett could come up with an argument, I leaned forward and stared right into the screen, unblinking. "Of course. As long as we are welcomed on the Crelanti Compound, we would love to team up with them."

My father frowned. But Caleb leaned forward as well. "Of course. You're always welcome here."

My stomach clenched, and I gave a curt nod before leaning back and allowing the conversation to resume while the rest of the Factions decided where they would go. Beckett's hot gaze lingered on me, his desire to talk pressing against my mind, but I pushed it out.

It was settled. I'd be staying in this torture pit a little bit longer.

# CHAPTER 16

The moment the screen went blank, I shot up from my chair and yanked my jacket off, fingers shaking as I tried my best to unhook each button without ripping it off.

"Are you all right?" Beckett came up behind me, his hand snaking around to hand me a tall glass of water.

I took it gladly, forcing a few sips down my parched throat. "I will be. Let's just focus on what we have to do."

Beckett nodded, knowing my moods and needs all too well from the past year. He removed his jacket, tossing it onto the couch where I had abandoned mine, and walked over to the dining table. It took a few minutes for Beckett to reset the Comms and link just to the other half of our team, allowing me to slump into one of the dining chairs and remove my aching feet from my heeled shoes. I downed the rest of my water, leaned my head back, and closed my eyes before pulling in a few deep, cleansing breaths to help refocus myself.

We had done what we came to do and now we could move

forward. That was what mattered.

Even if the lingering image of Logan's smug, smirking face still blazed in my memory. A face I had never wanted to see again, even though I knew it had been inevitable.

"Ready?" Beckett asked, pulling me from my daze.

I lifted my head, blinking rapidly a few times and sitting up straighter in my seat. I had no idea why I wanted to look less defeated than I felt in front of three people I trusted implicitly, yet I still righted myself. I fiddled with the cuffs of my black button-up, the wool skirt of my dress itching against my tights. "Yeah, let's start."

He nodded, flicking the switch on the monitor. The screen lit up, slowly sharpening into the image of the back half of our home Faction's conference room. Nolan and Emric were already seated at the head of the table and visible on the screen.

My gaze slid over to Nolan, a cup of what I assumed was coffee now gripped in his right hand, his hair a bit more mussed than before.

"Long time no see." I gave him a tired smile.

His lips curled up into one of those wicked grins that made my toes curl and my heart thump rapidly. "Always too long in my opinion."

"Saying you can't live without me?"

"Why would I want to?" He winked. My cheeks heated, my gaze fixated on him and only him, the ache behind my eyes lessening a bit.

"If you two are done openly flirting in our meeting, can we begin?" Beckett said beside me, pouring himself a glass of water and refilling mine. I nodded in thanks.

"I suppose." Nolan chuckled. "So, we need to figure out who will do the undercover work in Crelanti. It will probably be easier to have a pair of you stay behind, we just have to make sure they are from the same species."

"I'll be staying here," I proclaimed with no hesitation in my voice. All three men stared at me.

Beckett's eyes widened. "Are you sure? I'm happy to be the one to stay behind."

"Yes." I nodded, my eyes glancing between him and the screen. "Elliot wanted me at that meeting. I may not be going to the one that he told us about, but I am going to one. Maybe I'll notice something that another wouldn't, or it will give us a better insight into why he seems fixated on me."

"Kasha, it means…" Emric said.

"I know what it means." I cut him off, holding my hand up. "I can handle my brother. The last thing I need him to think is that I ran away from my responsibility because I'm scared of him."

Beckett sighed. "All right, fine. Liv and I will return home and help liaison with the visiting team."

"I've already assigned a few of the trainees to clean out the guest house," Emric said, pulling his glasses off his face and polishing the lenses with a cloth. "Should be done by this evening and set for whoever is assigned to come here."

"Perfect." Beckett nodded.

"Send Eden with you as well," Nolan stated, sitting up straighter.

I furrowed my brows. "Why?"

"'Cause I'll be the one to join you on the mission," he said matter-of-factly. "The Gammas can take care of the Pack while we are away."

My heart flipped. "You don't have to…"

"I want to." He stared at me through the screen. "For both our peace of minds."

I let out a deep breath, knowing he was right. I loved Eden, but having to be around my family for longer was going to be a struggle. Nolan's calming, settling presence would help, and I knew Eden would understand.

I nodded. "Okay then."

"Looks like I'm going on a trip." Nolan stretched his long arms above his head, leaning back in his chair. "I have a few things I should wrap up before I leave, but I can be there the day after tomorrow."

"Okay." I nodded, trying my best to keep a dopey smile from spreading on my face.

"Ready to have your favorite partner back?" I could see the flirtatious glint in his eye even through the digital connection.

Beckett groaned next to me, shaking his head. I pointedly ignored it. "I suppose. Let's just hope you can keep up."

He laughed, a deep, smoky texture laced throughout it. "Oh, sweetheart, just you wait."

"I'm sick of you two already," Emric mumbled. We all stared at him for a moment before the four of us busted into laughs, reminding me once again just how much I adored my team.

★★★

"Are you sure you don't want any of us to stay?" Beckett offered for the thousandth time as we walked outside the Château later that day, their three lectracycles already parked and waiting for them in the entry drive.

"Yes!" I shoved him, making him stumble a bit with a laugh. "There's no reason for you three to hang around here when you could be productive somewhere else."

Eden secured her bag to the back of the cycle. "I hate the idea of leaving you alone here."

"I'll be fine." I sighed. "I'll stay at the Château until Nolan arrives and then we will transfer over to Caleb's Compound. At least here I can stay in my room or hide in the crowds that generally mingle around. Plus, it will be nice to roam the city for a day or two before we have to start hunting the streets."

"Fair." Liv turned back to me, her backpack securely buckled across her chest. "Make sure you don't work the entire time, huh?"

"I'll try my best." I took a step forward, Liv's arms opening to me. I let her wrap her arms around my shoulders, pulling me against her into a tight hug. I settled a bit before backing away, Beckett already grabbing me in for another.

"Don't let anyone make you feel small," Beckett mumbled. "You are the one who decides where you belong, no one else."

"Thank you." I held him for one more moment before untangling myself. He gave me a warm smile, his white-blond hair ruffling in the chilled wind that swept across the drive.

"If anyone causes you trouble, you'd better let me know 'cause I'll kick their ass before they can try to defend themselves." Eden winked, giving me a final hug to help settle me a bit.

I laughed, shaking my head. "Please. You think Nolan will let you get a hit in?"

"If I ask nicely, maybe." She mounted her bike, shoving the key into the ignition, the gentle thrum of all three engines echoing off the stone walls and tall hedges around us. "Stay strong, my friend."

They revved their engines one more time before lurching forward and down the drive. I stood there watching, with my chest clenching a bit too tightly, until they disappeared through the front gate.

CHAPTER 17

I was already jittering out of my skin a few hours after they left.

Luckily, I knew what I could do to keep my mind preoccupied, but I needed some help to start my journey. I left the Château after an early lunch, weaving my cycle through the streets and towards the only other building in the city that rivaled the grandeur of the High Faction's residence. A place for all to find solace in the God and Goddess who saved us.

The Temple of Tranquility.

I parked my bike in the small lot in the back of the gold and black stone building, the spires looming over me with intricate carvings that drew the eye upward to stare. I gave them a glance before pushing my way inside the left tower, to Lunestia's sanctuary.

This temple of the Gods was nothing like the one I frequented in Seathra. This one was the original, the first constructed on the Isle after the Unity of Order, the only time Lunestia and Firenielle came to the Isle to bring peace between the warring species they had created out of love. It was then that all previous temples had been torn down and our current ones constructed, built to house worship for both the God and Goddess, so all species could be welcome. No longer divided, but one peaceful place for all.

This whole space was decorated in a mosaic style, every inch of wall and ceiling depicting intricately detailed pictures made of one-inch square tiles. To the left, the story of how Lunestia fell in love with Firenielle to create the Isle and, to the right, the story of the Unity of Order and how they finally brought our warring kinds to peace. Above, a fully black ceiling decorated with the moon phases ran down the center. Glittering diamonds encrusted it, perpetually cloaking the temple proper in the night sky us Varg Anwyns loved so much.

"Well, there's a face I haven't seen in a while." The deep, gravelly voice drifted down the aisle to me, snapping me back from my admiration of the beauty.

I smiled, my boots clicking against the marble floor as I made my way down. "Hello, Ahren."

The tall, lanky man stood in place waiting for me, his arms opening wide as I got closer, welcoming me into a warm hug. His jet-black hair contrasted a bit too harshly with the silvery white robes he wore, the hood gently resting on the crown of his head to keep his angular face visible.

"Or should I say Chaithea Ahren?" I snickered at my silly joke, his chest rumbling against my cheek. It was odd to use the official title of an acolyte of the temples, especially for someone who had a different title to me most of my life: cousin.

One of the few I had, he was the youngest son of my mother's sister. I didn't get to see him much growing up, as we were raised in Seathra and Crelanti, and Ahren was raised in the mountain territory of Luspan at his family's modest ore mine. But still, we always enjoyed our visits when we had them.

"Please, never call me that." He laughed, pulling away to look down at me. He was about Ollie's height but had none of the muscle. "Are you here for a visit to me or someone else?"

My shoulder deflated at that, my heart twitching at the memories I had long tried not to dwell too much on. It was in this temple that my mother's Last Rites were performed, Ahren being the Chaithea who had presided over them. A request that had been highly unusual since Ahren had been in his first year as a novice, and typically, a more experienced acolyte presided over funerals. But he was family, and we didn't want a stranger raising our mother's soul to Lunestia; we wanted Ahren.

It had been exactly what Mama would have wanted. I still believed that fifteen years later.

"To see you, actually." I refocused my mind, back to my whole purpose of being there. "I need to talk to you about a few things pertaining to a case I'm working on."

"I see." His face grew solemn. He had never kept it quiet that he prayed for Caleb, Ollie, and me daily. He was always nervous for our safety. Little did he know, we were safer than anyone on the Isle; almost invincible with our Ibridowyn blood.

Almost.

"Come," He gently placed my hand in the crook of his arm. "Best place to talk is in my chambers. No chance of prying ears listening in." He winked at me, guiding us to a narrow hallway hidden by a thick tapestry in the back right corner.

We walked down it, the whole area barely lit with dull sconces along the dark stone wall. A few twists and turns and a staircase down later, we arrived. The short wooden door looked so weak that a heavy puff of air would blow it down. Ahren pushed his way inside, revealing the expanse of his modest living quarters. A single bed sat in the back corner, perfectly made with plain blue sheets and blankets. A desk sat off to the right with a ceiling-high bookshelf next to it, stuffed full of too many books to count. At the front of the room was a cluster of blue velvet chairs surrounding the dark stone fireplace and a two-person dining table.

Minimalist and clean. Exactly what I pictured an acolyte would comfortably reside in.

He gestured for me to take a seat in front of the half-dying fire. I pulled off my black leather jacket, draping it over the back before settling into the well-worn and comfortable chair. I hadn't wanted to stick out or make it seem like I was there on official business. Technically, this was just a hunch my gut was telling me to follow through on. So, I had left my guard uniform behind and dressed in simple black pants, a gray silk top, and my leather boots. Inconspicuous and easy to blend in, just how I preferred it.

"So, what brought you to seek advice from me, cousin?" He handed me a glass of water before sitting in the chair across from me, a glass gripped in his own hand.

"I can't give many details with it being a case and all."

"Of course." He nodded.

"But something about what has been said by a suspect." I rubbed my chin. "They seem to have this idea that their actions are being guided by the Gods."

"If it's a case you're dealing with, I would have to thoroughly disagree." He chuckled, taking a sip of water.

"Well, something is making them believe that."

"They could just be delusional."

I shook my head. "No. I mean, yes, they are, but this person is intelligent. There has to be something in lore that they were able to twist to fit their narrative."

"I see." Ahren nodded, leaning forward to place his cup on the small table in front of us.

"Is there anything you have come across in your studies?" I asked hopefully.

Ahren had gone to university as a historian and fell in love with researching and learning about Ancient Times and details about the Unity of Order. It helped him find peace and a desire for truth, ultimately leading him to taking his vows. It was why he was assigned to Crelanti as his house of worship. He continued his study and research, even consulting with other universities for his writings to be used in historical texts. If anyone knew where I could begin, it was Ahren.

It was something about Elliot continually saying he and I were God and Goddess blessed. And that name he kept calling me, Rogthna, was obviously a lost Ancient Kazalonian word. He was using lore to show his worth to his followers or convince himself and them that this cause he had constructed was one blessed to be destined. Maybe, if I could figure out the root of the lore, I could learn what his ultimate goal was and learn his weakness.

It was a long shot, but at that point, we were desperate for as many answers as possible, and at least this kind of research would keep me busy during waiting periods of investigating and undercover work.

"About what exactly?"

I groaned. "That's classified. I'm sorry."

"I can't give you a direction if you don't give me an idea of what this loon is spewing." He gave me a pointed look.

"Fair point." I tapped my foot a few times, trying a new angle. "Are there any texts about who or why the God and Goddess would deem someone 'blessed'? Make them believe that they have been granted a greater purpose on Kazola?"

"Hm." He tapped his lips with his fingers a few times before standing up, his robes gliding along the ground as he walked towards his bookshelf. "Blessed, you say?"

"Yes." I turned in my chair, watching as he skimmed the titles on his shelves, fingers grazing each one as if they were telling their entire story through the gentle touch.

"Here we go." He pulled two hefty volumes from the stacks, walking back over to me. "This is the only thing I could think might help."

I looked at the slightly tattered books, both bound in black leather, silvery writing scrawled across them. The first was titled "Lore of the Isle: Truths Unknown to Kazola" and the second, "What of the Ancient Times?"

"What are they about?"

"Some of the more fantastical theories and ideas of what happened during Ancient Times, why Lunestia and Firenielle created our kinds, and what 'really happened' during the Order."

"Are there other evidential texts to back up the claims written in them?"

"For the most part no." He shook his head. "However, a true conspiracy theorist would be able to take factual text and manipulate it in a way to make it seem like it did. I remember reading a few lore speculations that reference God and Goddess blessings on people or places. Perhaps you can find something that will help."

I perked up. It was a starting point at least. "Do you mind if I take these with me? I can return them before I leave for Seathra."

"Keep them for as long as you need. No need to return them until you're finished with them." He gave me a weary smile. "I prefer fact to fantastical, and these are far from that."

I tucked them against my lap, the leather still supple even after many years of wear and tear. "Thank you. I appreciate this."

"I don't know what is taking you down this path, cousin." He leaned forward, placing his bony fingers on my shoulder and giving it a tight squeeze. "Please, promise me you'll be careful."

I leaned over the books, wrapping my arms around his into a tight hug of reassurance, hoping it was enough to calm his racing pulse, no words leaving my lips.

I wasn't the type to give promises I might not be able to keep.

CHAPTER 18

The next evening, I was packed, bag secured to the back of my cycle and parked out front of the Château when the rumbling of another lectracycle approached me. The winter sun was already beginning to set, a soft glow enveloping the entryway, warming my cheeks against the brisk air that blew across my bundled body.

A few moments later, Nolan pulled up, his signature grin already plastered across his face as he parked his cycle next to mine. Before I could mount, Nolan had dismounted his own, taking wide steps to close the gap between us.

He swept me up into his arms, crushing me against his chest, my heart leaping to finally feel him against me. I instinctively wrapped my arms around him, squeezing tightly. He buried his nose into my hair, taking a deep breath in, while I did the same by rubbing my cheek against his chest. My wolf hummed, stirring gently at that comforting scent of spicy citrus. I hoped his wolf did the same to my musky tonka scent. He pulled back slightly, leaning forward.

"I missed you, sweetheart," he whispered against my cheek before snaking his hand to cradle the back of my neck and guide my lips to his. I gripped him tighter, my legs shaking, head spinning at the warmth spreading through me.

"People can see us," I whispered against his lips, a teasing tone in my voice because, to be honest, I wanted them to see. No matter what they did to me, I was finding happiness.

"Does it look like I care?" he said, echoing my feelings on the matter. He closed the distance again, slipping his tongue through my lips to show me just how little he cared if anyone caught us in such an intimate embrace. I allowed myself to get a bit lost, letting the memories of the High Faction meetings and seeing Logan and Kyler melt away. They dissipated with each swipe of his tongue and press of his firm, passionate lips.

Far too soon, he pulled away, his cheeks reddened, lips a bit swollen and his eyes flickering from gold back to forest green. "I suppose we should go."

I grunted. "Way to ruin the mood."

He laughed, brushing his nose against mine a few times before straightening back to his imposing height. "I'll make it up to you."

"I'm holding you to that."

We mounted our cycles and turned them on, the vibrating hum underneath me loosening a bit of excess tension in my shoulders. I double-checked that my backpack was secured before giving Nolan a nod and lurching my cycle forward.

"How was the rest of your time here?" Nolan asked once we had

left the Château's grounds and worked our way through the streets of Ilfra. I could hear the concern in his voice.

"It was fine." I shrugged, taking a sharp left turn to take a shortcut to the edges of the city so we could make it to the travel roads quicker.

And it had been. I had spent the rest of the day before and most of that day reading through the texts Ahren had let me take. So far, not much had stood out to me, although I had bookmarked a few pages that I thought may lead somewhere with more extensive research. A few mentions of prophecies from the Ancient Times made me wonder what they could be and what was hidden within. It had been a good distraction.

We broke out into the travel streets, the Crelanti Compound about a mile west of the capital. My stomach knotted a bit, palms sweating even with the brisk wind blowing against my exposed hands. I knew it was the smartest decision for us to have switched with Crelanti. We boarded each other and I had already been there.

Still, it didn't stop me from loathing the idea of having to rely on Caleb for anything. And with this mission, I would have to collaborate with him. The whole idea left a sour taste in my mouth.

The Compound gate came into view all too soon, my fingers tightening around the handles. My vision started to blur, but I shook it out, forcing my eyes to shift for a moment to help sharpen my vision back.

"It will be all right," Nolan soothed, and my eyes darted to him next to me.

"Make sure I don't kill him, okay?"

"I can't make that promise." Somehow, I could hear the smirk in his words even in my head. *"I will probably be just as tempted."*

"Guess we'll have to watch each other's backs, then."

"Always." He winked just before we pulled through the open gate, the metal structure already starting to close after we broke through. It didn't take long for us to come to the small circle of structures that made up this Compound.

The Crelanti Compound was nowhere near as big as ours. It consisted of a training building, an office building for the Hierarchy, two long barracks for the trainees, Deltas, and Dairchtas, and finally, the Hierarchy penthouse building, which stood tall above the rest. All of the black brick buildings stood in a tight semi-circle, barely any space between them.

My chest tightened at the two figures standing in front of the penthouse building. Caleb was the first one, his dirty blond hair glimmering in the glow of the setting sun, his silvery eyes almost translucent. Next to him was Riley, the Ar Duts of the Shrivika Ibridowyn. Her long ginger hair hung loosely to her hips, her tawny freckled face and bright blue eyes full of kindness. I had met her a few times in the past during family visits to Caleb's Compound. She was the type of leader that was an absolute gem to everyone, and it fostered immense respect from colleagues and soldiers alike.

We parked our cycles in the small lot next to the building where the rest of the Hierarchies were and pulled our bags off the back before walking to meet the two of them at the entrance.

"It's nice to see you again, Kasha," Riley greeted, her hand outstretched. I grasped it, giving it a quick shake.

"Thanks for having us." I gave her a genuine smile. I had nothing against her or the rest of the people on the Compound. My struggle was with their Alpha.

I turned to Caleb, who hadn't moved from the front door. "Caleb." I nodded to him.

"Kas." He gave me a tightened smile. He turned to Nolan. "Nice to see you again."

Nolan gave him a tight nod, gaze appraising my oldest brother. "You two have met?"

Caleb shrugged. "A few times, when I would visit Ollie during his training. They were close."

"Oh." My shoulders slumped.

That made sense. Caleb had already been in the Guard and would have had clearance to go and visit Ollie during that time. Since I had yet to join, I hadn't been given the privilege, which meant I had only met Nolan this year. I always had to stop myself from wondering what would have happened if we had met earlier since there was no use dwelling on something that could never be.

I refocused, turning back to Riley. "Thank you so much for voting in favor of the mission."

She smiled at me. "You made a persuasive argument. We all need to work together if we're going to do what's right for Kazola."

"Thank you," I said again.

"I have to get back to training," she said, eyes gazing up to the sky briefly. "We have some evaluations coming up for the trainees that we need to get ready for, but I wanted to make sure I was here to say hello. You know where my penthouse is in case you need anything."

She gave us one more nod before she crossed the circular path toward the training building. I braced myself, turning back to Caleb, his posture as rigid and tight as mine.

"I'll show you where you'll be staying. Come on." He pulled the door open, disappearing into the building and down the gold and cream hallway that extended down the first floor. We followed, pressure building in my chest with each awkward, silent step we took through the halls of the imposing building.

Caleb cleared his throat, pulling a key from his pocket and opening the door we had stopped in front of, then pushed it open slightly. "Our larger guest suite is under renovation right now, so this is the only one available."

"That's fine." I peeked in, the sitting room partially in view.

Caleb cleared his throat again. "It's a one-bedroom."

"Oh." My shoulders slumped, realizing why my brother was acting so weird.

Well, this was certainly awkward.

I peeked over at Nolan, his shoulders a bit stiffer. Since we had only been romantically entangled for a short time, we hadn't even broached the subject of spending nights together and sharing a bed. My stomach knotted a bit, not in anxiety but anticipation. Along with the shivers running up my spine, I knew my opinion on the matter. However, I didn't know Nolan's.

"I figured Nolan could sleep here and you could stay in the guest room in my penthouse."

Red clouded my vision. "Absolutely not."

"We lived together for the first eleven years of your life." Caleb rolled his eyes. "You can survive your time here with me."

"Just because I can survive torture, doesn't mean I have to subject myself to it willingly." A growl crawled up my throat, my wolf itching to protect me. "I'm staying in the guest suite."

"Fine." He huffed, crossing his arms. "Then Nolan can come…"

"No," I said, letting the growl rip from my lips. "He will stay here too."

"I have a perfectly good bed in my place." His jaw ticked. "There is no reason why one of you should have to sleep on the couch or floor, especially when you're here to work. Rest will be important."

"We'll make do," I said through gritted teeth. Nolan stilled behind me, my gaze falling to the floor and my cheeks reddening.

Oh, please, Goddess, don't let Caleb read between the lines.

Caleb's gaze darted between the two of us, his brow wrinkled for a few moments before his jaw unhinged, eyes wide. "Unbelievable." He gave a haughty laugh.

Damn him to the depths. Why did everyone I know have to be in the Guard?

Nolan growled behind me, his body rigid, fists forming into balls at his side. He took a step toward Caleb, but I put my hand on his chest, giving him a slight push back. He receded.

"Shut your mouth, Caleb." My chest heaved, my breath shallowing. "You have no idea what you're talking about."

"Developed a taste for Alphas, I see." He sneered, an incredulous smirk gracing his lips.

I didn't even hesitate, didn't even doubt, my vision sharpening with the glow of my gold eyes before I reached up and promptly slapped Caleb across the cheek. He was lucky. The stirring of my wolf deep in my belly was tempting me to do a lot worse.

"Keep your mouth shut." My voice rumbled from my lips, deepening with each word I spoke. "You've lost every right to comment on the decisions I make for myself and my happiness."

I would make damn sure that he kept himself in line while he was there. Liv and Eden had been right during that dinner a few nights ago; the opinions of others shouldn't influence my happiness.

He shook his head at me, eyes hardened into an apathetic gaze. Back to being father's perfect Alpha. "Well then, you know where to find me if you need anything. Have a good evening, Beta Mallanis."

I looked up at him with a scowl. "You too, Alpha Mallanis."

I gripped Nolan's wrist and pushed us right past Caleb into the suite before promptly slamming the door in his face.

CHAPTER 19

We finished up dinner and the little bit of work the two of us had to complete before getting ready for bed. I took my time in the washroom, relaxing under the steady stream of heated water flowing from the gentle rainfall spigot that hung from the stall ceiling. It rinsed away the past few days, letting it loosen some of the muscles and aches that had built up with each passing hour.

I wouldn't go to bed anxious. As with most things in my romantic life, it had been a while since I'd shared a bed with another.

Luckily, this was something Logan hadn't taken from me that night.

Finally, there was a part of building a new romance that excited me. No lingering doubt or fear clouding my mind, trying to poison it. I was just ready to enjoy the next few hours with Nolan's warmth next to me. I had slept so deeply the few times he had put me to bed. I couldn't help but be curious if having him in my bed would help even further.

After I finished dressing and brushing out my wet hair, I left the washroom, Nolan giving me a quick peck on the cheek before going to clean himself up. I pulled out one of my books and jumped onto the four-poster bed, burrowing myself into the fluffy blanket and mountain of pillows. I settled down, losing myself in a tale of a lost princess, her three siblings desperately trying to help her remember her past life and her broody best friend who was obviously in love with her.

Almost an hour passed before Nolan emerged from the washroom, my attention instantly drawn to him. I couldn't help but openly admire him, his wet hair almost black and slicked back from his face. He wore nothing but a low-hanging pair of black linen shorts, a few stray droplets of water still clinging to his bronze chest and stomach.

I felt overdressed in my thin-strapped gray top, soft cotton shorts, and my underthings. If this was how Nolan went to bed, I could certainly get used to it.

"Enjoying the show?" he teased.

"Immensely." I licked my lips and wiggled my eyebrows at him.

"Glad to see my terrible influence has started rubbing off on you."

He turned back towards the bed, taking a few steps before stopping in his tracks, his eyes tracing the outline of the mattress. His jaw tensed, the muscles of his forearms and chest flexing. He looked ready to fight, preparing for potential danger. I sat up straight, dropping my book on the table beside me.

"Nolan?" I moved to the edge of the bed, kneeling. "Is everything okay?"

He just continued to stare, a haunted look overtaking his gaze. "Maybe I should sleep on the floor."

"What? Why?" I tilted my head, watching every movement he made.

He took a step back, angling to the closet. "I can see if there are any blankets and pillows in here and I can make a pallet. I think that would be best."

"But—"

I would have yanked him into bed if I hadn't caught the brief movement, fingers curling around the chain that always hung around his neck. The chain that kept something very special to him close to his heart.

Cleo's ring.

My heart sank. He wasn't holding back because he was concerned for me, he was holding back for himself. For the pain and heartache in his chest that he hid away from the world behind easy grins and carefree laughs.

I slowly padded over to him, his back still to me, hands holding the closet door handle in a vice grip. His breath was ragged, head downcast.

I didn't dare touch him, since whenever I was in those states, I disliked it. Instead, I moved to the side, leaning against the wall so he could see me and feel my presence without physical touch to potentially harm him.

"I'm sorry," I whispered, keeping my voice as gentle as possible. "I should have realized."

"Realized what?" His voice was rough, as if he needed to drink a gallon of water to quench a deep thirst.

"That the last person you shared a bed with was Cleo."

He let out a shuddering breath. "It's no big deal."

"Doesn't make it any less important." I looked him up and down.

"It shouldn't bother me." His other hand reached up to brace himself against the door in front of him, fingers curling into the wood. "I was looking forward to spending the night with you."

"Until you saw me in bed?"

He nodded. "I don't know why it didn't become real until then."

"Because it wasn't," I whispered. "Now it is, and your mind is trying to protect you from the pain you once felt."

"The last time was… the night before she died." His head dropped to rest on the door. "I just… it all came back to me when I saw you. And with what we are about to investigate tomorrow, who is obsessed with you… Goddess… it's all…"

"Nolan," I whispered.

"I want him dead."

"I know."

"I would feel very little remorse about taking his life if I had the chance." He growled, his nails extending slightly into sharpened peaks. "For feeling his blood drip down my fingers as I pulled my blade from his chest."

"I know that too."

"Does that make me a bad person?"

"No, it just makes you a person in pain," I said. "No matter how many people want to deny it, we are more capable of thinking about revenge than forgiveness, especially when we're trying to figure out how to cope with our own trauma. Just because you want to, doesn't mean you will. And I trust that you will make the right decision when it comes down to it."

"Do you believe that?" He peeked over at me.

I gave him a small smile. "I do."

"These emotions suck," he grumbled, standing up a bit straighter, hands falling away from the closet but his head still downcast.

"I'll agree with you on that."

"I don't want this to ruin our night." He slumped against the door, his eyes shifting to green from gold. They must have turned while talking. "I've missed you for the past week, and I was eager to have an excuse to have you in my arms for so long. Especially since most of our time here will be spent working."

I believed every word he said, and I understood why it might not be possible anymore when the idea of sharing a bed was apparently a trigger for him.

He did such a good job of hiding his pain. I wasn't sure if he did it on purpose or if he was trying to give me a safe space to process my own trauma, but that wasn't fair. His was just as valid as mine, and we were both going into this relationship with haunted pasts that threatened to ruin the budding beauty we were trying to grow together. If we weren't careful and truthful with each other, it could tear us apart before we even had a chance.

And that, I would not let happen. Not when I finally found someone I felt safe with.

"Then how about this. I'm going to get back into bed and read for a bit longer." I took a few steps back, inching slowly towards the bed. "If you feel ready to join me, you can. Or, if you would prefer to sleep on the floor or kick me out of bed and have me sleep on the floor, that's okay too."

"You are not sleeping on the floor."

"Just know you have options," I said, dropping onto the bed and scooting back onto my original side. "And there are no wrong choices. You make the one that's best for you and I will support it no matter what."

Slowly, he gave me a tired half smile. "Thank you."

I winked, settling into the mountain of pillows again and pulling my book onto my lap. I barely read the words but tried my best to make it look like I was preoccupied by the story while he stood there. Just as Vanessa had instructed me about exploring my triggers and finding ways around it, we would need to do the same for Nolan.

So, I would help create a space for him to do just that. I would let him see that I wanted to be his safety just as he was becoming mine.

Minutes passed by, my heart racing when I finally heard movement, but I didn't dare look up. I didn't want him to think he had an audience while making his decision. When I finally felt the mattress dip under his weight, I looked over, his green eyes gleaming in the low light from the bedside lamps I had turned on earlier. He leaned over and kissed the top of my head before swinging his legs up and tucking them under the covers.

I let him take the lead, keeping myself to my side while he adjusted the pillows and blankets around himself. I put my book down, already knowing I would have to backtrack a few pages so I could watch him a bit. My heart stammered at the sight of him, warmth filling the space underneath the covers, his body only a few inches away from mine. I pulled the blanket around me tighter, waiting.

"Come here," he whispered, wrapping his arm around my shoulder and gently tugging me towards him. I gave him no resistance, letting him settle me into the crook of his arm, my cheek resting on his warm chest.

Even though he settled me against him, I felt his body tense under me. So, I gently traced the lines of the runic tattoos that went up his arms and the tree root and branches that snaked along his pectoral muscles. I idly let my fingers wander, his breathing evening out a bit with each touch. I tried my best to avoid the chain that hung there, although my fingers snagged on it a few times.

"Does it bother you?" he whispered, his warm breath ruffling the loose tendrils of my hair.

I turned my head, resting my chin on his chest to peek up at him. "What?"

"That I still wear Cleo's ring." His gaze lingered on the ceiling, avoiding my gaze as best as possible.

"Of course not. Why would you think that?"

He shrugged, cheeks tinged with pink. "Something that always concerned me, even before we met was that if I started being with another woman, they would get angry that I still wore it."

"If someone got angry at you for that, then they aren't the right person to be with." I settled my cheek back on his chest. "I would never be angry at you for keeping someone you loved and miss close to you."

"Are you sure?"

"Yes." I kissed his chest. "She was a part of your life. I would never want you to forget her just because you're now with me."

"She would want me to keep living," he said, although it sounded like it was more for him than me. "If she's watching me from the After, I think she would like you."

"I hope so." I smiled.

His hand moved up, tangling his fingers into my hair and stroking along my scalp. "Thank you, sweetheart. For all of this."

He didn't have to specify what I had done; I understood. Just as he did whenever he helped me through a hard time.

"You do the same for me." I snuggled closer into his embrace, my eyes growing heavy at the comforting touch. We turned off the lights, letting silence and darkness settle as we just held each other. I waited for his breath to even out under my cheek before closing my eyes, sleep taking me.

CHAPTER 20

Three days. It had already been three days and nothing.

On our first morning on the Compound, Nolan and I had taken the time to formulate a plan for how we would discover the location of one of Elliot's meetings in Ilfra. After much discussion, and a bit of teasing from both of us, we knew all we could do was start going undercover in the city and try to find information about the assembly. After witnessing how he preyed on Lila, we decided to focus on the areas of the city that were similar to the lower sector of Eroste where the Black Howl resided.

From morning until late into the night, Nolan and I prowled the seedy streets of Ilfra, trying to find any sign of revolutionists or one of Elliot's schemes. We had a few Deltas or Derchtas drive us to the outskirts of the city and drop us off so we could spend most of the day on foot before meeting them for a pick-up. The routine had set in rather quickly, and unfortunately was becoming monotonous with no new lead showing itself.

"What if I just started punching people?" I mumbled to Nolan as we strolled along the streets of an area best known for back-alley prostitution. We had already hit the major spots I knew where drug trades went down, so the next areas were those with human trafficking. "Think that will get us answers faster?"

"Yes. That will make us fit in better." Nolan smirked at me.

"It probably would." I peeked down an alley, turning away quickly when the moans of pleasure reached me. "We're in the heart of the syndicates and crime families. Might as well act like it if we want people to talk."

I wasn't being serious. At least, not completely. I was a bit tempted to see if it would garner any results, but it wasn't like we had even stumbled across anyone who seemed to be talking about saving others or finding truth or any of the whacked-out phrases Elliot had used in the past to describe his movement.

"Careful. If you show just how malicious you can be, we might scare them away," he teased.

"I really hope we didn't miss this month's." I sighed, turning us down another road. "If we have to wait until next month, we're screwed."

"We'll figure it out." Nolan gently brushed his hand at the bottom of my spine before pulling away. "Worst case, only the team sent into the Seathra meeting will get in, but at least we will have some new information from that. Even if we aren't the ones getting to witness, it will still be vital information on how Elliot is convincing people to join the cause."

"I suppose," I mumbled.

He was right. What was important for this joint mission with the other Factions was getting as much information as possible about what Elliot was planning. However, a part of me stirred, my gut churning at the idea of not being one of those who would get to see what this was. I needed to witness it myself, to know what was going on. Elliot had wanted me at this meeting for a reason. I had to know why.

"Maybe if we…" I began, but I didn't have time to finish my sentence before getting distracted by something in the near distance.

BOOM!

An explosion. Heart-wrenching screams. The crackling of fire.

Nolan and I stared at each other with wide eyes for a moment before taking off, letting our senses follow the thick smoky scent of burning wood. We wound through the streets, feet pounding against the cobbled stone until we made it to the center of the eatery district, where a small cottage-like building burned with a raging fire, the glass of the windows already broken and the roof caving in on itself.

"Kasha…" Nolan whispered.

"I know."

The fire was too big, and with the explosion we had heard, it was more likely than not that foul play was a part of this.

I crept forward, not getting too close to the building but peeking down the narrow alley next to it. My eyes widened, focusing my hearing to confirm what I saw—a blur of shadows disappearing around the corner. I took a few steps in, pulling in a deep breath to take in any scents that lingered.

Refuge. Rotting food. The sour stench of rodents. Bright raspberry and peach.

There. That was a scent trail for someone.

I didn't know who, and I had no idea if they were connected to this fire, but it seemed too coincidental that whoever this person was ran away when the rest of the city folks were crowding around or starting to collect pails of water and sand to throw onto the fire.

Just a bit too suspicious.

"Got what you need?" Nolan asked.

I nodded. *"Yes."*

He tugged me away from the alley, bringing us back to the front where it seemed the fire already grew twice the size. What had they put into the building to make it combust so quickly? My skin itched to get in there and sniff it out.

It took all the control I had to keep myself rooted to my spot, to not run into that building and make sure everyone was out and safe. I wasn't a Guard right then, I was just another civilian watching a local business burn to the ground in black billows of raging smoke and cracking wood. I reached my hand down to Nolan's, grasping it as an anchor to keep me in place, his squeezing mine back, letting me know I wasn't alone in my struggle.

Finally, after what seemed like far too many seconds, a slew of local guards came running, a pressurized tankard of water pulled on a cart and placed in the front before they hooked long hoses to it and began to spray the flames while locals continued to throw water into different parts of the building. Any way to help.

"What do you think happened?" I asked, leaning in closer to Nolan.

He put his arm around my shoulder, tucking me in tightly to his side. *"I have no idea, but something just feels…wrong about all of this."*

"I agree." I wrapped my arm around his waist. *"We need answers."*

"I'm sure Caleb or his Faction will know some stuff when we return tonight."

"Probably." I looked around, eyes tracking everyone, most staring on in shock or terror. Finally, my eyes landed on those I was looking for. An older man and woman with three small children huddled around them, all of them clutching each other and some with soot smeared across their tear-stained cheeks or singed clothes. Those must be the owners. *"But I'm too impatient to wait."*

I shrugged off the plain gray wool jacket I wore and walked over to them, approaching slowly. A few steps away, I said, "Excuse me?"

The adults turned to me, the children's faces still buried in their mother or father's sides.

"Yes?" The man sniffed, eyes red-rimmed.

"I don't mean to bother you, but I thought you might want this." I handed it to the woman, who was in nothing but a quarter-sleeve tunic, loose pants, and an apron to protect her from the winter air. I at least had a sweater on, and I tended to run hot anyways. "It might help with the shivers a little."

"Thank you," she said, her mousy voice barely above a whisper as she grasped the coat and wrapped it around her shoulders.

"We're so sorry about this," Nolan said behind me, also handing his coat over to the gentleman, who wrapped it as best he could around his children.

"That bakery had been in my family for three generations." He looked over to the burning building briefly before returning his gaze to us. "The Gods must be angry at me."

"Don't say that," I soothed, heart clenching.

"Don't listen to those lunatics, Elian," the woman said, tugging on his arm. "They just wanted an excuse to invoke violence."

"Grace!" he hissed, eyes glancing at us in warning.

"It's not like we're the first." She wiped away a few stray tears.

"What are you talking about?" I took another step forward, closing the gap so our voices wouldn't carry.

"We are the third business in the past two weeks to get attacked in some way." Her cheeks were mottled red, eyes stone cold. "Vandalized by masked people screaming unknown profanities and claiming to be doing the Gods' work."

My cheeks drained of color. "Did they say why it was the work of the Gods?"

Elian sighed. "It's because we have a contract with the government. We supply specialty cakes or pastries to the High Faction for special occasions. All the other businesses had similar contracts with the High Faction or the local Garrison or Onyx Guard."

"This has to be Elliot."

"Yeah, no doubt about it." His voice was stiff, as was his posture. *"Looks like he's done hiding his people in the shadows and is ready for chaos."*

"And we have no idea how far his people are willing to go."

We talked to Elian and Grace for a few more moments, offering any help we could without giving up our identities. They had appreciated it but soon were called away by a local commander ready to take a statement from them. Nolan and I walked away to the outskirts of the scene hand in hand, my mind processing everything we had just witnessed and learned. I halted, Nolan stopping at the sudden lurch.

"Lea." My heart stopped, my mind racing. Lea had a contract with our Faction and handled all our weapon needs. "They could target her. I have to go. I must warn her!"

I tried to take off down the street, but Nolan pulled me back to him. "Lea will be safe. We will call Beckett and he'll put her under protective custody."

"We don't have our Comms." My foot tapped against the ground, my hands searching for my unit even though I knew I left it back at Caleb's Compound, not wanting to risk being caught with it while undercover. "Something could happen between now and then. She could be kidnapped, or her forge burned, or something even worse…"

"Kasha." Nolan grasped my cheeks between his hands, lowering his forehead to touch mine. "Breathe for me, sweetheart."

His voice was soft but determined, pulling me to focus so I could take a shaky breath in and a long exhale out. I kept repeating it for a few cycles, each inhale getting significantly stronger. Finally, I relaxed into his touch, my shoulders slumping.

"Lea is safe and smart," he whispered, that soothing, smooth tone still lacing each word. "She will be all right. Now, I hate to ask this, but can you reach Caleb from here? Families tend to have farther distances that the telepathic link can travel."

My wolf growled in my chest, but I ignored it and let Nolan's words soothe me as I reached out to someone I wished I didn't have to. It felt like stretching an aching muscle, one I hadn't used in a long time. It had been over a year since I had tried to form a pathway to Caleb.

"Caleb?" I called out, hoping he would let me in. *"Cal?"*

"Kasha?" His voice was surprisingly frantic, his pitch a bit higher than normal. *"What is it? Are you hurt?"*

"No, we're fine." I squeezed Nolan's hand linked with mine. *"But we just witnessed an attack on a local bakery that had a contract with the High Faction. They claim they were attacked because of it."*

"Do you think it's connected to Elliot?"

"Yes, but that's not why I'm reaching out." My gut trembled, tears threatening to prick at my eyes. *"Lea has a contract with us. I need you to reach out to Beckett or Emric and have them go and get her and put her under protective custody. I don't want her to be targeted, especially since she's closely tied to me."*

Silence fell, fear lacing my thoughts that he had disconnected. *"Of course. I'll reach out to them now. I'll have them keep me updated and I'll funnel any news to you throughout the day while you're away."*

"Good. That's good." I nodded, relief washing through me like ice water in my veins.

"She'll be safe, Kas. I promise," Caleb said.

I could have said something snarky back, letting him know his promises meant very little to me. But something about his voice and the desperation that was laced throughout the whole conversation gave me pause and sheathed my bitter tongue. So, instead, I said, *"Thank you, Cal,"* before severing the connection to him.

I took a few more deep breaths, leaning my head against Nolan's chest for stability before I pulled away and looked up at him, his gaze soft and focused completely on me and not the slowly shrinking fire and crowd near us.

"I still wish I could go home and be with her." My chest ached, my mind reeling at the fact that I would not be the one watching over her. I trusted my team and I knew they would keep her safe, but still, it wasn't the same as me being there for her. She had been through too much already.

"I know. I would too. But until then, the best way we can help is to find a way into a meeting and get more details on the uprising. That's what is leading people to attack, and the sooner we put an end to it, the sooner Lea will be safe."

I nodded, letting the logic seep into my frantic thoughts. "You're right. I know you are."

"You all right?" He kissed my forehead.

"I think so. I'll try to be, at least."

"So, where to next?"

I let my gaze wander, an idea sparking in my mind as the murky thoughts cleared away. "Follow me."

CHAPTER 21

I followed the trail of peach and raspberry, the sugary sweet scent becoming more potent the longer I followed from the alley where I first caught the trail. I had no idea if whoever was at the end of the hunt would know anything, but it was worth a try.

I lost the scent a few times, but by following logic and the layout of the city, I was able to find it once again. We ended up about two miles from the fire, walking down what had been named Traveler's Trail, the area of Ilfra that catered less to locals and more to anyone coming for a trip to the city. It was packed with different taverns, gambling houses, and theaters for people to enjoy. The paved streets were lined with performers busking for some extra cash or showing off their artwork and other talents.

Residents of Ilfa tended to avoid this area like the plague, making it the perfect place to hide in plain sight when you wanted to lie low after setting fire to a local bakery.

I focused on that peach and raspberry trail, trying my best to block out the onslaught of other unique scents trying to drown it out. I grabbed Nolan's hand, tugging him behind me, and pushed my way through the crowds and their wide-eyed awe of the brightly lit cobbled street.

Finally, I found the end of the trail, walking us into a blue and white striped building with the sign reading 'Seafarer's Tavern'.

My eyes darted around the half-packed tavern, the mid-afternoon crowd already starting to bring life to the space. The place was well lit, nothing seedy or run down about it. White lacy curtains hung around the full wall of windows, the tables painted bright white with navy blue chairs huddled around them. A bar took up the left side, and nautical paraphernalia decorated the walls from painted anchors, to mounted and stuffed fish, and even a giant helm.

And there, sitting at the bar, was the person I was looking for.

"That… is not what I expected," I said, my brows wrinkling as we lingered by the doorway to the tavern.

"Sure that's him?"

"Questioning my sense?" I side-eyed him playfully.

"Never." He winked.

I understood what he meant, though. I hadn't envisioned much when I followed the summertime fruit scent, but I didn't think the burly man hunched over a drink at the bar was the one I was looking for. That's the thing about scent patterns. They don't always make sense to someone until you get to know the person it belongs to.

"Follow my lead. I have an idea," I said, grasping Nolan's hand and pulling us to the bar. The seat beside the mark was empty, so I sidled up next to him and ordered two pints of ale. My stomach

churned at the scent of the hops I'd come to dislike, but I pushed it away, looking forward.

"Ask me if I'm okay."

"Are you okay, sweetheart?" Nolan asked, not missing a beat. He slung his arm over the back of my chair to rub small circles along my upper back, his fingers gently tangling in the ends of my ponytail.

I narrowed my eyes at him, and he responded with a wink. Shameless flirt.

"I just can't believe it happened." I traced the rim of my glass with my fingertips.

"It was certainly quite a shock." Nolan shook his head, dark hair falling against his forehead. "I heard that the bakery had been in the family for generations. Now gone from one little fire."

"The only silver lining is that the High Faction now loses one of their suppliers." I smirked, and Nolan laughed. Although to most it sounded relaxed, it lacked its usual mischief.

The burly man grunted at my comment, and not in a way that made me think he was upset by the ordeal I talked about. I finally turned to him, getting a better look. He was about as tall as Nolan, but twice as thick. He could probably take down an old building just by running into one of the walls. His face was tanned and heavily lined from what looked like too many hours in the sun and covered in a long, black beard that reached his heart. The hidden woodsy undertone to his typically brighter scent told me he was a Varg Anwyn.

And there, on the heel of his well-worn black boots, was a scuff of soot. Most would assume from lighting a pyre in his house, but

I knew better. He most likely got it from fleeing a crime scene.

"Did you see it too, sir?" I asked him.

"Might have heard about it." He kept staring forward, trained on the racks of liquor behind the bartenders that worked quickly to make drinks.

"We walked past it on our way here." I kept my words strained. "The building was basically charred rubble."

"Hm." Even under the bushy beard, I saw the satisfied smirk he tried to conceal.

Yes. My gut told me this was the man who set fire to that place, and it was obvious he had very little remorse. Now, all I had to do was get him to admit it.

If I wasn't undercover, I would have slammed the man's face into the bar and cuffed him, dragging him to the local garrison for imprisonment. However, he was more useful to me free, so instead, I ran my hand under the bar, placing it on Nolan's knee, and squeezed my frustrations out. He didn't even flinch, covering my hand with his.

"The crowd was whispering that it was done intentionally," I said. "Something about government contractors being targeted in the city."

"I've heard the same rumors." His beady eyes finally flicked over to me, the bright blue contrasting with his almost black hair.

"Sounds like these people are really trying to make a difference," Nolan said.

"From what I've heard on the streets, some don't find it fair that only a few benefit from the 'charitable' givings of the High Faction while the rest suffer," the man commented, venom in his words.

"You certainly did a good job at making sure proper justice was served." My heart pounded in my chest, Nolan holding his breath behind me.

"I have no idea what you're talking about," he grumbled, gaze darting away and his body recoiling. He scraped his chair a few inches away from mine.

"Well, then, I guess I will hold my thanks until I find the real person responsible." I went to stand, Nolan following and throwing down a few coins to pay our tab.

"Wait," he said, causing Nolan and me to plop back into our seats. "That's really what you would want to say to the person?"

"If the owners thought it was morally all right to work with… *those people* then they got what was coming to them."

My stomach soured at the words I was speaking, but I knew they were necessary. No matter how treasonous they were, I didn't mean them, and it would hopefully get me closer to those committing heinous acts.

"What would you know about it?"

I needed to gain this man's trust somehow; it was the only way I could find answers. Rule one of going undercover was making your fake identity as close to your real one as possible, helping to bring truth to your words. I reasoned with myself that was the only reason I spoke again.

"I used to believe the High Faction would protect me and keep Kazola safe." I took a deep breath, my fingers tingling. "But when I was assaulted last year and they let my attacker go because he had better connections than I did, I knew it was all a farce. They just care about their own power, nothing more. I had never felt more alone in my life."

My stomach sank. Not at the once again treasonous words, but the fact that a part of me believed them, a pang of guilt absent after I said my part. Nolan didn't speak. Instead, he took the hand that still rested on his knee and wound his fingers with mine, giving them a tight squeeze.

The man stared ahead, contemplating my words as Nolan slid his half-empty glass in front of me and removed the full one I clutched to take a long sip. Without missing a beat, I pulled his old glass closer, the illusion that I had been drinking this whole time hopefully solidifying.

"I'm sorry that happened to you. I went through something similar when my wife was killed. People don't deserve the treatment that has been given to them in recent years." He peeked back at me, his icy blue eyes filled with a raging storm that made my spine shiver. "We need to do something about it."

"Here, here." I raised my glass in a welcoming gesture, and a smile spread across his lips as he clicked his glass with mine.

I had him.

"Too bad there isn't anything we can do." I rubbed the back of my neck, feigning distress.

"Not necessarily." He downed the rest of his drink before slamming it on the counter, quickly gesturing to the bartender for another while standing up and pulling something from his back pocket. "If you want to meet others who think the same way as us, you can come to a little meeting we're having next week."

He slid the paper over to me, the trifold partially ripped parchment a beacon of hope for our investigation.

"What kind of meeting?"

"Just a gathering of those who want to try and find a better way for Kazola. If you become so inclined, you could even assist during the next… um… outing we have planned." He smiled at me. "Maybe it will help you feel less alone."

I opened the piece of paper, eyes scanning over the date, time, and location of this mysterious meeting. To most, it seemed like an innocent note. However, I knew better due to the crest stamped at the top of the page: an E and W intertwined with thorned vines—Elliot's crest.

We found it, and the meeting was the next week. I had to use all of my strength not to start dancing for joy.

Instead, I smiled at the man. "Thank you. I'll think about it."

His new drink was placed in front of him just as Nolan and I scraped our chairs back and left. He threw his arm around my shoulders, pulling me close to his chest.

"You are awe-inspiring, sweetheart." He kissed the top of my head.

"Couldn't have done it without you lending your strength to me," I whispered back.

We walked away from the tavern, but we didn't leave the city until we found a guard and reported exactly where they could find their mystery arsonist.

CHAPTER 22

We were back at the Compound an hour later, having found a few Guard members and hitching a ride back with them.

The first thing I did was rush to our room and grab my Comms unit to call Beckett. He confirmed that Lucas and Taylor had gone out and gotten Lea. To no one's surprise, she had refused to go until she finished all her orders. So, the two of them had sat in the forge with her until she was ready to go and had taken her to pack a few things before bringing her back to the Compound. She would be staying in the guest house for the foreseeable future, and a member of our team would escort her to work every day so no one got suspicious of her. My gut still churned at the idea of being away when she needed me, but Beckett assured me that I was exactly where she needed me to be.

So, I took a few deep breaths and repeated the words until I started to believe them as well.

Nolan and I cleaned up and changed back into our training

armor before heading out to the office building to liaise with Caleb and his Keturi members. They were all waiting for us in their conference room, almost a mirror image in blandness and set up to our own back in Seathra. Caleb and Riley sat at the head of the table, along with Brielle, Caleb's Beta, and Ivan, Riley's Dara. We took the two seats across from the four of them, my spine straight against the back of the well-used black cushion chair.

"I heard we have some good news." Riley smiled at us, warmth radiating from her. Caleb on the other hand, sat stiffly in his seat, Brielle and Ivan slumped in their chairs, obviously feeling a bit awkward at being in the same room as Caleb and me. At least Riley was acting normal.

I gave them a full report of what we had discovered, including the meeting time. Every single one of them congratulated us, even Caleb, although his wasn't quite as excited as the rest of the team's.

"I can pull together a tactical surveillance team," Brielle said, writing some notes down on a piece of parchment. "Get an idea of the place you're going and scout out the best spots for us to help keep you safe. It will…"

"No," Caleb's hard, steeled voice cut in. "I will lead the team and you can assist."

"Brielle is perfectly capable."

What, now he cares about my safety?

"Brielle will be my partner on it as always." He peeked over to her, giving her a reassuring smile. Brielle's didn't reach quite as far as his, her glance falling to the table in front of her. "But this is non-negotiable."

"Fine, whatever." I rolled my eyes. I wasn't in the mood to have

Caleb sour my and Nolan's success.

We went over the logistics and what we needed to do in the next week to prepare. By the time we were dismissed, we all looked weighed down by the heaviness of what we were preparing for. No one was immune from the pressure.

As I gathered my notebook, Nolan mindlessly tracing a circle on my upper back, my Comms unit buzzed in my pocket. I pulled it out, intrigue coating my tongue at Evette's name scrawled across the screen.

Caleb lingered. I shot him a scowl, but I wasn't going to let him bait me. So, instead, I answered.

"Hello, Evette." I smiled at the screen, Nolan peering over my shoulder.

"Hello, Kasha." She smiled back. "And hello to you too, Alpha Carrigan."

"Hello, Delegate." He nodded in greeting.

"What can I help you with?" I turned slightly so Caleb was no longer in my line of sight, although I could still feel the pressure of his stare on my spine.

"I know it's a bit last minute, but I wanted to invite you to a cocktail reception that we're holding at the Château. We have a handful of visiting Faction members in town, so we decided it was an easier way to talk about business and reconnect." Mango flew overhead before landing on her shoulder, his little face nuzzling against her cheek. "We just got notice that the first part of your undercover work was successful, and we would love to hear more about the next steps and celebrate the accomplishment with you."

My stomach churned at the idea. I had been to plenty of these receptions before. First as my father's guest when we lived here during the beginning of his time on the High Faction. Then later in life as a fellow Hierarchy member of the Onyx Guard. I knew the pomp and circumstance of it all. There were very few unknowns going into this that scared me, except one.

I still didn't know where I stood with the majority of the High Faction.

Father and Cole were still bitter and cruel towards me and what I had put all of us through. Evette had made her feelings clear about how she felt on the whole matter, backing it up by reaching out and inviting me. Kyler was still an unknown, but fury boiled my blood just thinking about his betrayal. As for the other eleven members, only the Goddess knew what they thought.

I gripped the unit tighter. I didn't know what to do.

"What do you think, Kas?" Nolan asked, looking down at me. "It's completely up to you."

I peeked up, his face creased with a combination of worry and trust. He knew I would make the best decision for myself and would be there to support me in any way I needed.

I looked up at Caleb, who had a scowl on his face. My eyebrows perked up. *"Are you going to this?"*

"Yup," he sniped. *"As is Father."*

My veins heated, something brewing deep in my chest knowing both would be there. A part of me wanted to run away. However, by the look on Caleb's face and the rigidness of his stance, something wasn't right. Did he not want me to go? Still too ashamed of his baby sister to even be seen in public with her?

Well, that made my decision easy.

"We'll be there."

★★★

An hour in, and already I regretted coming.

Not because I couldn't ignore the stares or the obvious whispers that followed Nolan and me wherever we went. It was because I had forgotten just how much I hated these stupid things, even before everything imploded in my life.

It was held in the receiving hall of the Château, the dome ceiling hovering above us, a glass and gold chandelier sparkling with the low glow of dimmed lights and the moonlight reflecting through the floor-to-ceiling windows. Two bars were set on opposite sides of the room, and at least half a dozen servers passed through the crowd of guests to hand out appetizers and glasses of wine and ale. Cocktail tables were peppered throughout, people gathering around them in laughter and vibrant conversation.

It was just a bunch of people acting in a way I knew wasn't completely them. Somehow, in a room full of investigators who dedicated their lives to finding the truth, we all put on the oddest masks when around the High Faction. And most of the Delegates weren't much better. They laughed and complimented, handing out advice and promises like they were rich and in supply. They pretended like they would follow through on said promises, and maybe they would, if it was in the interest of what aligned with their needs.

I hadn't realized just how bitter I had become towards them until I was surrounded by them, once again dressed in my formal uniform, the high collar of the black button-up shirt and thick coat choking me.

One of the few positives was getting to see Nolan in his dress uniform for the first time. I was used to seeing him in full black attire, but the cut and length of his intricate black jacket complimented his height, and I couldn't help but appreciate how good his ass looked in his tight dress pants. I hadn't even been a little ashamed when he had caught me checking it out in our suite when we were preparing to leave. In retribution, he had spent just as much time looking over me as I buttoned my coat, the tight fit helping to accentuate my waist and hips in a flattering way. It made my heart flutter something fierce, to the point where I had struggled to finish buttoning the coat and he had to step in and help.

Goddess, this man still made me weak in the knees and, of course, his flirtatious confident self knew and relished in it. I was just happy I was able to enjoy it without my past tainting every moment.

We kept our hands clasped together, deciding before we left that we wouldn't hide what we were to each other.

We spent the first hour socializing with other members from other Factions. Evette had joined us at one point and introduced us to a few people; mostly other High Faction members I had never really interacted with, which had included Imogene. All four of them were kind to me, not once acting awkward or uncomfortable around me.

After a while, Nolan led us to one of the low cocktail tables scattered about the room, sitting on the outskirts to observe and get a reprieve from everyone.

"Can I ask you something?" He swirled his glass, eyes appraising me over the table.

"Of course." I took a sip of my water.

"Why don't you drink?"

The sip struggled down my throat. "Maybe I just don't like the taste." I gave him a calm smile, trying to downplay it.

"Maybe, but I'm pretty sure that isn't the case."

"How?"

He gave me a pointed stare. "Do you really want me to analyze you right now?"

"Kind of." I couldn't help but be intrigued. I wanted to know what he had observed over the weeks. The way his mind worked always fascinated me.

"Fine." He put his glass down, leaning on the small table to crowd my space, and I instinctively leaned towards him. "I've been undercover with you to multiple bars now, where you've had to blend in. You usually have a decent knowledge of what's on the menu, showing that you've looked it over multiple times and have familiarity with it. Also, when you order your decoy drink, it's always something of a particular taste."

I wrinkled my brow. "What does that even mean?"

"It means that if you really weren't about alcohol but wanted something to help you fit in, you'd just order the cheapest option to have something in front of you. Instead, you order things in multiple price ranges, showing that you're not looking at the cost but at the quality and taste notes. Or that you already have favorite brands picked out and you instinctively know exactly what to order." He smirked at me. "How did I do?"

I frowned at him. "I hate you sometimes."

"No, you don't. You're enthralled." He winked. "Seriously, you don't have to tell me if you aren't ready, but I do think you used to drink and now you avoid it. I just wanted to ask to see if there was any way I could help."

I sighed. I wasn't even a little surprised that Nolan had observed this about me; it wasn't the first time. I felt stupid for my reasoning, a part of me ashamed, but I took a few deep breaths to push it aside.

"I don't want to get too into it here." I looked around the room, making sure we were decently alone and those closest to us were too preoccupied in their own conversations to overhear. "But one of the tactics Logan's defense used against my case was that I had been drinking that night. That I was too impaired to remember giving my consent."

"*Futeacha*." He swore under his breath, his grip on his glass tightening.

"To be clear, I had had two ales before I went off on the run with Logan." I shook my head. "It took at least four or five to start making me feel tipsy, let alone impaired enough to have gaps in my memory. The defense was weak, but still. The idea of drinking just makes me feel all sorts of anxiety. I don't want something like that to ever let anyone doubt my actions again."

"I get it." He leaned across the table, wrapping our hands together. "After Cleo, I wouldn't cook salmon anymore. Still haven't. It was the last meal I made her and now just scenting it makes my stomach roll in a way that I hate. It's devastating because I make a damn good poached salmon.”

I giggled, his admission and teasing helping to lift a weight from my chest. It made me feel less alone for my actions.

“Thank you.” I squeezed his hand back.

We fell back into silence, my eyes drifting across the room. I tried my best to control myself, but instinct from my past times in these events caught me, and I searched for them. I wasn’t even a little surprised to see them together. Father, dressed in a perfectly pressed black suit, not a hair out a place, and Caleb, in the same dress uniform as the other male Guards.

Ollie and I took after Mama, but Caleb had always been Father’s mirror image, and no longer just in looks but in mannerisms as well. They held their posture similarly, their glasses both filled with some kind of expensive whiskey, and they tilted their heads to the left when giving a polite laugh at something they probably didn’t find all that funny.

I hated them and loved them, I loathed them and missed them. It was utterly maddening. Maybe I was destined to live in this permanent stasis of confusion when it came to half my family.

Goddess, I hoped not.

My body seized when my oldest brother looked towards me, our gazes locking. I couldn’t look away, caught in the snare of those silver eyes that had once been filled with so much love and affection for me. The person who had protected me, who had loved me from the day I was born. We may not have been friends, but I had never doubted Caleb’s loyalty to me, and he never doubted mine to him.

Something flashed across his features, something I hadn’t seen directed at me in a long time. It looked like… heartache. Or anguish. Maybe I was reading too much into it, but the sadness in his eyes increased and the twist of his lips confused me. For the past year, he had done nothing but direct cold, steeled contempt towards me.

Not now. Now he stared at me with a longing that made my heart lurch and my fingers go numb. It was unexpected, mind-boggling, and an emotional twist I didn't need.

As quickly as he had revealed that part of him to me, it disappeared, back behind the curtain of cold steel, already a distant memory that I tried my best to shove away.

Tried, but failed for the rest of the evening.

CHAPTER 23

When Nolan and I needed a distraction, we defaulted to working out.

We had agreed with Caleb's Keturi team when they said we shouldn't venture out into Ilfra at all or risk being caught before the meeting even happened. The only exception was the Château since it was so well guarded and only if necessary. We needed to keep our fake identities intact, which meant relying on Caleb and his team to do all the necessary recon before the day of the meeting.

I spent the morning buried in the lore books, once again trying to find some kind of clue that Ahren had spoken of. Nolan tried to help, but the tapping of his foot and stilo made me feel violent yearnings, so I sent him away. When he came back, he had two plates of food that had obviously not been made in the barracks kitchen. No, he had flirted his way into Brielle's penthouse and used her kitchen for the past few hours.

I just shrugged, digging into my tuna cakes and avocado chickpea salad and ate while I continued to pore over the books.

By the time mid-afternoon had rolled around, we were both about ready to tear our skin off in frustration. I knew why I hated it, the idea of being captive hitting just too close for comfort, reminding me of my days in the hospital. For Nolan, I wasn't sure what made him look ready to punch anyone in his path, but I could sense it buried just below the surface. So, I had dragged him off just as he had me a few weeks ago, to a private training room set up almost exactly the same as our own.

We followed almost the same path as before. We stretched and warmed up before going through about an hour of sparring. Although, this time, the teasing and flirting had started then. Each of our jabs and punches and blocks was full of power and strength, just as the first time we went hand to hand. This time, however, our hands seemed to be perfectly placed, so he grazed my hip oh so gently for a brief second or I accidentally found myself brushing against his hard, defined chest. We moved like a dance, two partners stealing every touch we could in the delicate moment we were weaving, standing on a dangerous edge, that if we jumped off could end in heartache or the greatest high of our lives.

It was exhilarating and terrifying, but we never let up until we were both panting and coated in a slick layer of sweat, loopy smiles on our faces.

Finally, after we were both spent, from the flirting or the fighting, we broke off to do individual work.

I put myself through a circuit of training, using my body instead of weights this time to work my muscles. Not only did it make my body stronger, but my mind. It helped me focus, gave me something to breathe and push through. It gave me release from the sparks of energy that had been building up in me, to the point where it was overpowered by the pleasant hum of a body well worked.

I focused on that, on myself and nothing else for the next hour. Nolan wasn't there with me, Elliot was not still free, and unbound rage and hate weren't lurking in every street of Kazola. When I felt better, I worked better, and that was what Kazola needed. That was the soldier it needed.

I was pulled back to reality while on my third set of pull-ups, my body suspended over the floor with nothing but my hands grasping onto a bar that was rigged to the ceiling. I felt a prickling along my chest and neck, letting me know someone was gazing at me with a prowling focus. It was, of course, Nolan, weights still in hand as he sat on a bench and did bicep curls. But his gaze never left me, a gleam of promise winking in his bright green eyes as they slowly raked over every inch of me.

And with that wicked gleam and flirtatious smile, I lost it, one hand slipping from the bar, my body dangling from the ceiling.

I righted myself as quickly as I could, but it was too late to gain back any sort of composure, my muscles ready to slack under his watchful eye so he could pick up the pieces however he saw fit.

My mind may not have been completely ready for him, but my body sure was if the brief whiff of arousal that hit my senses was anything to go by. It may have only been there for a second before disappearing behind the salty tang of sweat, but it *had* been there.

And I hadn't been the only one to notice. Nolan's eyes glistened gold under the harsh lights. He dropped the weights, that grin still plastered on his face as he prowled towards me, footsteps graceful and soundless.

"Looks like you need a spot." He looked up at me, taking in a deep, heady breath, nose grazing over my exposed, sweaty stomach.

A zip of energy ran up my spine. "I don't know." I tried to keep my breathing as even as possible, my words steady. "You didn't impress me much last time you spotted me."

"Then let me prove to you how worthy I am." He walked around me, my body still but my hands gripping the bar and keeping me in place. Before I could take another breath, he leaped upwards, grabbing the bar above, his hands gripping the outside of mine. His body crowded me, cocooning me in warmth, his bare chest pressed against my back.

My body stilled, energy pulsing in my stomach, every inch of me aware of where I touched him and where there was still air between us.

"Is this all right?" he whispered in my ear, his teeth grazing the sensitive flesh.

"If you mean the closeness, then yes, it's absolutely fine." His body shivered against mine, a sigh of relief escaping his lips and brushing against the base of my neck. "However, I don't see how this proves you're a good spotting partner."

"Well, let me show you." He nipped my ear before wrapping his legs around mine, so every inch of my backside hit his front. "Ready to pull?"

"You expect me to focus like this?" Somehow, my voice came out in a squeak. Never had that happened before. What this man did to me was mind-whirling.

"Yes." He rested his chin on my shoulder. "Let's focus our closeness, specifically my closeness to your throat, on something you feel strong in. Let's make a new memory, slowly, where your focus isn't on pleasure. Well, not all on pleasure, at least."

My breath stuttered. "You think this could help?"

"I don't know," he whispered against my skin. "But I promised to help you conquer this fear. Can't hurt to try. If you had something else to focus on it might help quell some of the fear that instinctively rises in you when I'm close to this part of you."

I followed his logic through my tainted, lust-filled mind. It made sense, and I hadn't been able to come up with any except have him touch me there until it no longer scared me, and I had been too terrified by that, so I hadn't even mentioned it to him.

With this, at least I had something else to focus on. This, I might be able to do.

"All right." I nodded.

"We stop whenever you need to. You are in control." I nodded, but I felt his body tense. "Say it, Kasha. I need to hear you say it."

"I am in control." The words came out weak, and it felt that way in my chest. So, I kept repeating them in my head over and over.

"Good, now pull," he commanded, not as my Alpha but as my supporter.

I pulled us up, Nolan's strength only assisting where mine faltered, holding some of my body weight so it wasn't as heavy to flex my back and pull my face to the bar. We did a few reps before I felt the first touch, nothing but a whisper of his lips grazing over the curve of my neck, but it made me falter then freeze.

I didn't freak out as before, but the itching of anxiety crept along my skin, trying to warn me against something. Instead of listening, this time, I just breathed in and out.

I was in control.

I resumed pulling, allowing it to distract me partially, as Nolan had suggested. With each rep, my muscles relaxed into the exercise, and soon the hum of pleasure replaced the anxiety, sparks flickering along my throat.

Nolan noticed my shift, pressing firmer kisses. My muscles seized again, but I didn't falter this time. I kept yanking us upwards. I relaxed into his touch quicker, my wolf humming in my chest at the pleasure each one raked down my body. It swirled throughout me, tingles traveling up my arms and alighting me with a heat that swarmed every place my body touched his.

I was in control.

He moved on to gentle licks, lapping at the sweat that beaded there, a rumble of pleasure escaping his lips, echoing against my skin. This time, the anxiety barely felt like a tinge along my arms, easily ignored. My head fell back, giving him easier access, my eyes fluttering shut so I could commit to memory the delicious desire that raked through me with every lap against my hot, sweaty skin.

I was in control.

When his tongue reached my shoulder, he scraped his teeth over it, testing to see how I reacted to being touched there. My reps faltered once again, but not from anxiety, just the heady, mind-twisting pleasure of having him so close and touching me.

No longer could I control the heat pooling low in my belly, a fevered groan escaping my lips. His body tensed around me, my own melting into the tight embrace, desperate for more. Desperate for him.

I was in control.

"Kasha…" His teeth stilled on my shoulder, a low rumbling growl vibrating against my body, sending a deep shiver zipping down to my slick core. His legs were still wrapped around me, our bodies pushed together so tightly I could feel the strain of something hard in his pants pressed against my lower back.

And instead of finding fear lingering within me, I let out another greedy groan.

"Don't stop. Please," I whimpered, every inch of me alight with new pleasure and lust, begging to be fed by the man wrapped around me.

He gave my shoulder a quick nip before moving back toward my throat. We still hung there, and I had no idea who held us up; me, him, or both. But I didn't care. I gave into the lust and desire, nothing but him and me and our bodies learning the delicate dance of who we were together.

He reached the apex where my throat met my shoulder and stilled for a breath, pressing a longing kiss there. Then, without warning, he wrapped his lips around that sensitive flesh and sucked and licked, savoring every bit of me. I gasped, the sparks finally opening the gates of my desires, flooding me with heat and lust and a needy hunger I hadn't felt in a long time. It was ravaged and unfed, desperate for the man pulling the desire from me, mixing it with his own into a perfect concoction of us.

I pushed myself closer to his firm body, feeling every little inch molded to mine, and with my next yank upwards, his teeth latched onto the curve of my neck without breaking the skin as I teased him with my ass grinding against his aroused dick. A surge of feral craving consumed me, urging me to take him, to make him *mine*.

To let him make me his and feel the sharp, pleasurable euphoria that only came when a wolf Marked their chosen lover.

Never in my life had I needed it more, my wolf whimpering within me to let him Mark me, calling out to his in a desperate plea.

It was intoxicating, unlike anything I had ever felt. It was perfect. It was bliss.

After many seconds of losing ourselves, we collapsed from the bar, falling onto the floor in a tangle of limbs and sweat, both breathless and staring at each other.

He leaned forward, pressing a kiss to my forehead. "You are so brave."

And I believed it. I was brave in that moment.

My wolf howled within, left wanting and needy. I pushed him onto his back, swinging my leg over to straddle his hips, and threw my head back with a loud moan as I settled my core against his hardening dick, our sweaty, ruined gym pants the only thing keeping us from completely consuming each other. I grasped the side of his face, yanking him to sit up slightly to meet me halfway, crashing our lips together.

I filled that desperate, needy kiss with every bit of desire, affection, and pleasure that was frantic for everything that was him. I licked the outside of his delicious lips before pushing my way inside, tangling with his and allowing him to take control.

His hands snaked up, gripping my ass, pressing me firmer onto his arousal, lifting his hips to meet mine and setting a brutal pace of chasing whatever wild need we had just unlocked in each other. We were like desperate, horny teenagers, fearful that we would be caught at any moment, but I didn't have a care in the world. That twisted heat that had been building in my core grew quickly, winding me to a place I had missed.

"Oh, Goddess," I threw my head back, riding him with abandon and forgetting about everything except the promise of desire he was giving me.

My pleasure snuck up on me, crashing over me in a consuming tidal wave that made my body shake, his firm grip keeping me steady as I wrung out every little bit of lust that had been trapped within me since the day I met him. His movements turned wild and erratic, his back bowing upward as a guttural groan echoed off the walls. After a few moments, his gyrating hips slowed as we both came down from the incredible high we hadn't planned on when we entered the room.

I collapsed on top of him, both gasping for breath, his erratic heartbeat thumping gently against the press of my cheek to his chest. I couldn't help but giggle at our disheveled looks and the lack of control we had found ourselves in.

"You make me feral, sweetheart." He laughed, pressing a kiss against my forehead. "I haven't been this easy off the mark since I was a teenager."

"I would apologize, but I'm now oddly proud of that fact."

"You better not brag about this to people." The rumble of his chest told me there was humor mixed in with his words.

"No promises." I gently sat up just enough to look at him, leaning forward to steal a sweet kiss. "Thank you," I whispered against his lips, his grip on me tightening. "For more than just your support."

"Anytime." He winked before gripping the back of my neck and pulling me back down into an intoxicating kiss, reminding me once again, that it was safe to lose myself within this man.

It was my body, my pleasure. I gave it to who I wanted to, and I was choosing to give it to Nolan. He had earned it, and he treasured it and treated it with respect. I was safe and cherished.

I was in control.

CHAPTER 24

A hickey. The jerk gave me a hickey.

I wasn't complaining, since every moment of me receiving it still sent chills up my spine and made my cheeks flush. And even better, there was no shame and no fear. Nothing but pure joy at the lingering memory that I tucked away just for myself.

Just as the day before, I sat in the common area reading the lore books, already wearing my workout sleeveless top and pants, my feet bare. Nolan, after once again cooking us a lovely lunch of cheese-stuffed ravioli, that he made from scratch, and a spinach cream sauce, was now working opposite me on some reports. It was a comfortable silence, one that helped to focus my mind. The only sounds were the crackling fire we had lit for comfort, the scratching of our stilos against parchment, and the flipping of book pages.

It was nice, normal.

The silence was cut by a sharp knock on the door. Nolan got up, walking across the expanse of the room with his long stride, opening it to reveal Caleb standing there.

"I have an update for the two of you. Can I come in?"

Even from where I sat at the table, I could see the extra straight posture of his spine, his hands tucked professionally behind his back.

"Yeah?" Nolan asked me. I just nodded, not even standing up, but I did bookmark my page and drop the book onto the table. Nolan widened the door, Caleb striding in and heading right to me.

He halted a few feet away from me, a harsh glare carving down my face and towards my throat. It had been exposed in front of him before, and he always acted as though the long thin line that graced my neck was the beacon of our family's self-proclaimed shame. It wasn't uncommon and I was done hiding it for his comfort. Except, this time, he didn't stare at my scar but the bright purple bruise that stood right beneath it.

Of course he would focus on that.

I rolled my eyes. "Something wrong?"

He looked back up at me, snorting. "We did the preliminary search of the area they are having the meeting."

"What kind of place is it?" I asked as Nolan came to sit back in his chair. Caleb kept his rigid stance in front of us.

"A warehouse, obviously not in use right now, but well maintained. We did research into who owns it and it seems legitimate."

"Probably means the owner is on Elliot's side," Nolan said, rubbing his chin.

"What we thought as well." Caleb nodded, starting to tell us about the areas they scoped for his backup team to set up during the undercover job, all of which made perfect sense and I knew was the right call. However, as we continued, I felt the hot linger of his gaze slip every few seconds back to the hickey.

"Can you focus, please?" I kept myself still, twisting my fingers together to stop myself from rubbing the bruise; from hiding it from him. He would get no more of my humiliation. He wasn't worth it.

"Do you have no shame?" He glared at me.

I glared right back. As if I hadn't caught a few on him over the years. And this certainly wasn't the first time he had seen one on me. But apparently, this one bothered him beyond compare.

"I enjoyed my day off with my paramour." I shrugged, a smile gracing my lips as I looked over to Nolan, his cheeks tinged pink.

"You are an Alpha Beta team." Caleb shook his head. "This is highly unprofessional."

"Our entire Hierarchy knows. We don't keep it a secret," Nolan said coolly. "You know, our Hierarchy that has a married couple in it. And we sent in an official intent report to the High Faction, letting them know about it. We took all the necessary steps."

"Doesn't make it okay," Caleb seethed.

"Goddess above, Caleb!" I stood up, zips of energy pulsing up my arms and legs. I could no longer sit still. "Our parents met in the guard. Mom was Father's Gamma at one point and no one batted an eye at that!"

His jaw was so tight I was surprised he hadn't broken a couple of teeth under the pressure. I took a few steps forward, keeping a good distance between us. "Now, if that is all you have to update us on, we both have work to do."

"Whatever." He turned to Nolan. "I'd watch your back. She has a habit of shoving knives in the backs of her ex-lovers."

Nolan's features darkened, his eyes glowering at Caleb's cruel, cold words. He was shaking. I knew he was holding back his rising fury for my benefit.

However, they unleashed everything I had been trying to contain for far too long. My wolf flared, eyes sharpening gold. I charged forward, grabbing Caleb by the front of his shirt and slamming him against the closest wall.

Nolan just growled in angered approval at my rough handling of my brother.

I growled in Caleb's face, his wolf snarling right back. "Don't you dare say such slanderous things. You have no right!"

He leaned forward, his lips curling back from his teeth in a smug grin. "I won't take anything back."

My blood ran cold. I knew he was talking about more than just his horrid words to Nolan.

No more would I stand by and let him treat me this way. No more.

"Then I'll fight you!" I shoved away, releasing him from my hold. "One hour. Meet me at the training rooms."

"Fine." He straightened his button-up and stalked out, slamming the door behind him.

★★★

"You don't have to do this," Nolan murmured to me. We stood off to the side of one of the private training rooms, Caleb alone on

177

the other side.

"Yes, I do." I stretched out my arms, getting my muscles as nimble as possible before we stepped into the duel. "This is more than just what he said to you."

Nolan grimaced because he knew what I meant. I had fought him in pure anger only a few weeks ago, to get out everything I had repressed for far too long. But he had never been the true direction of that anger, just the conduit I needed to get it out, and happily took what I threw at him. There were many people my anger was directed towards and one of the biggest players was Caleb.

This fight between my oldest brother and me had been a long time coming.

I gave him a quick kiss on the cheek before heading into the center of the ring, Caleb already waiting there for me. We had agreed on hand-to-hand, no weapons allowed, only us. We fought until someone pinned the other or one conceded the fight.

I knew it would not be me.

We stood in front of each other, Caleb's cold, calculating stare already measuring me up. "Last chance to call this off."

"Never." I shook my head, taking my fighting stance. He just shrugged, taking his own.

"Go," Nolan called from the side. I didn't hesitate to throw my first punch, striking true, right at Caleb's throat.

I smirked. I wasn't dumb, I knew he had seen me fight before. Typically, I allowed myself to take the defensive first to learn my opponent, but not this time. I was fighting someone who I used to watch fight long before we were Bridos. I knew his style and I wanted to catch him off guard.

Plus, it felt extra satisfying to watch his shocked face struggle to breathe for a few beats.

As expected, he recovered quickly, surging forward and throwing a flurry of punches. I dodged most, but one connected with my side, my abdomen muscles flexing under the impact to absorb most of the shock and pain. It wasn't long before blood was finally drawn, a trickling lingering in my mouth from the rough impact of his fist against my jaw. I got him back with an elbow to the cheek, a bruise blooming along his sharp cheekbone.

With each moment that passed, it only seemed to fuel me more. More of my rage simmered to the top. More of my anger and hurt and utter helpless pain came forward, reminding me how I felt at my lowest. How his betrayal had contributed to it all. It was not pretty, almost unrecognizable within my soul. But it was there, and it was real and it was a part of me now. The only way to get rid of it was to expel it. To give it back to the person who had given it to me.

"Do you even know what you've done to our family?"

"You were one of two people I always trusted." My body shook, not from exertion but from the swirl of tangled emotions that were coming back, the ones reserved just for Caleb. "You were my big brother! You were supposed to protect me!"

"I wasn't there that night!" He snarled, throwing a few jabs to my gut, which I effortlessly dodged. "There was nothing to protect you from!"

"I don't blame you for what happened to me, you idiot." It rumbled from my chest, the darkness of my mind feeding into all the hatred, all the poison that I had absorbed because of him. "I blame you for turning against me. For saying terrible things about me. For believing *him* over me! For choosing to be father's perfect oldest son over your sister's sanity!"

"I had no choice. Not if I wanted to betray the truth." His concentration was still completely on the fight, his limbs nimble and smooth with each strike he tried to land.

I ignored such an infuriating reason.

"And it wasn't just me!" I aimed for his face, his body dodging it by a mere inch. "How do you think Ollie has been? Do you think it was fair that he had to go to the hospital, alone, to tell me you were all locking me up for three months? Do you think he enjoyed seeing me like that? Do you think Nana Aggie is all right that only two of her grandchildren visit her?"

It was overflowing from me, every unspoken word I had allowed to brew and fester in my mind, to blacken my soul into something unrecognizable.

"We all made choices." He threw another punch, landing on the side of my jaw, my neck snapping to the left with the impact, stars dancing across my vision for a few seconds, but I gained my composure quickly, blocking his next throw. "But it was your toxic choices that brought it to this point."

"I was raped." Finally, I had said it to him, no longer skirting the terrible word or hiding the truth. "By your best friend."

He tensed, his eyes finally wild and free, glowing gold. He charged, and I threw my next punch. Instead of blocking, he caught it, squeezing it into his grip and ripping me forward a few steps, keeping us locked together.

"Are you really going to keep lying?" Caleb growled in my face, spit lashing against my cheeks. "Do you have no shame?"

Heated, churning anger flared in my gut. "I have never spoken a lie when it came to what he did to me."

"You are lying! Stop!" Something poked at the back of my hand. I peeked down, his claws extending outward from his nail beds, scratching me. He was losing control.

"Why? Why do you think this?" I braced myself, strengthening my stance when taking a step towards him, our linked hands pressed against my chest. "Because Logan said? Because father did?"

"Because I saw the letters, Kasha," he screamed, the words echoing off the high ceilings.

"What are you talking about? Letters?"

"The ones you wrote to Logan after you slept together." His words were no longer yelled but whispered to me in the lowest of rumbles deep from his chest. Honestly, I had no idea which one I feared most. "The ones begging him to be with you. Wanting more than just a one-night stand. Wanting him."

I finally ripped my hand from his grip, a sting of pain radiating down my fingers, blood welling up from the shallow cuts his half-formed claws had given me. I ignored it, stumbling back a few steps.

I shook my head slowly. "I never wrote him any letters."

I tried to think back, to remember anything that would ever be misconstrued as a letter. But that wasn't me, even before. I didn't write letters outside of reports or professional correspondence. There was no way Logan could have taken one of the many I had written to him over the years into something romantic. And I never would have written a personal letter, especially to him.

Nolan approached hesitantly, coming to stand next to me, posture rigid. Without hesitation, I reached down, wrapping my uninjured hand with his, allowing it to be my anchor to reality.

"I know your signature, Kasha." Caleb's breath was shallow, chest heaving. "How else do you think they became the key piece of evidence in Logan's defense?"

So, this was the damning evidence that had swayed Kyler and the rest of the High Faction that voted against me. This was what had set Logan free. This was what had brought shame to me and my family. A piece of paper that proved me to be a pathetic liar who framed someone for a vicious crime.

And it was total and utter bullshit.

There had to be an answer behind this, and where they had come from. Logan and I had worked together for years, even before being an Alpha Beta team. He knew my handwriting. I don't know if he had the skill of forgery, but he was smart enough to find someone who was, and he had plenty of writing samples from our work together to create them.

Forgeries. That was what they had to be. I wasn't crazy; I hadn't written any letters. I had been viciously attacked and taken advantage of, and he had found a way out. I knew the truth and I would prove it to everyone.

But first, I needed to see the letters for myself. One step at a time, just like any investigation. I knew how to do this. I was strong and capable, and I would use that skill to get to the bottom of it.

I took in one more deep breath, calming myself until my fingers stopped tingling. I walked to the outer rim of the ring, picked up my bag, and flung it over my shoulder, Nolan following my lead.

"I will get my answer." I stormed towards the door, stopping to glare up at Caleb. His eyes returned to their cold, steely gray. "And you're coming with me."

CHAPTER 25

Nolan helped me make the calls I needed to request an emergency audience with two members of the High Faction.

Caleb trailed behind us as we walked quickly through the halls of the Château. All of us had taken a few hours to clean up and change before heading over, and it had been the longest time of my life. The stiff collar of my formal jacket made my skin ache and my chest heavy. I kept moving forward, my heart beating steadily, my gut letting me know that we were about to find a missing answer to so many unknowns from the past year.

When we made it to our destination, I rapped my knuckles against the door three times before letting myself in, as per the instructions he had given me when I requested his time. We gathered inside the office, the high ceilings dwarfing us in the space. The bay window in front of me let in the buttery light of the setting sun, illuminating the space and highlighting the unadorned gray walls.

"Kasha, Caleb." Kyler nodded to the two of us, standing up from behind the black wood desk that took up most of the back wall. "And you must be Nolan. Can I get anything for you to drink?"

"Kyler, dear, I don't think they are here for pleasantries." Evette stood from a plum-purple chaise lounge that sat off to the side. "They came to ask a question, so please proceed. I'm on the edge of my seat."

I took a step forward, shoulders pulled back as I stared at the two of them. "Caleb here mentioned that the evidence you all had been keeping from me was some kind of letters. Care to fill me in on the specifics?"

"We aren't at liberty…" Kyler began, but I held up my hand.

"Don't feed me the pre-rehearsed lines. Tell me the truth." I fixed my stare on him. "What are these letters Caleb spoke of?"

"These letters were the piece of evidence that was the deciding factor for the High Faction to exonerate Logan." She flicked her gaze to Caleb before looking back at me. "Well, those who voted in favor at least."

"Evette!" Kyler looked at her.

"Don't blame me. Her brother is the one who let the truth out." She shrugged. "I'm just filling in the much-deserved blanks."

My fists balled at my sides. "And what did these letters contain?"

"They were from you to Logan." Kyler's face twisted, and he squirmed in his seat. "Begging him to begin a romantic relationship with you after having slept together at a full moon."

"What?" I screamed, unable to contain the roiling boil of anger pooling low in my stomach.

"There were about eight of them." Evette kept calm, her silky voice soothing, helping to still my riled wolf. "They started very flirtatious and sappy, but by the end, they had threats in them. That you would make him pay if he didn't give you a chance."

I snarled, letting a bit of my wolf out, her raging chaos swirling within. Whatever these letters were, they were key to why my trial hadn't gone in my favor. Somehow, Logan had figured out a way to make them convincing enough to sway the High Faction, along with Cole's influence over many of them. I had to know why. I needed answers.

"Show them to me."

"We can't." Kyler sighed.

"Says who?"

"Cole." Evette moved forward, leaning against the desk.

"After everything you've watched her go through, are you truly going to deny this one request?" Nolan stood next to me, his jaw tense.

"There is a lot that happens within the High Faction that many don't see." Evette looked over at him. "Kyler and I would be risking our jobs and future on the High Faction if we went against Cole's orders. He is a branch Tribune. He has more power over us than you may think."

Nolan scoffed. "Sounds like excuses to me."

"You both say you want to be there for me, to help." I shook my head. "Do you really think keeping these from me is helping?"

They both had no response to that, eyes darting away from mine.

"Make the difference you claim to want." I looked at them, their postures rigid. "This case was about me and my life. Did it not raise suspicion at all to the two of you that evidence was deliberately kept from me?"

"Certainly did for me," Evette grunted, a smug smirk on her lips. She did admit to voting against Logan during the proceedings. Evette side-eyed Kyler, his pallor a bit peaked. "What about you Kyler? The mighty Varg that brought this case to us. Who fought for its place in trial. What do you have to say?"

Kyler shook his head. "It crushed me, Kas, but as I told you the other day, they were compelling evidence. I couldn't ignore it."

"Show them to me," I demanded again. "Why would I even want to see them if I wrote them? The case is over. It's not like I can destroy them to help me now."

"Kasha…"

I braced my hands on the desk, looking only at him. "You want to be the Alpha I once trusted? Then get me those letters. Prove me wrong."

He stared back at me, a range of emotions flickering in his gaze as he thought it over. Finally, he stood, pulling in a deep breath.

"I'll be right back." Kyler straightened his tie, his shiny leather shoes clapping against the marble floor as he left the room.

We stood in an uncomfortable silence, Nolan's hand rubbing gentle circles on my back, Caleb behind me out of sight, although I could feel his intense stare searing into my back. I refused to look. Refused to let him get to me. My fingers and toes were numb, and it was taking immense mental strength not to give into the murky fog that rolled through my mind.

I needed to stay sharp, to get the answers I had always deserved.

Kyler returned a few minutes later, a folder grasped tightly in his grip. He approached me, holding it up between us. "Here they are."

I ripped them from his hand without a thought, pulling out the stack of letters, and began to read. As I finished one, I handed them off to Nolan to look at, not wanting to keep anything from him. The swirl of anger kept rising within me as I read, my eyes sharpening to their golden hue as I continued. These letters were full of praise and sappy confessions to Logan. They pleaded and begged, talking about that horrible night as if it was some romantic dream come true. They read like a fantasy novel, and not a very good one.

How *dare* he spin a tale that made me look so maudlin and weak? Hadn't he taken enough from me?

"These are faked." My lips curled upward in disgust, my chest burning. "I would never beg a man to be with me, especially *Logan*."

"Shocker that you would say that," Caleb said, speaking for the first time since we left his Compound.

"Kasha didn't write these." Nolan backed me up, an amused, haughty laugh escaping his lips.

"And how would you know?" Caleb challenged.

"As the man currently romantically involved with her, I would never expect Kasha to write a letter like this to me. It's not who she is."

"You didn't know who she was a year ago." Caleb took a step forward, coming to my left and leaning over to look Nolan in the eye.

I pushed him back a few steps. "Neither did you."

"You're my sister." His jaw clenched. "I know you."

"And you're my brother." I turned to him, heart pounding erratically. "But you were never my friend. You don't know me as well as you want to believe. You never have."

"Kasha might have had to adapt over the past year, but in her core, she is the same," Nolan said. "I don't for one second think she wrote these, but if you don't believe me, show them to Oliver or one of our team members. They would say the same thing, I know that."

"Ky, we worked together for years! I was your Gamma." I threw them down on the desk, turning to him. "You know me well enough to know I would never write something so pathetic and sappy and… meek. Let alone leave a paper trail with my threats on them. If I really wanted to threaten him, I would have done so to his face."

He pulled a few of them towards him, eyes scanning. "It always churned my gut reading them, but I assumed it was because it was solid evidence proving you wrong."

"You never questioned it?"

"How could I?" Kyler's fingers pointed to the bottom of one of the letters. "I know your signature, Kas. I've seen you write it hundreds of times, and that is it."

I picked one up again, bringing it close to my face to examine the signature. My blood boiled, a growl itching at the back of my throat. "That is my signature."

"Of course it is because you wrote these," Caleb muttered.

I sneered at him. "Yes, it's my signature, but that is all that's true in these letters. The rest of it is a forgery. A good one, but…"

"Then how did your signature get on the bottom?" Caleb's face reddened, his eyes shifting to gold. Why was he fighting so hard to catch me in a lie?

"Isn't it obvious?" Evette moved forward, her hands skimming a few of the pages. "Logan wrote them and had her sign them."

"How?" Kyler asked, not defensively, but with curiosity laving every word, his brows crinkling.

"I was his Beta." I thought back to the before times when I enjoyed being in his presence. "We worked together on multiple projects, and he had many papers for me to sign throughout the week. He could have easily hidden them within other papers or contracts that had multiple pages for me to sign."

"And you just signed them without reading them?" Caleb looked at me.

"I would read them most of the time, but every once in a while, he would catch me when I was running out to training or on a case." I shook my head. "He would claim it was a report or order that was due immediately and needed it now. I would roll my eyes at him and call him a procrastinator, but I signed because he was my Alpha and I trusted him."

"And when it comes to handwriting verification, our expert only analyzed the signature, something else he might have known before creating them," Evette added.

I looked at her, my pulse steadying. She was right. That had to be it, and it would have been so simple for Logan. All he had to do was make sure the signature matched perfectly in case of any investigation and he was free to do as he pleased.

Caleb paled. "He wouldn't do that."

Evette shrugged. "He needed collateral, so he got some. He's an investigator. He knows what is needed to create plausible doubt against a court, and he knew how to forge it to his benefit."

"Oh, it gets better." I shook my head, memories flooding me. "He wasn't allowed anywhere near me after the attack; Beckett made sure of that. If my signature was needed, someone else handled the documents."

"So?" Caleb said.

"So, it means he collected these signatures before attacking me."

Kyler took in a sharp breath. "It was pre-meditated."

Silence fell at that spoken fact, my stomach churning, bile burning the back of my throat. He wasn't too drunk nor lost himself in the full moon that night. He knew what he wanted and was going to take it no matter what. He planned and plotted. He used and manipulated.

Somehow, that made it worse.

"Ky, we need to get a new analyst to take a look at these letters and compare the signature and the contents to handwriting samples again," Evette instructed, Kyler already collecting the letters and shoving them back into the file. "We need to verify Kasha's statement as soon as possible."

"We can't let Cole know about this. What we've learned can't leave this room until we have solid proof that this was tampered with," Kyler said, looking over all of us. I knew I could trust three out of the four, so I looked to the wild card in play.

"Can we trust you to keep a secret, Caleb?" I turned, but he was no longer beside me.

"This… I…. What…" Caleb was backing away, muttering under his breath. He kept shaking his head, steps heavy until he thudded against the wall by the door. His fingers tapped aimless patterns against his leg, the other scraping along his jaw. He continued to mutter, all of us staring at him.

"Caleb?" I took a step forward, my nerves tingling along my arm.

He looked up, eyes locking with mine. I lost my breath, his eyes swirling with clarity as if he had woken up from a year-long fever dream and could no longer discern reality from fantasy. Somehow, in that pained, twisted stare, I swear I could see the walls of lies he had built around him crumble into dust.

"*Cal?*" I reached out to him again, taking another step forward.

"*I—*"He shook his head, a single tear slipping from his left eye.

It was all he said before rushing out of the office, the door slamming shut behind him.

CHAPTER 26

The sun had fully set, and Caleb had yet to return to the Compound.

My stomach was twisted in knots most of the day wondering if something had happened to Caleb or if he had done something reckless in his agitated state. Nolan had tried his best to distract me, but this time, nothing worked.

Finally, after ignoring his team and Nolan's pleas for me to stay on the Compound, I hopped on my cycle and rushed away, following my gut telling me I had to go and find him myself.

I was trying not to overthink during the drive, but something about his broken look and pathetic words itched at something in my chest and stomach.

I made it to the Temple in record time, parking my cycle off in a side lot. However, instead of going inside, I circled the imposing building to the iron-gated entrance to the woods, the door slightly ajar, the whispering scent of vanilla tobacco still lingering on the air, letting me know my hunch had been right.

I pushed my way into the canopy of trees, following the winding path that broke off into smaller ones, each one leading to a burial plot owned by specific families or individuals. When a Varg Anwyn passed, they went through their Last Rite and burned under the full moon so their soul could safely leave their body and return to Lunestia's protective embrace.

It was there I had a feeling I would find my biggest brother, in a place we very rarely ever visited.

I sniffed, Caleb's scent pulling stronger until I came about half a mile away from my destination. It was strong, and I looked down to find a pile of clothes and a pair of boots thrown at the narrow path entrance that led to where I wanted to go. I sighed. Of course he didn't want to face me in human form.

I didn't know what state I was going to find him in, so I knew it was best to go in as prepared as possible. I swiftly piled up all of Caleb's clothes before removing my own and tying them into a haphazard bundle using my jacket before snapping my body into wolf form. It was amazing to have it come so naturally again, no longer a struggle to pull myself into the four-legged form that felt as ordinary as my two-legged one.

I shook out my gray coat, basking for a moment as the chilled wind rustled my fur before leaning down and gingerly gripping the bundle of clothes between my teeth, leaving our boots here. We would have to get them on our way back.

I trotted along the path, heart pounding as I broke through the trees and into the round clearing littered with dead leaves and pine needles. A lone grave was situated towards the back. As I expected, Caleb was there, his large wolf form huddled in a ball, dead leaves covering parts of him and his muzzle pressed gently against the carved gray stone.

Our mother's grave.

I trotted up to his curled-up form, dropping our pile of clothing off to the side before sitting back on my haunches next to him. He didn't move a muscle at my unexpected entrance. He knew I would show up eventually.

"You've been gone all day." I looked down at him, at the dead leaves that had shifted on top of his silver-gray coat. All three of us took after Mama for our wolf forms.

"Ollie was right all those weeks ago." His voice filled my mind, deadened and defeated. *"She would be embarrassed by me."*

I looked down, my heart lurching at the carved words:

Allona Mallanis. Dedicated Wife, Mother, and Protector of Kazola.

"Yeah, she would be." I wasn't there to coddle him or feed him consoling lies. He had spent the better part of a year hurting me and breaking the bond we shared. I wasn't about to forgive it all. *"You need to come back to the Compound. We have work to do."*

"I can't."

"Why not?"

"It's all falling apart."

"What do you mean?" I couldn't help myself. I was too curious.

"My life has been planned since the beginning, Kasha." He finally sat up enough to turn around and face me, gold eyes full of sorrow.

"Stop being cryptic, Caleb, and just explain!"

"Did Father ever make you feel pressured into joining the Guard?" Caleb asked. *"Or did you choose it because it was a family thing?"*

I thought for a moment. *"No, it just always felt right."*

"Ollie said the same thing." Caleb nodded. *"But that wasn't my experience. You and Ollie have called me Father's perfect child long before it became full of venom. But from a young age, that was what was expected of me. He always talked about how, as the oldest, it was my duty to carry on the family name in the Guard. We could be traced back to the original formation and no one would break that streak if he had anything to say about it."*

"I don't remember this."

"I made sure you and Ollie didn't know," he admitted. *"I didn't want you to think I was choosing the Guard out of obligation and not a desire to be a part of the family legacy like I knew the two of you dreamed of."*

I swallowed a lump in my throat, looking down at my front paws scratching aimlessly at the frozen dirt beneath me. *"You could have told us. We could have helped carry that burden."*

"Maybe, but I wanted you to look forward to your future without any of the guilt grooming father had started on me at a young age." His voice was breaking, even within our minds. This wasn't something he talked about a lot, if ever. *"You probably were too young to remember, but he would bring me to his Compound often, wanting me to see how things were run and what my future was to be. He would give me tests after tests, from case strategy to learning how to read social cues to be able to glean evidence. If I passed, I was rewarded in some way. If I failed, I was punished. Usually by not getting dessert or, as I got older, I wasn't allowed to spend time with my friends or go to events I had been looking forward to. I hated it, but I knew if I just pushed hard and worked, it would all be worth it when I was in the*

Guard."

"*How old were you when this started?*"

"*Around twelve. So, you were only five.*"

My stomach soured. I never had to do any of that growing up. I had a childhood while Caleb had been in Onyx Guard training long before it was legal.

"*He wanted me to break the record of the youngest promotion to Alpha. He said that our family name deserved that honor, and I was to be the one to bring it to us.*"

Which he had. We had all celebrated that promotion announcement. Father had been so proud of him, bragging to anyone who would listen. Caleb had stood by his side, preening with happiness over every kind word Father doled out for him.

"*Everything was going according to plan. I had made those goals and continued to follow through on any new ones Father put in front of me.*" He rested his head back on his front paws. "*You and Ollie joined, and that seemed to make Father even happier because you both were naturals at it and rose through the ranks like the good soldiers, and Mallanis children, you were. That is, until a year ago.*"

I looked down at him, waiting for him to talk about the turning point in all our lives.

"*It all began to fall apart when you brought that case forward.*" He looked over at Mother's grave again. "*Father was telling me we had to protect our legacy and that you were risking all of it. He said it was my duty as the oldest to stand by him and follow his lead like I always had. I figured at first, he would want us to stand as a united front, but the next thing I knew, he was talking about having to stay impartial and how he would be on the side of justice and truth, no matter the bloodline.”*

I snorted. *“Exactly what I expected him to say.”*

“Well, for once, I questioned his words and asked him how he could not take your side. He told me to go and see Logan, that I wasn’t hearing the whole story.” His body trembled. *“Father was the one to convince me to listen to Logan’s side. And as I had always done, I followed orders.”*

“Why would Father want that?”

“My guess is he had seen the evidence that Logan’s defense had submitted for the case and knew that with it, true or false, you would lose. And we couldn’t be associated with that in his eyes.”

Heat burned in my chest, twisting from the anger I had held for my father for so long into blinded fury mixed with extreme betrayal.

How could he?

“So I went to Logan, listened to his side of the story and, when I told him I didn’t know who to believe, he showed me the letters.” He looked up at me. *“They convinced me to do what I always did—follow Father’s orders. He had raised me to do that. To be his loyal soldier, and it had never steered me wrong. So, I didn’t question it. Then the handwriting came back as matching yours and it solidified Father’s plan. There was no turning back after that. I knew I had to choose between my father and my siblings, and I chose the one I always had in the past.”*

Bile rose in my throat, my stomach twisting, but I pushed it away. I needed to focus on Caleb’s words and figure out where we would even go from here.

“But just a bit of digging into those letters brought doubt to my mind.

In the past, I would have ignored it, convinced myself that it was lies trying to get me to distrust my morals, but for once I let the thought through. And it broke through so many things I had come to accept as truth for far too long." He shook his head. *"All of that realization came crashing down on me in that office. All my actions that I thought were mine to make were just blind faith instilled in me from a young age. I followed them because of a desperate need for acceptance and control. That's not an excuse, but it's the honest reason why I chose the path I did."*

I blinked at him a few times, listening to the whistling of the wind breaking through the bare branches of the trees.

"I don't know what to do now," he admitted.

"How about we start with turning back into humans?" I suggested, my back legs going numb from sitting on them for so long.

"Yeah, sure." He sighed, standing up and following me over to the pile of abandoned clothes.

I gingerly used my canines to pry the knot open and grabbed my clothes before disappearing behind one of the trees near the clearing. A couple of minutes passed before we both emerged, my eyes looking over Caleb again. His shoulders were slumped forward, his face still full of regret and pain. I ignored the tug in my gut as we settled back in front of the grave a few inches apart, both of our gazes trained on the stone, allowing silence to fill the distance.

He looked over at me, his dirt-caked blond hair sticking to his forehead. "My mind feels broken. Like I can no longer trust the thoughts that pass through it, scared they don't belong to me but to those I let guide me for most of my life."

I rested my chin on my knees pulled against my chest. His words held so much weight, but it was a feeling I knew well, just in a different way.

"You need to learn to shut the voices out and listen to your own mind, heart, and soul." His shoulders sagged. "What are they trying to tell you? Find the small voice they're trying to drown out."

He sighed, dragging a dirty hand over his face, smudging more grime onto his cheeks. "I've locked that one away for far too long, but I can finally hear it again."

"And?"

"Investigate," he whispered, almost more to himself than to me, but still, I heard it loud and clear. "Find the truth."

My heart cracked, an unsettling combination of relief and pain snaking from my chest and down to my stomach. A part of me had hoped that he would come to my side when his loyalty to Father finally crumbled. I had hoped he would protect me once again.

Yet, I knew that was an unrealistic expectation on my part.

"I understand." I nodded, my voice just as quiet as his.

"I know you want me to take your side. After everything you've been through, I wish I could give that to you." A tear slipped down his face, his silver eyes glinting in the moonlight. "But I can't, not without looking at the case and investigating evidence myself. I blindly gave my loyalty to Father, which has turned me into a mindless soldier, not in control of myself as he led me to believe. The only way to get that control back, to finally have my voice back, is to dig into the case myself."

In the end, both of us were investigators, and he needed to seek and learn the truth in his own way and time. I knew what really happened that night, and I trusted in his ability to seek and find it.

This wasn't forgiveness, but it was understanding, and it was a better step than the ones we had been taking for far too long. It helped lift a weight that had been burdening my heart and soul. It hadn't disappeared, but at least it wasn't as crushing.

"I look forward to hearing all about it when the day comes." I didn't know what else to say, an awkward silence lingering in the air.

"But for what's about to come, for the Elliot case." He reached over, squeezing my forearm in solidarity. "Please know I am on your side. I know you're doing right by Kazola, so please, let me help you in any way I can."

My throat was clogged with too many emotions, ones I didn't completely trust. I was learning to hope again, but with Caleb, after everything he put me through, I wasn't sure if I had any left to spare for him. I prayed to Lunestia that I would find some again. That maybe we would look back on this day and know it was his first step to redemption in my eyes. Our first step back towards each other.

My heart and mind clamored with each other, and it took a lot more effort to force them away, knowing I needed to focus.

I shook it off, clearing my throat. "Well, you can start by coming back to the Compound with me so we can finalize the last details of the operation in a few days."

I stood up, reaching my hand out to his. In more ways than one.

He looked up, his silver eyes alight in the moonlight, with

a sliver of hope breaking through the heartache reflected. He grasped my hand tightly, anchoring to me as he stood back up. "Let's go."

We each patted Mother's headstone before starting the long hike back in silence.

CHAPTER 27

The walk to the warehouse increased in foot traffic the closer we got to the towering building's entrance.

We had ridden partially there with Caleb and his team, helping them set up the surveillance station about three miles west of the meeting location. It was also there that we set up my and Nolan's Comms unit on our persons. Similar to when I went in bugged to my counseling appointment a few weeks ago, we had muted our units but kept what we said on our side of the connection open so anything going on around us would be recorded.

But this time, we took it one step forward. Using the bulky winter coats we were wearing as the perfect place for hiding them, we had sewn them inside, fashioning the coat so that the tiny lens looked like a shiny black embellishment that decorated the bottom half. In reality, it was sending the meeting right back to Caleb and his team.

It was a risk carrying them on us, but the more people who could watch and hear gave us a better understanding of Elliot's plans.

Even on the cold winter day, fluffy clouds danced across the bright blue sky, the sun warming my face. Beads of sweat formed along my hairline by the time we made it to the front entrance. We broke through the threshold and into the lions' den that Elliot apparently had everywhere.

"Goddess," Nolan whispered under his breath.

It wasn't the musky warehouse, the high-beamed ceilings, and plain beige walls. It wasn't the makeshift stage set up at the south wall or the podium that stood in the center of it. What took my breath away and made my heart thump rapidly in my chest was the number of people crowded around the stage.

I estimated there were at least two hundred people crowded into the space, and that didn't include the guards that were lined up around the stage, their plain blue shirts and black pants all matching. They stood completely still, eyes watching everyone, making sure no one got too close to whoever would be gracing us on stage.

This many people were willing to listen? So many doubted the High Faction?

"Where should we go?" Nolan whispered into my ear, his arm snaking around my waist to make sure we weren't separated in the throng of people.

"Mid-way if we can even make it there," I whispered back.

The point was to blend in, and seeming too eager listening at the front was not a look we wanted. Instead, we would let others surround us, giving us a semi-safe place to listen and learn.

Nolan used his tall, muscular form to gently weave us through the crowd, stopping us when we were surrounded. My breath shook a bit at the claustrophobic pressure building on my back. I just breathed through it, reminding myself why I was there.

For Kazola.

"Are you seeing everything okay from here, Caleb?" I asked.

"All set with both of your videos." He would be watching mine while Brielle monitored Nolan's.

I put my arm around Nolan's waist, pressing our sides together, his arm moving upwards to rest on my shoulders. I looked up at him, his strained smile giving me little reassurance, but at least he was with me. We stood in silence, waiting for something to happen. My fingers dug into Nolan's side, my feet swaying from side to side as I counted down the seconds, waiting, waiting, waiting…

A cheer erupted from the crowd the moment a lone man walked onto the stage, his long, gangly arms open wide in welcome to everyone. His inky black hair was slicked back, the long curling tendrils perfectly sculpted to show off his angular face and sharp cheekbones. He wore a suit, similar to the one I saw Elliot wearing in his video message, but not as high quality. Where Elliot's had looked like a second skin molded to his form, this man's looked a little loose on him in some places. Still, he walked with his head held high, confidence leaking off him with every step he took toward the podium.

"Chu Fui na Déithe!" he yelled across the room in opening, his voice booming off every surface. "By the blood of the Gods, we are here today. We have gathered as concerned citizens of Kazola, lovers of our country, ready to see the atrocities stop!"

Cheers rang out in agreement. I looked around the room, noticing a healthy mix of overly eager people and those who huddled into themselves, obviously guarded and unsure about what they had stepped into. I was unsurprised, seeing as this whole meeting was meant to sway people to their side. I wouldn't be surprised if the cheering fans were plants or encouraged to come to help boost those who were nervous or unsure. It made Elliot's revolution seem stronger. Although, with the amount of hollering people mixed in, my heart shook at the idea that maybe it already was.

"Life on this island has always been about peace between the species, for all of us to live and thrive and grow while technologies and advances gave us a better quality of life." He paused, scanning the room with a rueful smile. "At least, that is what the High Faction has tried to feed you. But what if that is all a lie? How is it that after a hundred years of ley line electricity gracing our Isle that it's still unavailable to residential buildings? Of course, the High Faction's Château is perfectly outfitted with modern conveniences. And let's not forget their precious Onyx Guard and their high-tech equipment. Tell me, why can't we have lectracycles? Why should we continue to walk or ride horses and carriages while they blow past us? And don't get me started on their Comms Unit communications when we still have to resort to Falcon mail."

My stomach dropped as more and more people who had seemed hesitant mumbled in agreement. The ley line issue was due to a lack of electrical mines needed to pull the energy and distribute it. Yes, it was discovered a hundred years ago, but it took nearly twenty-five years for the first mine to even be a success. New ones were being developed and built, but it took time. The High Faction had communicated to us their plan to have residential electricity available within ten years, although they hadn't announced it to the public in case there were any delays. This ultimately was the reason for regulations of lectracycles and Comms as well. They used electricity that we didn't have enough of for the entirety of Kazola to have access to at once. Once residential electricity was opened, the next phase was more widely spread technology.

Of course, only those with the proper clearance knew any of this, making it easy for Elliot's crew to use it to their benefit and make it seem like the High Faction was withholding life-changing advances from most of Kazola, creating plausible doubt in their minds.

"And of course, there are the archaic practices of their detox centers." He gently removed his suit jacket and threw it across the podium before rolling up his crisp white sleeves and bearing his forearms to the crowd. An audible gasp rang out, the lingering black lines surrounding the thick veins of his forearms were visible from even my vantage point.

The telltale signs of a Blackthorn addict.

Or a past one, because his strong voice, pink-cheeked complexion, and powerful stance were far from the typical addict. That answered why his suit hung around him. He probably lost unimaginable amounts of weight when he was still using.

"Do you know how many of those programs I went through, only to be back a few months later?" He shook his head, looking down at his shoes before returning to stare at the crowd. "Too many to count. I was killing myself with those horrid drugs. Until, one day, a stranger told me there was a better program. One that would help and have me back into a future within a matter of weeks. Weeks!"

"Like Lila," I said to Caleb and Nolan.

If only we could have spoken to her, but her pack was too good at keeping their people away from us. Besides, as an Elliot follower now, I highly doubted she would be willing to openly discuss it.

"That is why I stand up on this stage, to tell you about the man who not only created the program that saved my life, but who wants nothing more than to see Kazola bloom to its full potential. We have waited far too long for a savior to bring us back to the path our God and Goddess wanted for us." He paced in front of the stage, abandoning the podium. "But no longer should you hold fear. For our new leader has come for us. He will bring back strength to this world."

He pulled away the fabric with a flourish, revealing a portrait of the man himself. Elliot. He preened, spine straight, chin raised high, hand resting casually on the waistcoat of his three-piece suit. His eyes pierced through, watching. Even though I knew it wasn't possible, I felt like his gaze lingered directly on me, a shiver running up my spine and making me nuzzle into Nolan's embrace even closer.

"Does he think he's a King or something?" Nolan sneered.

"More like a Dictator." My jaw clenched. My wolf stirred in my chest, but I had to push her down. Any flicker of aggression could give us away. So, I pulled in deep breaths, making sure my eyes stayed their deep blue and my claws didn't peek out.

"This man is a Gods Blessed miracle, who will no longer halt progression but welcome it with open arms and work tirelessly to make it available to every citizen on the Isle. He will make sure we are no longer oppressed under the High Faction's greed and the guards' watchful gaze. When we rise up…" His forceful voice was cut off by a blood-curdling scream echoing off the high ceilings, everyone freezing around us.

"Guards!" someone screamed as a swarm of black-clad soldiers ran into the room, grabbing for anyone in sight.

The Onyx Guard. They had shown up and they were here for a fight.

"Caleb!" I screamed, my fingers shaking as they clutched Nolan's arm to try and stay secured in the wave of people desperate for escape around us. *"What is going on?"*

"This isn't us!" Caleb said frantically. *"I didn't approve any kind of raid, I swear!"*

"Cole?" Nolan asked us, suspicion crawling through his words.

"What gain would he have to go against the entire High Faction?" I shook my head. I knew he was a bastard who hated not getting his way, but this was too far even for him.

"You two have to get out of there!" Caleb said, pulling us to what was important; the pure pandemonium surrounding us. *"There is a back hallway on the south side of the building. It leads to loading docks. Try your best to get there."*

Nolan secured his grip around my wrist, tugging me forward and pushing his way through the crowd.

It was made worse that we needed to go against the wave of people and attempt to avoid any of the guards that brutally slashed clubs and battering wands to incapacitate people. Their all-black leather armor only made the imposing figures even more terrifying to the crowd of citizens wanting to escape with their lives intact.

I flinched as we passed a poor young woman, a blue-eyed brick wall of a Guard whacking her across the head with his club, her body crumbling to the floor. It took all my training not to scream out, wanting to punish a rogue Guard for using such force. That wasn't how we were trained. We used physical strength first, then non-life-threatening weapons, and then blades if all else failed. Even then, we would go through an extensive post-investigation to make sure our actions were the only option.

Nolan continued to tug me along, his focus on the back wall. The double door we were meant to find came into view. I let him take the lead, pulling me along because my focus was on everyone around us, my eyes finding any Guard members I could. Their uniforms seemed standard issue, but every single one I saw was a broad-chested man, not one woman in the mix. As a Guard leader who had been on multiple raids, that wasn't right.

So, I looked closer, taking in every detail of the men, from the black leather chest plate and bracers, the form-fitting under clothes, to the thigh sheathes secured to hold their clubs and wands. And that was when I noticed the fatal mistake the men had made.

Not one of them carried an Amalgam Blade.

It didn't matter if we were instructed on raids to use non-killing force, we were required to wear our blades at all times in case of an emergency. So why would none follow procedure? Unless they had no way of accessing the standard issue blade…

"These aren't Guards," I whispered to the two of them. *"They are*

imposters making it look like the Guard is arresting people.”

Nolan crinkled his brow, looking back at me as he continued to shove his way through the wave of people. *“What would be the point of that?”*

“Fear.”

This was how Elliot had grown his militia over the years, or at least partly. Talking hateful words against the High Faction, instilling the small seeds of fear into people’s minds, and then reinforcing them in a staged traumatic situation that would ultimately make them flee right into Elliot’s ‘safe’ embrace. It was similar to how he had gotten Lila on his side. The manipulation was disgusting. My skin crawled, and I wondered how many other moments over the past years we’d been hunting him had been a part of his master plan.

“We’ll figure out the particulars of why when you two get out!” Caleb yelled again. *“Are you at the door?”*

“Almost,” Nolan said, using his shoulders to shove the last of the people out of the way, allowing us to sprint the final distance around the make-shift stage, towards the door, and flinging it open to safety.

Or at least, what we thought would be safety.

“Well, hello there.” A horde of fake guards stood on the other side, the brutish men smirking with a glint of amusement in their eyes as if everything was going according to their plan.

“Caleb…” I don’t know what I was going to say, but I didn’t even have time to finish.

We barely took a breath before they lunged at us, four sets of hands grabbing at me while the other six sets surrounded Nolan.

"Get your hands off her!" Nolan snarled, elbowing one of the men in the nose and throwing an uppercut to another, both of them screeching in pain. But there were still too many. One of the uninjured moved in front of Nolan, taking his club and ramming into Nolan's solar plexus. My partner doubled over in pain, wheezing for air.

Fury, unlike anything I'd ever experienced before, clouded my vision with red. No one touched him. No one hurt him. No one got away with it.

No one.

"You'll pay for that!" I growled at the guard who had hurt Nolan. I flung myself around, twisting and contorting my body to make it as difficult as possible for them to keep a hold on me, and out of the corner of my eye, I saw Nolan doing the same.

We snarled and lashed out, my arms desperate to reach out and feel his warm fingertips against mine. Just one touch to know he was all right, to know we would get out of this together.

"Kasha!" he screamed at me, his long arm breaking through the wall of muscle in front of him.

"Nolan!"

"Enough of this!" the obvious leader yelled, his stone-cold glare assessing the situation. "Hold them still."

He walked up to Nolan first, pulling out a long, black device that looked like one of the battering wands. Except this one was forked at the top, two prongs of metal glinting under the harsh factory lighting. He clicked a button at the base of the contraption. Nolan and I stilled, staring at the flicker of miniature lightning dancing between the two prongs. This man had harnessed a piece of nature straight from the sky and into this metal stick.

What in the name of the Goddess was that torture device?

He touched the sparking end to Nolan's side, my paramour clenching and groaning in pain, his body convulsing in spasms before his eyes fluttered closed and his body slumped into the three men that held him.

I screamed at the top of my lungs, not caring that my voice was grating my throat harshly. He had hurt my partner. Mine! Every inch of my wolf wanted to escape, and I was happy to oblige, my shirt and pants starting to press painfully at the seams, my claws extending from my fingernails, and my bones beginning to pop into the proper place for my beast to emerge. I let out the desperate howl of a wolf whose chosen one had been hurt. All I could hear in my head was her fury-stricken words.

Protect, avenge, save.

Get to Nolan! She screamed at me with a ferocity I had never heard before.

Yet, it didn't even faze the soldier as he moved over to me. A cruel smirk graced his lips, his hulking form towering over me as his men held me in place. I had nowhere to escape to, even with my wolf wanting to tear their faces off.

"Sweet dreams." His rancid breath whispered across my face before he pressed something firm against my belly. My body convulsed with the force of a lightning bolt before everything went black.

CHAPTER 28

I woke with a start from the blackened pit of forced unconsciousness.

My mind was a bit behind my body, catching up when I felt the jerking pull of chains binding me to a stiff metal chair. Ropes I probably could have managed to escape from, but chains mixed with whatever torture device they had used on us made me slump back in defeat.

Us. Nolan.

A low, snarling hum pulled my attention to my right. Nolan sat in a matching chair and chains, but he had obviously been awake longer than me. His spine was ramrod straight, eyes aglow with yellow fury, staring down the group of men in front of us. His lips curled upwards to bear his sharp canines to the room, daring them to get closer even though he was incapacitated. He looked like a feral, defensive animal keeping the most precious thing to him safe from harm.

And that precious thing was me.

My heart warmed a bit, a brief flicker of hope, forgetting that we were utterly screwed.

I lolled my head back and forth a bit, pulling out the pretense that I was still clearing from sleep to give myself a few extra seconds. *"Caleb?"*

"Kasha!" My brother's frantic voice filled my mind immediately. *"Where are you? Are you all right?"*

"I think so. But we've been captured. Tied up with some hulky-looking goons." I let out a low groan, letting my eyes flutter closed for a few seconds as if whatever they had done to me pulled me back under. *"Do you still have eyes and ears on us?"*

"No." His tone turned poisonous. *"Whatever they hit you with damaged your Comms."*

No shock since it looked like they had mildly electrocuted us. We'd have to get new units.

"Do you need us to come in?" I could hear the desperation in his voice, the itch ready to pounce and save us.

"Not yet," I said. *"We need to let this play out. It was obviously a trap that Elliot wanted me to walk into. I want to know what this is about."*

"Kasha..." He growled.

"I'll be careful."

"Most of the civilians escaped, so I have to believe it's just you and Elliot's men. We are waiting close by, ready to infiltrate when you give the signal. And you will give a signal."

"Of course," I agreed, letting my head loll back up. *"We aren't letting these men get away."*

"We'll be waiting," he said. *"Rip him a new one, little sis."*

"I plan to." I laughed, shaking off how almost normal that conversation felt. Well, as normal as a conversation between two soldier siblings could be.

I turned my attention to the room, trying to focus on my new surroundings. A few of the men that had taken us lingered around the room, stationed against the wall in a perimeter formation. Some had weapons in their hands, while others lounged back as if having us chained up meant they could let their guard down. That was their first mistake.

"Thank the Gods you are finally awake." A silky voice pulled my attention to the front of the room. "I was getting bored waiting for you. Although, this growling mess next to you has served as a little entertainment."

Nolan let out another low snarl for good measure, while I kept my mouth shut, staring at the man in front of us. It was the same lithe man that had been shouting Elliot's praises on stage. He still had his jacket removed and his shirt sleeves rolled upward to reveal the black scarring from his old drug habit. However, now I could make out the deep hazel-green hue of his round eyes and the slight wave that rippled through his slicked-back hair.

"You must be Kasha." The alluring-voiced man smirked at me. "I'm Ezekiel."

"I don't care." I curled my fingers around the arm of the chair, forcing myself to stay still, to calm my racing heart.

He sat behind a desk, the simple gray wood unadorned, not even a stilo or paper to break up the thin coat of dust that had settled. So, obviously, this wasn't his typical place of business, just the empty space they used for their meetings. Well, probably not any longer since we now knew of it.

"Well, I certainly care about you." He looked me up and down, his thumb gently brushing against his lower lip. My stomach revolted at the appraising sight.

"Stop looking at her." Nolan shook next to me.

"Calm, sweetness," I soothed him, gently coaxing a light shushing sound through the connection.

His shoulders relaxed a bit, although his eyes and fangs stayed shifted. *"Only because you called me a cute name for the first time."*

I smirked. I had, hadn't I?

It would have warmed my chest and sent fluttering through my belly had it not for the aching pinch in my back from the heavy chain keeping me tied to the awful chair.

"Goddess above. This is not the time for us to be flirting!"

"Eh, there's always a spare second to be flirtatious with you."

"Ahem." Ezekiel cleared his throat. "Are you two done staring lovingly into each other's eyes?"

"Not quite." Nolan gave me a wink before turning back to the man, but his voice reached out to me again. *"It's you he wants to talk to, so I'll follow your lead."*

I turned back to Ezekiel. "You were droning on about what now?"

"That I was happy you chose my meeting to come and enjoy." He leaned forward, bracing his arms on the table.

"Your meeting?"

"Oh, yes." He nodded, eyes glinting with an underlying meaning that itched at my mind, glaring realization breaking through my thoughts.

Futetcha. Fury boiled into my veins, racing through my entire body and alighting me with burning fire that desperately wanted to escape. We all should have realized from the start that Elliot wasn't just egging me into joining the Seathra meeting. He had planned so far ahead that he had prepared everyone.

Always ten steps ahead of us and counting. Would we ever find ourselves on an even playing field with this man?

"Besides Elliot himself, you are a treasured guest to grace my group this evening."

I scoffed. "Please. I'm nothing more than a toy he likes to chase around." I didn't want this man to know just how deep my fear of Elliot and his plans were embedded within me.

He tisked. "That is far from the truth, and you know it. You're his favorite."

"No, I'm not." My body chilled, Nolan stilling next to me.

"Of course you are. You're his *Rogthna.*"

"What in the Goddess does that mean?" My lip curled upward, my calm façade slowly breaking.

A low, rumbling chuckle escaped his lips. "Oh, don't worry. You'll find out soon enough."

A shiver ran up my spine at his ominous words, my gaze unable to look away from the preening man.

He snapped his fingers, one of the guards moving forward to hand him a neatly wrapped package. An almost identical one to the brown parcel that Lila had given me a few weeks ago. I had a sneaking suspicion I knew exactly what was in there.

"He wanted me to tell you that he hoped it was informative and he looks forward to talking to you again soon." His index fingers traced the edges of the package, his eyes never leaving me.

"Start closing in," I shot out to Caleb, keeping Nolan in the loop this time now that his rabid mind had cleared up a bit.

"On it."

"Maybe I don't want to see him again," I challenged, trying to draw this out to give Caleb and his team time to arrive.

"Are you willing to take that risk?" he asked, my stomach dropping.

No, I wasn't.

"He said you'd know what to do with this." He pushed the package to the edge of the desk before leaning back in his chair and waving absently to a few of the guards. "Release them and escort them to the edge of the property."

"Caleb? Status?"

"Coming up on the back entrance now, the other half going through the front."

I hid my smirk, Nolan obviously doing the same judging by the squirming in his chair as a weathered-looking man unlocked and unwrapped him.

"You think it's that easy?" I looked down at the blushing man removing my chains.

Ezekiel chuckled. "Of course. Why not?"

"Did you really think we'd let you just walk away?" Nolan stood from his chair, rubbing his red-rimmed wrists a few times before reaching his hand out to me, which I gladly took, pulling myself flush to his side.

"What? Are you gonna arrest almost two dozen trained men?" Ezekiel scoffed. "Even you two aren't that talented."

"Are you sure about that?" I taunted, their eyes narrowing at the glee filling my voice.

Ezekiel's eyes went wide a beat too slow. It was too late, and he knew it.

"Oh, biggest brother…" I sing-songed, my voice echoing off the walls. Like a siren call beckoning him, the door burst open, an amber-eyed Caleb at the front of the group ready to fight, and we were plunged into anarchy.

CHAPTER 29

It was a whirlwind getting back from the warehouse to the Compound, but we eventually made it.

By the time we arrived, Caleb and his Keturi were set up in their conference room, the large Comms screen on the wall lit up with the picture of the stoic High Faction, all waiting for us to arrive.

"Report," Cole barked at us. Nolan and I hadn't even sat down yet.

I rolled my eyes, taking my time to pull out my chair and settle myself. I kept the package hidden on my lap, allowing the rough brown paper to slide against my numb fingertips, the sensation grounding me. I told them the entire story, not stopping or allowing anyone to talk over me until I recounted every second.

"If we had just infiltrated as I suggested, at least we would have some of them in custody," Cole seethed.

"And then we wouldn't have known he was using scare tactics or whatever he has passed on to Beta Mallanis," Evette shot back.

"What's in the package?" Kyler asked, cutting off the argument between the two Delegates.

"I guess we're about to find out." I placed it on the table, Nolan's hand snaking out to rest on my knee and give it a tight squeeze.

I wasn't shocked in the least bit to find a similar contraption to the first message he sent me through Lila. However, there was something different about this screen when I powered it up.

"There isn't a video message, just words." I crinkled my brow, biting my bottom lip.

"What does it say?" my father asked.

I glared back up at the High Faction before returning my attention to the device in my hand. "It just says 'come back when the clock strikes zero' with a counter winding down." I did the math quickly in my head. "Three days. It also says to make sure I return to Seathra before then."

Stillness overtook the room, my fingers trembling as I laid the device gingerly in the box. I was sick of this man's games. He talked as if we would one day be comrades in arms, like he could convince me to join his side. Yet he played with my mind and my body, torturing me to try and get ahead of him. He baited me, taunted me, and I was *sick* of it.

There were very few people in the world that tempted a feral side of me that craved bloodshed, but Elliot Wells was dangerously close to joining that exclusive list.

"You should head back tomorrow morning," Caleb spoke up, my gaze finding his across the table, his silvery eyes mixed with concern and perseverance. "You've been through too much tonight and it's late. Better to get a good night's rest."

I nodded, agreeing with him completely until a voice from the screen cut in. "Who says she's leaving?" Father growled.

I looked over at him, my insides rolling with heat. "If we've learned anything from hunting Elliot for years, it's that following his orders is the best way to keep others safe."

"We should try to hack into that device," Jasmine suggested. "Maybe we can use it to locate him somehow."

"The likelihood of us cracking that device before the countdown is over is slim," Imogene reasoned. "Our Alchemists would need at least a day, probably longer, to understand the tech, let alone hack into it. The safest thing to do is to have Beta Mallanis follow Elliott's directions. Let us hear the message before we complete any plans. The device will still be available for testing and investigation afterwards."

"Doesn't mean she has to follow the orders to go to Seathra," Father said. "She could take the message here."

"And what if lives are at stake? Hm?" I stood up, hands braced on the table in front of me, my growing claws scratching at the shiny surface. "If he sets a challenge for me, and me alone, and I'm not there to take it? Who will die because you forced me to stay? Lea? Oliver?"

Father's face drained of color at the mention of their names.

Good, he should be scared. Elliot and this whole revolution should have scared them to the core.

I was done listening to the High Faction's constant bickering, nothing more than inflated egos willing to oppose those who they thought were the enemy within their own team. I was ready to fight, to take down the hateful group of people threatening my country.

Politics be damned, I was going to save lives like I vowed to do ten years ago.

"As High Tribune Imogene said, the best thing for Nolan and me to do is to return to Seathra and take the message when it comes through." I leaned forward. "Then we can figure out how to beat Elliott at his own game. Sound like a good plan?"

An array of looks decorated the screen, from Evette's proud smirk to Cole's dark glare, with a smattering of resigned nods passing over the rest of the High Faction. Good, I wasn't in the mood to deal with more of their bullshit in fighting. It wasted time.

"So, since we've settled that little argument," I sat back down, raising my chin in defiance. "It's time for Nolan and me to begin preparing to leave. Feel free to send on any additional news that may pertain to the call. If not, we'll talk in three days."

And with those final words, I cut off the High Faction's connection.

***

We were packed and ready to go by the next day, mid-morning sunlight streaming down and warming my chilled skin from the frigid winter air. I was trying my best not to obsess over what the message would be this time; what Elliot would try to bait me into. He could hurt me or those around me. He could manipulate me or kill again. With him, nothing was off the table, and that lack of knowledge set every nerve ending in my body on full alert, tingling from any little brush of the long sleeves of my shirt.

Suffice it to say, I did not sleep well the night before, even with Nolan's protective arms wrapped around me the entire time.

When we approached where our cycles were parked, my steps faltered at the sight of who had arrived in the time it took to get the last of our stuff. Caleb stood there, his hands shoved deep into the pockets of his workout pants, eyes downcast until we were right in front of him.

"Hey," I weakly said, my heart thumping a bit too hard.

I wasn't sure where we were anymore, or what we would become. The talk in the woods had helped lessen some of the burden I had been carrying for a year, but the lack of trust was still there. We were in an awkward in-between of repair and destruction that I didn't know how to maneuver through.

Ugh, this day was already terrible.

"Do you mind if I talk to you for a moment?" he asked.

"Sure."

Nolan took my backpack from me, placing a chaste kiss on my forehead before turning away, my footsteps following Caleb across the way to give us a bit of privacy.

"I wanted to give you an update before you left." His hand twisted in front of him, his face pale and sleep-deprived, bruises blooming under his eyes. "The new handwriting analysis came back."

I pulled in a ragged breath. "And?"

Even though I knew the answer, my palms still sweated as if I was back on the witness stand.

"They came back as fraudulent." He couldn't even look me in the eye, his feet shuffling back and forth. "You were right."

"Oh." I bit the inside of my cheek, awkwardness creeping up the back of my neck.

"Go ahead, say it."

"Say what?"

Finally, he looked up at me. "The one thing you adore saying to Ollie and me."

I couldn't stop the chuckle from escaping. "I told you so."

"Yeah, you did." He nodded. "I used my spare time the past few days to review your case as well. Go through all of the details like I should have at the beginning of all of this."

"And?" My shoulders pulled back defensively.

"And you know as well as I that he said, she said circumstantial evidence takes up most of the file." My heart lurched because I did know that. It always pissed me off, made me feel hopeless, like my voice and pain didn't matter. "However, the faked letters already show he had planned something. It shows motive. Along with Beckett's testimony and medical evaluation, it will help make your case stronger."

"Stronger, but still not solidified?" I was reading between the lines, and his fidgeting body showed me that he wasn't ready to fully commit. He still had a voice of doubt, and it sounded like my father. Or Logan. Or both. They had been in his ear for far too long now, and it would take him a long time to shake off the manipulation they had planted in his mind, if he ever could.

"They could still counter the argument." He rubbed his fingers across his forehead as if to relieve an aching muscle. "Beckett's your friend. They could question the validity of him doing your medical exam. He could come up with an excuse for the falsified documents, saying he just put down in words what you had verbally threatened him with."

"All of that is bullshit," I snarled, his reasoning making the heat in my chest rise at a steady pace.

"Even so, I know how Cole and those in his good graces think, Father included. But I came up with a plan that will put all circumstantial evidence to rest and will make everyone who doubted you shut up, including me." He continued to rock back and forth.

"How?" I whispered, my heart thumping, but my darkened thoughts warned me to not get my hopes up, not when it came to Caleb. I had been burned too many times.

"I'm going to see him during the Blue Moon," he said, shoulders pulling back slightly, his words laced with a determined conviction. "I'm going to prove he bears the *Marc Gealach,* and, if he has one, I'll arrest him myself."

As a Varg Anwyn, one of our gifts from Lunestia was our ability to see what was known as the *Marc Gealach*, her beautiful crest that only appeared under the moonlight of a special moon phase. Blood Moons, Harvest Moons, Super Moons and Blue Moons.

They were found all around Kazola, branding the skin of those who had committed terrible, disgusting acts. Murderers, war criminals, pedophiles… and sexual assaulters.

She had given it to us so we could track down wrongdoings easily, the Wild Hunt nothing short of a frenzy in the Ancient Times. Feral wolves prowled through the night, soaking up the added strength the special moon had given them and killing anyone who bore Lunestia's crest before the sun rose.

Of course, the wildness of it all caused a lot of issues. Varg Anwyns who had enemies used it as an excuse to kill them in cold blood and walk away, where loved ones of those who bore the crest claimed that the wolves were killing Shrivs and Humans to try and eradicate them.

So, when we had come back together in peace and created the Onyx Guard, new protocols had been put in place to make sure none of that happened again. All military Varg Anwyns would be out on patrol searching for anyone that had the *Marc Gealach*, listening to the call and pull of it. If one was found and arrested, they would be brought to the closest military base immediately, where three other Varg Anwyns had to sign off that they had also witnessed it on the guilty party.

After that, the accused would be held in jail for six months while a case was built. If not enough evidence was found to go to trial, we would be forced to let them go. However, when it came to those who bore Lunestia's mark, there was always evidence and witnesses. If you were caught, there was a very small chance you would ever see the outside of a jail cell again.

It was the perfect place to prove Logan's guilt. With Lunestia's guidance.

"Goddess, I completely forgot that we had a Wild Hunt coming up." I wiped my hand down my face, beads of perspiration smearing across my cheeks.

I usually loved the hunts during the special moons. I had missed the last one a few months back, the Harvest Moon having occurred during my first month of hospitalization. Being forced to stay in that room had been absolute torture, making me desperate to get out and hunt down wrong-doers. I had thrown myself against the door so many times trying to escape that I had dislocated my shoulder and the staff had to sedate me for the rest of the night.

After that, I realized I had lost track of the special moon cycles. I just couldn't let myself think about them. And even now, when I was ready and able to participate again, Elliot came in and pulled my focus so violently, it had vanished from my forethought.

"You've had a lot more on your mind recently."

I crinkled my eyebrow. "How did he hide during the Harvest Moon six months ago? The High Faction ignored it?" I realized I had never asked my team, still too lost in my own blackened depression while I healed in my confinement.

"He had been called away by his uncle to assist with a specialty project sanctioned by the High Faction," Caleb sneered, his words venomous. "With what I know now, it looks like our High Tribune helped hide him and, since the case was already closed, there was no reason to call him out for it."

"What's going to stop him from doing it this time?"

"I proved my loyalty to Logan over this past year. He has no reason to doubt me." He squeezed his hands into white-knuckled fists. "I already called him this morning to talk about it. After too much ass-kissing and feeding him ego-boosting words, he invited me to spend the Blue Moon with him and Cole at their family estate. Apparently, that's where they spent it last time."

I was speechless. He was willing to use his precarious place between Logan and me and go undercover. He was going to risk his status in the Guard, his relationship with the High Faction, our father's opinion of him, and seclude himself with a violent wolf to get answers. For me, for him, and for everyone who doubted me.

He was on the precipice of finding his own way, in learning what he truly believed was the right path forward. I could still see doubt in his mind. I could see he was struggling to give in to the truth, probably because it would break down even more of what his world had been over the past years.

I could relate in a twisted way, and it softened my heart a fraction more, although my walls were still widely constructed around myself when it came to him.

A part of me screamed to tell him yes, wish him luck, and send him on his way to do what he should have done a year ago. But the more logical side, the one who planned and executed undercover missions dozens of times, couldn't help but go through the list of all the possible things that could go wrong. He would be alone with two people who were determined to keep their violent tendencies a secret. He could be a sitting duck if he went in alone.

I shook my head, finally finding the correct words. "There are too many unknowns. You can't do it."

"I'll have backup waiting on the perimeter," he assured me. "Brielle has already agreed to lay in wait on the outskirts and infiltrate when I call her in."

His Beta. So, he wouldn't be going in alone. "She did?"

"Well, first she smacked me on the back of my head, said *finally*, and then agreed." He smirked. "She hasn't liked me very much recently."

I scoffed because I knew that. She had written me after the trial and I knew she had tried to transfer a few times, but there had been few Beta openings and ended up stuck here.

Still, two people against Logan and Cole; it seemed too risky. "You don't know where you're going, what they plan to do during that time, or what they will try and get you to do. It will be their stronghold, and that is just too damn risky for you to do this. You just can't…"

Even with all the anger, I refused to see him hurt. I didn't want him to risk himself leaving this world just to get answers I was desperate for.

"Kasha." He grabbed my shoulders, shaking me back to reality, my body freezing. "Let me do this. This might be our only chance to bring him back in and force Cole's hand in this."

"The risk…"

"You are worth the risk," he urged, hunching down to bring our gazes level. "You are my sister. Born by Blood, Bound by Loyalty. Let me prove that to you. Please."

I stared into those bright silver eyes that had been a comforting constant in my life for the first twenty-seven years. He would do this. For me, for us, for our family bond. He would do whatever it took to prove that his wrong-doings were worth risking his life to make it up to me. To show me where his true loyalty lay.

I did something I hadn't done in a year. I lunged forward and wrapped my arms around my biggest brother.

His arms didn't hesitate to wrap around my waist, pulling me closer, the familiar scent of tobacco and vanilla enveloping us within the embrace. It had been so long. Too much had passed, too much had happened. I wasn't sure if any of this could make up for what he had done.

But it was a start.

CHAPTER 30

"How would you feel about taking a detour?" Nolan nudged my shoulder with his.

The apple I was eating with my lunch hovered a few inches from my open mouth. "How big of one?"

"One night," he said. "If we go right to Compound, we're just gonna be sitting around watching a clock tick down. We might as well try to distract ourselves a bit."

"You're not wrong." I snorted, tossing the core of the apple into the trees. After a few hours of driving, we stopped on the side of the road to have a quick lunch. "Why the sudden change, though?"

"I've been your paramour for what, almost a month now?" He traces a pattern on my knee. "I don't like that in this time we've spent most of it working. You deserve better than that, especially with what you're going through."

My heart lurched at that. I couldn't believe it had been that long, even longer if you counted the fact that we had been skirting around our feelings since very soon after his arrival in Seathra. But work and Elliot had been priorities above our romance. I was a workaholic, and so was Nolan. We didn't care too much on the daily. However, he said I deserve better than that, and so did he.

I reached down, lacing my fingers with his. "What did you have in mind?"

***

"Goddess above, this place is stunning." My eyes didn't know where to settle in the beautiful room we'd checked into. "How did you find out about it?"

"My dads came here last year for their anniversary." He hung our bags in the armoire, shucking his jacket off and hanging it up as well.

Nolan had brought us to a small town in Seathra known as Ravach, which was located on the coast. It was rumored that every spot in the cliff-like city had a view of the ocean. I wasn't sure if that was true, but the bungalow in the small inn we were staying at was nothing short of luxurious. Each one spaced out and enclosed in tall hedges to give as much privacy as possible. Inside was well decorated in soothing, coastal tones with a canopy bed in the center.

"I love it." I threw myself down on the bed, my back sinking slightly into the plush mattress that was decorated in a cream, lapis, and buttercup quilt and pillows. Gauzy white fabric that twisted around the mahogany frame hung above me.

"What's most special about them, though, is what each room has outside." He grabbed my hand, running to the double doors on the opposite side and swinging them open, revealing a pool that looked like it belonged hidden behind a waterfall.

I gasped at the stunning view, the sun already setting over the vast ocean that drifted on for miles. To the left and right of the pool, lattice work walls rose, circling around and covered in vines so as to not obstruct the view but keep the pool area private. The circular pool itself was made of sand-colored stone, the glittered water reflecting the witching hour sunlight, sparkling like jewels coating every inch. It wasn't very big, only about ten feet in circumference, but the perfect place for a soak and to enjoy the serene setting.

"They use special irrigation to bring salt water up from the ocean and deposit them into the heated pools so you can use them all year round." He crowded behind me, hands gently squeezing my shoulders. "Want to take a swim with me? I made sure these were in the room since we didn't have our own."

He held out his hand in front of me, dangling scraps of fabric from his fingertip—a scarlet red swimming set.

"Well." I bit my bottom lip, the temptation just too sweet to pass up, warmth pooling in my lower belly. "I guess we might as well take advantage of all the amenities."

We made quick to dress, me hopping into the bathroom and putting on the strapped bandeau style top and matching high-waisted bottoms that had ruching along the sides, accentuating my curves in a special way yet keeping my tummy covered. I pulled one of the rolled white towels off a shelf near the shower and wrapped myself in it. I had no idea why I was nervous and self-conscious, especially after what we did in the gym the other day. But there was a charge in the air, licking my body with needy heat and begging me to enjoy every moment to come. I wanted to. I craved it, but it didn't make the fluttering nerves in my stomach dissipate at all.

With one final breath, I came out of the bathroom, the doors to the pool still swung open, Nolan already sitting within its depths. I tiptoed to the edge before dropping the towel and slowly lowering myself, shivering from the sharp contrast of the bitter winter air and the steaming water. I settled quickly, wading to the opposite side where Nolan stood, his arms resting on the ledge that overlooked the ocean. I pressed myself against his back when I reached him, wrapping my arms to grasp him just below his sternum. I rested my cheek against his taut back, the muscles rippling at the contact, a surge of his spicy citrus scent surrounding me.

"Do you like it?" He whispered, his hands reaching down to grasp mine and tug them upward to give a kiss on each.

"It's lovely." I ducked under his arm to situate myself in front of him, looking up into those intoxicating green eyes. "It's exactly what I needed."

"Good." He cupped my face, dragging it to his to place a heartwarmingly delicious kiss on my lips. I tried to deepen it, reaching my arms to snake around his neck, but he pulled away, twisting me around so I leaned against the edge of the pool, chin resting on my arms as he crowded around me, creating a safe cocoon with his body.

I relaxed into his hold, comfortable silence falling around us as we both stared out into the horizon. It was absolute perfection, and already my mind was melting away the stressors of my life to focus on the moment. Pleasure and devotion swirled in the air around us, mixing in this perfect little slice of paradise that we had found ourselves in.

I knew what I wanted; I wanted him.

"Nolan?" I nestled into his embrace more, my chest rising slightly deeper than normal. "There is something I need."

"What is it, sweetheart?" he whispered against my ear, dragging his nose along my temple.

"I—" My breath hitched, my back feeling the effects the water was having on him pressed against my backside. "I want you."

"I want you too."

"I know you do." I looked over, catching his gaze with mine, my eyes shifting to a glittering gold. "And I'm ready to explore more."

Heat flared in his eyes, his own shifting to gold. "Are you sure?"

I nodded. "I need you."

"You're wish is my command." He chuckled against my cheek. "You'll tell me to stop if it's too much?"

I nodded again, but there was no lingering sense of fear waiting for me, no anxiety expecting the moment to eventually be ruined by my trauma. I didn't focus on that. I let myself just feel the safe, comfortable place Nolan had created for me.

They had not taken this from me. I was finally realizing that all this pleasure could be mine, with a partner I trusted with my body and my heart. I think I finally found him.

I went to turn around, to wrap my body around his, but he halted me, pushing against my back harder and locking me in place between his body and the edge of the pool.

"Shh," he whispered, my body squirming against him. "You want me? Then you have me, but let me earn you. Let me seduce you the way you deserve."

I stilled in his grasp, his arms moving from the stones in front of us to trail up my sides, a shuddering breath escaping my lips. My body relaxed into the touch, focusing on nothing but the feeling of his fingers trailing along my wet, heated skin.

"I love all of your tattoos." His fingers traced the words written on my right bicep, the touches featherlight and dragging light sparks across my skin. "I know what these are." He leaned down, trailing a few kisses over the Onyx Guard Motto and my sibling vows before righting himself again, chin resting gently on my left shoulder, his lips tracing the tattoo there. "And this one."

A moan escaped my lips, my head falling back to rest on his shoulder. "They…uh…" My mind was hazing over, my body heating a lot faster than the warm water that surrounded us. "All matter to me for a specific reason."

"Mmm," he hummed against my skin, tongue darting out to lick a few drops of water off the crest before trailing his lips to the back of my neck and down a few inches on my spine before they reached the next tattoo that inked my skin. "Then what does this one mean?"

My mind blanked. Utterly gone was any fact about what was there and what it meant because all I could focus on was the lightning pulses running up my spine at every lingering touch of Nolan's lips.

Where a few days ago was a heady, lust-filled frenzy of devouring each other, this was slow and methodical. An alluring temptation meant to wind me to the brink and leave me dangling over the edge for as long as he wanted me to hang before letting me fall into bliss.

And damn, was I loving every moment, every swipe of his tongue and lusciously laced word he whispered to me.

I moaned, knowing this was only the beginning.

"Kasha," he taunted, wrapping one arm around my hips to band me against his body. "Are you still with me?"

"It's uh… I got it after my first successful case as a Delta." The memory finally returned to me in flashes of pictures.

"Tell me about it." His hand on the front of me began trailing upwards, teasing the edges of my swimming top, gently pushing into it to tease the underside of my breast.

"Lucas and I had been sent to assist with a string of deaths in a little town near the border of Adro. Everyone thought they were accidents, but we ended up discovering that someone was using snake poison to force people to have strokes." I moaned at the first brush of Nolan's fingers against the hardened tips of my breasts. My Goddess, were his fingers magical?

"We caught him on the full moon." I moved my hands into the water, reaching behind me to grasp at Nolan's thighs, starting to draw my own teasing circles just under the rippling hem of his swimming shorts. "That's why it's a snake wrapped around the moon phase."

"I love it." He grunted when my fingernails dug into his thighs, his tongue tracing along the twisted pattern of the snake that went up the top half of my spine before sucking deeply on the head that sat just below my neck.

He finally turned me around, grasping my hips and yanking me up, my legs wrapping around his waist, my body shivering as more of my torso was exposed to the cold air. He held me tight with one arm, his lips now finding my collarbone and tracing downward to lick at the top swells of my breast. His free hand found my ribs, trailing the final tattoo he had yet to explore. "And this?"

"Lucas, Taylor, and I got it together after our most recent promotions to Beta and her Gammas." I turned my head, wrapping my fingers into the wet strands of his dark hair and trailing kisses along his temple and down to his jaw. "Each line of the triangle represents one of us. Music notes for me, a paintbrush for Lucas, and a stilo for Taylor, who loves journaling and writing."

"Beautiful." He said, but I wasn't sure if it was in reference to the tattoo or my breasts, his lips moving to suck at the tip through the thin material of the top. I threw my head back, gasping breaths escaping as I clenched my thighs around him and started to slowly grind up and down against his quickly hardening length, a pulsing ache at the apex of my thighs building more and more pressure with each swipe of his lips against my body.

Everything he was doing to me was divine and I needed more; so much more of him.

"Nolan… I…" My chest heaved, my mind lost in the haze of lust swarming around us, body completely at his mercy and melting into his arms, waiting for him to do whatever he had planned.

"I want to taste you." He growled into my neck, backing me up against the wall of the pool. "Can I?"

I sucked in a deep breath, my heart stuttering and my mind screaming *yes, yes, yes,* but somehow, I was unable to say the words to him directly.

"Please, sweetheart." He lifted me to sit on the end, fingers curling into the edges of my swim bottoms. "I want to worship you."

I could only nod, my gaze fixated on the stunning man sitting below me as he slowly removed my bottoms and tossed them to the side of the pool. He pressed his face into my spread thighs, taking a deep whiff in. "You smell divine."

He didn't move closer to my center, and whimpers escaped my lips. His fingers dug into my hips, teeth nipping up and down my legs, but whenever he drifted closer to my core, he hesitated before pulling away and trailing back down. I let out a deep, frenzied growl, my body ready to snap at the painstaking teasing he was inflicting on me.

"Nolan."

"Yes, sweetheart?" He nipped at my thighs, rolling his cheek against it to peek up at me through his long eyelashes, gold eyes glinting with wicked pleasure as my body squirmed underneath his tight hold.

I gripped his hair, yanking him to look at me, to see exactly what I needed. "Devour me, sweetness."

He growled, needing no other probing to take exactly what he wanted, his tongue finding my center and giving a deep, sensual lick across it. I didn't care if anyone was close by as I let out a scream of pure ecstasy, my thighs gripping Nolan's head closer, my fingers tangling in his hair to keep him exactly where I needed him.

The pressure in my core sang to new heights, winding up and up and up. His tongue took its time at first, exploring every inch of me, before settling on my clit, my legs beginning to shake around him, badgering me to the edge. All I could think about was what was weaving inside of me, my desire reawakened, begging to come out and play.

"Goddess, Nolan… I'm… I'm…"

"Give me your pleasure," he rumbled against my core before licking and sucking earnestly, that final pull on my little bud my undoing.

I threw my head back, white flashes blasting across my closed eyelids as my release consumed every inch of my being. I let it envelop me, my fangs popping out, claws scratching against the rough stone below as I quaked with the desire Nolan had reawakened inside me.

He kept licking fervently against my sensitive core, sinking a finger deep inside me and not letting up for a moment while I allowed myself to lose control for once. My eyes rolled back, the desire and pleasure of giving myself willingly encircling me into a cocoon of safety, allowing me to explore a part of myself I thought was long gone.

As the last wave of euphoria settled into my veins, a light buzz of post-haze wrapped me in a delicate, sated state. He pulled away, placing a delicate kiss on my thighs before helping me drop back into the pool, my body sweaty even though I had been exposed to the chilled air for the past few minutes.

I wrapped my arms around him, my body perking up a bit at the pressure of his strained swim shorts against my stomach. I reached down, tracing my fingers along the edges, teasing them into the waistband.

He gripped my wrist gently, using his other hand to lift my face gently with his finger under my chin. "You don't have to. I'm okay."

"I gave you my pleasure," I whispered against his jaw, peppering it with light, fluttering kisses. "Now I want yours."

I pushed his swim shorts down, exposing him to me just below the surface of the water. I took a firm grip on him, a guttural groan escaping his lips, rumbling against me as he melted into my touch. I didn't hesitate to continue, stroking up and down his hardened dick, exploring how he liked to be touched. I played with my grip, the glide of my strokes, and the speed at which I moved my hand up and down across him. I watched his face with raptured attention, his eyes fluttering closed when he particularly liked one of my movements, his abs flexing against my knuckles. When I rubbed my thumb over the leaking tip, his body shuddered under my touch, a whisper of my own pleasure coursing through me once again.

"Kasha..." He moaned my name, encouraging me to grip harder, quicken my pace, and help him chase what had been building in him during his seduction of me.

His breathing increased, the ragged breaths puffing against my cheek as he leaned down to nip his teeth at my earlobe. I pushed him against the wall, our labored breaths mixing as he grabbed me by the back of my neck and crashed our lips together, his pliant against mine, letting me devour him as I continued to stroke up and down.

Finally, with a deep cry, he pulsed under my touch, hips gyrating into my hand as his sticky cum shot into the pool, washed away by the water. I slowed with the settling of his hips, dragging out every bit of pleasure he could give me, the final shudder rocking through him as he once again took control of our kiss and consumed me with gratitude.

CHAPTER 31

The tension in the conference room was palpable the moment we crossed inside, the entire Hierarchy packed in, some standing others sitting. All eyes found me the moment we came through.

We had arrived back to Compound by mid-morning and made quick hellos, Grayson taking Elliot's package from me right away to set it up in the conference room before it was time to meet with them all. After taking an hour to clean up, settle in, and check in with Lea, we finally trudged over to the office building to watch the final minutes count down.

"It's all set," Grayson said, pulling out the chair at the head of the table for me. I wordlessly sat in it, the odd boxed screen sitting in front of me, the counting clock only a few minutes away from zero. I gripped my knees under the table, my heart hammering against my chest. Nolan took up a place behind me, Grayson moving away to fiddle with the stationed Comms unit.

The only stipulation for us taking the package back to Seathra was that the High Faction would call into the room while I listened to Elliot's newest message. I understood, but when their foreboding, stern faces showed up on the screen mounted on the wall across from us, my stomach twisted, bile rising in my throat.

Everyone muttered hello to the Delegates just as the screen hit the last ten seconds. My pulse moved a bit faster, my breathing hitching for the last three, two, one...

His face appeared instantly, once again dressed in a well-tailored suit, this time in a cerulean blue with a matching vest, crisp white shirt, and heather-gray tie. His eyes lit up the moment the connection took, a dashing smile appearing on his full lips.

"Hello, *Rogthna*." He smiled at me, my stomach curdling. I waited, a long pause filling the video before he finally gave a little chuckle. "You can actually talk back now."

Fire burned in my veins, desperate to escape. There were many things I wanted to say, to scream, but I reined it in. "What do you want?"

"Many things, lovely, but for now I am here to offer you a deal." He smirked, leaning forward on his elbows, fingers laced under his chin. It was too casual.

"What kind of deal?"

"One I think you might have a great interest in." He smirked. "More of a challenge, if you will."

Nolan stiffened next to me, but I kept my eyes on Elliot. "What kind of challenge?"

"The Blue Moon is in two weeks."

I rolled my eyes. "You don't say." I leaned back in my chair, crossing my arms in a protective yet relaxed stance. I was trying to tick him off, making him think I couldn't care less what he said, hoping to get him off-kilter.

Unfortunately, he continued, unfazed. "I will allow you to hunt me on that night."

I straightened. "Excuse me?"

"I will give you a section of public woods that I will be in, and if you can hunt me down, fight me, and capture me, then I will turn myself over willingly," he said. "I even promise to give you any information you want and assist in the disbandment of my militia. I will do everything in my power to not make a martyr of myself."

My heart thudded, my mind already analyzing every word he just spoke, figuring out if participating was worth it. To get him off the streets, could I risk myself in one of his games? I didn't have a good track record of keeping up with him. But I was learning, and this opportunity was one I knew was once in a lifetime. He was coming out of hiding and he was giving us a chance.

Me. He was giving me a chance to catch him.

"I'm assuming there are rules you are going to make me follow?" I needed to know everything; it was the only way I could decide.

"Well, no killing, for one." He tilted his head. "I may be willing to let myself be caught, but I am not interested in losing my life quite yet."

"And?" I pursed my lips.

"And only you can participate. No one else from the Onyx Guard will be allowed within the set arena I have created," he said. "If any of my guards catch a whiff of them, I will make sure they are dealt with."

"What else?"

"That's it." He held his hands out as if it was a simple gesture. "Catch me and I'm yours."

"And if I don't catch you?" I narrowed my eyes.

He shrugged. "Then we continue with this little chase as if nothing happened."

"What do you get out of this?"

"Besides the potential to see you once again?" He winked.

I sneered. "The real reason."

"I'll tell you when you catch me." He tilted his head. "So, do we have a deal?"

There were already so many loopholes that I had identified, ones that he could exploit but I couldn't. But there was one that was most important to me, that I couldn't let him keep in his arsenal of manipulations. Not for a game such as this.

"One caveat to this little hunt of yours." I stared him down, my jaw tightening. "You will not take or hurt anyone in my Faction, my family, or my friends. If you so much as touch one of them, I will not hesitate to put my blade through your heart."

"Do you really believe I would hurt those closest to you?" he whispered, eyes narrowing.

I scoffed. "You would have to have honor for me to believe that."

His face betrayed nothing, although his fingers tightened around themselves as he leaned back in his chair. "Are you claiming I have none?"

"Honor is proven with actions." I raised an eyebrow. "All I see is a power-craving man who likes to take lives."

"You have so much to learn, *Rogthna*." He shook his head, but the gleam in his eyes said something entirely different.

"Do you accept my stipulations or not?" I gritted through my teeth, my fingernails starting to sharpen, pinching into my thigh.

"I do." He nodded. "Do you accept my challenge?"

I swallowed, finally looking up to gaze around the room. I had been ignoring the weight on my neck that they had been causing, but the fear and trepidation that mixed in my Faction's eyes was nothing compared to the hunger that seemed to radiate from the heavy gazes of the High Faction on the screen. I already knew what they wanted, but still, yes was far from the tip of my tongue.

I didn't dare look at Nolan. I already knew what his eyes would say. They would say no. But I couldn't seem to say that either.

"I need time to think," I said, turning my attention back to Elliot.

He smiled at me, warmth blooming across his face. "Of course. I wouldn't expect anything less from you. You have twenty-four hours. I will call back on this same machine at the same time as today. Once you accept, we will send you the coordinates for the course."

"Very well."

"Talk to you soon, *Rogthna*," he said before the screen went black.

I finally let out a breath that had been caught in my chest, my body slumping back in my chair. My mind whirled, not exactly sure what Elliot's motives for this were. To embarrass me? To hurt me in some way? I gained the potential to capture him, but what was in it for him?

It didn't make complete sense in my head.

"You will take the hunt." A voice cut through our silence, my eyes looking up to the High Faction. It had been Mitchell who had spoken.

"You can't just force her to do this." Nolan seethed next to me. My hand reached out to grasp his, and I hoped it calmed him down. "We need to discuss it."

"We have already," Evette said. They must have muted the call after Elliot had given the challenge. "And we cannot give up this chance. If Kasha wants to take the hunt, she can."

"Kasha will take the challenge." My eyes turned to the right side of the screen, my father ramrod straight in his chair, his cold, detached eyes finding me. "We will not let such an opportunity get away. Not when this is a chance to stop a potential war before it begins."

"Do you have so little care for your daughter's life?" Nolan took a step forward, pulling from my grasp.

"Nolan," I chided, trying to grab for him again, but he flinched away. My heart ached at that.

"I've known my daughter since the day she came into this world, Alpha." My father leaned forward. "She would never be able to give up this chance, not when it meant the potential to save thousands of lives. Giving in to fear is not in her blood."

I stiffened, hating that he was talking about me in such a way, as if he was privy to my innermost thoughts. Unfortunately, though, he was far from wrong. This challenge was dangerous and reckless and had too many what-ifs to be a safe move. But it was our only move at this point, one chance to catch a man that was ready to rip Kazola in half. Who knew who would be lost in the break?

Maybe, if I caught him, I could finally get an answer as to why he was fixated on me.

"I'll do it," I blurted out. Nolan whipped around to look at me, his eyes shifting, lips curled in a snarl, although he was able to contain the noise.

"Very well. Time to prove your new worth, Beta," Cole said before the line cut off and the screen went dark.

"You aren't doing this." Nolan growled from the left. I shot from my chair, growling right back, everyone stiffening around us.

Somehow, I had forgotten most of them were there. I looked around, my nerves suddenly jolting along my arms at the audience we had. I shook my head, turning back to Nolan.

"Out," I growled at him, pointing to the door. He glowered at me, eyes still burning gold as we retreated away from our gaping friends.

CHAPTER 32

I slammed the door to my office the moment we crossed the threshold, unable to bottle up my ire any longer.

"What in the name of the Goddess was that back there?" I pushed him, his feet stumbling backwards. His face was still hardened, giving away nothing. So, I pushed him one more time for good measure.

"That was me being the voice of reason." He pushed me right back, his palm warm for the brief second it connected to my shoulder. "Since you have decided that throwing all caution away is the best course of action."

"It's not the best course, Nol, it's the only one!" I threw my arms into the air. "Do you really think I would make this decision lightly? Playing his games has too many risks to count."

"Then why do it?" His white-knuckled fists shook at his side. "Why agree to the hunt?"

"Because like it or not, his sights are set on me. He will do anything to have the opportunity to let his disgusting obsession out." The words were painful to say, like razors slashing against my tongue as I let them free, but we both knew the truth.

"Then let us handle the fight!" He slammed his fist onto my desk, then kicked it as if it had personally offended him. "You don't have to take on every burden alone. Not when we can keep you safe and protected."

"I'm not taking on a burden." I shook my head, trying to calm my racing breath down. Yelling and screaming wouldn't convince him because he was just like me. Facts, truths, and logic; that was how I could win him over. I just needed to break through this intense wall of protectiveness he had been building for weeks.

"Then what would you call this?"

"Taking control of an uncontrollable situation." I took a step forward, his eyes tracking my every movement as I made my way toward him. "We have two weeks until the Blue Moon rises and The Wild Hunt begins. We can prepare, plan, theorize…"

"But that is all it will ever be, theories." He shook his head, a few tendrils of dark hair falling against his forehead. "We can never truly know what twisted schemes he has planned for you at the end of the hunt when you finally catch up to him. What then?"

"I fight…"

"And if you lose?"

My heart dropped. "Do you have so little faith in me?"

"My faith in you knows no bounds." His heated gaze bored into me. "But that doesn't mean he won't take you away from me given the chance."

I froze, my lips parting on a deep inhale. It was at that moment I realized a truth I had been too blind to see before.

It wasn't just my life he was trying to protect, to keep out of harm's way.

I wanted to believe it was just his need to protect me, a tug on the bond we had been strengthening over the past few weeks. Yet, I knew it was so much more than that. So much more darkness that lurked beyond that bright, confident personality he let everyone see.

I closed the distance between us in as few steps as possible, his body going rigid as I approached. I grasped his face between my hands, his jaw ticking at my tender touch, eyes downcast at the floor.

"Nolan, please, look at me."

He hesitated for a moment before obeying, his beautiful green eyes jolting my heart. I knew that look well. He wasn't just being overprotective. He was in pain. Deep-seated hurt he was trying desperately to hide from me. He was hiding from his own trauma, one we had only talked about in fond memories and beloved moments of his. We never brought up the darkness within, the ending that crashed his life down four years ago.

"I'm not Cleo," I whispered, his eyes flashing pain, heartache, and turmoil; words I very rarely ever associated with my partner. He was the light to my darkness, the laughter to my tears. We had fallen so easily into our roles towards each other, it was easy to forget that his past was almost as dark as my own.

His hands instinctively darted out to grasp my hips, pulling me closer to him, my hands still grasping his warm cheeks. "I can't lose you. I barely survived it before, and if it's possible I…" His words trailed off, his face leaning into my left hand.

My mouth dried. "You… what?"

He closed his eyes, taking one deep breath before fixing his alluring gaze onto mine. "I love you. More than I ever have, and yet it grows with each day I get to call you my own."

His words were beautifully intoxicating, my mind reeling in euphoric bliss for a few seconds as I grasped exactly what he was telling me.

He loved me. Me. The broken Varg who was trying her best to rebuild herself into a stronger wolf. He loved me. All of me. Every little bit.

He loved me.

No matter how many times I repeated it to myself, I couldn't completely grasp it.

Even worse, I was completely lost for words, even though what I should have said was obvious.

We weren't Mates, not technically, although the past few weeks of stolen time and tender moments had shown me a future that was becoming more and more of a reality. He made me want it, crave it, and finally, I wasn't scared of the possibility.

So, why couldn't I say it back?

Why was I so scared to take that step, to give that part of myself to him? It was almost as bad as my flaring desire to let him Mark me and claim me, to take me to his bed and help me eradicate every dark moment of my past with bliss.

But something inside kept me so still, so scared to move forward, even though I knew I wanted it all.

He turned his head, placing a gentle kiss on my palm. "You don't have to say it. I wasn't even planning to say it now."

Damn him. He always knew what I needed to hear.

I swallowed, my voice rough. "Then why did you?"

"It just felt right." His thumb traced circles, heating my skin through my shirt. "I'm not trying to guilt you into agreeing with me or pressure you to let me lock you in a tower and keep you there until Elliott is dead…"

I scoffed. "I'd just break out."

"I'm well aware." His eyes gleamed with a wicked teasing humor before settling back into the serious moment. "I just… I can't go through that again. You are my future, Kas. I want you there with me."

"I want that too," I whispered with sincerity.

"Then why are you doing this? Why play his game?"

I let my hands fall from his face, placing them on his shoulders. *"Tsio a Chisain."*

He sighed. "Protect the Peace."

"I took that oath. We both did." I leaned into him, my chest pressing against his, a bit of the tension in his body melting into my touch. "It has been weeks, and with each day that passes, Elliott's acolytes and armies grow. They are the biggest threat against our oath, ready to tear it down and destroy everything good about Kazola. We can't let that happen."

He dropped his forehead to mine. "I know."

"He's giving us a chance to bring the fight to him. We can't pass it up." I squeezed his shoulders. "I wish it didn't involve what it does, but it's the only option we have. That's why the High Faction is sending me in. That is why I have to do this."

He let out a ragged breath, his body trembling against mine. "I hate this."

"So do I."

"If anything happens to you, if he captures you…" A growl rumbled from his chest, his eyes flashing gold. "I promise to find you and bring you home to safety. I won't rest until you are back in my arms."

I leaned up, pressing my lips against his, greedily tasting him in a moment I couldn't quite explain but knew I would cherish forever.

"I know you will," I whispered against his lips. "With you out in the world, I can never lose hope again."

"I love you," he whispered once more before wrapping me into a hug.

He surrounded me, his spicy comfort helping to calm my racing heart, those words bringing me warmth and peace, settling my soul, knowing that my future was right in front of me. Even if I wasn't ready to utter the words myself.

CHAPTER 33

The bliss of Nolan's lips was ripped away from me with the bang of my office door.

I jumped back, my eyes widening at the sight in front of me.

"Oh, Goddess." My mouth gaped at my older brother, his fingers still clutching the door to my office.

This was not good. This was really not good.

"What in the name of the Goddess did I just witness?" Ollie slammed the door behind him, closing all three of us into the confined space, his eyes already flashing gold. "Someone better start talking."

"Um…" Nolan looked between us, brows furrowed in confusion. "I was kissing Kasha?"

"So, I didn't hallucinate that just now?"

Nolan straightened. "Um… no."

"And why are you kissing my baby sister, Carrigan?" He took another step forward. Every movement was controlled, purposeful as he strode around the room trying to either keep his composure or wait for the right words to be muttered so he could pounce on Nolan.

"You didn't tell Oliver about us?" Nolan looked at me, eyes brimming with confusion and a bit of hurt.

"No, I didn't." I rubbed my temples.

"Why not?"

"Nolan and I are seeing each other, Ollie." I sighed, letting the words hang between the three of us, the shifting of tension filling the room at an exponential rate. "Romantically if that wasn't already obvious."

"I'm going to punch your lights out, Carrigan," Ollie growled, stalking forward, ready to throw down.

"That's why," I said to Nolan before throwing myself between them and shoving Ollie to take a few steps back. "Cool it, Oliver. We don't have time for your overprotective bullshit."

Still, he growled over my shoulder at Nolan. I shoved him back again.

"How long?" he asked, looking at me.

"A little over a month now," I said, leaving out the fact that Nolan and I had been interested long before that and in complete denial over it.

"Why didn't you tell me?"

"I had enough going on in my life!" I said. "Finally, *finally*, I was enjoying a piece of it after a year of utter hopelessness. Forgive me for wanting to keep it that way, at least for a little while."

"I'm not that bad," Ollie grumbled.

"You have threatened and challenged every man I've dated since I was sixteen!" I threw up my hand. "My first paramour broke up with me because you threatened to hunt him."

"He was too weak for you."

"Goddess above." I rolled my eyes.

This had been Ollie every time I had chosen a man to spend my romantic time with. He would threaten or challenge them. I wasn't sure why he took it upon himself, but I guessed it had to do with the fact that he was the only one to pay attention when I had started dating. Caleb was well on his way to rising in the ranks of the Guard, Father was still frozen in time from Mama's death and too distracted as a member of the High Faction, and Nana Aggie couldn't have cared less as long as I was happy.

Somehow, that had translated to Ollie that he had to be the one to vet all my potential romantic trysts. My first had quickly cracked under the pressure without any kind of physical confrontation. Unfortunately, every one after that had taken up Ollie's challenges. All of them had lost pathetically.

"Wait a second." Nolan rubbed his jaw. I could see he was hiding a smirk behind it. "Is that why you came back from a family visit with a cracked rib and a black eye once? Right before we were transferred to our new units as Deltas?"

Ollie smirked back. "Yup. I believe his name was Dillion."

"It was Declan," I deadpanned.

"Whatever."

Nolan tilted his head. "You said your sister had done that to you."

"I did." I crossed my arms. "After he finished kicking Dec's butt, I got in a few punches of my own."

"I never should have taught you how to fight." Ollie rubbed his ribs as if a phantom pain still haunted him from the day I had pushed him up against one of the trees in the wooded clearing and given him a piece of my mind.

"But you did, and I made sure you remembered." I smirked at him.

"Mmm, sexy," Nolan whispered in my head, and I blushed.

"Come on, Mallanis," Nolan said, a wry grin on his handsome face. "It's me. You know you can trust me."

"Wrong thing to say." I shook my head, groaning.

Ollie's face darkened. "Yeah, well, looks like you need to show me if that's the truth."

"I'm not fighting you, Oliver."

"Not willing to fight for my sister?" Ollie stalked forward, an inch away from me, my back pressed against Nolan's front. I wasn't moving from this spot, even just to make sure that my office didn't get messed up in a potential brawl Ollie might start. I didn't have time to reorganize it.

"I'm willing to do anything for your sister. But I highly doubt this is it."

"It's fine. Just do it." I rolled my eyes. "My last few dates didn't get scared away by Ollie's big brother routine, and I trust you way more than I did them."

"You sure?" He looked down at me.

I just shrugged, a little too used to the whole ordeal and ready for it to be behind us. "You two fight, but you do it in the training ring."

Nolan nodded.

I whipped back to Ollie. "And once this one fight is over, you back off and let your grown sister make decisions for herself? Promise?" I poked him in the chest for good measure.

"Yes, Little Shadow. I promise." He gave me a weak smile that I didn't return.

"Let's just get it over with." I stalked out of the room, both men on my heels.

Goddess, this should be interesting.

★★★

Only twenty minutes had gone by and already the gossip of Nolan and Ollie's fight had made its way through all my friends.

Which was probably why most of them were now crowded into one of the private training rooms which I had taken over for this little fight Ollie was insistent on. Almost the entire Hierarchy was there, and I tried my best to ignore the bets being made on who would win. Unfortunately, this would not be the first time they had witnessed one of Ollie's little outbursts.

"Heard there was a fight to be seen." Lea approached where I stood in the corner, trying her best to disguise a smirk. I was keeping myself away from Ollie and Nolan, letting them stretch and prepare themselves alone.

"Of course someone told you," I mumbled, slumping closer to the wall.

"You should have just told him when he was here a few weeks ago." She knocked her shoulder with mine, leaning against the wall next to me.

"And we would just be right where we are now."

She shrugged. "But it would be over."

I just grunted. Honestly, I always knew that the longer I put things like this off, the worse it would be when the truth finally came out. Still didn't stop me from doing it to delay things that made me overly anxious just thinking about.

"Little Lea!" Ollie strutted towards us as if it was just another day and he wasn't about to try and beat my paramour to a pulp. "Come to see the show?"

He winked at her, but she just shook her head. "You're so predictable, Oliver."

He grasped his chest, faking offense. "Why would you insult me so? I have never been called something so heinous in my life."

"Why can't you just let one of your sister's romances go?"

"Need to make sure he's good enough for her." He flicked his gaze over to me, giving me a little smirk. "Only the best for my little shadow."

"Didn't you know him for years before Kas even met him?" She raised her eyebrow, challenging him.

"Many," I answered for him, a frown settling on his lips. "He was even the one that encouraged me to get to know Nolan better."

"Ah." Lea nodded, a lovely smile spreading on her lips. "So, do you not trust your own judgment in people, Ollie? Or are you just too prideful to admit that you're excited for the two of them?"

He sidled up next to her, wrapping his arm around her shoulder and shaking her a few times, her arms still crossed against her chest. "Come now, little Lea. Just because he's my friend doesn't mean he gets off easy. There is a process to these things. You know that better than anyone, seeing as I've beaten up a few of your past lovers as well."

"I hate that nickname," she grumbled, and that got a little laugh out of me. Ollie had been calling her that since she was five and she had hated it the entire time. That seemed to just egg Ollie on more, and it soon became the only thing he called her.

He leaned forward, dropping a wet, sloppy kiss onto her cheek. "Oh, please. You can't get enough of me."

"Sure, if you say so." She scrunched her face, wiping away at the flamed cheek his lips were just pressed against.

"Mallanis, are we doing this or not?" Nolan called from the center of the room, arms loose at his sides, ready for the fight to begin.

"Gotta go." He wiggled his eyebrows a few times before turning his back to us and heading straight to Nolan.

"First to draw blood?" Nolan suggested, cracking his knuckles in the process.

"Works for me." Ollie shook his arms out. "Let's see if your footwork has improved over the years. If I remember correctly, you used to be a bit clumsy with those big feet."

Eden and Liv quietly approached, standing to my right with Lea still on my left.

"This is gonna be good." Eden chuckled.

I shook my head for what felt like the millionth time, turning to catch Nolan's gaze looking at me, barely paying attention to Ollie as he explained his typical speech of why he had to do this. For me. "*Good luck,*" I said to him. He winked in response before turning back to Ollie, both taking their fighting stances.

"Begin," I yelled from the sidelines with a shake of my head.

Hoots and hollers filled the space, my team cheering both men on as they circled each other for a few seconds, sizing up their prey. They had matching cocky smirks on their faces, obviously both excited for such a fight. I wasn't surprised in the least; it was in their blood at this point.

Finally, Ollie made the first move, starting with a series of jabs to Nolan's chest before ducking and moving seamlessly into an uppercut to his chin. I breathed a sigh of relief when Nolan dodged all of his efforts perfectly. Nolan took the opportunity to aim low, swinging his leg out in hopes of knocking Ollie off balance. It didn't work, and Oliver jumped back gracefully. They continued, no one making contact for the first few seconds.

Then, Ollie lunged, clocking Nolan right in the cheek, a crack rebounding off the walls. My wolf leapt in my chest, a growl escaping my lips at the sight of Nolan hurt. I took a few steps forward, and Liv yanked me backwards.

"Breathe, Kas. He's fine, see." She pointed right at Nolan. I focused on him, noting that a deep bruise already bloomed on his tanned face, but no blood dripped from it. He just laughed at the rough impact of Ollie's fist before rounding and sending a well-aimed kick right at Ollie's ribs, a matching crunch ringing out. He lifted his shirt, confirming no blood had been drawn.

I took in a shaky breath, pushing my wolf back down, settling her. I turned to Liv. "Thank you."

She shrugged. "I was the same way with Beckett. Especially when we first joined the Guard and he was taking beatings from training. I don't know how you lot do it with a full wolf form tempting you to attack. I could barely handle it with the traces of

Varg in my Brido body."

I snorted a laugh, unsurprised that Shrivika Bridos felt a surge in territorial urges after blending with Varg Anwyns. Our wolves were known for being protective of what we considered our own. And apparently, my wolf was very adamant that Nolan was mine.

I refocused back on the fight, the two of them throwing jabs and punches, no more landing.

"So," Ollie grunted between dodges, "you think you're good enough for my sister?"

"I think she makes me happy and I her," he replied, throwing another aimed punch to Ollie's face and missing.

"And you think that's enough?" Ollie challenged. "Happiness doesn't always last."

"No, but it should always come back to that," Nolan argued, dodging Ollie's right hook. "In the end, a partner should be the one you can trust and rely on, even when life isn't the best, or even at its worst. That's what she and I are trying to build together."

"Doesn't mean you can," Ollie pushed. "Not if you aren't willing to give everything for her."

"She is the greatest thing that ever happened to my life," Nolan growled, aiming right for Ollie's solar plexus. "I will never see her harmed. And if someone slipped through the cracks, I would hunt them down and make them bleed for every drop of blood they took from her."

"You'd give your life for hers?" Ollie reached forward and grasped Nolan's shirt, bringing their faces close together. Ollie's glittering gold eyes examined every movement of Nolan's.

"I protect those I love," Nolan said.

"Love?" Ollie tightened his grip.

Nolan inched forward. "Love." He snarled low, Ollie's eyes widening before Nolan tilted his head back and then shot it forward, landing a perfect blow right to Ollie's nose.

"*Futeacha*," he swore, dropping his hold on Nolan to grip his face, blood pooling in between the cracks of his fingers.

First blood drawn. Nolan won.

Claps rang around the space, people cheering Nolan's name as he sauntered over to me, gaze still glowing gold. The moment he was in front of me, he wrapped his arms around me, swung me around, and tilted me downward before crushing his lips on mine. The cheers increased at our joining for a few seconds before Nolan pulled away, his lips still hovering over mine.

"Nothing to worry about I guess." He winked.

"I probably shouldn't admit this, but that was *hot*," I whispered in his ear, nipping the lobe with my teeth.

He chuckled darkly. "Keep that in the back of your mind." He righted us, giving me one last kiss on the cheek before pulling back. "Right now, you might want to go help Ollie."

I gave him one last smile before walking past him and into the center of the ring where Ollie still nursed his bleeding nose, Beckett now next to him pressing a handkerchief against the gushing wound.

"Let's go get you cleaned up, big bro." I moved his arm to sling it over my shoulder, Beckett taking up his other arm and helping me to drag a mumbling Ollie out of the room.

CHAPTER 34

Oliver's grunts of pain were the only thing that filled the room's silence as Beckett reset his cracked nose.

He could barely sit still. "If Carrigan ruined my face, I'm going to ruin his." I scoffed in response, and his eyes narrowed at me. "No sympathy for your injured brother in pain?"

"Not when it was self-inflicted and completely avoidable." I smirked at him, earning me a death glare but no response, because he knew there wasn't one when I was right.

Ollie whimpered like an injured puppy when Beckett snapped something into place. "Your nose will be fine. You just need to keep this brace on here for the next day while your bones heal." Beckett picked up an arched piece of plastic and metal, pressing and molding it to Ollie's purple nose.

"Ugh, this is annoying." Ollie squirmed under Beckett's expert touch like a toddler at their first physician checkup.

"You're worse than your sister," Beckett mumbled, securing the last bandage. "You're all set. I'll leave you two alone for a minute."

He dropped his gloves in the trash by the bed Ollie had taken up in the infirmary and gave me a quick wink before striding across the room and closing the door to the secondary office he had here. I leaned back on my hands, sitting across from Ollie on the neighboring bed, my feet barely scraping the floor.

"Feel better?" I asked.

He sighed, tension releasing from his shoulders. "You really like him, don't you?"

My cheeks heated. "Yeah, I do."

"And he…loves you?" His bright eyes sparkled under the harsh lighting, a softness overcoming his features as he waited for my answers.

"Yes, he does." My heart stuttered at the admission.

"Please tell me that wasn't the first time you heard it."

I laughed. "Oh, no, of course not. The first time was so long ago. Almost an hour has gone by."

"Oh, Goddess." Ollie let his head hang. "Please don't tell me…"

"That you interrupted one of the most romantic moments in my life with your overprotective bullshit? Yeah, you did."

"Well, at least I helped put on a good show for you."

"Goddess above," I mumbled, rubbing my forehead.

"He makes you happy, I can see that." He looked me up and down before standing up and shuffling over to sit next to me. "But that's not all. You still have something weighing on you."

"How can you tell?"

He shrugged. "I can feel it. You have something sitting on you. Something new."

My throat quivered, my gaze falling to my lap. What I was

being forced to participate in, wouldn't be a secret for long. The High Faction knew, and now, with all the other Factions involved with the hunt for Elliot and his allies, it was only a matter of time before a report was sent out with details of my mission to capture him. Between my squabble with Nolan and Ollie, I hadn't taken a minute to realize the actual weight that had been placed on me with this decision.

I was going in alone to face one of the most dangerous men against Kazola. One who was utterly obsessed with me, and I knew had an ulterior motive for getting me to play his game. But I had no other option and I refused to back down from the challenge when there was still the possibility that I could win.

Still, it was going to be a lot to process and prepare for over the next two weeks. For once, I was hoping time would slow down, that I could take a moment to enjoy those around me and what I loved to do every day. I wanted to play my piano for hours and read as many books as I could. I wanted to cuddle with Nolan and go running in the woods under the moonlight with Lucas and Taylor. I wanted to sit around a fire with Eden and Liv and talk about the most random things. I wanted to share a cup of coffee with Beckett. I wanted to go to Nana Aggie's and have brunch with my brothers and Lea.

I wanted to do so much over the next two weeks, but I knew none of that was possible. Not when the weight of this responsibility forced me to work, work, work until I felt somewhat prepared. Although, my gut was telling me no matter how much I worked, I would never feel ready.

I looked back up at Ollie, so many questions passing over his face. I leaned my head against him, dropping my temple to his shoulder. "There is something I need to tell you."

"You're scaring me, Little Shadow. What's going on?"

"A lot." I lifted my head back up, realizing there was one more person I needed to tell. I pulled my Comms unit out, typing in a name that made Ollie's eyes widen.

"Caleb?" He looked at me with a gaping mouth. "Why?"

"A lot happened while I was in Crelanti," I said. "But if I'm going to explain everything to you, I'd rather not have to explain twice."

The unit rang a few times before Caleb's face came into view, a casually surprised smile on his chiseled face. "Kasha." His smile faltered when he noticed who was next to me. "Oh, hey, Ollie."

"Kasha needs to tell us something," Ollie said, a deep frown settled on his usually bright face.

"What's wrong?" Caleb leaned forward, posture rigid and alert.

"You two need to promise me you'll let me get through the whole story before you blow up." I looked between them.

They both mumbled their agreement before I launched into the explanation of everything. They had both kept their word, but the moment I finished, their voices boomed around me.

"Goddess, you two are loud," I grumbled, not even picking up what they were saying in the cacophony of profanity and angry words.

"You are not doing this," Ollie growled.

"I agree," Caleb said, his cheeks reddening.

"You have no say." I shook my head. "The High Faction has approved, and I've already decided to accept. If I don't participate,

I don't want to think about what Elliot will do."

"We can find a loophole," Caleb suggested.

I shook my head. "There will never be loopholes where Elliot is concerned. All we can do is play his game and hope I survive."

They both fell silent, pensive looks overtaking their faces. They knew I was right after both of them had worked these past two weeks on the hunt for information on the rebellion. We had no way out except through.

"I hate this." Ollie broke the silence first.

"You two just have to trust me." I wrapped my hand with Ollie's and squeezed as I looked at the screen and gave Caleb a reassuring smile. "It's all you can do."

"I'm coming here that night," Ollie announced. "I'll work with your team on the back end."

"It's a Blue Moon Hunt, Ollie, and you're an Alpha." I shook my head. "You can't just abandon your team."

"They'll understand." He assured me.

"Do you want me to come too, Kasha?" Caleb asked, hope brewing in his gaze.

"No." My fingers squeezed tighter around the unit, my pulse picking up. "No, you need to stick to the plan we have. Please. I won't be able to concentrate if you don't."

He nodded solemnly. "I understand."

"Now what are you two talking about?" Ollie asked, looking between us. Caleb took over, admitting to everything that had happened and how he was trying to make up for the year of betrayal that had stained our relationships. All three of ours.

"You're really going to do that?" Ollie quirked an eyebrow.

"Swallow your pride and potentially prove yourself and your beloved father wrong?"

Caleb winced at his words, my own insides squirming a bit. I didn't miss the use of *your* instead of *our* when it came to father.

"I am going to find the truth." Caleb regained his composure, looking right through the screen at Ollie. "If that means admitting that I was wrong all this time, then I'm ready."

"Are you ready to grovel at our sister's feet when you do?" Ollie sneered.

Everyone thought Ollie was the happy-go-lucky one of our family, but what they failed to realize was that he had the hidden capacity to hold even more ire against those who had hurt him or those he loved. Even more than me, and that was saying something.

"I will be ready to grovel at both of your feet," Caleb said without a single waver in his words. "I hurt more than one sibling this past year."

His face still did not betray him, but I could feel the loosening of Ollie's muscles next to me. Relief. It was a step, even if he refused to show that to Caleb through the Comms connection.

My chest settled for a few moments, looking between the two of them. I wasn't sure what would happen, if the words we pledged so many years ago could ever hold meaning again. But maybe one day we would all be willing to try, to find ourselves back in a similar place. Not the same, but one where we could exist in an altered bond that meant just as much.

Born by Blood. Bound by Loyalty.

"I just have one more question," Caleb said, his forehead crinkled inward.

I sighed, not sure if I could take many more. "What?"

"None of this explains why Ollie's face is busted."

My chest splintered a bit, a laugh escaping me at Ollie's deep frown. "That would be from his fight with Nolan."

"Ah." Caleb leaned back in his chair. "He finally found out about you two, then?"

Ollie's eyes widened. "You knew?"

"They were just here for two weeks." Caleb smirked at me. "And they were horrible at hiding it from the moment they arrived."

"I can't believe you told him first," Ollie grumbled.

"I didn't, he guessed." I knocked my shoulder against his. "But in fairness, I also knew he wouldn't threaten Nolan with his fists if I did."

"Well, maybe you'll be in luck." He winked at me. "Maybe there won't be anyone else for me to fight anymore."

My heart beat swiftly at that. Something about when I was with him, it just felt… right. Normal, which was something I craved more than I realized. I was me and he was him. We were both a bit broken and cracked in places, but it didn't make us care for each other any less. We felt no need to repair the other or 'fix them'. We just wanted to be by each other's side while we tried to heal ourselves.

It was a romance a past me would have scoffed at. But this me, the new me, needed it. A bond that gave me something I thought I had lost. Peace.

But I couldn't tell him all of that, so instead, I just said, "Yeah, maybe."

CHAPTER 35

Since everyone knew I was moving back onto Compound, Lucas and Taylor had taken it upon themselves to move as much of my stuff out of my Eroste place as possible. They had been the ones to watch over Lea while she finished up the last of her orders and helped her move stuff into the guest house on our own Compound. It was a generic version of one of the Hierarchy houses, situated at the end of the row, but it worked for visitors.

The boys had assumed I would still be living with Lea in the guest house and moved all my clothes and things in there. It was the next morning when I had finally peeled myself out of Nolan's bed and over there to collect some of my bath products to see how extensively my Gammas had set up the space for me. Along with my essentials, they had moved some of my personal touches into the second bedroom. They had hung up some of my artwork, covered the bed in my worn-in quilt, stacked a few of my favorite books on the desk, and somehow even figured out a way to get my piano shoved in the corner.

Those two would get a very extensive vacation when all of this was over. I would send them anywhere in Kazola they wanted to go. They had earned it a while ago.

Even though Nolan and I had decided that I would stay with him most nights, I chose to keep it all here for now and just grabbed a refill on my hair wash and favorite body oil back over to Nolan's. I loved spending nights with him, but I couldn't help but be tempted to flop down on the bed and curl up with a book or sit at the piano. It might be good to still have a space that was just mine. For now, at least.

I shoved the few bottles into my bag, trudging back downstairs to find Lea in the kitchen already.

"Wow, you'd think it was just a typical morning," I joked, shuffling into the space as she moved around the kitchen as if we hadn't moved out of Eroste.

She pushed a few things around on her plate, the last bits of eggs and sautéed spinach lingering. "Except this time, it seems you're going to be more of a part-time roommate as I'm pretty sure I never heard you come home last night."

"I may have spent the night at Nolan's."

"Ohhhh," she teased, giggling. "Good for you. You deserve this."

"Thank you." I looked down, my fingers playing with the strap of my bag. "But don't be packing up all my stuff just yet. I'm still your roommate, just not every night, I guess."

"I think I'm all right with that." She winked. "Want some coffee?"

"Sure. I can have a cup before I head out." I sat down in the chair across from her at the granite island.

She flitted about, grabbing a cup and preparing it exactly how I liked it, her chaotic curls flurrying around her like a halo. She dropped the cup in front of me and settled back in her seat with a deep breath. "Now, update me on all you've been through these past few weeks."

I took a deep sip, allowing the caffeine to start working its way through my system before I started in on the tall tale that had become my daily life. I couldn't tell her everything, half of it was confidential at that point, but I gave her the highlights. Everything that happened with Caleb. Nolan and my relationship progression. My father still being a jerk. But I had to end it all by letting her know what we had learned about Government contractors being attacked. I needed her to get a better understanding of why she was having to stay here.

"Honestly, I'm not that surprised," Lea said, standing up for a moment to drop her plate in the sink, refill her coffee, and settle back across from me.

"What do you mean?" I wrinkled my brow.

"Don't get mad."

I frowned. "No promises."

She sighed. "Well, I had heard rumors about a few vandalizations and threatening letters around Eroste. Mostly to contractors who I knew worked with you or exported stuff to the High Faction."

I choked on my sip, my chest constricting around the liquid as it painfully slithered down my throat and into my stomach.

"Have they reported them?" I sat up straighter, trying to clear my throat.

"Most of them, I think." She swayed a bit, but I could tell by her twitching nose that she was trying to make this seem fairly normal. "They went to the local garrison."

"Have you gotten any threats?"

She stared down at her hands, rolling her bottom lip between her teeth. "One or two."

"Lea!" I moved our cups away, sloshing a few drops of coffee in between us. "You should have told me. We could have gotten you out of there long before now."

"I know. That's why I didn't."

I sat up straight. "What? Why?"

"Because I figured you'd make me stop working." She shrugged.

I gaped at her. "To keep your life safe? Um, yeah, Adelaide, I would have made you stop working. It's considered the logical thing to do."

"I suppose, but I'd really just like to get back to work." She leaned over the counter clutching her hands. "You can send me with plenty of guards and I'll happily still stay here, but please, Kas, I need back in the forge."

"Lea, what's going on?" I flipped my hand over.

I had known this woman since we were kids. She was kind and devoted and a hard worker, but she had always known when she was taking things too far. She had the self-preservation of a soldier even though she was far from one. If she had been threatened even once, she would have told me. What had changed?

Well, one thing had, and my gut was telling me this was all connected.

"Lea." I leaned forward as if we needed to whisper, even though we were alone in the house. "Is work a coping mechanism for you? After what happened at the Tavern?"

She swallowed. "Work keeps me distracted. It keeps me focused."

"Distracted from what?" I said, keeping my words soothing, my thumb rolling a circular pattern on the back of her hand.

"The memories." She shook her head, tapping her fingers against her temple. "They don't stop when I'm just sitting with myself. The screaming and the yelling and all the blood. The chaos. It's just… it's stuck in there and I don't know how to get it out! But I can make it quiet down and that's with working and moving."

I scraped my free hand down my face. I had recognized some warning signs with Lea since the hostage situation, but I kept saying I would let her come to me. Maybe I was getting too distracted with my own life and was using it as an excuse to put my friend on the back burner.

My stomach soured at the thought. She had been there for me when I needed a shoulder to lean on outside of my Faction. I should have been there for her long before it got to this point.

"Is this why you've been working extra hours and going out almost every night?" I asked. A solemn nod was her only response. I sighed. "You could have come to talk to me. We could have worked on a way to help together."

"I know, but…"

I gave her a questioning look, trying to get her to continue. "But?"

"There's more to the story," she whispered, eyes downcast. "I didn't stop at that tavern by chance. I had been planning on meeting someone there for a date."

I tilted my head. "Who?"

"His name was Will." Her hand was shaking in mine, the color draining from her tawny cheeks. "He was the brunette guy that was strung out on Blackthorn."

I stilled, remembering the brunette man who had been preening around the tavern, rambling about 'saving' everyone. The high Shriv who had impaled himself on a broken table leg when Nolan had been about to take him in. I kept my composure, but my insides started to scream, my wolf growling at the idea that Lea had been in more danger than she had even let on.

I needed my wolf to breathe because she wanted to go and find Will and revive him, just to rip his throat out. She was even more vicious than she was before she left me.

I squeezed her hand tighter. "You never told me that you knew them."

"Not them, him," she emphasized. "He had passed through town a week before that happened. His horse had thrown a shoe and asked for help. We got to talking and he invited me to join him for dinner when he was going to be closer to the area. I luckily had a delivery around that time, so I said, why not? But then he showed up already strung out and covered in black veins with two friends right behind him. The moment they crossed the threshold, pandemonium ensued and there was no escaping."

I processed everything slowly, pulling it into what I now knew about Elliot. It was no coincidence that some of his followers had found my roommate. He had already started calling me out at that point, and I had known him as Benji for well over a year. He had even met Lea before since I'd brought her to the bar a few times. He knew she would be a weakness and had sent one of his men out to… what? Hurt her? Convert her? Get her close to use against me?

How *dare* he try and harm those in my life?

At least a bit of myself was calmed knowing it must have gone wrong. He used his ability to get people off drugs as a selling point for his revolution. I highly doubted having those three go rampaging on Blackthorn was part of the plan.

Still, there were a lot of questions about that night that needed to be answered still. However, the time was not now. I turned my focus back to what was important.

"Why didn't you mention this before?" I asked gently, keeping our fingers laced in hopes of grounding her a bit.

"I was embarrassed. I didn't want it in any reports, scared people would think I was involved."

"You could have told me unofficially," I said. "Besides, none of us would have thought that. We were there. Your fear and unwillingness to participate was obvious."

She shook her head. "No. You didn't need the burden. I should be able to handle this myself. You shouldn't have to deal with a mess like me."

"Lea, I'm a mess!" I threw my arms up, gesturing at my neck. "What made you think I wouldn't understand?"

"Because the things you went through were horrific! Utterly disgusting, and still you find a way to come back to this job and put your life on the line to protect people like me."

I dropped my chin to my chest. I was scared it would be something like that. It was easy to compare one experience to another and feel unworthy of help or ashamed that you may need it. I knew I had been like that through my trauma, and that had led me to some destructive places. I didn't need to see Lea find herself in a place she couldn't come back from. A shiver raced down my spine at just the passing thought.

I looked back up, my best friend squirming in her seat.

"The first thing they teach us in therapy is that there is no one way to cope with trauma." I shook my head. "Just because I went through a few does not invalidate the one that you went through."

"I just didn't want you to think less of me. Or that you couldn't rely on me anymore." She shrugged. "I liked being someone you felt safe with while you healed, and I didn't want that to stop."

I snorted. I knew that feeling well.

"Past psycho-physician aside." I rolled my eyes, Lea letting out a tiny laugh at the sarcastic mention of Vanessa. "My sessions always helped me. They helped me discover the root of things and come up with healthy coping ideas. Multiple, just in case one of them wasn't available for me. Like when I had to stop working for instance."

She bit her lip. "Yeah, I suppose."

"Maybe it's time to find one for you." I nudged her hand, her deep brown eyes peeking up through her thick eyelashes.

"Yes, maybe it is time." She tapped her fingers on the counter. "I'd really like to stop reliving it all the time."

I walked around the counter, pulling her against me to rest my chin on her head as she stayed seated. "You're going to be all right.

I'm here to help. We can help each other."

Her arms ran around me, her face buried against my chest. "Thank you."

I smiled, placing a kiss on the top of her head. I would do anything I could to help her.

Just as she had helped me.

CHAPTER 36

I wanted to throw the old dusty book clear across the room.

My head ached from reading all the tiny words written on the pages and still nothing had panned out in a way that would allow me to understand what Elliot wanted.

"Maybe we need to accept that without more knowledge of Elliot's plans, we may not be able to pull any connections." Nolan patted my hand across the table, one of the books propped up in front of him.

"I don't accept that reality," I mumbled, scraping my fingernails along my scalp, trying my best not to rip my hair out.

After I had taken the final call with Elliot a few days before and accepted his challenge, he had given us the coordinates for what he called the "playground" that I would be hunting him in. It was a large area of public woods not too far away. We had been sending scouts out, trying to see if any traps were being set, getting an idea of the terrain, and keeping an eye out for anyone who was in the area. We weren't sure if we were technically allowed to be scouting up until the day of the hunt, but in all fairness, Elliot hadn't made it an expressed ruling to the challenge.

We knew how to work within loopholes as well.

The only other way I knew to prepare was to try my best to exhaust my lore theory. The more I read and knocked out as a possible motive, the less hopeful I was to find something, yet I couldn't stop. My gut churned with each idea I read, and somehow, I knew this one was connected. I was becoming pretty good at reading between the lines with Elliot, and the Gods had something to do with it. I just knew it.

Still, with a lack of evidence, my gut was starting to look a little pathetic.

"What other motives could be pushing him?" I groaned, leaning back in my chair, my neck barely supported while I stared up at the bland, beige ceiling tiles.

"He's a power-hungry megalomaniac?" Nolan shrugged. "Sometimes, they don't need a deep-seated reason if they are smart and can easily manipulate people by preying on their fears and insecurities."

"Yeah, I guess." I dropped my stilo, standing up and stretching my arms and legs out a bit. "It just seems too easy. And if there is one thing we know about Elliot, nothing is ever easy."

Nolan rounded the table, coming to stand in front of me. "But going in circles like this with the lore could cause more stress that you don't need right now. Not when you should be focusing on what is going to happen in a little over a week."

My stomach dropped. I had been training as often as I could, from working on hand-to-hand combat with Lucas and Taylor to going for runs in both my wolf and human form through the woods to try and pick up speed. Liv and Eden had been setting up tracking courses for me throughout it as well, trying to get me to pick up scents quicker and follow them to the source. Beckett had made me sit through some field medic training, just in case I fell into a trap or needed to patch myself to finish the hunt.

It wasn't like I wasn't already extremely proficient in all of these things, but we were all on edge as the hours blew past us. We all needed to feel like we were doing something to prepare.

But when my body needed to be rested, my mind needed to be worked so as to not feel like I was going crazy lying in wait. My usual ways of playing piano or reading were no longer helping. I needed to feel like I was doing something to protect myself. So, of course, investigated lore became the obvious choice.

"You need to rest; to take care of yourself. Or let others, perhaps me, take care of you in certain ways you seemed to like in the past." Nolan leaned down, his breath tickling my lips. "Maybe I could give you a bit more of that special worship tonight."

My stomach tightened at the lingering memory, my cheeks and other body parts heating fiercely.

"Mm." I moaned against his lips, stealing a quick kiss. "Yes, I think that can be arranged."

"Knock, knock," A sing-song voice came from the hall, banging on the door to the conference room. I jumped right away from Nolan and crossed the room in two steps, ripping the door open to see if my sense of smell was lying to me or if the woman I thought was on the other side was actually there.

"Nana?" I balked at the lithe, tall woman waiting there, a plate of what looked like her famous pistachio chocolate chip brownies clutched in her hand. Enough to feed my entire Hierarchy, of course.

"Hello, Moonlight." She pushed her way inside, dropping the plate on the chaotic conference table.

She shouldn't have been in there, but between her late husband, son, and grandchildren all being in the Guard, she had maintained her security clearance from when she was a State Alchemist long after she retired.

So, technically, I wasn't breaking any laws not rushing her out. I was more scared of her anger than the High Faction's.

Besides, by the irritated look on her face, she couldn't care less about the papers, notes, and maps now surrounding her. Her focus was on me.

"According to Oliver, you have had quite the adventure the past few weeks."

"Goddess above." I groaned, slamming the door closed and meandering back towards Nana, who was hovering near Nolan. My stomach dropped, and I instinctively put myself between them, taking back Nana's attention. "What did my idiot brother say now?"

"Well, he didn't go into too many details." She crossed her arms. It didn't matter that I was the leader when she was on the Compound. She still held her presence with authority, and I wasn't about to overstep. "But he mentioned that you'd been out of the territory for a few weeks, working with the High Faction on some things."

"This case of ours has taken a lot of unexpected turns," I tried to console her. Of course, she wasn't buying it.

"And that is your excuse for not only missing bi-weekly brunch but using your brother as your messenger falcon instead of writing me yourself?"

"I thought it was more personal coming from Ollie." I shrugged, giving her an innocent smile that used to work on her when I was an adorable little girl, but I had a feeling it lost its effectiveness the older I got.

She flicked my nose. "Not an excuse, young lady. I raised you better than that."

I shot Nolan a withering stare when he tried, and failed, to contain his laughter.

"Yes, Nana." I rubbed my stinging nose. "So, you decided to seek me out instead of writing?"

"Well, dear, unlike most grandparents, when my grandchild drops off the face of the world, I hunt them down so I can make them feel guilty about it." She gave me a cursory look, eyes darting between Nolan and me. "And who is this?"

I perked up, pointing to the man next to me. "Oh, Nana, this is Nolan."

Nana frowned, her lips pursing as she looked at him, her neck craning a bit to take him all in. "So, you're the one that stole my granddaughter's job?"

Nolan's brows crinkled in confusion. "Well, I was assigned."

"Do you not think she's qualified?" She took a step toward him, gently pushing me away.

"I didn't…"

"Do you think she's undeserving?" Nana kept pressing on,

moving forward to stand right in front of Nolan.

"Of course…"

"'Cause let me tell you, you'd be wrong!" She pointed her long, bony finger at Nolan, staring up at him with that look only a seasoned mother knows how to make. The one that elicits guilt even if you didn't do anything wrong.

"Um…" Nolan wasn't one to look flustered, but my grandmother's withering stare was all it took to make his cocky façade crumble.

I couldn't stop the laughter from bubbling up.

"You could help, maybe." He frowned at me.

I shrugged. "But this is entertaining."

"What is going on?" Nana looked between us, confusion rimming her gaze. "I thought we didn't like him."

"Ouch," Nolan mumbled, but a smirk once again graced his pillowy lips.

"We didn't." I shook my head, biting my bottom lip.

"Luckily, I'm quite the charmer when I want to be." Nolan reached over, snaking his arm around my shoulders and pulling me to his side. I wrapped my arm right around his waist to secure us together.

Nana took a step back. "Excuse me? What is this?" She flicked her finger back and forth between the two of us.

I let out a deep breath. "Nolan and I are seeing each other, Nana."

"You're paramours?" She raised her eyebrow.

"Yes." I nodded, squeezing Nolan's side a bit tighter, his grip on my shoulder squeezing back in comfort.

"Hm." She took the two of us in, looking over Nolan's face with a little too much attention to detail. "Well, the two of you would give me the most beautiful great-grandbabies."

"Nana!"

"Oh, ma'am, I very much agree with you on that fact." Nolan winked at her, a laugh finally trickling from her lips. I, in turn, punched him in the stomach.

"Ah, and once again, I'm the last to know." She shook her head at me. "Tell me, Nolan, do your parents know about my dear granddaughter or are you hiding your romance as well?"

Nolan chuckled. "I told them very soon after we started seeing each other, ma'am."

"Good." She reached up, patting his cheek gently. "Point one for you."

Nolan beamed at the compliment.

"I was going to introduce you when we had time to come out to your house so you could meet properly." I pleaded with her. "We just needed the case to stabilize first."

"You all spend way too much time in here if you have this much evidence on your board. You could have spared half a morning to introduce me to your handsome paramour." She tisked, looking over at the investigation board. Nolan looked at me, but I just rolled my eyes. "Oh, how strange. Why do you have a picture of Mason on here?"

My head whipped over to look at where Nana stood pointing at a sketch drawing that Lucas had created weeks ago. Except, the man Nana was pointing at wasn't known as Mason.

We knew him as Elliot.

CHAPTER 37

Any Hierarchy member that was on Compound had been summoned for an immediate meeting. All of us needed to be there to listen, and lucky for us, Nana Aggie loved all of them and was used to the procedures and ways of us Guard members. She just sat at the conference table, waving hi to everyone as they walked in, sipping the tea I had gotten her while encouraging people to eat her brownies.

And not one of them batted an eye while grabbing one. We all knew Aggie would answer our questions without hesitation.

"So, you know this man?" I moved the picture across the table.

"His name was Mason." She nodded, tracing her fingers along the ink drawing Lucas had created from memory. "Mason Wright. He was a junior Alchemist in my first lab. We worked together for about a year before I transferred to be with your grandfather in his assigned Guard territory."

"What do you remember about him?" I asked.

"He was a brilliant scientist. We all saw that very early on." She looked down, smirking at the picture. "He was eager to develop, wanting to spend time with all of us seasoned Alchemists to learn as much as possible and help. Within six months, he had helped break multiple obstacles for projects and bring new twists that made engineering even more efficient. By that point, everyone wanted him on research teams. By the time I left, he was about to start leading his own projects. Faster than any other junior Alchemist I had ever seen."

"Figures he would be an actual genius." Nolan grunted.

"Like we didn't already know that," Liv scoffed. We were all on the edge of our seats, my own heart rapidly beating at this new development in our investigation. Elliot knew my grandmother. Did he know we were related? Was that why he had fixated on me?

"Did the two of you have any kind of relationship outside of a professional one?" My stomach revolted at the idea, and I prayed to Lunestia that the answer I wanted was the truth.

"Good Goddess, Kasha. No!" She shook her head. "I was already engaged to Papa by that point, and Elliot was much too young for me and my subordinate! What kind of madness would make you ask such a question?"

"He, uh…" I looked around the room, wondering how many details I should divulge to her. Everyone's resigned looks let me know it was up to me. "Mason, or Elliot as we know him, has decided to set his attention on me, and we haven't figured out why."

Her face contorted in disgust. "And you thought it could be because of me?"

I squirmed in my seat. "I need to exhaust every theory, no matter how disgusting."

She just shook her head at me, prickling crawling up my neck.

"Wait, Nana. How much younger is Mason than you?"

Things weren't lining up. I trusted that Nana knew who this man was and that they did have some kind of connection. But Nana was in her eighties, and although we Vargs and Shrivs aged slower than humans, making her look in her sixties, Elliot looked no older than mid-forties, even with his Shriv bloodlines.

What in the Goddess's name was going on?

"Only about eight years if I remember correctly. I was thirty when he first arrived." She shrugged. "He was pretty young when he started in the lab, right out of university."

"Maybe Elliot's his son?" Eden suggested.

"I'd be surprised," Nana said. "This looks exactly like him just many years older. Plus, he was very dedicated to his work. Was never one to get romantically involved, but I suppose I didn't know him well enough to say that with authority."

"Did he have any specific devotion to the God or Goddess?" Beckett asked, moving the conversation in the right direction.

"Hm, devotion isn't the best word. He wasn't an acolyte by any means." She tapped a finger against her chin. "But he was dedicated to the idea of discovering everything they had to offer Kazola. He believed we would discover certain technological advances when we had earned it. It was certainly a unique perspective, but with his hard work ethic and incredibly talented mind, people didn't care what motivated him to keep working."

"Was there anything special about his... outlook on life?" Beckett prodded. It had been decades since Nana had seen him, but she was still as sharp as ever. Hopefully, something would come up.

Nana just rolled her eyes. "Besides being almost neurotically clean." She pursed her lips a bit, brows scrunched downwards for a moment before she sat up straight. "Oh, he did like to talk about the fact that you could trace his lineage back to the first Shrivika family. Even though we are all technically descendants, his bloodline has stayed completely within the Shrivika species. He was always quite proud of it. I assumed that was where his whole God research came from."

Something nagged at the back of my mind. The first family. A descendent of the God…

"Wait a second," I ran to the table, flipping through one of the books. "Yes! I knew that sounded familiar. There is a very convoluted theory that a group of acolytes created decades ago. The wording seems similar now with this new information."

Just as Nolan said, we needed something more into Elliot's past to better understand and get a new perspective. Who knew it was right in front of me the whole time?

"Read it out loud." Nolan came up behind me, putting his hand on my shoulder, the warmth comforting.

I cleared my throat, my fingers tracing along the words as I read. "There are many lost words and moments from the Unity of Order, but through fragments and extensive excavation, a group of archaeologists and theologians were able to tie together some of the lost pieces that could change our society forever. This includes the final words spoken by Lunestia and Firenielle, which some believe to be a prophecy warning. 'There will come a day when those who protect Kazola will no longer be worthy of their titles. But fear not, for when a pure descendant of Firenielle, untainted and devoted, bonds with a Child of Lunestia who has returned from death, they will usher in the newest age for Kazola and all who inhabit its sacred lands.' We have no clear picture of when this will happen, but we must be wary and ready for when it does, praying that our salvation will protect us from those who wish to harm."

My fingers shook against the page by the time I finished, my stomach twisting in knots. I turned to Nana. "Thank you for all the answers, Nana. Would you mind waiting in my office for now? I'll be over in a moment."

"Of course, dear." She gave me a solemn nod, leaning down to kiss my forehead before walking out the door, closing it with a soft click behind her. I slumped even farther into my chair, my muscles aching already.

"Kasha," Beckett whispered, his already pale complexion draining of all color. "Does he think you are that Child of Lunestia?"

It was the obvious reasoning. It all clicked together, even if my mind was scrambling to come up with any reason why this was *wrong.*

"But..." I shook my head. "I never died! You saved me before I did."

My body was trembling, my heart racing and my mind unable to contain the overwhelming rush of darkness that was pummeling me from the inside out.

"You were close, Kasha. You had minutes to live when I finally got you to take my blood." Beckett sat down next to me, Nolan's tight grip on me re-centering me back to reality. "The physicians at the hospital had marveled, at least those who were not privy to the secrets of the Guard and the Ibridowyn. Once we got you to a physician who knew the truth, they all knew we had saved you just in time and that your heart never stopped beating. But…"

"If one of those physicians was an Elliot follower." I dropped my face into my hands, shaking my head back and forth. "And if they truly believed in this half-baked prophecy, then they could have said they found the Varg Elliot had been looking for."

"I think we found your link, sweetheart." Nolan kneaded into the taut muscles twisting around my neck, trying his best to help me through.

All of this made little sense to me, but when I dug deep and let myself think like Elliot, twisting my mind to the deranged levels he had found himself in, it came together. Combining an unknown prophecy with an addiction to power, unmatched charisma, and a genius mind, it was the perfect cocktail to give Elliot the insane confidence he had in himself and the movement. Add the ability to convince others as well, especially those who were in vulnerable or altered states of mind, and it wasn't far-fetched to see how his cult had grown so much.

He knew every move, but for once, we knew facts about him before he was ready for me to know the truth. Finally, I could feel clarity in the whirlwind chaos that he had been weaving around me. Still, it raged on, but I was able to see a bit of light peeking through the darkness.

Hope. I would latch on to it and make sure it brought me through until the end.

I breathed in. I breathed out. I focused. I listened. I pulled myself out of the darkness and looked up at the group of friends that surrounded me.

"He may believe this, but we all know it's fake." I curled my fingers into fists, my soul settling with determination and strength. "He thinks this will be his rise to power, but I will make sure it's his undoing."

CHAPTER 38

Two weeks went by far too quickly.

Lost in the preparations, training, and researching, I didn't notice time flowing by me until suddenly it was the night before my hunt for Elliot. A night that I could have spent any way with anyone, and they would have given in. But there was only one who would make the night bearable, who would make sure it was as best as it could be, even with the looming threat of the hunt mere hours away.

"Did you like dinner?" Nolan reached across the table, pulling away my empty plate and taking it over to the sink.

"It was perfect as always." And it had been. A honey garlic roasted pork loin with green beans and buttery mashed potatoes. Hearty, perfectly seasoned, and completely satisfying.

The conversation was quiet and stilted throughout the whole meal. No bantering, no teasing, just random talks about work and things that happened throughout the day. We were both tense, stuck in an awkward place of knowing something big was coming but refusing to talk about it.

But I was done with it all.

This wasn't what I wanted. I wanted a night with him, the man who made me happy, who made me feel alive. With so much darkness looming into my future, threatening to take me back to places I had hoped to never return to, I needed to feel stability. I needed a reminder of how far I had come. I needed Nolan, the embodiment of how hard I had worked to grow and heal myself. Being with him, having him as my partner in so many ways, helped me to recognize that strength.

I walked over towards him, the moonlight reflecting through the window, casting his handsome face in an ethereal glow. Moving up behind him, I wrapped my arms around his torso, pressing my forehead against his back, the toned muscles underneath his soft cotton shirt tensing.

"You should wash the dishes later." I kissed him gently, peppering them down his spine.

He turns around in my hold, moving his hands to cup my face, palms still a bit damp with water. "Are you sure? I just wanted to spend the night with you."

"And I want that too, but in a much more specific way." I pressed my body tighter against his, molding myself against him.

I wouldn't go into the next day with regrets. I knew what I was ready for, what I wanted, and he was right in front of me. With that, I wanted to give all of me if he would accept it, and in turn, I would adore him, take him, make him mine.

Together, as one. That was what I wanted on that night. Nothing more, nothing less. Just him and me, two sides of the same coin, ready to start a new journey.

I pushed up onto my toes, brushing my lips against his in invitation. He took it in stride, pressing our lips closer together, slowly moving against each other, memorizing everything. I relished the heat coursing through me, settling into my veins and growing with each passing of his lips against mine. I let my hands wander from around him, coming to the front to slide under the hem of his shirt, a moan escaping me, devoured by his own lips.

"Kasha…" His breath came out ragged, my fingers continuing to play with the sensitive skin just above the waist of his pants, goose-flesh pebbling under my ministration. "I want you. I just want to make sure we haven't been moving too fast. I don't want you to have any regrets with me."

I moved my hands up his torso, tracing the planes of his chest with my fingertips ever so slowly before gripping the neckline of his shirt and tearing it in two.

"Does that answer your question?" I challenged.

He growled, throwing me against the island behind me, taking my shirt in his grasp and shredding it into strips of fabric, throwing it behind him. "Does that?"

We crashed back together, lips and teeth mauling at the other's, attempting to devour what was growing between us. I gripped him tightly, my fingernails running up and down his back, clawing at him. He lifted me without any effort, my legs wrapping around his hips. Another moan let loose at the feeling of his hardened dick pressed against me, our pants the only thing separating us. I gave a slow, cursory rock, drawing a strangled noise from him.

Without breaking contact, he moved us, our lips still fighting each other for dominance, the slaps of his bare feet against the floor and stairs a faint noise in the background. He shoved his way through a door, my mind dizzy with pleasure before he threw me down, my body lightly bouncing onto the feathery, plush mattress in his bedroom.

He flicked on the table side lamp, casting a faint glow into the large room. He looked down at me, my pants half unbuttoned, which somehow happened in between the kitchen and here. My chest band was askew, one of my breasts having escaped, my puckering nipple already hard and begging for attention. I shook with need, dampness settling in between my thighs, the slick growing with each slow rake of Nolan's gaze over my body.

I scooted forward, my eyes never leaving his, a sizzling connection pulling us together. My fingers reached out, tentatively tracing the top of his waistband. His own reached out to my breast band, a sharp nod from me all it took for him to reach down and pull it over my head. His fingers dipped down to graze each of them, swirling inward until he reached the peaks, giving them a few swipes with his thumb before pinching them in between his fingers. My mouth hung open, a strangled cry escaping at the biting pleasure.

He kneeled, fingers skimming down my belly, gripping my pants and pulling them down along with my undergarments, exposing all of me to him. His breath caught, and he looked back up at me. "You are devastatingly magnificent."

I smiled, leaning forward and coaxing him to stand up again. He had seen all of me before, but I had yet to see him. I looked up at him for permission before removing his pants, pushing them down, his feet kicking them away. I leaned back, drinking all of him in, the two of us exposed to the other.

He was stunning. The sharp planes of his body molded into each other, the well-defined muscles of his arms and chest decorated with his tattoos, sliding downward to slightly narrow hips and into strong thighs and legs. My breath stuttered at the sight of what I really wanted to see, his impressive dick standing at attention, already glistening with a bit of moisture. Ready for me.

Goddess, I wanted him.

I didn't let myself overthink it. I pulled him down onto the bed, throwing my leg over his hips to straddle him. He sat up, wrapping his arms around me to anchor us together. His lips pressed against mine for only a moment before exploring. I rocked against him, my body buzzing into a tight winding of pleasure settling deep in my stomach. He moaned against my throat, the heady sound shivering through me, my head moving farther to the side to give him more access to my smooth skin.

For the first time, I knew what I wanted.

I tangled my fingers through his hair, pressing him closer to that sensitive spot. "Bite me."

He stilled, moving away just enough to stare up into my eyes. His forest-green gaze locked with mine. "Kasha… I…"

"I want you with me tomorrow, Nolan." I pressed a kiss to his forehead, the flood of truths washing through my body allowing my words to flow freely from my lips. "I want to be every bit yours as I feel right here." I took his hand from my waist and pressed our intertwined fingers against my chest. "You are what I want. What

I've always wanted. Someone to challenge me and cherish me all in the same moment. Who sees me, darkness, and light, good and bad, and loves me for it. I need you every step of the way. I need to know that when I get back, I will be exactly where I belong. With you." I gripped his fingers tighter, locked between our bodies, my heart hammering against them. "I belong to you, sweetness. I have never felt surer of anything in my life."

His lips curled into that intoxicating smile that took my breath away. "I need to know you're sure. This will be your first bite. I want to make it perfect for you."

"You are what I want." I said it with all my heart, with as much conviction as had settled in my soul long ago. "You are who I choose to share this moment with. You, and only you."

His eyes flashed gold before he crashed his lips into mine, devouring me. His tongue traced the seam of my lips, begging for entrance, and I happily obliged. His hands skimmed over my back, my body shuddering under the delicate touch. With one final nipping suck of my bottom lip, he pulled away, rolling his forehead against mine.

He mumbled against my lips. "I want your bite first."

"What?" A tear slipped from my eye, my heart bursting with so many emotions they were spilling out.

"I'm yours too, sweetheart." He kissed my cheeks, taking my tears with each brush of his lips. "I feel it in my bones that I belong to no one else. So, I want you to make it so. Claim me."

My fingers shook a bit, my heart swelling full of acceptance and bliss. It was traditional for the male to claim the female first. It was how we had always been taught. How the pretty stories about a claiming bite went.

But I was far from surprised that Nolan didn't care about any of that bullshit. He cared about me, my comfort, and my needs. It had been taken away from me the first time, so he was giving me all the control. The first bite. The first step towards forever together. It was mine to take.

And I would happily take it.

I leaned forward, brushing my lips against his racing pulse, the cool brush of the metal chain of his necklace tickling my lips. Using my hands to move it over a few inches, I found the perfect spot, the place I would make him mine. Claim him.

I didn't hesitate. I didn't think. I bit.

His scream throughout the room was nothing but pure ecstasy, his hips pushing upward to grind his thick girth against my core. My teeth gripped his delicate flesh tighter, rocking myself against him, the first rattling orgasm flowing through me, making my head spin. It gripped me, and a whine filtered through the cracks of my lips as I rode higher and higher into the pleasure he was giving me. It was perfection.

I finally let go as the rush of pleasure dissipated, throwing my head back to catch my breath. However, it was far from over. Nolan's arms snaked around my hips, pushing upwards and over so I was on the bed, his body crowded and flush against my own.

"Claim me now. Take all of me," I breathed into his neck, my tongue darting out to lick at the fresh bite wound, soothing it, his body shuddering underneath me.

He leaned down, kissing me slowly and romantically, my insides already clenching again, winding up for the promise of more bliss to come. He settled his hips against mine, the tip of him teasing my entrance, gently pushing forward to move us together.

My breath caught, my eyes fluttering closed to feel and memorize every agonizingly slow inch he gave, connecting us for the first time. Nolan was not my first lover, but never had I felt so content, so in need of being linked together. It was the first time that, when he bottomed out flush against me, it felt right. Complete.

"Are you all right?" he whispered into my ear, nuzzling his nose against me.

"I'm wonderful." I arched upwards, moving my hips so he slid inside me, showing him exactly what I needed.

He began to move in and out, starting with controlled, gradual movements that made a desperate whine rattle through me. He laughed, the rumble jolting against my neck as he licked what I assumed was the spot he'd chosen. But he didn't bite. He picked up the pace of his hips, hitting that perfect spot to make the pleasure spin up and up, tightening around my insides, my face and body tingling with longing and promises of pleasure. I begged, wrapping my legs around his hips, digging my heels into his tight ass to force him even deeper, closer, letting it enrapture me.

He reached his free hand between us, allowing his thumb to delicately play with my clit, my head spinning with the extra jolt of ecstasy it caused. It was the final push I needed over the edge, and when I screamed out my final release, the dizzying euphoria overtaking every inch of my body, his teeth broke my flesh. It made the rush of his addictive self swirl even higher, my vision blacking out for a brief few seconds as I let myself revel in all he gave.

I rode with him, his thrusts moving deep and erratic, grunts pressing against my throat as he let go himself, giving me his pleasure, his Mark, and his soul, just as I had started to give him mine. It was perfect. It was bliss. It was us.

As we both came down from the intoxicating moment, he gently pulled out and rolled us onto our sides. His arms kept me close, our sweaty bodies coated in each other, pressed together wherever we could find it. We panted, my hands moving up to wipe away a few strands of his hair from his sticky forehead. He gave me that beautiful smile, and my soul settled, content to never leave the protection I always felt when close to him.

Mine. He was mine.

"I love you, Kasha," he whispered in between soothing licks over my fresh wound.

My heart lurched, words once again escaping me, fear gripping my tongue in a vice. Instead, I settled within his warm, comforting grasp, nuzzling my face into his neck, pulling in a deep comforting breath of our mingled scents, a tiny preview of what I knew was just the beginning for us.

CHAPTER 39

Unsurprisingly, sleeping the night before the hunting challenge was almost impossible.

I was able to get a few hours before I finally gave up, untangling myself from Nolan's long limbs and dressing in comfy clothes, including one of his large knit sweaters, before tiptoeing out of the house in hopes of not waking him.

I assumed I would just mindlessly wander around the Compound, my first destination the woods to let the breeze of nature pass through me, hoping it calmed my jittering nerves.

The last place I expected to find myself was the jail cells, a place I had been avoiding since my return. I walked down the steps, my booted footsteps echoing off the eerily quiet space. I walked the path I had been before but never expected to find myself there at that very moment. I should have been with those I cared about most, but I had too many questions, ones I wanted to give one last attempt at gaining answers to before I faced Elliot.

Vanessa was lying on her cot, her back towards me, but even

with the even breathing making her side rise and fall, I had a feeling it was all fake.

"Elliot issued me a challenge," I said, trying to get her to turn around, yet still she pretended to sleep, although the hitch in her breath at Elliot's name proved she was far away from dreamland. "He wants me to hunt him under the Blue Moon. Tonight."

Silence continued to spread between us, my throat tightening, fingers rubbing against the cool metal poles.

"I took it." I didn't know why I was telling her all of this. Some part of me believed she deserved to know. "Maybe you'll have a cellmate before the night ends."

"Do you have a death wish?" She finally rolled over, although she still didn't sit up, her body curled into itself as she positioned herself on her left side to look at me. "If you think you're getting away victorious, you do not know that man."

"I think I have no other choice," I stated, taking a step away now I had her attention.

She scoffed. "You'll be in my prayers to the Gods today, Kasha."

"Last chance, Vanessa." I leaned against the wall across from her cell. "I don't know what will happen tonight, but I have a gut feeling I will be seeing Elliot again. You can either tell me your story or risk letting him have the opportunity to skew it in his own twisted way."

"What does it matter?" she mumbled into her pillow.

"I want the truth," I said. "Between my two options, I believe you are the one to give it to me."

Vanessa groaned, sitting up, her shoulders slumped. Her prison outfit hung over her thinning body, the plain gray shirt and matching linen pants making her look like a young child playing dress up in her parents' clothing. She hadn't been eating enough if I had to guess, just blood to keep her from going feral and little bits of food and water to keep her alive. She wasn't eating for strength and sustenance, that was for sure.

"I'm going to tell you part of my story. Not all of it, but something that may be able to help you in case tonight goes wrong." She rearranged herself, pressing her back against the hard concrete wall and pulling her leg up onto the bed. "It all started when I met the man I ended up… marrying."

My stomach soured. "To Elliot?" My mind couldn't help but remember the citizenship paperwork that had the surname Wells listed on it.

"Gods above, no!" She shook her head, thorough amounts of disgust laced in her tone and creased across her face. My shoulders loosened. Thank the Goddess. "He was someone close to Elliot, though I didn't know that at the time."

I crossed my arms across my chest to keep them from fiddling. "Go on."

"I met him while I was studying for my psycho-physician certifications. I was about halfway through my program when he came through my clinic. I needed extra cash to pay off some of the schooling debts, so I would pick up shifts in the emergency department to help with small cases, minor lacerations, or patching since I had the basic skills to do so. He came in need of stitching on his hand." She let out a scoffing laugh, the whisper of a smile on her lips. "The bumbling fool had hurt himself cutting up some vegetables. Was never much of a cook."

My heart dropped. I could see the lingering memory in her eyes. It was a happy one.

"He had been an excellent patient through the whole thing, asking me to distract him with conversation while I stitched him up, so we talked about every random thing that came to my head." She bit her bottom lip. "I thought I sounded like a fool, but he told me it was exactly what he needed. The next day, after my shift, he was waiting outside with a cup of coffee." She ran her fingers through her hair, itching at her scalp. "Said he couldn't stop thinking about me and had somehow caught enough nerve to come back and ask me out on a proper date. I couldn't stop myself from accepting because I'd been thinking of him too. Next thing I knew, I was in a whirlwind romance with him."

"How did you find yourself saying yes to joining Elliot and his cause?" I asked.

"My husband had slowly started to tell me about it a few weeks into our seeing each other. He explained the pain and struggles he had faced in childhood that led him to the cause. He told me about the things the High Faction was keeping from Kazola. I wanted to deny it at first, but it was hard with what I did for a living. I had too many patients under my care in the clinic who seemed to feel similarly, as if the law had let them down in some way." She let out a bitter laugh. "That, along with the facts that James fed me, made it easy for me to be interested in meeting with Elliot."

"A successful one, apparently."

She nodded. "You've met him. He's charming and utterly convincing."

"You're not wrong there," I mumbled.

"He made me feel seen and heard and gave me solutions he wanted to implement to make all of those horrible cases I dealt with rectified or, even better, never happen again." She scratched at her nails. "He didn't try and convince me with pretty words but facts and plans he had to make Kazola better for the people. It didn't take long for me to realize between that and my loyalty and love for my husband, I wanted a part of it. I wanted to help too.

"Everything was fine at first," she said. "I finished my degree, married my husband, and started using my skills to help some of those within Elliot's budding militia. Some were coming to us with dark pasts, and I was able to counsel them and give them a safe space to express their anger and hurt."

"And use it to help Elliot's cause?" The bitter taste of the words lingered on my tongue.

Redness spread across her cheeks. "I thought it was helping at first. These people were there to be an ally for Elliot. I had given him reports as if I was signing off on someone being okay to work a job."

My stomach rolled, my lip twitching. "You sang a very different tune when you started seeing me."

I couldn't help but let that jab fly. She had wanted me to feel safe in that room all those weeks ago. As if she was there for me and not for the High Faction. And I had believed her.

"I changed my stance on the matter long before you and I began working together." She banged her head lightly against the wall. "At first, I would just tell Elliot if a certain patient was progressing well. Then he started asking for more details. I would refuse to answer, and he always seemed to take it just fine. That is until I caught him snooping around my patient files."

I snorted. "Unsurprising. He doesn't seem like the kind of man that takes no well."

"I learned that lesson that day." She shook her head. "He tried to sweet talk his way out of it, but I started becoming suspicious about what exactly he needed from my file and why he was taking such a vested interest in specific ones."

"Did you find out why?"

Her face paled. "I started paying attention to what he was asking me, and I had a disgusting idea of why he might need to know. I knew he had been an Alchemist and still played with experimenting with others who had an interest in technological advances for society. I wondered if the two were connected somehow, but I tried to convince myself that he would never cross ethical lines. But I couldn't get the question out of my head, and I knew I wouldn't know any peace if I didn't put it to rest. So, one night, I stole my husband's keys and snuck into one of Elliot's research buildings."

"What did you see?"

"Lines being crossed." She rocked back and forth, her eyes darting between unknown spots on the floor. "Ethics being bent."

I took a step forward, leaning towards the bars. "Vanessa, what did you see?"

She shook her head furiously. "No. I cannot tell another soul what I saw in there. I would never wish anyone to hold that knowledge if they didn't have to."

"It might help..."

"No!"

"All right." I nodded slowly, the last question I had for her pressing against my lips. "Did you betray me to Elliot when you realized we were hunting him?"

I had been wondering for a while, if she was running from them, how we were able to connect her to him. How he was able to learn the things about me that only she would have known.

"Yes and no." She took in a shaking breath, her cheeks reddening. "I didn't go to him. In fact, when I realized you were investigating him and he was most likely close by, I went nowhere except the clinic and my apartment that was only a three-minute walk from work. I even stayed late most nights, so I was in a guarded building. I should've known that was a waste of time."

"So, what happened?"

"He found me," she whispered. "He discovered I had taken up a position at the clinic and somehow figured out that I was the one working with you. I don't know how. He probably has followers working at the clinic and they told him I was treating you. He might not have even known it was me until he got to my office. But I arrived one morning, a few days after you had transitioned your eyes for the first time. He was sitting in the chair you always sat in, my notebook laying in his lap, reading it like it was the most enticing book." She shook her head. "Fear froze me in place, especially when he called me by my old name. I knew I was caught. Then I saw it was your file he was reading. Everything I had written and your medical history as well. I didn't even think. I leapt for it, but of course, he was too fast, incapacitating me before I could even get my hands on the papers. I thought he was going to either kill me or drag me out of there so my husband could do what he wanted with my betrayal. That didn't happen, though."

The pieces were falling into place, my stomach churning, anticipating the last piece of the puzzle she was about to admit.

"He told me I had a choice. Either I stop him from reading the folder and I die." She looked me right in the eye. "Or I sit quietly, let him finish reading your file, and he left, keeping my location a secret from my husband."

"You chose to live."

"I chose to betray you!" Tears streamed quickly down her face. "I chose to sacrifice the trust you had in me so I wouldn't die."

"Self-preservation is a strong need." I leaned my head against the bars. "I can't say I forgive you, but I at least understand."

And I did understand wanting to live. To escape from a situation that was obviously traumatizing to her was a basic, natural instinct. It didn't stop the hurt from festering within me—betrayal does that—but this knowledge might start to help me heal. Maybe finally releasing this secret would help her heal as well.

"I should have done more, but I knew he would kill me and take the file with him, so either way, he would get his hands on your information." She gave me a watery smile. "I am so sorry, Kasha. I should have tried to fight harder, but I'm not strong enough to fight him, even if he needs to be taken out for Kazola's safety."

"That's why I need to hunt him tonight."

"Elliot is capable of so much more than you could even fathom," she warned. "He could lead the world to greatness with his mind but instead uses it to manipulate everything. To make everyone move the way he wants like his little dolls. You have no idea what he has planned for you tonight, but it will be cruel, and you won't realize how stuck you are until it's too late. He always gets what he wants."

Every nerve in my body zipped with energy at her statement, my mind and soul knowing there was nothing but truth in her words. I knew the risks, I had for weeks, but hearing it from one of Elliot's victims just solidified that there was a chance tonight would end in nothing but pain and heartache.

Even so, I couldn't let that stop me. Fear would no longer make my choices for me.

Tonight, I would protect Kazola, even if it meant my own life was forfeited in the process.

"Thank you for telling me your truth." I looked her up and down one last time, giving her a weak smile before turning to walk away.

"Please. I know I don't deserve anything from you, but promise me something."

I turned back around. "What?"

"If Elliot asks about me, or if you see my husband and he asks about me." She squeezed her eyes shut, a stray tear escaping down her cheek. "Please, don't tell them anything. I don't… I can't…."

"I promise," I vowed, her eyes opening to look at mine. "As I promised when we first brought you here, you're safe with us."

She sighed. "Thank you."

I left without another word, my chest hardening around one fact. Vanessa may have betrayed me, but I still had a duty to protect a victim from those who had hurt her.

And I would do exactly that.

★★★

The first peek of the moon settled on the starlit horizon, the dusting arch of glowing blue the first glimpse of the hunt that was about to begin.

My team and I stood on the perimeter of the hunting zone Elliot had given us, a stretch of public woods about twenty miles west of the Compound. Just as we knew Elliot would use loopholes, we decided to do the same, setting up a camp right outside the designated area. They may not have been able to cross into it, but at least we could be in communication through the telepathic connections. With Nolan and Ollie there, there shouldn't be any spots in the zone where we couldn't reach each other.

The more I tried to sit still, the more I paced around the clearing everyone had set up in, my fingers beating random patterns against my leg. Everyone gave me a wide berth, but I could feel all their gazes following my moves.

Luckily, none of them mentioned the bright red bite mark that rested on my throat opposite my scar. I hadn't tried to hide it, the black sleeveless top of my simple hunting outfit showing it off in all its precious glory. Although, I had caught a few sly smirks and laughs from them when they thought I wasn't looking. I couldn't help but preen because even in all of the darkness and fear, I had found a place to find a shred of light.

It gave me even more power swirling in my chest and heart, my driving factor to walk out of this and back into the arms of the man I had Marked, who had Marked me.

My fingers mindlessly stroked over the healing bite, my stomach flurrying with delicate butterfly wings. I would win this fight for him. For our future.

"It's almost time," Ollie announced, all our gazes turning to the horizon, the final quarter of the moon slowly rising above the tree line. Ollie strode across the clearing, the first to reach me and pull me into a crushing hug. "You come back to us, Little Shadow."

I squeezed him tightly. "I will."

He pulled away slightly, looking down at me. "You better not leave me alone with Father and Caleb."

I snorted. "Well, when you put it that way."

He gave me one last wily grin, leaning forward to press a kiss to my forehead before passing me off to the next set of arms. The entire Hierarchy was there, waiting to wish me luck and pass along any form of support and love they could. I hugged them all in turn, trying my best to shut off the small voice in my mind warning me it might be the last time I saw them.

I would not give in to that voice. I would fight, and I would do my best to win.

I walked up to Nolan last, his handsome face creased with worry, eyes expressing love and fear turning through the amber gold of his shifted gaze. I fell right into his waiting arms, wrapping myself within the spicy comfort of Nolan. He leaned down so his nose found the arch of my neck, burying it against me and pulling in a sharp breath. I didn't want to ever let go.

His lips brushed over the bite mark, a groan escaping him. "Come back to me. Please."

I reached up to stroke the one along his juncture, my thumb tracing the pattern, a hum rumbling in his chest. "This Mark is my promise that I will fight every moment to return to the future we have. Together."

He pulled back a bit, resting his forehead against mine. "I love you, sweetheart."

My heart squeezed at the beautiful words, a part of me begging to tell him, to let him in.

To tell him before it was too late.

Before I never saw him again.

But I couldn't, my fear once again getting the better of me, gripping my heart and clouding my mind with dark thoughts.

Something I would have to work on, with him by my side.

Instead, I pressed my body against his, pulling his lips against mine and not caring that we had an audience as I showed him exactly what he meant to me. I darted my tongue out for one final taste, tracing his lips lightly before he gave me entrance, taking in my fill of Nolan.

I struggled to break the kiss, praying that the spicy taste stayed on my palette for the next few hours. He stared down at me, cheeks flushed against his tanned skin, chest rising and falling heavily. His fingers dug into my hips, pressing them against his in one final, silent plea for me to stay with him.

Oh, how tempting it was to let him steal me away, to never leave the protective, trusting place he had created for me over the months.

But that wasn't the reality we lived in.

"I'll be back soon, sweetness." I gave him a wink before I forced us to untangle from each other's embrace and let go.

I walked to the edge of the tree line, a few feet before the threshold, staring at the sky, my heart beating out the final seconds of waiting. The moon had risen, the bright blue beams filling me with the power of my gifts from Lunestia. I turned back for one last glance at my friends, my family, giving them a final nod and looking at their worried yet encouraging faces.

It lasted only a heartbeat before I forced myself to turn back toward my mission.

I pulled in one final breath, sent a final prayer up to the Goddess, and ran straight into the thicket of dark trees, every heightened sense on edge, ready to pick up my next prey.

The hunt had begun.

CHAPTER 40

My wolf was on fire, burning with need through my veins to let her free and take down any devious person who may cross our paths.

The heady, addictive moonlight bathed my body as I ran through the woods, the bright blue rays sinking into my skin and adding to the fuel, awakening that part of me that was designed for this.

We were wild. We were free. We were hunters.

And that night, we hunted for those who were hurt or killed. We hunted those who took what did not belong to them. We hunted the evil of this world.

It was all that my mind could concentrate on, the wind whipping through the plated braid of my hair, my arms already covered in a thin coat of sweat and drenching my top. I was focused on one thing and one thing only, taking down what was arguably the worst evil currently walking the lands of Kazola.

My wolf was fully aware that we had prey, that we were here to take him down and she was reveling in it. She had been hidden away for so long, to have such a challenge dangled in front of her was giving me an extra zip of energy to keep pushing forward through the empty branches and underbrush that prickled at my ankles, my thick military boots protecting my flesh.

As the first hour passed, she itched and clawed inside me, desperate for me to let her free. She wanted to hunt in the form that Lunestia intended us to hunt, but I refused her that one caveat. If necessary, I would transform, but I needed to stay in human form. For one, I didn't know what Elliot had planned and if I needed to talk or negotiate or be able to use my thumbs, I had to stay human. And second, I really didn't want to be naked in front of him. Ever.

Ugh, what a disgusting thought I had to consider.

Luckily, the Ibridowyn in me was enough to curb her down. After running south, I stopped, catching my breath, and honing my senses on what was around me. I closed my eyes, listening to the peaceful sounds of the winter woods, the movement of animals and insects non-existent. Nothing but the wind bristling the branches above or sweeping dead leaves around the ground, no crunch of boots or pounding of feet anywhere to be heard.

I pivoted my focus, looking for scent instead.

He had sent over a piece of cloth a few days ago, drenched in the scent of sandalwood and orange blossom. My stomach had heaved when I first got a whiff. Did I know it was his scent? No. For all I knew he was sending me a decoy. But my instinct, my gut, told me this was Elliot. He had scent marked for me. He wanted me to find him.

He was ready for a fight, and I knew that he would not evade me for long, because that was what he wanted.

But that was okay. I wasn't fearful, I was driven. If he wanted me to find him, then I was ready to get to the end.

And that was what I focused on. I moved forward, slowly and methodically, trying to pick up any trail of his essence. I stayed upwind, the only direction that I would be able to get a good whiff of someone on the air. I had a feeling he was staying upwind to attract me to him. It was only a matter of time before I did. So, I pushed forward, walking, walking, walking…

There. Got him.

The floral sweet scent enveloped me, my wolf snarling within my chest, but my own escaped through my lips. We had found our mark, our prey.

We had found Elliot.

I launched to the west, my focus on nothing but that trail of scent, the potent smell getting stronger and stronger with each pounding footstep against the frozen earth. My wolf could sense it too. She stirred and pushed me and told me to hunt, capture, take. It was another mile until I broke through a thicket of trees, skirting to a stop when I knew I had reached the end. I pulled my weapons slowly, eyes scanning until they landed on exactly what I was looking for.

And there he was, standing in a small clearing of trees, dressed in a long-sleeved black shirt and stretchy black pants and boots, similar to what he used to wear in the Tavern. He looked normal, peaceful under the starlit sky. Non-threatening.

But I knew better.

I had found Elliot Wells.

The *Marc Gealach* was so simple, nothing more than a glowing circle with the moon phases cut through it in a diagonal line. But it was there; I saw it.

Right in the center of his forehead, branded by the truth of the Goddess herself.

All of it a beacon for my feral, extra-aggressive wolf to let herself free and take. Him. Down.

So, that was exactly what I did.

I did not allow for taunting words or conversation. I launched myself at him, an Amalgam gripped in each hand with wooden blades protruding from one side. I swung, aiming right for his jugular, but his long blades parried them away, the silver daggers glinting under the moonlight.

Silver. The deathly element of the Varg Anwyn.

Lucky for me, I was an Ibridowyn now and it didn't hurt me the same.

Still, I needed to be cautious. He could maim me enough to capture me, to pull me into his grip and steal me away. I would not let that happen.

I was taking him down.

We began a fierce crash of strength, his eyes aglow with the intense red of the Shrivika. It was unnerving to say the least, to see him in such a way. I had known him as the carefree bartender of the Blood Moon and the cold, calculating psychopath that made up these games and taunted me. Never had I seen the well-trained, brutal warrior he was now. His strength matched my own along with his skills, hands expertly wielding the two blades with sharp precision and deathly aim. He knew what he was doing, his eyes focused on nothing except me, his own mark, his own prey to destroy.

We were both there for a purpose, but only one of us would come out victorious.

We continued throwing jabs and strikes, switching between the offensive and defensive whenever we got the chance. He towered over me by a good half a foot, but I used it to my advantage, aiming lower and focusing on getting a maiming blow to a fatal organ, but I had yet to meet anywhere on him. He lunged, aiming one blade for my thigh and I took the opportunity it presented. Using my left hand to block, I struck my right hand upward, slashing my blade and connecting with his warm, soft flesh.

I hummed in feral delight as crimson liquid bled from the strike to his face.

He snarled, wiping away the thin stream of blood now dripping down his perfectly shaved cheek, and charged me. His shoulder rammed into my solar plexus and sent me flying, the air punched from my lungs as my back impacted to the ground with a crack.

I screamed, but luckily, I knew nothing had broken, my body squirming to get up. He was already there, towering over me, lips curled upward, fangs protruding out.

He raises his hand above his head, the blade arching down towards me, a bloodthirsty scowl plastered on his face as he put all his strength into the vicious stab that was aimed right at my chest.

It was with seconds to spare that I rolled away, avoiding the heart-piercing jab he was hoping for.

I kicked out, both my feet colliding with his left knee, causing him to stumble but not fall. It was enough time, though, to scramble to my feet and out of the vulnerable position I had found myself in. We continued our fighting, but I knew we would just block each blow and give pointless jabs. It was no use; we were too evenly matched.

I stumbled away from him, his own feet moving him in the opposite direction as we regrouped and struggled to find a way past the stalemate we were locked in. Brute strength and even technique were not enough. We were both too good at protecting our fronts and our vital spots for either one of us to take an advantage. I needed to change tactics. I needed to get him vulnerable. I needed to get him on the ground by whatever means necessary.

It meant tricking him instead of overpowering him. And that was how I would beat him at his own game.

I focused on Lunestia's Crest on his head. I focused on my duty to the Goddess and to Kazola.

I focused all of that and pooled my strength, giving it my all as I launched myself towards him, leaving my body open, taunting him with an easy kill. He aimed upwards, swiping across chest level to me to keep me at a distance, but that was exactly what I anticipated. I dropped to the ground and rolled, missing the blade. I used the momentum, sliding past him until I was behind him.

I didn't hesitate, twirling around and swiping my blade right across the back of his knees with all the strength I had, severing and damaging the delicate muscles that would keep him standing with strength.

His wails filled the air as he collapsed, his body stumbling forward, legs giving out from underneath him. One hand lost grip on a blade to catch his fall, his hands and knees keeping him upward as he groaned in pain. I scrambled back to my feet, taking the advantage and kicking him down, my boot smacking against the base of his spinal cord. He collapsed, flipping over onto his back and writhing in pain.

I slammed my foot down on his wrist, his gravelly scream echoing into the woods as his fingers released his final blade and I kicked it away before I crouched down and threw my body weight on him. I straddled him, using my hips to press down on his chest and restrict air flow, my blade pressing against the delicate flesh of his exposed throat.

I did it.

"I win." A smug grin escaped me, the wildness and addictive adrenaline rush of the hunt seeping into my veins.

"Are you sure about that?" He was completely relaxed under my body weight, making no effort to try and break free. He just stared up at me with those glassy blue eyes through disheveled salt and pepper hair.

He was too calm. Too relaxed. Too sure of his words as they left his lips.

I had him pinned with a deadly weapon ready to pierce his pale skin and he was acting like this was just any other day.

What did he have planned?

I spat at him, a growl tempted on the tip of my tongue, my wolf begging me to let her loose. *To rip out his throat like he deserves.*

But I couldn't, because I made that damn promise when the challenge was set and, unlike Elliot, I had a conscience.

I breathed through the murderous need that my wolf had let loose under the protection of the Blue Moon. Although, it was common knowledge that Varg wolves got a bit feral during the hunt, a fact Elliot most likely wanted to use.

What a sick monster.

A slow, creepy smirk spread across his lips. "You may want to stand. I figure you wouldn't want the others to see us in such a precarious position."

"Others?" My heart pounded, my muscles tensing around my neck.

What others?

CHAPTER 41

Ye were downwind, and I hadn't been able to smell the onslaught of scents that filled the small clearing.

Varg Anwyns. Shrivikas. But no humans.

They emerged, like a ghost army from the shadows, surrounding us in a circle that made my stomach drop. I skirted to stand up, taking my defensive stance even though it was no use. I was outnumbered.

I wasn't surprised and I couldn't even be angry that others had joined the field. He had only specified that *my* people couldn't cross the border; he had never said anything about his own. But anger and fury pooled in my gut and swirled when my eyes locked with what each member of his team gripped in their embrace.

Soldiers. Members of the Onyx Guard.

All of them were still dressed in their full uniforms, some unconscious, slumped in the grip of their captors, others struggling with little strength to break free. Drugged most likely. Taken who knows when, although they looked fairly clean, a few smudges of dirt and sweat but that was it. And luckily, no signs of torture or injury that I could see or scent.

How dare he cross this line.

"No." I shook my head, snarling at Elliot who now stood in front of me, dusting off his sweaty black clothing. "You lied to me! You forfeit the game."

"And how did I lie to you?"

"You took Guard Members!" I pointed my blade at all the helpless soldiers, my fingers shaking. "You broke the rules I set and you agreed to!"

"Ah." He wagged a long finger at me, taunting me like a little child in need of reprimand. It made my blood boil. "You said I couldn't capture a member of your Faction. Take a closer look, *Rogthna*. What do you see?"

I pushed through the anger and my wolf's blood lust to bite this disgusting man and gazed at each of the captured members. I studied their faces, a mix of men and women, Shrivs and Vargs, short and tall, dark-skinned to light. They were Guard.

But I did not recognize any of them.

A loophole. He had found a loophole.

I cursed myself. I was so focused on those I loved, I didn't even consider that he would take innocents. But it seemed no matter how hard I worked to get in his head and think like him, my moral compass was just too pure compared to his blackened, tainted soul.

I wasn't sure if I was happy or saddened by that fact. If I had let myself spiral down to his level, maybe we wouldn't have been there at all.

"I will give you two choices, Kasha." Elliot hobbled in front of his men, his hands reaching out to brush the cheek of one Guard member.

I growled, warning him. "Get your hands off!"

He just laughed at my false bravado. "Choice number one. I take all of my seized spoils with me and leave you behind. Let you walk right back to your Faction, your family, and your lover." His gaze flicked to my neck, and it took all my strength not to clasp my hand around my Mark. I wasn't ashamed of it, but it felt disparaging to let his eyes stare at it for so long.

But that wasn't my focus.

Pressure built in my chest, my sweat-soaked black tank top clinging to my skin and making me itch. I knew where this was going. I knew the other option before it even left his lips.

"Or choice number two." He turned to me, chin raised. "You come with us willingly and we let all of them run to freedom."

Agony. Pure emotional misery swirled within me. It consumed me, raked over me, and tried to possess me.

An impossible, heartbreaking, and villainous choice to make.

And I knew I would have to make one.

If I went with him, I was giving him exactly what he wanted. Something about me was special, and I had yet to figure out exactly what that meant to him. I knew I was a part of his plan to take over Kazola—by the sounds of it a very important one—and I would be handing myself over to him to use as he saw fit.

Could I let him have that boost in strength?

My gaze went to the fallen soldiers, to my brothers and sisters in arms. There was fear in their eyes and weakness in their limbs. I had no idea how Elliot got them or how we hadn't heard any reports of missing guards, but that didn't matter now. He was willing to take them all.

They were Ibridowyn. They couldn't die, I knew that for a fact. But there were so many fates worse than death. He would torture them. He would pry for information. And, now knowing that he was once an Alchemist, he may have known how to do the reversal. He could make them vulnerable. He could take away their invincibility first and then their lives.

So many lost.

Or just one.

I swallowed down the utter turmoil and fear that was brewing. The darkness that was threatening to consume me. I shoved it down because I knew there was only one answer, and I needed to find my last shred of strength to do what needed to be done.

"Fine," I whispered, one of my blades falling from my fingertips. "I'll go."

"An excellent choice," Elliot drawled, his words too sweet and sickly. My stomach once again revolted. "Remove the rest of your weapons."

I whimpered like a weak fool but listened. I dropped my second Amalgam and began to unhook my black leather thigh strap that had a few throwing daggers. I took my time, pulling my focus inward, and reaching out miles beyond where I was, craving a connection.

There was one more person I needed to hear. I needed his voice one last time.

"Nolan." I reached out to him, the connection instant even with miles between us. *"I'm sorry."*

"What's going on?" His voice was frantic, desperate. My heart ached because I knew the pain I was about to cause him, but there was nothing I could do. I prayed to the Goddess that one day he would understand why I had no other choice.

"I don't think I'll be back soon like I promised." I dropped the last of my weapons. Elliot smiled.

"Very good." He nodded, reaching out to someone to his left, a long black stick exchanging to his hand.

"It was a trap like we thought." I wasn't sure how much time we had, so I needed to be quick. *"But we weren't sick enough in the head to anticipate what he was capable and willing to do to get me."*

"No…" he whispered.

"He kidnapped other Guard members. At least a dozen." Elliot switched on the weapon, a burst of energy escaping the tip. The same weapon they used on me at the meeting.

I swallowed back my fear, focusing on Nolan. *"It's me or them, Nol. If I go with him willingly, he will let them all free."*

"Don't you dare!" he yelled, but I knew his anger wasn't at me. It was hiding the pain I could almost feel pulsing in my own chest. He was cracking. Elliot was taking me away from him. It was Cleo all over again.

Another promise I broke.

I tracked every movement Elliot made, his slow, limping paces stalking towards me, blood soaking his black pants from the deep cuts I had inflicted. He was drawing out the moment to begin my torture now. I snarled at him. "Let them go first. I want to see them walk away."

"Very well, *Rogthna*." He waved his hands, and his men released the Guards, some stumbling away, others falling to the ground, still unconscious from whatever was given to them.

"Run!" I commanded them. "Take them and go!"

The mixed group stared at each other, unsure if they should stay and fight or listen to me. Their fingers flexed, their muscles tensed. They sensed the danger; they knew what would happen if they ran. I would be taken.

But if they fought, they would be taken too, and I would not let that happen.

"I am Beta of the Seathra Faction, and you are in my territory," I snarled at all of them, my stomach sinking, swirling with so much self-loathing that I was going to do this. "You follow my orders. Now, go!"

If any of them were equal or above me in station, they could have refused, but I knew none of them were. I could sense most of them were Deltas and Dairchtas, maybe a few Gammas or Treasus in the mix, but Elliot would never risk a Keturi member to be here.

Which is why they all stood at attention and began to gather their fallen brethren. And they ran.

I let out a slow, pained breath. At least I had saved them.

"I have to go," I finally admitted to Nolan. *"The captured Guards are on their way to you now. Protect them."*

"No!" Nolan snarled. *"Fend them off, Kasha. I know you can do it. I'm coming for you."*

The last of the victims disappeared into the dark, finally leaving me alone with Elliot and his men. I focused back on him, his steps once again resuming, his weapon sparking and aiming right towards me.

I suppressed a cry. Not because I was scared of the weapon; I knew the pain I was about to be dealt. What made me whimper inside was the slow, methodical raising of his hand, the sparking tip aimed at the left side of my throat.

For my scar.

"I trust you, sweetness," I whispered to him, silent tears falling down my cheeks.

"Kasha, please just hold on!" He was screaming. Even in his mind, he sounded breathless, and I knew he was running towards us. He was determined to get to me. But it was far too late.

"You made me a promise," I whispered, my eyes trailing the movement of Elliot's weapon getting closer and closer to my skin. *"I know you'll keep it. Find me, Nolan. Bring me back home to you."*

"KASHA!" was the last thing that sounded through my mind, the pain and screams of the man I loved ringing in my ears when Elliot pressed the flickering tip to my neck.

First, there was a burst of pure pain.

And then, there was nothing but darkness.

CHAPTER 42

Nolan

Two hours and thirteen minutes.

That was how long I had been separated from her, since she sprinted into the thicket of trees, hunting the man that had been tormenting her for weeks.

The man who had taken Cleo from me.

And now he was trying to take Kasha from me as well.

My feet pounded against the frozen ground, her voice still echoing in my mind, even though the connection had been severed, a sharp, obliterating pain wracking my body the moment she was ripped from consciousness. I could feel it, whatever he had done to incapacitate her.

He had hurt her. Put his hands on her.

Taken her.

I refused to believe it, even though the truth lingered in my tensed muscles from the intense severing of our mental connection. I knew it was futile, even as I pushed myself to the limits of my stamina, forcing my steps to speed up, letting my wolf and her delectable vanilla, musky scent guide me to where she was.

Get her. Save her. Don't lose her.

The wolf in me was propelling me harder and faster, begging me to find the bright light that had helped us take the final steps out of the shroud of grief that had consumed us for the past four years. My saving grace to emerge from the pit I had found myself in. She reminded me that hoping and dreaming were still alive and well. She reminded me to live every day to the fullest and find the little joys wherever I could.

She reminded me to live.

Almost there…

Finally, I broke into a clearing, and the trail stopped, her scent already dissipating into the biting, chilling air that blew around me in a gentle breeze.

"Kasha!" I screamed, hoping for any whisper or sound that would let me know she was still there, that I hadn't lost her. "Please, sweetheart. Answer me!"

She should have been there, but the abandoned area held no people, just her discarded weapons. I couldn't have been that far behind, our connection only severed two minutes ago, but it had been enough. Elliot had gotten her.

I stumbled to the pile of her things, a handful of daggers and her discharged Amalgam blades lying helplessly there. Collapsing onto my knees, I dug through them, trying to find something, anything, that could give me a clue to find her.

But there was nothing. Only the remnants of her existence in a handful of weapons. I pulled the closest one to me, gripping it tightly in my hand, body shaking as the truth washed over me.

She was gone. She was gone. She was gone.

I didn't just howl to the bright blue moon above. I roared as loud as I could, my pained, pitiful wails begging Lunestia to bring her back.

Bring her back to me.

I snarled, those terrible thoughts coming back with a vengeance that only past trauma could cause. I didn't keep her safe, I didn't keep my promise. She was gone because of me. She was gone because I didn't have her back.

I knew they were all lies, but the ripping of my heart within my chest made the words hard to ignore, festering within. The noises escaping me were foreign, my claws pressing tightly against the tips of my fingers, my joints aching to shift, to give over to the animal within and hunt for the man who had taken her from me.

Hunt. Kill. Bleed.

It was all my wolf wanted, and I was tipping over the edge, wondering if giving in, letting him find Elliot and ruining anyone who stood in my way, would give me relief from the turmoil that was overtaking me with each passing second.

Something pounded into my back, grasping my arms to my side so I couldn't escape. I struggled in their grasp, thrashing back and forth in hopes of taking them out, my survival instincts kicking in, desperate to escape, so I could go to her.

"Let me go!" I growled, gripping Kasha's blade even tighter in my grasp, refusing to let go of the last thing I had left of her. The last thing that she had held in her hands before he took her.

"Stand down, Alpha," Greyson grunted in my ear. "You're going feral."

"I don't care." I kept fighting him, trying to shove my elbows backwards to get a good hit in his gut, but he had me perfectly pinned, just as we would a frantic suspect trying to withstand arrest.

Someone gripped my wrist, trying to force the blade from my hand. "No! Don't take it!"

"Alpha!" Eden's voice broke through the fog, through the gutting pain that my wolf was howling from within me. "You have to let go. You're hurting yourself!"

She slammed her fist against my wrist, forcing my grip to open and the blade to fall and clatter to the ground. I finally looked down, a stream of blood dripping from my now open palm. How did that happen?

"You were holding it by the blade, idiot." She held it up in front of me. I tilted my head, taking in the crimson-coated wood.

It was nothing compared to the gutting pain deep in my core. It felt like a scratch compared to that.

"She's gone." My voice broke over the words, the truth slipped from my lips to hit me square in the chest as I finally admitted it. The first tear slithered down my face, blurring my trained gaze on the forest floor.

"Nolan," Eden whispered, gripping my chin to make me look at her. "We're searching. The whole team is canvasing the area."

I shook my head, my soul already knowing they wouldn't find her.

I slumped into Greyson's hold, giving up the struggle. He let go, keeping his hands on my shoulders just in case I started to fight again, but there was no use.

"She's going to be all right," Greyson said, shifting so he was finally in my line of vision. "She's a survivor. She will come back to us. To you."

I looked between my two Gammas, their military training helping to keep their faces sympathetic and calm, but their eyes betrayed them.

Fear. Hurt. Pain.

They were just better at controlling it, but Kasha was close to them. She was a part of their family. They were feeling this deeply. We all were.

A howl rang out in the air, Taylor's wail full of sadness, closely followed by Lucas and Ollie responding in a similarly pained cry.

Eden sat up straighter, gaze drifting to the trees unfocused, her lips falling into a deeper frown. She was talking to all of them, reporting in, knowing I was not in the right headspace to have others talking directly to me.

"They didn't find her, did they?" I whispered, her bloody red hair glinting in the moonlight as she shook her head.

Silence settled between us as I stared up into the Moon, the rays bathing me. I pulled in a deep breath, her final words brushing through my mind as if Lunestia herself was reminding me of the oath I made, determination flooding my veins.

"Find me, Nolan. Bring me back home to you."

"We will get her back," I said, reaching out and taking the Amalgam blade from Eden's hand and wiping it off on my shirt before grabbing the second discarded one. "I will find her."

I pushed the two wooden blades back into the handles before shoving them into the holder around my belt, unable to part with the last piece of her I had. I would hold onto it, never letting it leave my side until I could return it to its rightful owner. Until she was once again safe in my arms.

I had made her a promise. And a promise was something I never broke.

CHAPTER 43

Kasha

The last thing I expected to wake me up was the shining sun.

My head pounded, a groan escaping my lips with each little movement I made to try and gain my bearings. I finally peeled my eyes open, wincing at the brightness of the light filtering through the sheer white curtains that framed a bay window just off to my left.

I blinked a few times. This couldn't be right.

I used every inch of strength I had to sit up and take in my surroundings, my fingers curling into the soft, plush blanket below me. I looked down, my body lying on top of a large bed big enough for two people at least, decorated in a sky blue and pewter gray blanket and pillows. I slowly looked up, seeing the rest of the space occupied by a bedside table, a wardrobe in the corner, and a fireplace right across from me, flames dancing within the pyre. Two doors were to the left of me, one closed tight, the other slightly ajar to reveal a washroom decorated in the same breezy style as the bedroom.

It was a bedroom, not a jail cell. A cozy, well-decorated, inviting bedroom.

I must be hallucinating.

Yet, no matter how many times I blinked or shook my head, it was all still there. The crackling of the fire, the rumpling of the sheets fisted in my hands, and the creaking of the windows against a winter wind whistling outside. I scooted to the edge of the bed to look out the window, but there was nothing but trees. Did he take me to some kind of cabin?

I dropped my feet to the ground and stood, walking over to the floor-length mirror beside the wardrobe on shaking legs to take in the damage that had been done to me. I had been washed and redressed while unconscious, my stomach clenching at the thought of Elliot being the one to handle me while unable to fight. I couldn't let myself think too much about that, not when I needed to focus on the situation I had found myself in.

At least he didn't dress me in something frilly and bright. I was still in full black; a clean sleeveless top and breathable, form-fitting pants. I had no shoes on, not even socks to keep my feet warm. I could have argued that the only reason I was dressed that way was because I had just gotten out of bed, but I knew the truth. I wouldn't be able to get far in the winter cold dressed like that.

But it wasn't just that fact that made my heart ache. What made my legs want to collapse to the ground was the lack of Nolan's bite on my neck. I had to have been out for days if it had disappeared completely. I had a new marking, tangled with the scar on the other side of my neck. A web of angry purplish lines that crawled up my neck and down my shoulder, intermingling with the Moonlight poppy tattoo on my left shoulder. It must have been from the bright, buzzing light he had touched to my skin. I had had a similar wound on my stomach for a few days after being hit by that thing at the warehouse.

My body started trembling, tears stinging the edge of my eyes as I let the memories of my last conscious moments come flooding back. The hunt. The fight with Elliot. His threat. Nolan screaming in my mind to wait for him. Telling him I trusted him to hold his promise but forgetting to tell him that I…

Goddess, why didn't I tell him?

I needed to stop. To pull it together and trust in my team. In Nolan. I knew he would keep his promise and find me. And while he searched, I was in the lion's den, poised to get anything I could to stop Elliot from enacting whatever plan he had to take over Kazola. All past actions proved that he wouldn't hurt me, and it wasn't like he had an Ogdala Dagger to be able to threaten my life. While I waited for them to rescue me, I could use it to my advantage. To the investigation's advantage.

Then Nolan would find me, and I would tell him. I would see him again. I knew in my heart and gut that this was not the end.

I let those thoughts wash over me, pulling in the deepest breaths I could to stabilize myself. The logic and the trust helped my muscles loosen and the chest-heaving sobs dissipate. I would make it through this. I was strong and capable and there for a reason.

Or at least, I had to keep telling myself that so I would hopefully survive the fight I was able to enter.

I took a few more minutes to calm myself before moving to the closed door, the cool metal of the doorknob biting into my skin.

To my surprise, it didn't hesitate to pull open. What was going on? I peeked out, looking up and down the stretch of undecorated hall I was in. The walls were painted beige, the doors all a matching chestnut. Besides that, nothing adorned the space or made it seem anything special.

I focused, trying to dredge up a bit of strength from my sluggish mind and body that must have still been a bit drugged with something. Luckily, I was able to pick up on something a few doors down, the shuffling of papers and a tapping noise. I tiptoed out, each step light as I prayed that the floors didn't creak with my movements. It didn't take me long to realize which door the noise was coming from; the only one cracked open just an inch, a warm glow emanating from it.

I peeked in, heart thudding too loudly within my chest as I got my first glimpse at Elliot since the night in the woods. He was in a well-decorated office, sitting behind a polished, hand-carved desk. He looked so calm and… normal sifting through papers and writing things with a black stilo. You wouldn't know that a monster lurked just beneath.

"No need to linger, Kasha. You can come in," he said without looking up.

I didn't hesitate, pushing in and charging, a snarl escaping my lips as I poised to leap over the desk and tackle him. However, I didn't make it far before a towering man caught me in his grip, yanking me towards him. With my body still weak from whatever they gave me to keep me asleep, I wasn't able to escape the vice around me.

I looked up, my lips curling at the brutish man who thought it was a good idea to keep his hands on me. Based on his height and hulking build, I had to guess he was the man that had been with Elliot all those months ago when he had taken me from the Blood Moon. I still couldn't pick up a scent, but this time I saw his face.

His amber skin was a bit weathered, putting him at about forty years old if I had to guess, a jagged claw-like scar running over his left temple and cheek. His russet eyes matched well with his black hair peppered with grays. He didn't even budge as I tried to break free, his lips curling upward in a smug smile to reveal his sharp fangs; a Shrivika then.

"Now, now, James. No need to be hostile." Elliot finally looked up, a wicked glint in his ice-blue eyes. "She promised to behave, and she would never break a promise. Would you Kasha?"

Patronizing prick.

"I suppose," I gritted through my teeth, using every ounce of self-control to not lash out at him again. It would do me no good, especially if I wanted to try and use this time to gain information. Making him think I was a feral wolf so early on would not help.

"Good," he said with a nod, James releasing his grip on me. "Please sit. You must be famished. Shall I call for some lunch?"

"How many days has it been?" I continued to stand so I wasn't in a weaker position. He knew me well enough to know I hated pointless pleasantries.

Elliot dropped his stilo, leaning back to look up at me. "Three days."

"Who changed and washed me?" I couldn't stop myself. I needed to know the answer or I would never feel clean again.

His eyes softened. "One of my maids. *She* has been keeping an eye on you since we arrived."

It didn't evade me that he emphasized the *she*. His knowing my past with Logan was the reason I was asking. Damn him for knowing all of this about me, but at least it quelled a certain anxiety that had been settled in my mind since waking up. Allowed me to focus a bit more.

"Where are we?" I crossed my arms, spreading my legs a bit more to stabilize my stance.

His lips parted to speak, but a knock interrupted us, a petite woman strolling in without Elliot telling her to enter. "Here are the reports you asked me to pull."

"Thank you, doll." Elliot looked up, giving her a kind smile and taking the offered stack of papers.

The new lady was about my age and stood a few inches shorter than me, although she was probably about my height with the three-inch red heels she wore with her black silk wrap dress. Her copper brown hair was pulled back in a tight bun at the nape of her neck and her bright red lipstick made her light olive skin tone and hazel eyes pop.

She looked nothing like Vanessa, yet that perfectly poised and put-together look shook me to my core. Was that something the ladies in Elliot's cult were expected to do? Maybe all of them based on the way Elliot dressed as well.

A sardonic smile pulled upwards on her full lips. "Ah, I see the prisoner is awake."

I just growled in response.

"Be nice, Ari," Elliot chided, barely looking up from his desk.

"Very well." She sighed, turning back to me. "Nice to see you again."

My heart fell at that last word. "Again?"

"Oh, Elliot didn't mention we've met before?" She propped her hip against the edge of his desk, and he was completely unfazed by it, as if it happened every day. It probably did. "Although, you didn't exactly see my face the last time."

My sluggish mind took a few moments.

"You!" I snarled, trying to launch myself at her to scratch her eyes out, but James was there once again, banding his arm around my waist and yanking me backward. "You stabbed me, you bitch!"

"Oh, please. You were fine." She rolled her eyes, smoothing the tight fabric of her skirt. "Besides, you stabbed me right back."

She had me there, but still. I was the one attacked in a filthy alley outside the Blood Moon while I was out with my friends and brother. I was just protecting myself, for Goddess sake.

"You better hope I never find out where you sleep," I grumbled under my breath.

She rolled her eyes. "Like you'll even get your hands on a weapon here."

I turned to Elliot, reeling with anger and confusion. "If I'm so important to you, then how come you seem completely fine with the fact that she attacked me?"

"Yes, yes." Elliot finally gave us his attention, dropping his stilo and leaning back in his chair. "Arielle was instructed to keep you preoccupied when I noticed you might be getting closer to figuring out who I was. I needed to delay you while I was dealing with a particular… issue for the next few days."

A chill ran up my spine. That 'issue' must have been the poor

Varg Anwyn male we had found eviscerated the next day. I pushed past it, noticing that I couldn't scent Ari either. Just like James and when she had attacked me in the alley.

What in the name of the Goddess was this magic?

"Why can't I smell any of you?" I shook in James's hold, making him clutch me tighter. I supposed he still didn't trust me to keep myself calm. Smart guy.

"Sorcery," Ari sneered.

"Science." Elliot ignored her. "A creation of my own. I found a way to crush up dried wolfsbane plants and weave it into fabric. Most people in my inner circle have an arsenal of clothing they can wear to make sure no one can track them while they are out doing business for me."

"Is your inner circle only Shrivs or something?" Seeing as I was surrounded by them, I had to assume.

"Nope." He shook his head. "Some of the clothing is double lined so the Vargs can wear them as well without it irritating their skin. Although, they tend to only wear it when absolutely necessary."

I clenched my jaw. He was so willing to tell me anything. He had said he was ready for me to learn the truth, but I didn't realize that meant such transparency. It shook my nerves. I didn't trust it one bit. One's truth could be another's downfall.

"I see," I bit out.

"Impressed?" He smirked, winking at me. Ari just rolled her eyes next to him.

I grunted because I had no other response that I wanted to say out loud. Unfortunately, I was impressed. And I hated that I was.

He didn't deserve it, and it made me want to rip his throat out even more.

"You never answered my other question." I finally shook off James. He released me from his hold but still hovered right behind me. "Where are we?"

He stood up, rounding the desk to stand a few feet away from me. "Let me finish up a few things while you eat, then I can show you around."

"Giving your prisoner a tour of her cage, huh?"

He gave me an unamused frown. "If a beautifully decorated five-bedroom home is considered a prison to you. But of course, I want to show you around town as well."

"Town?" I perked up, my spine straightening. "We aren't in the woods?"

"No." He shook his head. "Although our house is located on the outskirts, accounting for the wooded view from your room."

"Our house?" I snarled. I did not like being lumped into a unit with him.

"Well, we'll both be residing here, so I suppose it is ours." He looked me up and down, his hard stare appraising every inch. It took every effort not to look away. "You have nothing to worry about though."

"There is plenty to worry about."

"Worries that I hope to prove wrong as our days together continue." He took another step forward, my feet firming into my stance to stay strong. "Bridget will bring you some lunch and I'll come get you in an hour. Then I can begin showing you there is nothing to worry about."

"What is your game here, Elliot?" I said, speaking his name for the first time to his face.

His eyes smoldered, that flirtatious smile I had come to know many months ago returning to his handsome face. "You'll see soon, my *Rogthna*."

CHAPTER 44

Kasha

B ridget was a sweet girl, full of smiles and kindness in her big brown eyes. She not only brought me a well-laid-out tray of roasted salmon and dill sauce, sautéed green beans, and sourdough bread, but she took a small bite of each and a sip of the tall glass of sparkling water with lime. She made sure I watched, to see that nothing laced the food I was about to eat.

I knew she was doing it to set my nerves at ease, yet it had the opposite effect. It made my skin crawl, my instinct already telling me that Elliot instructed her to do it. He knew I wouldn't trust the food, that I wouldn't eat if it wasn't tested. He knew too much about me and I hated that it wasn't all forcibly learned. Some of it, he had gleaned from our times talking in the Blood Moon, when he was just the kind and cute bartender, and I was the patron.

Lies. So many lies that sparked a fire within my chest, flooding my veins with determination.

As I ate, my stomach clenched at food for the first time in days. She rummaged through my wardrobe, pulling out a knee-length black fleece coat, fleece socks, and a pair of black leather ankle boots. More clothes that looked like something I would have picked out for myself. She found me a brush and some ties so I could braid my hair. She tended the fire, making sure it warmed the space of the room and even asked if I wanted a chair so I would have an additional sitting space in front of the hearth.

She thought of everything and did every task with a smile on her face. Perfectly primed in her knee-length black skirt and plain black button-up shirt, hair pulled back. Absolutely perfect.

A shiver ran up my spine. She also reminded me of how Vanessa always seemed so perfectly put together. Apparently, there were some things she just couldn't shake off habitually, even after leaving Elliot's acolytes years ago.

Once I was fed and dressed, she led me through the halls and down a flight of stairs, depositing us at what looked like a front entrance, an arched entryway with stained glass windows and a carved black door. Elliot stood in front, dressed in the same outfit he wore in his office, a black vest and pants and a silk black button-up underneath. His tie was black as well, with flecks of gold dusted along it, catching in the light he stood under. He gripped a wool jacket of his own, taking his time to put it on and button it up.

As I watched, my eyes caught on the two black leather sheathes secured to his belt. Only the hilts showed, the smooth handles crafted from what looked like a slab of opaque blue stone with flecks of silver swirled within it. The cross guard was made of black metal, carved swirling patterns embossed in them, but nothing too intricate. The pommel was also made of black metal, with his crest imprinted on it, an interlaced E and W.

Daggers. If I had to guess, one was made of silver, the other wood.

My heart thumped in my chest, my mind already plotting how I could get close enough to pull the proper one on him.

"Ready?" he asked with a warm smile, arm outstretched for me to take.

"As I'll ever be," I grumbled, ignoring his offered arm and shoving my hands in the deep pockets of my jacket.

He shook his head without a care, pulling out a key to unlock the door in front of us. My stomach clenched. So, I was free to wander the house but not the streets. Wonderful.

A gust of chilled air whipped around us the moment we stepped out. I squinted at the bright sun, the position telling me it was sometime in the mid-afternoon. After locking the door again, he walked us down a cobbled stone path lined with bushes, any remaining leaves dried and cracked from the winter chill. It led to a tall, wrought-iron fence, the gate also locked from the inside. He quickly unlocked it, and we stepped out onto a steep street, the house we were in the only one occupying it.

We began our descent in silence, my eyes taking in every blade of browned grass and crack in the pavement below my feet. I memorized every detail, trying to pull any facts that I could.

"We're in Luspan," I said, not needing his confirmation from the mountain ranges I saw in the not-too-far distance. Luspan was known for the mountains, its primary export jewels and metals that were mined from them.

"Yes." Elliot led me farther down the road and took a sharp

left, depositing us in the middle of what looked like a village center. The circular space was outlined by different buildings, all of them made of bright gray stone and glass walls to best show off different wares, food displays, or bright artistic exhibitions. There were benches in the center, wrapped around a tall statue of Elliot's crest. A banner weaved through the intermingled E and W with the words I had come to know well over the past few weeks carved into it: *Chu Fui na Deithe*. For the Blood of the Gods.

Perfect. Just perfect.

It wasn't just the fact that it was immaculately kept, but that there were people. A full village worth. It was as if I was walking through the Eroste Market with how many littered the streets.

My eyes shifted around. It was a town, with houses, shops, and buildings. People mingled, laughing and talking in clustered groups. Yet, something seemed too familiar, and not because it was just another village. What caught my eye was the flashing of the walls surrounding the space, peeking out from behind buildings and disappearing behind trees and mountain views. Those walls were something I was too used to.

"This was a Compound." I twirled around, most likely making a fool of myself, but I didn't care if people were staring. My eyes trailed the cement bricks and turrets surrounding us.

Elliot smirked. "Very good. It's the old Luspan Compound that was abandoned for a larger plot of land in the southern part of the territory."

"How?" I stopped, facing him. "How did you get your hands on this?"

"I purchased it, of course." He cocked his head at me. "Well, actually, a dear friend of mine purchased it from the High Faction first, wanting to use it as a space to begin building his new mining business. However, once it was in his name, he sold it right to me. Just as we had planned."

He was too smart for his own good. A trickster in every sense of the term.

He took me around, showing off some of the cafes and shops that he particularly liked. People waved to him and even approached to ask him how his day was. You would think he was just a typical resident of the town if it weren't for the bows and salutes everyone gave him or the reverence glinting in their gazes as they watched him talk.

"Why are all these people here?" I demanded when we left the bakery his household apparently bought bread from every day. "Are they trapped?"

"Of course not." Elliot kept his features schooled, as if my accusatory question was completely expected. "They are here because they want to be. They believe in the country I'm trying to rebuild for them."

"Keeping them in a guarded, enclosed space is not freedom." I shook my head, eyes darting to the turret towers, seeing armed guards watching all of us from above.

He stopped us near the statue, my skin prickling. "They know they are safer here until we have reformed Kazola into a peaceful country. Until then, they're protected by those who believe in the cause. They couldn't ask for a better place to live."

"You've brainwashed them." I snarled, taking a bold step forward, pushing into his personal space, attempting to crowd him and catch him off guard. "These people are your prisoners just like I am."

"These people," he closed even more distance between us, his lips curled up in a sneer, "see the true potential for Kazola. They are dreamers, visionaries for the future. They want to feel heard and seen. Not just another body on the isle that the High Faction watches from their gilded Château."

"That's not what they do!" I defended, my loyal Onyx Guard upbringing flaring to life within me.

"Really?" He smirked down at me, leaning forward to whisper in my ear. "I don't think that's what you believed when they dismissed your case. When your father tried to make you believe that you were shamed for what you went through."

I glared right back at him. "Don't you dare talk about things you have no business knowing about."

"You are more like all of them than you think." His breath was warm on my cheek, his nose gently grazing my flushed skin. "You'll see. I know you will."

"Don't hold your breath." I jerked away, bile rising in my throat at the intimate touch. "Suffocating yourself is an awfully stupid way to go."

He laughed, relaxing his posture once again. "Well, now that you've gotten an idea of where your new place of residence is, it is time for me to get back to work. James here will take you back home and help if you need anything Bridget can't tend to."

He waved at someone from behind me, peeking over my shoulder to see the man from his office stalking towards us.

"A prison guard." I rolled my eyes. "Fabulous."

"James is my second in command and typically my personal guard." He raised his eyebrow at me, a frown settling on his lips. "But I want you to have the best while you're here. One of the few people I trust to take care of you."

I gave him an unintelligible grunt in response to his 'kindness'.

"Welcome to Folanoch, *Rogthna*." He tilted his head in goodbye before walking away and disappearing down one of the many streets that webbed away from the center.

Folanoch. A word I had read in one of the texts Chaithea Ahren gave me. Old Kazalonian for Sanctuary.

Well, this just kept getting better. I pulled in a few more deep breaths, calming my racing pulse and soothing the burning blush on my cheeks. Once I felt more in control of myself, I turned back to the man lurking behind me.

"So, I'm stuck with you?" I grimaced at James.

"The feeling is mutual." He glared right back. "Stuck being your babysitter is the last thing I want."

I huffed. "Then help me escape and you don't have to."

"Funny," he grumbled, grabbing my arm and pulling me back towards the house. Towards my new cage.

CHAPTER 45

Kasha

A note arrived for me later that day, "inviting" me to have dinner with Elliot.

Could I have said no? Sure. Even if they had taken me kicking and screaming, I would have found a way to knock myself out if it meant getting out of the dinner.

And a part of me wanted to do just that to spite him for taking me and holding me against my will.

But after having a little temper tantrum in the privacy of my room, convincing myself that I would not take orders like a dog, I calmed myself down with my breathing techniques and thought like the soldier I was.

In the short time I'd been awake, Elliot had proven that he wanted me to be 'converted' to his cause, that I would fit in. He would treat me like a member of the community, even if I didn't want that. And although it was the truth, I never would be, it didn't mean I couldn't use it to my advantage.

So, I went to the wardrobe and pulled out a modest midnight

blue dress, the high neckline going straight across my collar bone and the long sleeves covering my tattoos, but the dip in the back made the head of my snake ink peek from the top. It was form-fitting to my curves, the hem falling just below my knees. After pairing it with a silver wedged heel, I knew I was ready. I was confident in myself without feeling on display. I looked like I had put in effort without sacrificing my comfort.

It would have to be my perfect armor for the evening.

The dining room Ari silently led me to was unexpected. With a mansion this large, I expected to be shown an elaborately overdone space with seating for twenty and the two of us seated at opposite ends. Although I suspected that space probably existed in some part of the house, that wasn't where we were dining. Instead, we were in what looked like an atrium of some kind, three of four walls completely made of glass, even the roof, starlight reflecting through the frost-coated panes. Heat was not lost within the space, however. A fireplace kept the room toasty, so we would be comfortable.

Elliot stood from the intimate two-person table, a smile on his lips. "Thank you for joining me."

I didn't return the smile, and I didn't say anything back. I didn't trust myself.

A servant came through, dropping a hearty plate of roasted chicken, fingerling potatoes in an herbed butter sauce, and a white asparagus and tomato salad. Smelled pretty good. But already I knew Nolan cooked circles around whoever the chef was. I took a few slow, testing bites and sips for potential poison, not detecting anything.

I looked up to find his amused gaze lingering on me. "What?" I asked.

"Did you think I was poisoning you?"

My shoulders slumped. "Can't be too safe. Who knows what you plan for me."

"It would be rather obvious if I poisoned you." He shook his head. "And wasteful."

"There are poisons that can make things look natural." I leaned back. "Read about one that can cause a heart attack."

I didn't mention it was in one of my fiction books.

He just laughed it off, tucking into his food and letting me enjoy mine. We ate in silence, barely looking at each other. It wasn't until my portion was half gone that he cleared his throat, causing me to look up.

"You should come with me into town again tomorrow," he said, my stomach twisting. "I can introduce you to more people, maybe even take you to the council house."

"You're on Kazola land still, Elliot." I cut off a piece of chicken, the knife scraping a bit too violently against the plate. "You still answer to the High Faction, even if you think that having your own fake council building makes a difference."

He just shrugged. "For now, maybe, but not forever."

I gripped my fork harder. I guessed we were doing this. Well, it was what I came to dinner for—to learn.

"So, what is your plan?" I took a casual bite of potato, chewing it thoroughly before swallowing and continuing. "Overthrow the High Faction by force? Claim Kazola for yourself? Like a Dictator?"

"Leader," he said calmly. "I would be a leader."

"Dictators are types of leaders." I shot back, a frown settling on his lips.

"There are too many voices on the High Faction." He dabbed his lips with his napkin.

"Those voices represent the people."

"They represent people in power who argue and never actually agree on anything," he argued, the lines on his forehead deepening. "They go in circles and struggle to come to a consensus. And when they do, half of the time people are bribed or coerced into agreeing. Maybe even threatened, who knows?"

I swallowed a lump in my throat. I had recently started to learn that there was an air of truth to his words. Still. "How would you even know that?"

"I learned from experience." His gaze hardened as if recalling a potent and terrible memory. I bit my cheek, wondering if it had to do with his time as a State Alchemist. I would keep that bit of knowledge to myself for now, but I had a feeling it was all connected somehow.

"So, what is your plan, then?"

"A Monarchy of sorts." His eyes cleared, a relaxed smile back on his face, already the practiced politician he wished to be. "Led by one Shrivika and one Varg Anwyn. A King and Queen, bound through their vows to Kazola. They would lead together, to give a voice to all."

"And what of the Humans?" I challenged. "Shouldn't they have a voice too?"

"The God and Goddess blessed us to protect Kazola. They gave the Isle our species to be the ones who gave the humans a safe place to live." He tilted his head. "They need to leave us to the job that was gifted to us. Trust in it like it was intended."

"Protectors, not overlords!"

"Some may argue that they could be one in the same."

I pulled in a stuttering breath, willing to calm down the anger building in my veins. It wasn't the time.

"So, you plan to be the Shrivika King?" I raised an eyebrow. He was saying many treasonous things, but I needed to hear the truth from him.

"Yes." He nodded without hesitation. "With you as the Varg Anwyn Queen."

I gaped at him, my mouth hanging open in the most unladylike gesture. But I didn't care; I had never considered myself a lady.

"Absolutely not!" I threw my napkin on my plate. I tried not to gag over my next words. "I would never lead with you or… Oh, Goddess… marry you."

He balked. "And I would never do that with you!"

"You have flirted with me since the day we met!" I challenged, remembering how he was in the bar, all of it starting a year and a half ago.

"Flirting got you to open up when I knew you were a Guard and I wanted to gain your trust. It ended up becoming habit, I guess." He shrugged as if it was nothing. "But, no, Kasha, I do not want to marry you. You're a child compared to me."

"Yet you want me to lead?" I rolled my eyes. "And how… what would happen when we die? Who would take over?"

"We would each have consorts, to marry and to birth heirs

from." He sat tall. "Who would take over our respective seats upon our passing."

My food churned in my rolling stomach. "You are a special brand of crazy."

"Some may say crazy, others a visionary." He didn't seem the least bit fazed by my words. "But I know the prophecy, one I have a feeling you are already aware of."

My veins chilled. "How did you know I was researching?"

He smiled smugly. "I didn't, but I knew you were smart and cunning. You make sure to cover every base."

"Then you'll know I found the prophecy in a research tome that is considered to be outlandish and not recognized by many acolytes or researchers."

"To them, it's something to write in a book." He leaned forward. "But I was raised on that prophecy. It was a place of pride in my family. We knew we were the bloodline to complete it."

I snorted. "So, the crazy was hereditary, then."

"We are meant to bring a new life to Kazola. The one Firenielle and Lunestia meant for us."

"One flaw in your plan. I didn't die that night."

"According to doctors, that is untrue."

"Even if I had, even if by some delusional twist of fate I was the one from this prophecy of yours," I shook my head, a bitter taste flooding my mouth at the words I was saying, "I am no leader. What makes me qualified to make and uphold the laws best for Kazola?"

"You have experienced enough at the hands of the High Faction," Elliot said. "You need to realize that there is power and knowledge in that, making you more qualified than half of the men who sit on that council."

"I am no Queen."

"You have been through too much in your life, *Rogthna*," he said. "After this past year, the betrayal of your leader, the court case…"

"I will not talk about that with you." I glared at him.

He looked at me steadily for a few moments before whispering, "Then tell me about your mother."

I slammed my fork down, the rest of the cutlery and plates rattling under my shaking hands. "Do not test me."

"I'm just trying to understand how you can still be a part of the Guard, to trust the High Faction, when they have been letting you down from childhood."

My blood boiled, my jaw tense. "It sounds like you already know the story."

"I may have looked into it." He rested his arms on the table, leaning forward. "But I want to hear it from you. The full truth, not just the basic details."

I stood up from the table, my chair pushing back. I paced towards one of the glass walls, looking out into the black night, the leafless trees looking like haunted sentries assigned to keep me caged.

"My mother was in the Guard." I would play along, talk about that very first tragedy in my life, just to prove that no matter what, he could not break me or get to me through them. They were my memories and my history, but I was in control of how they affected me. Me and no one else.

"She retired when I was around ten, when my father did." I crossed my arms against my torso, my fingernails biting into the soft velvet fabric of my dress. "He had gotten a position as a High Faction assistant, and Mother just wanted to finally be able to raise her children without work getting in the way. And that was exactly how it was until I was thirteen."

"What happened?" Elliot whispered, still sitting at the table, although I could see him through the reflection in the glass, his posture rigid.

"One of her last cases had been taking down a drug trafficking ring. The greatest accomplishment of her career, they used to call it. Then, one of the dealers got out. They believed that he wasn't as ingrained in the ring as the others and deserved a lighter sentence. Along with the good behavior and community service he completed, he was given probation. But they didn't realize that he had been in the same prison as one of the leaders." I held back the tears, the memories that still make me crack to this day. "And that leader had somehow convinced him to get revenge for them all. He hunted down my mother and killed her, in cold blood."

It had been a devastating night. She had gone out with friends, Ollie and I at home alone while father worked late. We had been practicing a duet on the piano, me playing and him singing, as a gift. Her birthday was in a few weeks, and we wanted to surprise her.

I hadn't heard Ollie sing since.

"And he's in jail now, right?"

I growled, unable to stop myself. He already admitted to knowing the facts, so he knew the truth. He was trying to bait my anger, and it was working.

"No." I turned back around, steeling my features. "Somehow, he got off on a technicality. Evidence improperly collected, stored, and tested."

"I am so sorry for your loss, *Rogthna*," he said, the words dripping with sympathy and pity.

I scoffed, gracefully settling back into my chair, posture straight and facing him. "I do not need it. It happened so long ago."

He just nodded, waving to the server in the corner to come and take our abandoned plates away. "Would you like dessert?"

I wanted to laugh. As if something sweet would make this whole situation all right. But that was when I realized that it wasn't the lack of sugar or difficult story that was causing that gnawing pit to slowly form in my stomach. It was hunger, as if I hadn't eaten a bite of dinner.

Elliot had said I had been asleep three days, which meant it had been four since I last fed on blood. That was why I was still hungry. I needed the rest of my necessary sustenance.

"I need…" My voice trailed off, realizing I wasn't asking for a glass of water or another portion of food. I was a Varg Anwyn, and I needed blood. That wasn't typical.

Wow, for the first time in my life, I was wishing to have been born a Shrivika. It would have made the whole moment a lot easier.

I would need to feed; it was inevitable to keep my strength up. I peeked around the room at James and the other guard. I couldn't give up the secret of the Ibridowyn. Elliot had been an Alchemist, so he knew the truth, but I couldn't risk giving it to anyone else.

I would just have to find a way.

"Yes?" Elliot's eyebrow raised.

I just shook my head. "Nothing."

Elliot's eyes gleamed. "If this is about your need for blood, these two are already very much aware of the truths about the Guard."

My eyes flared golden. "Excuse me?"

"I do not keep secrets from my closest." He nodded to the two of them. I peeked over, but in soldier fashion, neither of their expressions gave anything away. I turned back to Elliot.

"Fine," I said through gritted teeth. "Then can I please get a blood donation from the local blood bank?"

"Who says we have one?" he asked, but I gave him a look that told him I wasn't stupid. He laughed. "All right, we do, but you can feed from me instead."

I sneered, trying not to gag at the image his suggestion brought up. "Absolutely not."

He stood up, straightening his tie and jacket before slowly walking around the table to tower over me. I looked up, but I didn't stand, waiting.

"You either drink my blood from a bag or my wrist, or you starve," he said. "Your choice."

I curled my fingers into the skirt of my dress. "I'll find someone else."

"Express orders that no one else can feed you." He unbuttoned the cuff of his shirt, rolled up the crisp pressed sleeves, and bared his wrist to me, inches from my lips. "So, what will it be?"

My stomach dropped, my mind and stirring wolf competing against each other within me. I could feed. His blood would keep me strong, but I didn't trust him. There was always a reason for his actions, and he was making it so I could only feed from him. Nana said he was a genius to a terrifying level sometimes. My mind went through a flurry of possibilities from somehow getting hooked on his blood like a drug to lacing it with a poison that didn't kill him but somehow hurt me.

My active imagination was having too much fun with the possibilities.

Even if it wasn't anything like that, feeding from someone created dependency, which was exactly what Elliot wanted from me. He wanted to break down my walls and find ways to manipulate me to his side. Making me feed from him, to let him take care of me in that way, would be giving him power over me. He could withhold it if I didn't behave the way he wanted me to or use it as a means to torture me. Even just for that, it was too much of a risk.

No, I would not give him that power over me, even if it was at the risk of my own health. It would be my decision. I would just have to find a way through.

"No." I knocked his wrist out of my face and promptly stood again. "If you'll excuse me, I am done eating for the night."

I didn't let him say another word as I sauntered out, my head held high, even though I was already trying to figure out how long I would survive without blood.

And, ultimately, when the starvation symptoms began to set in.

CHAPTER 46

Kasha

I woke up on edge the next morning, my body a bit too sensitive to everything around me.

The bed sheets scratched my skin, and I ripped them off, even though they were as smooth as silk. This was a common anxiety response for me most days, but I couldn't help but wonder if the hunger was already starting to cause symptoms.

Maybe it was both.

Bridget woke me up with a large spread of breakfast and I ate greedily, trying to build up my strength since I would slowly be depleting into starvation. I had to do everything I could to stave it off as long as possible.

She ran me a bath and pulled out my clothes to dress in. She tidied up the room and even dropped a stack of books she had pulled from a local bookstore since Elliot had let her know I love to read fiction titles.

And she did it all with a perfect unwavering smile on her face.

I was trying hard not to let it freak me out every time. It wasn't her fault she had been brainwashed.

I was flipping through one of the books mid-morning when a sharp knock interrupted me. I walked to the door, ripping it open, expecting Elliot to be on the other side.

"Oh," I sneered, "It's you."

"Like I'm so very happy to see you as well." Ari waltzed inside, a knee-length burgundy wool coat over her sleek black A-line dress. Her matching black pumps were muffled by the plush carpet in my room. "Get your coat. I'm taking you somewhere."

"Pass." I flopped into the chair in front of the fire, turning my back to her.

"That wasn't a request, Beta," she bit out, saying my title as if it was a swear word meant to offend me. "Elliot would like to see you."

I squeezed my fingers into fists. I hated that he was summoning me like one of his followers, a need to rebel biting inside of me. However, I decided to use the time to figure out as much as possible about him. If he was asking for me, I had to assume he was about to show me another piece of this deadly game he was playing. I couldn't pass up the chance to learn, observe, and possibly use the information against him.

I let out a heavy sigh, dropping my feet to the floor and grabbing a coat from my closet. "Fine."

She nodded before striding out the door, my footsteps quick behind her as she led me out of the house, and down the way towards the town. However, before we made it to the city center, we took a sharp left, heading up a quiet street, leading to a dark red and black brick building that I could make out in the distance.

"Where are we going?"

"You'll find out when we get there," she spat at me.

I rolled my eyes. "I see we are going to be the best of friends while I'm here."

"I'm here to assist Elliot in any way I can," she stated, pride lacing her voice. "I don't need your approval to do that."

"Seriously, what is your problem with me?" I asked, not really in the mood to play a guessing game the entire time I was there. I hated her too since she stabbed me and was happy to play along in holding me hostage. Elliot made it seem like I was some destined monarch. So, if that was what he wanted, why did she seem so annoyed with my presence?

"You will bore him once you take your place." Her hair swung in a long-curled ponytail down her back. "Then you will just be his partner on the throne, and he will no longer be so obsessed with his attentions."

"You can have them," I grumbled.

"So unappreciative." She glared at me over her shoulder. "Thank the Gods that you are a Varg Anwyn and not a Shriv. You wouldn't be worthy then. Not like I am."

"What, are you trying to be his consort or something?" I laughed, saying it in a sarcastic manner, but by her silence and strained, angry look, I had hit the nail on the head. "Ew, seriously?"

"He is blessed by the Gods!" She turned on me, her face turning splotchy and red, eyes shifting to crimson. "It would be an honor to be bound to him and help to carry on his family line to rule Kazola the way it was meant to."

My face twisted in disgust. "Please tell me you don't mean those words."

"You wouldn't understand." She whirled back around, picking up the pace towards the tall, mansion-like building. It was obviously an addition to the town when he had renovated since no Compound would have such a classically beautiful building on its property.

She walked in the black metal front door and brought me through a few halls before pushing us into a room, the echoes of our footsteps the only thing ringing between us.

And there he was, in a navy suit, a burgundy tie contrasting with his crisp white shirt. We were in some kind of antechamber, the grey stone walls bare and only a few seats off to the side decorating the space. The only thing to catch my eye was the enormous double doors, one carved with the moon phases, the other with a snake slithering up it.

"Thank you for joining me today, Kasha." He gave me a warm smile, one I didn't return.

"What do you want?"

"Thank you, Ari." Elliot gave her a slight nod, dismissing her. She frowned as he turned his back on her, stalking away with her chin jutting into the air. "Follow me, *Rogthna*."

He crossed the dimly lit room until we reached the imposing doors and pushed inward, flicking on a light switch so the entire space was lit for me to see. And damn, what a space it was.

The room was opulent on a whole different scale from the Château. The ceilings raised high, making me wonder if it took up all three levels of the building. White marble floors glinted under my feet, the expansive space echoing each one off the black carved walls. My eyes drifted upwards, multiple crystal chandeliers hanging from the rafters in a diamond pattern to properly light the space, including the balcony that encircled the entire room a floor above to overlook the wide-open space.

"What is this place?" Chills skated across my skin, making me pull my jacket tighter around me, although it did nothing to dissipate them.

"The Throne Room." He gestured to the dais at the front, walking forward, my feet following. "It's a stand-in, obviously, while Folanoch is the Capitol of my people. But once we take over Kazola for good, we will move it to its proper place in the Château."

"Plan to make yourself a castle?" I mocked.

"It will be easier to transition within those halls where all the records are kept," he explained. "Plus, the country will already be in a state of change with a new regime. It will be better for the masses if the main building for the country stays the same. Now, come."

He walked us across the room, the marble floors slippery from a fresh polish. Luckily, I was in boots so I could grip better. I would have been on my ass if forced to wear heels. We reached the dais at the front of the room, but instead of stopping, he walked up to stand next to the light-absorbing black Throne. Obsidian stone was my guess.

"However, these will be coming with us when we move there." He placed his hand delicately on the carved top, stroking it like it was his pet. "I had them custom-made for the Shrivika King and Varg Anwyn Queen who will lead Kazola into a new age."

A shiver ran up my spine as I turned to the matching white throne to the right of him. I knew that stone well, although I had never seen anything carved from such a large slab of it. Moonstone, the opaque, milky white glittering under the crystal chandelier. The moon phase was carved up the back, his motto, *Chu Fui na Deithe*, imprinted just above it, so it would hang over whoever sat in the seat.

I stumbled back a step. "I will never sit on a throne."

"Never say never." He smiled down at me. "This throne was meant for you, and I cannot wait to see the day you take your rightful place. With me."

"Why are you showing me this?" I shook my head, crossing my arms.

"To give you an idea of the future I have planned." He stood in front of his own throne but didn't sit. "We could do such good for everyone. No longer would people have to worry that the High Faction will debate or drag on their case. There won't be endless negotiations and nothing getting done. You and I will be the ones to take cases, and we will make judgments swiftly and efficiently, so those hurt by wrong-doers can find peace right away. So, they can begin to heal when the evil is expunged from this world."

"Expunged?" My eyes went wide. "Would you kill every person who breaks the law?"

"No." He shook his head. "However, we would certainly execute more than the High Faction does."

The High Faction didn't believe in black and white, meaning the death penalty wasn't something that was used often in Kazola. Only those who were truly malevolent lost their lives. Elliot, for example, would be a prime candidate.

Everyone else was given punishment, ranging from community service to a lifetime in jail. We tried our best to rehabilitate people who could still be contributing members of society while letting those who had hurt too many waste away their final days in a cell.

I had a feeling, with Elliot, death would be the preferable method of justice.

"Taking a life shouldn't be easy, Elliot."

"It never is. But are you trying to tell me that there aren't a few criminals that walk free that you wouldn't like to see bleed?"

I clamped my mouth shut, keeping that darkened thought within. However, my scowling face was obviously giving too much away because he smirked down at me and said, "I thought so."

"You know nothing about me," I bit out, my claws pressing at the edges of my nail beds, begging me to scratch his eyes out.

"I'm sorry that this transition hasn't been the easiest, *Rogthna*." He changed the subject briskly, giving me a solemn look as if he cared.

"You kidnapped me." I crossed my arms. "How would that ever be easy on me?"

"I had other plans to have your Varg Anwyn friend be here with you, to make it more comforting," he stated, my veins running cold. "However, a few loose ends made a mess of my plans. Thank you for taking care of them, by the way."

"Are you talking about Lea?" I took a step down, away from the imposing throne, my breath loosening a bit. "Does this have to do with the tavern attack?"

"That was a misstep." He sighed, righting his tie. "I assigned

William to go and find your dear friend Adelaide and get to know her. As your only civilian friend, I figured she would be perfect to bring to the cause. I wanted her here for when you arrived, to help make it more comfortable for you."

I growled, taking a prowling step toward him. "You targeted my best friend?"

"I knew she would be good for you here," he explained as if it was completely normal to use my best friend as a pawn. "However, William had been with some friends earlier that day and somehow, they had convinced him to try Blackthorn. Of course, they took too much, and the three of them went to William's meeting and ruined it."

I snarled, lunging at Elliot, my claws fully extended as I scratched at his pretty, perfect face, his feet stumbling back at the impact. Blood welled up at the scratches I had left behind, starting at the edge of his right eye all the way down to his bottom lip. He reached up, eyes wide as he grazed his fingertips through the drips of crimson skating down his face.

Pure delight washed through me as I watched a few drops stain his perfect white shirt.

"Stay. Away. From. Her." I stalked towards him, crowding his space, ready to strike again if necessary. The only reason I wasn't ripping his eyes out was because I knew there was more to learn. I knew I was still missing something.

Particularly what Vanessa had seen that sent her running. Maybe it was the key to understanding everything.

Then, to my utter despair, he smiled, eyes lighting up with glee at my violent outburst. "This is why Kazola needs you as its

Queen, *Rogthna.*" He pulled out a handkerchief, wiping away the blood on his face, the cuts already starting to heal.

Wait, why so quickly?

"You will keep them safe. You will protect them with a fierceness none of the High Faction has." He shoved the soiled cloth back into his pocket. "That is the Queen they need. That is the Queen they want."

He sounded so sure. Nothing could break the confidence he had in his mission.

Sounded like a challenge.

"Now, come." He began striding across the Throne Room towards the front doors. "I have to change out of this shirt and should have time for some lunch with you before I have to head back to work."

I bit back another snarl, pulling in shaky, angry breaths to try and calm my unsettled wolf. This was going to test every bit of patience I had.

Luckily, I had been trained for this.

CHAPTER 47

Nolan

One week and six days.

Almost two weeks since she had been taken, and I had barely slept in that whole time. No shocker to anyone.

I parked my bike in front of my house. The rest of the team that had come with me to the unsuccessful raid parked in their usual spots around the Compound. I didn't say a word to any of them as I strode across the way and towards the office building, my focus only on one place.

I had already gotten the message from Ollie right before my raid that his was also a failure. It had been the last two locations that Vanessa had given us of old safe houses and hideouts that she knew about in Elliot's network.

And I was determined to get more places to search. The traitor hidden in the cells would give me more.

"They were all dead ends," I said in a way of greeting, her body still upright even though it was well past midnight. "Give me new ones."

"I have nothing more for you. That was the last location I was aware of," Vanessa said, her face hardened, just like the last few times I had come down to the dank cells to question her. I was becoming her least favorite person with each visit, but I didn't care.

She hurt Kasha.

"There has to be more!" I slammed my palms against the bars, pain zipping up my arms at the impact but I easily ignored it. My insides were humming still with the adrenaline from the raid, and I was determined, my mind only focused on getting another lead. Finding another way. Bringing her home to safety.

"There isn't!" She insisted.

"After everything you did to her, the betrayal, you would let her rot with him?" I urged, my words barely my own, fueled by the rage my wolf-self was encouraging. He hadn't been able to settle since the moment she was snatched, as if a piece of him had shattered and couldn't be fixed until she was back next to us.

"I told her not to go," Vanessa grumbled, wrapping her thinning prison blanket around her tighter. "I told you all not to underestimate him and yet you did. I told you all the places I know but that it had been five years since in their company and still you wanted to waste your time raiding."

"She is suffering because of you," I snarled, not sure if my words were true. "She is alone and imprisoned because of your betrayal." Those didn't feel right, yet they still escaped my lips with ease.

"I get that I made mistakes. I get that because of me, Kasha has been found and taken." She trembled, contrasting with the fiery conviction laced through every word she shouted at me through the bars separating us. "But do not take out your anger on me and use me as an emotional beating bag because you can barely keep control of your emotions over this whole mess!"

I took a step back, finally letting rationality settle into my bones, silencing my feral wolf. She wasn't wrong. She wasn't completely right, but ever since coming into our custody weeks ago, she had been trying to help. Giving information, telling Kasha as many details as possible.

I rubbed my hands over my face. "I'm sorry. You're right."

"I wish I could give you more, Nolan." She took a step forward, pity and hurt in her gaze as she stared at me. "You have no idea how badly I want you to find her after everything I did. But he is just too good, too calculating. The moment she chose to take his challenge was the moment she forfeited herself to him, and only a miracle will save her now."

I nodded at her, with no words to respond because I refused to believe what she said. I didn't break promises.

★★★

Somehow, I found myself at the guest house instead of back at my own where I should have been trying to sleep. Kasha may have been sleeping with me for the few weeks leading up to the chase, but most of her belongings were still being stored here or at her townhouse in the city.

Why? Why hadn't I asked her to move them in with me? In the home that should be considered ours? I had been too afraid to push her to take a step she wouldn't be ready for.

As per usual, it was times of tragedy that made one look at their past decisions with regret, even if they were the right ones at the time.

I wandered upstairs to the tapping sound of a broken tune being played on Kasha's piano. My heart fluttered, even though I knew it wasn't her up there sitting by the black and white keys. I had yet to hear her play, something I planned to rectify soon, but based on her passion for the instrument and the stories Ollie used to tell me, I knew she was much more proficient than the terrible sounds currently emanating from the instrument.

When I crossed into the bedroom, I wasn't the least bit surprised that Ollie was the one sitting on the bench. He had gotten back to the Compound with Caleb from their raid about an hour before I did, the two brothers almost as determined as I was to find their baby sister.

Caleb had arrived in Seathra the same night Kasha was taken after his… somewhat successful undercover mission. He was keeping fairly tight-lipped about it, wanting to tell Kasha everything first. Plus, we were all too focused on finding her anyways.

He was in the other guest house, but Ollie had been staying there with Lea instead of in my spare bedroom. He seemed protective of his sister's best friend, almost as much as Kasha was, and I knew Kasha would appreciate that Ollie was looking after her while she couldn't.

Their father had stayed at the Château, claiming he was more useful there. I was fine with it; I didn't need my anger toward him distracting me.

"Hey," I said to get his attention, the obvious exhaustion I'd been carrying with me for weeks seeping into every syllable.

He turned, looking at me with an equally tired expression, dark circles rimming his eyes that carried no hint of their usually teasing gleam. "Hey. Nothing, huh?"

I dropped next to him on the bench, my shoulders sagging. He already knew the answer, since I was alone, but I think he needed to hear it to completely accept it. "No, it was another abandoned property."

"We were idiots to think these would pan out." Ollie's fingers slipped from the piano in front of us. "He's too smart to leave locations going when someone who escaped knew the location."

"We had no other leads."

Silence fell between us, my eyes roaming over the tight space filled to the brim with her things. Her books and music and drawings. Everything that made her who she was. Everything that made her the woman I love.

My heart clenched. I had to find her. Alive. There was no other option because, if she died, if I lost yet another love to the same man, I knew my sanity wouldn't survive it.

And I wasn't sure if I would be strong enough to try and fight it.

"You're perfect for her, you know," he said, shocking me to my very core.

"Really?" I couldn't help but joke, even when we were both struggling to hide our heartbreak. That was just how Ollie and I naturally were around each other. "The threats and need to draw blood from me in a fight said otherwise."

He shrugged irreverently. "I knew even when she was a teenager that she would need someone who didn't hold her back. Even more, she needed someone to encourage her to go after everything she wanted in life, to show her just how special she was. Yet, at the same time, knew the precarious balance of protecting her when she needed it.

"None of those other punks would ever have done that. I don't think any of them would have known where to begin." He looked over at me, those blue eyes almost identical to his sister's misting over with tears. "But not you. You balance her, steady her. After everything she's been through, she deserved to find happiness with someone, and to have that someone remind her that there can still be joy in life among the heartache."

"I told her I love her."

Ollie chuckled, rubbing the back of his neck. "Yeah, she told me. Sorry for kind of ruining that moment."

I playfully punched him in the arm. "Bashing your nose in was punishment enough. Still looks a bit crooked."

"Oh, bullshit, Carrigan." He shoved me right back, yet still traced his nose with his fingers for a brief second before dropping them back to the keys, plucking at them once again.

"She didn't say it back," I whispered. I wasn't heartbroken over it. I knew it wouldn't have been easy for her and the last thing I wanted was to make her feel like she had to say it just because I had. When she whispered those words to me for the first time, I wanted her to say it on her terms and no one else's.

Still, it stung knowing there was now a chance I would never hear them uttered from her beautiful lips.

"Even before everything that happened, she was terrible at admitting her feelings. All three of us are. Our father isn't one to encourage emotions." He shrugged. "It was only solidified in her mind after the trauma. But she let you in. I can tell just by the way she looks at you. She loves you. Might just take her a bit more time to catch up and say it."

"Yeah," I said, dropping my chin to look down at my lap.

"Hey." He shook my shoulder, making me look back up at him. "We will find her. I can feel it in my bones. There is no way this is how she is taken from us forever."

I tried not to let tears slip from my eyes at his words. I had been good about only letting them fall in the privacy of my bedroom, and I wasn't planning on breaking that. Even if it was Ollie next to me. "I don't even know where to go next. It seems like an aimless abyss now."

"I have an idea." Eden's voice came from behind. Ollie and I turned towards the door to see her hovering there, Greyson right behind her with a comforting hand on her shoulder.

"What?" I stood, rushing over to her. Greyson's eyes flashed, a direct warning not to get too close or to push too hard. In only a matter of weeks, I'd come to learn what many of his silent facial expressions really meant, and this was one to take seriously.

"There is one other person besides Vanessa that we know who has had contact with Elliot." She twists her fingers in front of her, but still strong enough to keep eye contact with me. "And much more recently as well."

"Your sister," I finished, so she didn't have to say it out loud. She nodded solemnly in response.

Truthfully, I had already thought of that, but I hadn't wanted to bring it up right away, not when we had a more direct link in Vanessa. Lila was a messenger compared to the high-profile standing Vanessa had had in Elliot's inner circle.

Plus, I knew Kasha wouldn't appreciate me pushing my Gamma closer to her family. She wouldn't have wanted me to take the risk unless absolutely necessary.

"She won't know any specifics of the location." Eden sighed. "She wouldn't have earned enough trust. But if we can get an idea of what she was surrounded by, see if she can tell us something that might at least give us a better perimeter to search within. It's worth a shot asking."

I look down at my Gamma, her face doing little to hide the conflicting emotions that skated across her delicate features. "Are you sure?"

"For Kasha?" She straightened her shoulders, taking a deep breath. "Yes."

CHAPTER 48

Kasha

Three days. It took three more days for the first symptoms of blood starvation to settle in.

It was easy to ignore at first, the pin-jab prickles all along my skin something I was used to with my anxiety. However, it became harder to ignore with each passing hour until it overtook my entire body, wrapping me in an uncomfortable blanket of hunger.

It kept me on a razor-thin edge, my body ticking and desperate for a release of… something. I knew what I needed. Blood. I needed to feed, and I knew I could find my way to desperation if I wasn't careful.

I looked up at the ceiling of my pretty room, legs slung over the overstuffed chair in front of the fireplace. I was trying anything to keep myself distracted, but it was almost impossible at that point to turn to those tasks that used to help. The deep, gnawing hunger felt like my anxiety but on an entirely different level. This was primal, desperate, and eager to unleash itself on me at a moment's notice. I didn't have a piano to sit at, and the book in my lap wasn't doing anything to distract me, even though it was a story that would typically enthrall me with its beautifully strong fairy-born heroine and the two princes vying for her attention.

I had used working out to help the past few days, but the pushups and sit-ups I could do in my room were no longer enough. I needed to punch and jab, feel the biting of impact against my knuckles. Something to distract me from this God-dess-awful hunger.

Well, maybe I could make that happen.

I strode across the room, pulling open the door, James's una-mused face staring at me with a frown.

"What?" he said, his words blunt like a torture dagger.

"Take me to a gym." If he was going to be rude, then I was going to be rude right back.

He scoffed. "Who says we have one?"

I looked him up and down, his hulking build enough of an answer. "Call it a lucky assumption."

He rolled his eyes. "Why do you want it?"

"To bake a cake." I spat, leaning against the doorjamb and crossing my arms, keeping my stance relaxed to make him ever annoyed at my impertinence. "Why do you think? I want to hit something."

His eyes glinted, fangs peeking out from his smug smirk. "Hun-gry, are you?"

I glared at him. "Extra energy from being locked up against my will."

"You had a choice." He strode forward. "You could have let us take the others."

I shook my head, not in the mood to explain his stupidity. "Look, can you take me to the gym or not?"

He pursed his lips before letting out the deepest sigh of annoyance I'd ever heard. "Fine, go get changed and I'll get you soon." He stepped forward, pushing me back into the room, and slammed the door, a click letting me know he'd locked me in to wait for his impending return.

★★★

The gym was as state-of-the-art as the ones at the Compounds. The equipment looked up to date but was well-worn from use, all the guards most likely milling in throughout the day. Right then, however, it was empty. James must have gone there to clear it out before coming back for me.

I beelined for the row of punching bags in the far-left corner, completely bypassing the row of free weights and benches. I should probably have worked on rebuilding my muscle, but that wasn't enough. I ignored the neatly stacked tape on a table behind the bags and just started whaling on one, my knuckles bruised and small cuts busting open along them with each jab. I kept up a steady pace, trying everything I could to make the horrible itch of my hunger go away for just a few moments.

It wasn't enough, though. The lifeless punching bag was too boring. I needed movement and challenge. I needed something to make this stupid buzzing lessen across my body.

I halted, leaning my hands against the bag to steady it, my gaze running across the room. James was the only one with me, sitting in a chair in the corner, a stack of papers in his lap. I may not have known exactly what they were about, but I had read enough reports to know when someone was slugging through some boring work.

My shoulders perked up; maybe that was an opportunity I could take advantage of. At the very least, maybe I could get a few punches in. The idea of punching my annoying, hulking shadow a few times was immensely tempting.

I pushed away from the bag, sauntering over to the corner he sat in, and stood in front of him, arms braced on my hips.

"What? Our gym not good enough for you?" he asked, eyes never leaving his reports.

"If you're just going to sit there, you might as well fight me."

He glared up at me. "Pass."

I leaned forward, a smirk curling across my lips. "What? Scared a girl is gonna beat you?"

"Baiting me won't work," he taunted, returning to read the stack of papers.

I blew out a loud breath. "I thought you were supposed to keep an eye on me."

"I am."

"Well, Elliot made it seem like you have to help me with whatever I need."

His shoulders tensed, eyes peeking back up. "And?"

"And I want to fight someone." I looked around the room, pretending to search for a person in the crowd. "You seem to be the only one available to fulfill that need."

"You're a brat," he snarled, throwing the papers onto the floor next to him.

I shrugged. "I've been called worse."

He took a few deep breaths, rolling his eyes before standing up and removing the black sweater he had been wearing, leaving him in a plain white sleeveless shirt. His corded muscles flexed, arms stretching above and behind him. He rolled his neck a few times, the bones cracking under the slight tug he gave on his chin.

"You done?" I raised one eyebrow at him.

"Just stretching." He smirked, the scar on his face deepening into his cheek. "Let's go."

We went out to the training ring, the two of us circling around a few times to size the other up. I didn't care about winning, I cared about hitting and punching. I needed to move, to stop the stupid pin pricks, to get my mind back to center as best I could with the growing hunger rumbling in my belly.

I lurched forward, aiming for his face first. He dodged, allowing me to swing downward and get a hit into his abs, the muscles flexing under my touch. He growled, eyes flashing Shrivika red, my own sharpening to my favorite golden hue.

Yes, this would help.

We continued in silence, throwing and blocking. With each punch thrown and each one absorbed when he caught me, the buzzing eased, quieting to a slight ripple that was easy to ignore.

Thank the Goddess, this was working.

I sent a flurry of jabs, most of them missing before I caught him right in the chest. He blew out a shuddering breath, stumbling away. He looked up, darkness clouding his once bored gaze.

I thought he would rush me, but instead, he said, "How is

Haelyn? Is she okay?"

I took a few deep breaths, trying to understand what he was asking. "I don't know who that is."

"Yes, you do." He stared at me, begging me to try and understand. I racked my brain, thinking back to everyone I knew connected to this revolution.

Then it clicked, my memory bringing me back to the stack of papers I had found hidden in Vanessa's office. One of them had been real: Haelyn Vanessa Wells.

"You knew Vanessa?" I took a step forward, my heart lurching at his curt nod. She had told me so much before I went on my hunt, it was no surprise that I was meeting someone from her past. She had mentioned she had been higher up in Elliot's inner circle. "You were her husband, weren't you?"

"I *am* her husband." He growled, charging forward with a flurry of blows that I sidestepped. "Just because she ran doesn't make my vows to her any less real."

"Hate to break it to you, but it doesn't seem like she wants them anymore." I aimed for his face, my fist connecting with his cheekbone. He spit out a chunk of blood, unfazed as he slid back into a fighting stance.

"I love her." He threw his own punch, the strong force hitting my back, directly on my right kidney. I stumbled. "She was my everything, and I was hers."

"She left you."

"She left Elliot." He kept throwing and I let him. I let him get it out.

I could see it, the rage simmering under the surface. He most likely had to play pretend that the fact his wife left him didn't bother him at all. He was Elliot's second and if he showed love for someone that wasn't a part of the cause, he was a weak link. He was protecting himself, and it probably made the pain even worse.

But with me, the one person he was forced to be near that hated Elliot, he could show his truth. It was written all over his face, laced in every word he spoke of her.

He continued. "She left his cause. She was forced to leave me because of it."

It sounded like a comforting lie he told himself every night to get him through the pain. I couldn't help but feel a prick of sympathy deep in my chest. "You could have gone with her."

He growled again. "No. I couldn't."

I stared at him. Three words spoken, yet I could tell they were loaded with secrets I had yet to uncover. James was hiding something, and maybe, just maybe, if I figured it out, I could exploit it. I could use it to help take down Elliot and escape.

"Is she his sister or something?" I blocked his right hook. "The papers I found had the last name Wells."

He shook his head, aiming for my stomach, barely nicking my ribs as I dodged. "All of those in his inner circle have taken the surname. When Haelyn and I married, she took it as well."

Huh, that was interesting. He was creating himself a family and then probably used that loyalty to exploit them. Similar to how Eden's family ran things.

"Do you know why she ran?"

He grunted under the impact of my left jab, giving me one right back in the chest. "She had been spooked by something. Tried to convince me that what we were being told wasn't as it seemed. I tried getting her to explain, but she seemed too horror-struck to talk about it."

I ducked, punching upward, hitting right into his solar plexus. He stumbled, and I took the opportunity to punch him again, knocking him off balance, his hulking figure collapsing to the floor. I loomed over him, pushing my boot into the center of his chest to pin him, taking the win for myself.

"You should have listened to your wife." I narrowed my eyes at him, digging my heel a bit harder into his chest, a groan escaping him.

"I told her to go talk to Elliot, but she refused." He let his head drop to the ground. "A week later, she was gone, and I haven't seen her since."

"No idea what she saw?"

"No." He narrowed his eyes at me, his lips curling upward. "And even if I did, I wouldn't tell you."

Damn, he had caught on to my little manipulation. I wasn't surprised, but at least I had gotten a little bit of information. Although I didn't know how useful it was going to be, at least it was something.

I released him from under my foot, taking a step back. He sat up, eyes flashing bright red. "Elliot didn't tell you? He found her months ago."

"He wouldn't let me see her." He shook his head. "He wouldn't tell me anything."

"I'm sorry, but I can tell you that she's safe." I reached out my hand, his sweaty palm clasping mine as I helped him to rest on his knees. "And I'm sorry about this as well."

His brow pinched inward at my odd comment, giving me the opening to lunge for him, grasping onto the back of his neck and chin before snapping it to the left, his body crumbling to the ground in front of me.

CHAPTER 49

Kasha

He wasn't dead. That would be just too damn easy.

He was knocked out while his Shrivika body repaired the shattered bones I had created in his spine. But at least it was enough to give me a chance to escape that I wasn't going to waste. I reached down, searching his pockets before I came upon the ring of keys I knew worked on the front door.

The moment they were in my grasp, I hesitated, staring down at James's prone form. My mouth watered, my nose pulling in the rich scent of his pumping blood, the artery on his neck beating steadily.

I had to be quick. I didn't know if someone would come and check on us, but I couldn't pass up this opportunity to get my strength back.

Picking up his arm, I turned his hand over, exposing his wrist. I didn't hesitate to clamp my sharpened teeth into his warm flesh, taking insatiable slurps of blood from him. I didn't care that it was dripping down the sides and onto the mat below us, and even staining my shirt a bit. I took as much as I could, feeling the gnawing tingles along my body disappear and my muscles and mind sharpen and strengthen. I took more than I probably should have, but I needed to be careful since I wasn't sure when I would have this opportunity again.

It would have to be enough.

I peeked my head out of the gym, looking around and finding no one. I knew Elliot was out of the house, but who knew if more guards were around? Still, I kept to the walls and slowly made my way along the halls, down the stairs, my heart racing when I got the first look at the front door. My fingers gripping the keys tingled, my teeth digging into my bottom lip as I tried all the ones that looked like they could fit. Too many seconds passed, sweat forming along my hairline. Another, and another, and…

Click.

The lock gave way, the first rush of frigid air drifting into the house. I didn't linger, grabbing the first coat I could find hanging next to the door and bundling myself in it, even though it was obviously a size or two too big. Not caring, I ran out, down the path, and towards the center of town.

I started looking for a way out, to get away and try and locate the closest town in Luspan and report myself found. I kept to the outskirts, but I knew from the beginning it was a lost cause. The walls from when it was a Compound were still strong, no hidden holes, and it was well guarded by Elliot's team. There was no getting out; I was still stuck within its grip.

Still, I was free and away from Elliot. This was my first opportunity to try and figure out what in the name of the Goddess was going on with the place. I wandered around the town, keeping my head down and the hood of my coat flipped up, hoping no one noticed or recognized me. Everyone seemed so happy, delusionally so. It was disturbing, too perfect, making my skin crawl.

My eyes caught on a clinically white brick building, obviously ostracized from the rest of the town. My gut churned at the imposing structure, the bleached color letting me know this was one of the new constructions that must have happened when they built the town. It reminded me of the different medical clinics, my skin prickling at too many bad memories.

However, the one other place it reminded me of was the Alchemist Labs.

I had only been in a lab once, when I went through my Ibridowyn conversion. Lila and Ezekiel had mentioned a detox center. Could that be it? Something about it called to me, my instinct letting me know this could be important; that searching in there could give me the necessary information to take home to my team when they found me.

I moved towards the building, skirting to the back and looking for an alternative entrance to the double doors that stood out front. I finally found what looked like a service entrance, unsurprised by the locked door. Reaching inside my coat pocket, I pulled out the keyring and tried a few, and the door gave in.

I found myself in a back hallway, a few open doors showing off storage. I poked through a few, hoping to come across anything that may help me blend in…

I perked up, finding a box of lab coats and uniforms. Ditching my jacket, I threw on a long white coat, hoping it was what most of the people in the halls wore. I tucked the keys in one of the pockets, I drifted until I found a stairwell and headed upwards, ready to discover what the place had.

No shocker, it led me to a long hallway lined with doors, exactly like one of the wards I stayed on during my time at the clinic. I saw a few other employees drifting by, luckily in the same lab coat as me. I walked down, pretending to just blend in. There were viewing windows in each of the doors, although a few had curtains pulled over them. As nonchalantly as possible, I approached one of the closed-off windows, peeking at the clipboard hanging next to it. Stacked lines of information were jotted on it in mismatched handwriting:

"Crila, Joren. Age 32. Shrivika. Committed for Blackthorn. Day seven of treatment. Dosage: half diluted."

My brows wrinkled. I understood it was a patient profile, but what did the dosage mean? Were they giving a medicine to help with the addiction? At least I could confirm that I had found one of his detox centers. Lila never mentioned where she had gone, just that she had been safe. However, since she had met Elliot, I could only assume it was here.

I walked down the long hall, gently glancing into a few other rooms where the observation window was open. All those patients looked almost completely normal, a few ticks or paled complexions, but nothing like the detox centers I had witnessed that belonged to the state. When I peeked at their charts, none of them had been in treatment for longer than three weeks.

Lila hadn't been lying. What was going on here?

I looped around and headed back to the stairs, deciding it was time to explore more. I found one more level of detox patients and quickly went to the fourth floor. The long hall mimicked the others, rows of doors with observation windows and clipboards hanging next to each one. However, something about this space, the moment I walked to the level, made my skin prickle and my gut churn. Something was very, very wrong.

Would I dare walk forward and learn what horrors could be there?

I knew the only answer was yes, even though a small voice was telling me to run away.

I took a few steps forward, peeking into the first door I found with an open-view window.

A man recovering from something, half his face covered in bandages. The other half looked melted off. One arm was almost black, decaying flesh encroaching almost up to his elbow. Low moans of pain strangled from his lips, my stomach revolting, making me move to the next open window.

This one made my heart sink. I kept myself to the side since two physicians stood with the patient. One was injecting the young man, while the other pulled out a scalpel, going right for his chest, cutting a clean line right over his right rib cage.

"It's for the betterment of Kazola," the one who had injected the patient said. My hearing honed in to listen through the shut door. "You are going to help so many people by being a part of this study."

The man thrashed in their hold until whatever drug they had just given him took effect, then they started peeling away at his flesh.

I ran from that too.

Finally, I found a room that was less horrific, although that wasn't saying much as I took in the sight. This one had a clipboard next to it, a single line written across a piece of parchment:

"Patient A, test three."

No name, no treatment day, no species, nothing to make this person an individual. There were more notes scribbled at the bottom, but nothing I could make sense of without the proper degree. I looked inside once again, my heart lurching. A young female, probably no older than twenty-five. She had no signs of being a drug addict, but she didn't look well. Clothed in nothing but a thin, white slip, she lay on the bed, the blankets tangled around her feet. Her entire body was covered in a shiny layer of sweat, bright red lesions and rashes covering every inch of her sandy skin. She shook gently, pained whimpers drifting through the door.

Was she sick? Were they treating her? It looked like no disease I had witnessed, but I was no physician…

"I thought you would be a better spy than this." A voice jolted me away from the door, and I braced myself against the wall as I turned to face Elliot.

"Hey, I escaped from the house, didn't I?" My insides trembled but I refused to show him my fear. He could punish me or hurt me, but he would not get my fear, which belonged to me alone.

He chuckled. "If you wanted to see the lab, all you had to do was ask."

I swallowed. I wasn't sure if I wanted to see more. Elliot either didn't see my apprehension or didn't care. He held his arm out, daring me to take it and let him give me a tour.

"What is this?" I gestured to the window I had been looking in, the young woman letting out another strangled, desperate moan. "What is wrong with her?"

Elliot stopped next to me, looking in as well. He shrugged. "Seems the neurotoxin antidote we've been working on might be moving slower than we expected. Good catch." He winked at me, pulling a stilo from his pocket. He wore a matching lab coat to the one I had stolen over his usual three-piece suit.

"Working on?" My shoulders tensed.

"Yes." He nodded. "We wanted to see if we could counteract poisons specifically used to attack the nervous system."

I gaped in horror. "You're experimenting on people."

"They are willing participants."

"Did they know what they were signing up for? Were they sick beforehand, or did you poison them to test your serum?" I pushed back, following him as he strutted down the hallway, turning a corner and opening a new door. He gestured for me to walk through, and with a huff, I obeyed.

We found ourselves in an office of sorts, minimalistic and nothing like the one in his house with old-world opulence. All this had was a glass desk and three chairs, one behind and two in front. I whirl back around to him, slowly clicking the door closed. "Well?"

"Well, we needed to poison her to see if we could treat her." He said it so casually, like it was completely normal.

"That is not how experimenting works!"

I didn't know much, but Nana had explained a bit over the years that it took at least a few rounds of testing on synthetic materials and smaller creatures before testing on people was even allowed. Just by the way that poor woman was suffering in the room, my gut told me that those pre-testing steps hadn't been taken.

"It's quick and efficient. It helps to give us a better basis to understand why it's not working in our biology when it's working on animals." He walked around towards the desk. "Why waste time when we can perfect it quicker and help lives sooner rather than later?"

"You are torturing people!" I kicked the chair in front of me. I was pissed that he thought this was okay. "They surely didn't allow you to do this when you worked for the State."

I held my breath, wondering if he would admit to being the Alchemist my Nana had said he was, or if there was another explanation.

He let out an amused laugh.

"I shouldn't be surprised you figured out my past." He leaned against the front of the desk and smiled at me. "How is Agatha anyways? I haven't seen her in many years."

My mind spun. It *was* him that had worked in the lab. So why did he look at least thirty years younger than Nana when she had said he was only a decade below? Still too many holes in what was going on.

"When did you retire?" I ignored the personal question and went straight to learning more. He always said he was open to showing me the truth. Now we'd see how open he really was.

"I didn't." He raised his eyebrows in challenge. "They fired me."

"Let me guess, for testing on humans before approval?"

His impassive face gave away nothing. "Among other things."

"Even with that, you have found ways to keep creating and testing." I gestured around the room to represent the whole building. "And instead of trying to help Kazola, you use what seems to be the most effective treatment in drug addiction ever created to recruit soldiers to your cause. To brainwash them into believing you're a savior instead of being a decent person and opening true treatment centers. It's despicable."

"I created these serums many years ago." He smirked down at me. "When I was still a State Alchemist. It could have been theirs if they had desired to take it. But they didn't, so I use it for myself instead. Their loss."

I took a step back, chills running up and down my spine. "Impossible."

"Why?" He tilted his head, tucking his hands into the pockets of his coat. "Because the High Faction would never try and halt the safety and lives of those struggling with addiction?"

"They have state centers!" I argued. "They are trying to help, unlike you, who is using treatment as a brainwashing technique or blackmail."

"It would mean toppling the underbelly of Kazola, putting an end to the crime families and drug trade." Elliot tilted his head. "And they didn't want to do that."

I had no words to respond, so I just shook my head. He took my silence as an opening to continue.

"You see, taking down the crime families could topple Kazola. It could create mayhem," he said. "They may be hurting people, but in the end, they contribute somewhat to the economy. Plus, if we take away their drugs that they make money from, then who knows what they will start selling. It could lead to mass incarcerations that they don't have space for, or the tumbling of the economy if handled incorrectly. They would rather let them have the idea of power in their world and control it than stop it and risk Kazola."

I swallowed a lump in my throat, my mouth drying out. "I don't believe you."

He didn't seem fazed by my words. "Your choice. But this is why I have been starting my own drug trade and slowly pushing the major families and traders into tight spots. When I do take over, I will have control of both the High Faction and the Crime Families. I will be the first to have actual control over all of Kazola. We can stop the illegal trade in a controlled way that won't hurt the economy, slowly phasing it out until it no longer exists. The war on drugs will end."

My skin prickled, my mind trying to wrap itself around what he was saying. On the surface, it sounded like it could be positive for Kazola and help. But the churning of my gut, the doubt in my mind, knew it was too much power for one person to wield. If we let him take it, he would abuse it. He was too clever and cunning not to.

"Ah, you're finally here." Elliot smirked, looking over my shoulder. I peered over, seeing two guards waiting a few feet away. "Please escort Kasha back to our house. Her tour of the lab is complete."

They both nodded, waiting for me to move towards them. Instead, I turned back to Elliot. "I'm surprised you aren't bringing me back yourself."

"Unfortunately, I have more work to do." He took a step forward, crowding into my personal space. "However, before you go…"

He delicately gripped my right arm, lifting it and pushing back the sleeve of the stolen lab coat. He examined my forearm, my stomach churning, trying to tell me to escape. Before I could even pull away, he twisted my arm in a swift motion, yanking it back in an unnatural way, the bone crunching under the pressure.

I screamed, the sharp pain radiating up my entire arm. The bastard had just broken the bone. Intentionally.

"What in the name of the Goddess was that for?" I screamed as he let my arm go, the loss of support causing another jolt of pain to engulf my forearm.

"That was for feeding off someone without my permission." He nodded, my skin already starting to bruise. "You'll be fine. It's just a hairline fracture. A medic will meet you at the house to wrap it for you. But your accelerated healing will sap away that extra bit of strength you gained."

"Monster," I mumbled under my breath, cradling my injury against my chest, suppressing the whimpers that wanted to escape.

"I'll be back tonight for dinner. Have a good rest of your day, *Rogthna*." He waved over his shoulder, completely unfazed that I was in pain or that he hurt me. He pushed past the guards and into the hallway, the hem of his lab coat billowing behind him.

"What does that even mean?" My heart clenched, unsure if I was ready to hear the answer.

He peeked back at me over his shoulder. "Chosen."

CHAPTER 50

Nolan

Two weeks and one day.

Each hour that passed was torture, and I had to force my mind not to spiral. I just kept praying to Lunestia to keep giving Kasha hope. To give her a sign that I was coming. That I would find her, always.

For all I knew, the Goddess wasn't even listening, but at least it brought me comfort.

It was only fitting that it was gray and bitingly cold as my Gammas and I raced through the streets toward the lower district of Eroste. I had given Eden time to prepare, even though this had been her idea. I knew she was doing it for Kasha, for her sister-in-arms. Even so, this was not an easy decision for her, and although I had to constantly convince myself not to push, I hadn't.

The only thing keeping me from shoving Eden onto the back of my bike and driving her here myself last night was Kasha's voice in the back of my mind.

Protect her. My life is not worth Eden's sanity.

And although my unsettled wolf completely disagreed, I knew that was what she would say, and I would respect that. I would do this in a way that would make Kasha proud. That would make me worthy to be hers forever.

We finally slowed, Eden leading us to the side alley that flanked the Black Howl. We parked our cycles in a line, and Eden gripped her handlebars tightly for a few breaths before dismounting. Grey and I followed her toward the front door.

Toward answers, and ultimately toward Kasha.

I would get them one way or another. No matter what it took.

She whirled on both of us, Grey and I taking a step back at the cold, detached look in Eden's usually expressive green eyes.

"I know she is your everything, Nolan." She poked me in the chest. "But you've barely scraped the surface of the den of vipers we're about to enter. You have to let me take the lead with this. Trust that I want her home as much as you do and keep your cool."

I balled my fists at my side, white knuckles aching. I knew she was right, but I was on a razor edge of sanity with each passing day, and I wasn't sure when it would finally break.

"I'll try my best," I said, giving her a solemn nod.

She sighed. "I suppose that's the best I can ask for."

"What about me?" Grey asked, his arms crossed against his chest, face unreadable. Also normal for him.

She smirked up at him. "Be yourself."

He turned to me, giving me a wry smile and clapping me on the back. "Good luck."

I shoved him, a deep, soft chuckle escaping his lips as we entered behind Eden into the Tavern, the room already half full when it was barely noon. All eyes were on us, even though we had worn plain clothes instead of any of our military gear. It didn't matter, though. When Eden walked over the threshold, a pulsing tension filled the air, centered completely on her.

She ignored it all and went right to the bar, a petite young woman perking up the moment she saw us, the complete opposite reaction to everyone else in the room. "Little Sprite!"

Little... what?

Even in the dire circumstances that brought us there, I had to suppress a laugh at *that* nickname for my chaotic Gamma.

"Never call her that," Greyson warned me. *"Unless you want to find your ass on the ground."*

"Noted." I nodded.

Eden grabbed the woman's hands before she could wrap them around Eden's neck and pull her into a hug. "Lila, we need to talk, please. It's important."

Lila looked over Eden's shoulder to Grey and me. "What's going on?"

"You're not in trouble." Eden squeezed her hands, bringing Lila's focus back to her. "But... we need to ask you a few questions in private. Please. My friend... she's... please?"

Lila's face softened, gripping her little sister's hands back. "All right. We can go to the office."

I ignored the pointed stares as Lila led us to a back hallway. The black and gold décor followed down the winding path until we made it to a lone door. Lila pushed in without even knocking.

It was just as you would expect an office for the cover of a crime family. Opulent and big, a black-painted wooden desk sat in the center with a deep maroon wingback velvet chair behind it. Floor-to-ceiling bookshelves lined the wall behind it, but everything on it was obviously decoration and not for use. A six-person long conference table was off to the right of the desk, with a bar cart right next to it, and to the left was a black velvet couch with gold stitching embellished throughout.

The whole place screamed over-compensating prick. Lure them in with shiny objects in hopes that they don't realize how inept he is, most likely with both his mind and his dick, depending on who he brought through the doors.

"Where is Mylo?" Eden asked, a noticeable tension building in her shoulders.

"He's traveling. Just don't touch anything." Lila turned, sitting on one of the chairs at the long executive table. "What's going on?"

Eden let out a deep breath, striding over to her sister but not sitting, keeping the higher position. *Good. Show her who's boss, Gamma.* "My friend Kasha has been kidnapped. By Elliot." Her voice was grave, desperate to hide the true pain Kasha's loss was causing her.

Lila just laughed, shaking her head. "That's what this is about? Oh, Little Sprite, he didn't kidnap her. He would never. She must have just gone with him."

I growled, taking a step forward, but Eden shot me a withering stare, warning me back into place. I had to trust my Gamma.

This was going to be near impossible.

"No, Lila." Eden shook her head, gnawing at her bottom lip.

"He tricked her. Sent her on a wild chase with promises he never intended to keep and, when he finally got close enough to her, he snatched her."

Lila still looked unconvinced, pity in her eyes as she looked up at her younger sister, but Eden just continued. "We have been searching for weeks but have only reached dead ends. You said you met him at your rehab center. Where was it, Lila? Please tell me. It could save Kasha's life."

"I didn't know where I was." She shrugged irreverently, as if a person's life didn't hang in the balance. "And even if I did, I gave my oath to them. You just have to trust that Elliot is doing what needs to be done. She's there for a reason."

Her words were practiced, spoon-fed to her by those who had taken her vulnerability and spun it to their own needs. It just made the anger rise, my insides shaking and rumbling for me to act, to do, to protect.

Eden was going too easy on her, treating her with kid gloves when what we needed was answers.

I could get those answers.

"Calm, Nolan." Greyson's smooth voice invaded my head, his eyes darting over to me in warning. *"Lila's skittish, and Eden knows that. Trust."*

I clenched my fists again, keeping to my place near the desk, but with each passing second, my control slipped away little by little. Eden needed to hurry up, or I was unsure if I could keep my promise to her.

"Please, Lila. You know I wouldn't come here, begging for your help if I wasn't scared for my friend's life." She grabbed her sister's hand, squeezing it tightly. "Elliot took the person that is like…" Eden cut herself off, squeezing her lips together as if forcing the words back where they came from.

Anguish filled Lila's eyes, her voice quiet. "Like a sister to you?"

Eden didn't respond, regret and guilt flashing across her face. It was answer enough for Lila it seemed, confirming her question, making the pain sink deeper into the creases of her forehead.

As quickly as the hurt flashed in her eyes, she covered it, pulling her hands from Eden's grasp to flatten her well-pressed skirt over her legs and straightening her spine. "I can't help you. I don't know anything."

"Liar!" I finally snapped. I crowded into Lila's space, Eden quickly backing away, Greyson right there to help catch her stumbling steps. Rage built in my veins, bubbling over, refusing to be contained any longer the more traitorous words she spoke.

How did he do it? How did he get people to believe him? To obey him with such dedication? After everything he did, everything he was known for, they still followed. They trusted him above all else. They saw him as their savior when all he wanted was to fulfill some kind of God complex he easily masked behind a charming persona.

How long would my sweetheart last there? Could she survive?

All I had was my belief in her, and that needed to be enough.

I yanked the blade I had been carrying for weeks from its holster, slamming it on the table in front of Lila. Her body flinched at my rough impact. "Do you know what this is?"

"I-I think you all call it an Amalgam Blade," she stuttered, her face paling. Gone was her sister, replaced with a fuming Alpha struggling to keep his wolf at bay. I tried my best to rein it in. I didn't want to scare her too much, but if fear were the emotion to finally get through to Lila, I would use it.

"Correct, but this isn't mine, it's Kasha's." I braced my hands on the table in front of her, leaning closer so she couldn't ignore my looming presence for even a second. "It is the last thing I have of her because that precious savior of yours took her from me. From your sister."

Lila shook her head emphatically. "No, that's not true."

"You think Kasha wanted this? She has vowed her life to fight men like Elliot." Everything within me darkened, but I pushed on, letting it fuel my every word. "But if you can't do it for Kasha, for her safety, do it for your sister. Do it for all the times I know you let her down. Do it because you want to make her happy. You feel hurt that she considered Kasha her sister? Well, then give her a reason to finally look at you like the sister you should have been!"

I'm not sure where the words came from. Maybe from my desperate need for answers, but I knew it wasn't just that. Seeing Eden there, surrounded by the life they had planned for her, would have been shocking under any other circumstance. My Gamma had pulled herself from what most would consider impossible circumstances, a jail sentence to live her life as a criminal, and instead built herself not only a life separate from them but a place as a hero.

I would not let someone hurt her. Especially someone who claimed to still want to be her family.

"Nolan…" Eden's voice drifted from behind me. I looked over my shoulder, both her and Greyson looking at me with a mix of shock and awe at my outburst.

I gave her a small smile before whispering into her mind, *"I mean every word,"* before turning back to Lila.

Lila stared up at me, cracks breaking through the mask she was putting up as a happy, lovely person following Elliot's orders. She was warring within herself, struggling, and doing a horrific job at hiding it. Good, just one more push. One more…

Before she could answer me, a bang from the front pulled my attention away, my body shooting straight up from its crowding position over Lila.

"Rumor had it we had some Guards here." An imposing man strode in, his pointed chin rising high in the air. "Of course, seeing as they uphold the law, they would never start questioning someone without due cause or allowing them to summon their attorney."

"Silas," Eden sneered, disgust taking over every word.

"Eden," he said with just as much venom. "What can we help you with?"

"We were just asking Lila some questions pertaining to a missing persons case." She crossed her arms, every bit of warmth she had carried into this room to console her sister vanishing, replaced with the cool, calculating Gamma I knew her to be in certain situations. Fighting ones.

Who was this man to her?

He delicately placed his hand on Lila's shoulder, giving it a tight squeeze, my own body instantly tensing at the possessive gesture. "Well, then you should be aware that questioning someone without giving them the right to an attorney is against the law. Or did

Lila refuse to have me brought in to support her?"

I snorted. "You're an attorney?"

"Personally hired to handle the Bralechi Pack's business dealings and needs." He preened.

"So, you're Mylo's Second, then?" I tilted my head, knowing the answer before he even had to say it. He didn't have the build or the dominating energy needed to be in that position, and I had a feeling that pissed him off.

"No," he forced out from his sickly-sweet fake smile that only a lawyer would know how to make. "I'm just one of his closest friends and trusted business associates."

"That's a fancy way of calling yourself his loyal little lapdog," Eden spat, my eyebrows shooting up at the poisonous words. Damn, my Gamma had sharper teeth than I realized. "Can we please proceed with why we're here?"

"Sure, but I'll be staying." He smirked.

"That's unnecessary. I'm just talking to my sister."

The conversation was devolving quickly into who held the most power in the room. My skin started to itch, wanting to get back to the real reason we were there. For Kasha.

"Funny, I thought you weren't a part of this family anymore, Eden?" He took a step away from Lila, towards Eden, her muscles tense as he approached her. "Is that not true?"

"Just because I refuse to associate with criminals, doesn't mean I can't speak to my sister," she ground out through her teeth.

"You know that's not how it works with us, sunshine." She flinched at the nickname, her eyes darting to the door as if expecting someone else to walk through and call her that. "Once you start blurring the line between one member of the Pack, it's only a matter of time before you fall right back into your place with us."

"I am loyal to the Guard," she snarled, her fingers brushing over the hilt of her blade, making both Greyson and I follow suit in case of a fight. "I know exactly where my place is."

"That's the thing, Gamma." Silas spat her title out, his thin lips curling into a sneer. "You can dye your hair and mark your pretty skin with dozens of inkings, but it can't hide the truth. That's Bralechi blood running through your veins, Eden. You can't outrun your birthright."

She stepped forward, crowding into his personal space, her face eerily calm as she grazed her nose against his. Pure fury lit her gold eyes up as she whispered against his cheek, "Watch me."

They stared each other down, showing me just how little I knew about my Gamma and her elusive family. Seemed that what she had told me was only scratching the surface of the pain and hurt these people had put her through.

And they were doing it even more by trying to keep information about Kasha from her. The person who had been more of a sister to Eden than the woman now sitting in front of her that shared her blood.

Even more ire rose to the surface, my claws finally poking through at the tips of my fingers. If someone didn't say something helpful soon, I knew my wolf would be impossible to control. I wouldn't be able to stop the near-feral beast from breaking free and hurting all those in the room who had hurt the ones we cared about.

"Mountains," Lila whispered before I gave into the temptation, her gaze trained on the floor.

Eden whipped around to face her sister once again. "What?"

"When they were escorting me once into the town before they brought me back here," she said, looking up at all of us, "I saw that we were surrounded by mountains. Which means we were most likely in Luspan."

My heart cracked, veins flooded with all the shaking energy I had left, the thick control it had over me slowly loosening me from its rage-fueled hold.

Luspan. A direction. A place to finally start searching.

"Thank you," I said, with as much appreciation and gratitude as I could muster, my body sagging into a slowly building exhaustion that was catching up to me.

Eden walked over, placing a delicate kiss on her sister's forehead. "This means everything to me."

Lila grabbed her wrist, looking as if she was going to say something, but instead, she just gave her sister a smile and a quick squeeze. "I have to get back to work," she mumbled before scurrying past us and back to the bar.

Silas leaned against the desk, a murderous look on his sharp face, but I didn't care. We had a lead, a more focused location.

"*To Luspan,*" I said to them, my heart aching and my insides clenching.

Almost there. Almost back to her.

"Always a displeasure, Silas." Eden blew him a mocking kiss before strutting towards the door, Grey and I once again flanking her a step behind. She had been perfect, facing something that most would cower away from. I was once again in awe of my Gamma and the power she wielded.

But just as we reached the door, Silas's voice drifted to us. "I'll tell Lachlan you said hello."

She hesitated for a moment but never did her face waver or her confident stance slouch. Instead, she pursed her lips gently before continuing out the door, Greyson and I on her tail.

It wasn't the time to wonder who Lachlan was, my mind too preoccupied with Kasha and the news we had just learned.

One step closer.

CHAPTER 51

Kasha

James was no longer alone; at least two more guards were always with him.

He had not been happy when I had been shoved back into his care. He rarely talked; I was lucky if I got a grunt in response to my questions. And even worse, Elliot had added Ari to my guard rotation, meaning I was forced to spend even more time around her. The bitch always looked like she was forced to control murderous impulses every time we had to be in the same space.

Luckily, Elliot still told them to let me go to the gym, although I could not convince one of them to fight with me again. Was I surprised? No. But the blood lust was getting worse with each day that passed.

Foggy brain. Lethargic muscles. And the buzzing along my skin had shifted to a light burn as if I was sitting too close to a fire but not close enough to cause damage.

If I worked out, it cleared some of the slowness and helped me stay sharp, at least for a little while. Then I would go and eat or try and read. Usually, I could only last an hour before I was forcing my chaperones to bring me back so I could lift weights, or run on the treadmill, or punch the living daylights out of the suspended bags.

That day, I chose the latter. I was on day eighteen of capture now. Officially over two weeks away from home. They were coming, I knew they were. I just had to be patient. I was territories away, for Goddess sakes, in the middle of nowhere on what was technically private land. They needed enough time to find me, to figure out where Elliot had taken me, and they would.

Nolan would.

I would not give up hope. I would tell Nolan that I loved him one day, I knew that in my very bones. In my heart. This was not the end; it was just the unfortunate circumstances I found myself in. It would pass, and then I would be back home.

It would happen.

Or at least, that was what I kept telling myself to get through the days and the hunger.

I focused back on the bag in front of me, not caring when my guards all scrambled to attention. At least, until I heard them all salute and whisper.

"Can we help you, Sir?" Ari said in the overly accommodating voice she always used around Elliot.

I peeked around the bag, my nose wrinkling when I saw him enter the room. He waved them off, the three of them settling back to their posts, Ari sneering behind his back when he had passed her without a glance. He was focused on one thing, and it was not them.

"Are you sure you aren't overworking yourself, *Rogthna*?" he drawled, gliding across the room toward the punching bag I was beating the shit out of.

He was dressed in workout gear himself, a gray shirt, black loose pants, and boots. Similar to how he had been dressed in the woods, the shoulder holster secured tightly to him, the hilts of his twin blades peeking out.

My eyes drifted to them. I needed to find out which one was which.

I looked back up to him, a frown settled on my face. "What else am I supposed to do while I'm here?"

"I've offered plenty of options." He stood behind the bag, steadying it for me. "We could go to dinner, go shopping…"

"I do not want to go on a date with you!" I tried not to puke when I said it yet again. He had been offering every night at dinner, wanting to take me out somewhere special. "I have a partner."

"A partner who couldn't protect you," he stated as if it was nothing more than a plain fact. "Besides, they are not dates. How many times do I have to tell you? You're too young."

He told me that often, yet his obsessive attention didn't help to drive that point home.

"A partner who trusted me to take care of myself." I spat back. "But a psychopath decided to play dirty and kidnap me."

He just shook his head, laughter bubbling through his lips. "Whatever you say."

"What do you want?" I kicked the bag with a jolt, Elliot stumbling back a few steps at the swift swing. My chest burned a bit at the delight of seeing him falter.

"I need to work out as well." He shrugged. "You aren't the only one who likes to keep in shape."

I scoffed. I, unfortunately, was aware of this seeing as we were very well-matched during our fight in the woods. I bit my lip, my poor pride still healing from that disgusting memory.

"Would you like to spar with me?" He pointed over his shoulder, to the mat I hadn't stepped foot on since snapping James's neck.

"Seems unfair." I dropped my fists, sizing him up. "I'm weakened by starvation."

"You could remedy that quickly." He flashed his wrist to me.

I snarled. "Absolutely not."

It wasn't safe and I would not rely on him, become dependent. I didn't trust him to keep his blood clean and safe for me, even if it was taken directly from his veins. If anyone could find a way to make their blood addictive, it was Elliot.

I just needed to stay strong until my Faction came for me.

Breathe. I am stronger. I am free. I will always be free.

"Then I'll go easy on you." He walked backward towards the mat. "Look, I'm giving you the opening to try and punch me. Besides, no weapons this time."

He removed the holster from his body and slung it over a chair that lined the side of the sparring mat. Probably for guards who were resting before their turn.

"You can leave us." He waved to the guards. They all hesitated for a moment and then scurried out, eyes downcast. Ari was a bit slower, glaring at us over her shoulder, or more specifically me, before she disappeared on the other side of the door. He then made his way to the center.

This seemed off. Elliot didn't do anything without reason, which meant he was there for more than just a quick workout and letting me get out my frustration on him. He wanted something, but I couldn't figure out what it was. Was he looking to get me closer to him? Was he trying to wear me out quicker? Or was he just playing another game to make my head spin?

It made me even more curious to figure out what he wanted. So, I walked to the center of the ring and took my fighting stance, watching him mimic the action. We stared at each other for a few seconds, and I willed myself not to move. I didn't have the energy to spend. I had to lie in wait and see what he was willing to do.

He started with a false jab to the left, his right hand ready to punch me in the gut, but I dodged both. He was meticulous, even in fighting, and he was moving with me in each pace as we circled the room. I did my usual, taking up the defensive and formulating a plan before working my way slowly into the offensive.

And he took all of it in stride, barely breaking a sweat and smiling through the entire thing. He was watching my every move, not just to anticipate, deflect, and protect himself, but to observe as well. His eyes were alight with interest as if I was just putting on a show and not actively fighting him.

I growled, annoyed, and lunged, uppercutting to get a good, cracking hit against his chin. He stumbled back, shaking his head out a bit before righting himself and jumping right back into the fight.

"Do you like fighting, *Rogthna*?" He dodged my left hook, skimming downward and aiming a punch to my chest, but I jumped back just in time.

"Of course I do." I dodged to the left, missing a jab to my face. "I'm a soldier."

"But it's not just work for you, is it?" He smirked. "You like to watch people succumb to your strength. You like to win, to draw blood."

My veins chilled, my fingertips prickling. Where was he going with this?

"It's okay to admit it," he coaxed. "I love knowing I have the power to take what I want. It's thrilling, no?"

"How can you even admit this to me?" I shook my head, my heart racing, my mind trying to understand the motive behind his words.

"Because people have hurt me." He swung at me, and I dodged, my muscles starting to weaken, barely missing. "They have tried to take everything from me, labeled me a fanatic. They wanted to silence me, and I chose to take that back."

"You have chosen destruction!"

"Destruction of corruption for the betterment of Kazola," he argued once again, even though I didn't believe a word. "People have hurt you too."

"Don't you dare talk about my past!" I snarled, throwing a flurry of jabs he easily blocked.

"Logan tried to take your dignity, your pride, and your honor." He punched with more strength and speed, stalking me around the ring as I tried my best to keep my distance and move around. "And that man, that criminal, who took your mother away from you? He killed her in cold blood."

"Shut up!"

"She never saw you grow up. She never saw you become a Guard." I kicked out, aiming for the delicate place between his thighs, but he shoved my foot away, my steps fumbling. I snarled. "She'll never see you fall in love."

"You do not deserve to talk about my mother!" I bellowed, forcing back the tears his words were bringing to the surface.

"Then tell me this. Is there not a part of you that wishes to watch them bleed?" His eyes were wild, but his movements were calculated and true.

It was becoming impossible to dodge them all, my stomach and ribs taking a few hits, but I stayed upright through the pulsing pain in my abdomen, the ache of fresh bruises already blooming.

"Don't you want to see them get what they deserve?" He smirked. "Don't you want to take from them? Give them a taste of their own medicine? Give in to the darkness I bet you have to hold back and smother every day?"

My body froze, mind reeling because no matter how badly I wished to deny his disgusting claims, I couldn't.

There was a part of me—a tiny, dark part of me—that had wished it.

I would not be remorseful if they died. I would never shed a tear for them and would even enjoy watching them bleed. I would want to know what their blood felt like seeping between my fingertips. I knew I had the power. When I was strong, I could take from them just as they had taken from me.

It was black, inky, and gross, but never would I revel in the power I had to destroy them. Never would I hunt them down and take their lives. It would make me no better than them. And that was my only saving grace; that I was better than them.

I was better than the man in front of me as well.

He was crazy and dangerous, and I needed to stop him. All I needed to do was get to that dagger that I had now slowly moved us closer to. All I had to do was get one good roundhouse kick to his solar plexus, send him flying, and then I would have mere seconds to grab a dagger before he gained back his breath and was on top of me.

It was a long shot, but it was the only way to potentially put a stop to the madness.

I was slower and weaker. I shouldn't have been able to win this. But it was my chance, most likely my only one, to end this.

I drew in my strength, I prayed to the Goddess, and I focused on returning to my family, my Faction, and Nolan. I took all of that hope, love, and devotion and pooled it into my center, swirling it, thriving off it, and discovering that last burst of strength that would get me through and help me survive.

I spun. I kicked. I ran.

I lunged for the holster hanging over the chair. Fifty-fifty chance of picking the weapon that would hurt him, even kill him.

I didn't have time to think. He was screaming, charging me from behind. So, I grabbed, praying I had picked the right one, and twirled around to face my captor.

I briefly caught sight of the wooden tip before arching it over and slamming it right into his heart.

CHAPTER 52

Kasha

My throat dried at the pooling blood that seeped between my fingers still gripped onto the dagger.

The scent was intoxicating, my gaze locked and mesmerized by the sticky liquid that spread and coated my hands. My mind filled with the small, feral voice that had come to reside there over the past few days, tempting me to lean forward and drink.

To take. To feed. To give in.

I shut it down. He would die at my hands, which meant I could finally feed from a safer source. My eyes twitched, fingers going numb, but I stayed true to what I needed to do for my own safety, even if starving myself seemed far from it. My gaze roamed upwards, to watch the light leave Elliot's eyes. I wanted to watch them dim, to see the moment I won.

But it never came.

He was staring down at me, pain etched along his face, but no fear. Not an ounce of regret or desperation for life. He was just smirking, a laugh bubbling from his lips where even more blood spilled, staining his teeth crimson. Sweat coated him, limbs shaking from adrenaline, all the signs that his body would shut down shortly.

And he wasn't scared.

And that was when I felt it, something my own body did. His skin and bones and organs trying to repair themselves, even though the dagger was still inside him. There was only one reason this would be happening. Only one species on the Isle of Kazola. One who was created, not born.

"Impossible!" I seethed, ripping the dagger from his chest and throwing it onto the ground.

"Are you so sure about that?" He laughed some more, throwing his head back against the wall. "Damn, that hurts like a bitch."

"I stabbed you in the heart!" I ripped at his shirt, exposing the gaping wound even more, gently pressing my fingers against his throat to measure his pulse. It wasn't strong by any means, but it was gaining steadiness, not dissipating like it should have been.

Any Shrivika would be dead by now, no matter how strong or how recently they fed. A wooden dagger to the heart was almost an instant kill.

He should be dead in my hands.

"We're more alike than you think." He grabbed the front of my shirt, his grip weak, but still using it to anchor us together.

"This can't…" My mind was far too fuzzy from the adrenaline mixing with the lack of feeding. I knew what I wanted to say, but I couldn't. If I said it out loud, it would be a reality, and there was no way that this could be the truth.

"Say it," he sneered, licking his blood-coated lips. "I dare you."

"You're an Ibridowyn," I whispered, daring myself to take that one final step in hopes that he would deny it, even though I knew the truth deep in my bones.

"Yes." He winked at me.

I punched him across the face, needing an outlet for the rising rage that was boiling over within. He was a Brido, so he could take it.

"Cheap shot." He rubbed his jaw, a hint of amusement still gleaming in his gaze.

"How?" I demanded, taking a step back but not moving too far away. I needed him in fighting distance, in case I wanted to hit him again.

"It was quite simple, actually." Somehow, he was still standing upright, his hands now clutched over his chest, muscles shaking. It was obviously taking a lot of effort for him not to sink to the ground, but apparently, he was going to face me on his feet.

"Tell me," I demanded. It was an empty demand, but it didn't stop me.

"Well, when the High Faction rudely fired me, I was still given an opportunity to go back to my lab and gather my personal effects." He rolled his head against the stone wall, looking up to the ceiling as if reminiscing. "They forgot I had been assigned to do the next round of Brido injections that week, and I had the vials already set up for when the new Guard members came through. I slipped a vial into my pocket before they came to check my things. They searched my bags and the pockets they could see. Luckily, I had always been one to create hidden ones in my clothes."

"Paranoid from the beginning, huh?"

"I'd say it's smart on my part." He looked back at me. "I began to formulate my plans for the Prophecy almost immediately after I left. Once I knew it was time to begin gaining my inner circle and followers, I injected myself."

I hated how much this made sense, how pieces were starting to come together and create some form of logic around the anarchy that moved around him.

"How old are you?" Another question that had confused us with Nana's tale.

"Seventy-four." He preened as much as he could with a gaping hole in his chest. "I look good for my age, don't I?"

I gagged, my tongue sticking out and bile rising in my throat. He had flirted with me a lot when he worked in the bar. And I let him.

Goddess, I would never be able to forget that.

My mind raced, trying to bring together different questions that I knew were listed on the board back at my Compound. With each day I spent there, more and more of them were being checked off. I wasn't sure if he was giving me too much trust or was confident that I would never return to my Faction and family, but he had certainly loosened his lips since bringing me there. I supposed if anything was worth this, it was the clarity I would bring back to them when Nolan saved me.

I stilled, my body covered in chills.

Something clicked. Something that mattered to one of the most important people in my life. A question he had always wanted answered.

And I think I finally found it.

"Cleo." I pointed to Elliot. "The Brido you killed. She figured it out, didn't she? She knew you were a Brido and that's why she had her Ogdala Dagger when she went to confront you."

It made sense. Nolan had told me about the case at the beginning of his time there, saying he just wanted answers on how his fiancée had been killed and how Elliot had gotten the one weapon that could kill her.

"She was a smart woman." He looked me up and down. "Apparently, that lover of yours has a type."

I snarled, my white-knuckled fists shaking at my side. "Don't ever talk about him."

Never would he be worthy to utter Nolan's name. I would have stabbed him again, but I needed more answers.

"So, you took her weapon and killed her with it?" I shook my head. "Have you no honor?"

"Actually, I killed her with the Ogdala Dagger that I have." He shrugged. "It took me a few years to obtain the right materials, but once I had a few suppliers on my side, it was easy to gain and forge my own for safety reasons. We fought and I won."

"Their Faction's blade was found in her chest."

"I couldn't let them think I had used my own." He rolled his eyes. "So, I shoved hers in the wound before dumping the body."

"Just when I think you can't get any worse."

He snorted. "You should be thanking me. If I hadn't gotten her out of the way, he would be blissfully mated to that woman, and you would still be all alone."

I was on him once again, shoving him into the wall, my finger wrapped in the tattered remains of his shirt. "You are a disgusting piece of trash if you think I would thank you for causing Nolan four years of unresolved pain. I would gladly give up my now happiness so he would never have to experience the trauma that *you* put him through."

He stared at me, pulling in a deep, unsteady breath before that obnoxious smirk spread on his lips, watery, pink blood staining his teeth.

"You look hungry, *Rogthna*." He leaned towards me, using one arm to keep himself upright on the wall. "Your pupils are dilated, your fingers shaking. And your scent is souring a bit."

I hissed, my insides quivering, begging me to take some of the copious amounts of blood that still leaked from the healing wound. "I'm fine," I gritted through my teeth.

"No, you're not."

He raised his hand, his blood already starting to dry, but he went back to his wound, rubbing it around and coating it even more. I was mesmerized, unable to control myself because all I could do was lust after the warm, sticky liquid that I needed, craved to slurp at and drink. The whispers in my mind grew stronger, urging me to do it. To take it, to feed…

Which was why I didn't even notice when he reached for me, blood-coated fingers sliding across my lower face, trying to force their way into my tightly closed lips. Marking me, tempting me, his essence and scent now surrounding and mixing with my own.

I screamed, stumbling away with tears pricking at my eyes. My entire body felt on fire, consumed with the need to lick my lips. It would give me strength. It would make me feel better.

Give in.

I collapsed to the floor, my fingers desperately trying to wipe away the sticky substance, but it only made it worse, my own fingers coated in it from when I stabbed him. I howled, my wolf itching and scratching, trying to get to me, to protect me, to find out what was wrong.

If only I could give her the ability, but over the past few days, she had dimmed a bit, my lack of feeding weakening her as well. I knew that little voice that was tempting me to feed had been her. She wanted strength again. Blood would give it, so she couldn't understand why I was depriving us. Her feral, basic instinct was to keep strength, not willingly give it up.

It twisted my soul every time I had to ignore her. I just had to believe it was the right move for both of us in the end.

"Soon, *Rogthna*." He took a few stumbling steps forward, finally falling to his knees across from me.

I didn't have the strength to respond, ripping my shirt over my head and scraping violently at my face, desperate to remove as much of the blood as possible before I did something I would forever regret. I needed to get his blood away from my lips, even if it meant scratching my skin off.

I let out one gasping weep before pulling them back in, but it was enough. He had heard it.

"James!" he shouted, the front door immediately banging open, the hulking man striding across the room quickly.

"I told you this was a stupid way to show her." He slung Elliot's arm over his shoulder.

"You knew?" I gaped at him.

"That the God and Goddess have blessed him with immortality?" James looked me up and down like I had grown a second head. "Of course. Most of us do."

"What?" I creased my eyebrows. That was never how we had explained the transformation process that the Alchemists put us through. It was simply just the procedure. A procedure that was completely reversible. Although it protected us while we were in the guard, we far from considered ourselves immortal, since it could be taken from us on a whim if necessary.

Which meant Elliot had never told them but built his own reality around his new species designation. He was using it as a manipulation tool to gain followers and power.

I wanted to throw up, my body physically rejecting that reality.

"The other guards will bring you back to your room," James shot at me, starting to walk and half drag Elliot along with him.

I was stuck in place, watching them slowly hobble away. Too many emotions pooled in my stomach, warring with the information I had just learned. I wanted to cry, to scream, to tear at Elliot again, even though I knew it would be a fruitless endeavor.

He was so much more dangerous, so much more in control than I could ever have guessed.

It was then that I finally admitted it to myself. Elliot could get everything he wanted.

Kazola. Power. Revenge. Me.

It was the worst kind of pill to swallow; bitter, terrifying, and lonely. Everything that was swirling in me started to crack me from the inside out.

And when he looked over his shoulder and winked, he knew he had demolished something within me.

CHAPTER 53

Kasha

I couldn't work out anymore. The hunger had surpassed that coping technique.

Three more days had passed since I stabbed Elliot in the chest. I had woken up the next day feeling weighted down by lead, my stomach constantly rolling with nausea, my body covered in cold sweats, and every inch of me twitching in bed. So much of my strength had been sapped, my Ibridowyn abilities following.

I had been trying to reach out to any guards, to see if I could mentally connect with someone in the area. But those who I had strong pathways with were too far away and I didn't know many guards in Luspan to even try and form a connection. Now, with my body so drained and weakened, I didn't think I could mentally connect with anyone unless they were standing right next to me.

I needed blood; my wolf was getting restless.

She itched at me from the inside out, whispering to me, tempting me. If I drank blood, I would feel better. I would feel strong. I could fight Elliot. I could do my job.

I refused.

Then, she resorted to threatening me. She told me I was a bad Varg Anwyn. She told me I was weak. She told me she would abandon me again because I wasn't giving her a safe space.

Even though it terrified me, I still refused.

I had no idea anymore if this was my wolf talking or some kind of blood-deprived torture that I was creating within my own mind. Late-stage hunger symptoms included hallucinations. Had I reached that point already? Based on some case studies I had read about when I was training in the guard, they tended to be more visceral—people or objects or animals appearing to you, not voices. But I supposed I could have reached that point.

I tried not to think about it too much as I went about my day, no longer leaving my room as I had no strength or desire to venture out. It was late afternoon when James barged into my space. I had somehow gotten the strength to shower, the ice-cold water painful against my sensitive skin, although it did ease a bit of the warmth that now covered every inch of me.

"Get up," he demanded, eyes narrowed on me slumped in the chair, staring into the fire.

"Why?" I rolled my head to look at him, his form a bit blurry with my unfocused gaze.

"Elliot wants to talk to you."

"Ugh." I somehow managed to stand, my legs shaking, but I was upright. He moved back towards the door, expecting me to follow. Of course, I did, because at that point, I was too weak to argue.

Had walking always been this annoying? I didn't like it anymore.

Finally, we made it to the office I had first seen when I had woken up. Elliot stood in front of his desk this time, leaning against the edge with his arms crossed. So calm and collected, as if this was just any normal day. Nothing rattled this man, which just set me off. Too bad I was too weak to do anything about it.

He just stared at me, looking me up and down. To James, it looked like we were in a stare-off, but I knew what was really happening. The light knocking in my mind, something clawing at the edges, begging to be let in. He was trying to mind speak with me.

He was an Ibridowyn, and he had that ability.

I strengthened the barrier I kept around my thoughts, refusing to let him in. It was a struggle, feeling it deep in my muscles even though it was typically second nature, but I held it firm. He could deprive me of blood, but he would not get into my mind.

Yet.

"How are you today, *Rogthna?*" He looked me up and down. "Looking a bit pale."

"What do you want?" His pleasantries were particularly grating on my nerves that day.

"I have a gift for you." He smiled, that devious glint in his eyes sending a ripple down my spine. I swallowed, trying to keep my face as neutral as possible. "Bring him in."

The door burst open behind us, one of the nameless guards dragging in a man. His face was covered with a bag, his clothing dirty and torn, skin smeared with sweat and dirt. I wasn't sure if he was homeless or had been in a holding cell somewhere in the town, but I figured both were an option.

The guard dropped him in front of Elliot, the man collapsing onto his knees, trembling. Muffled sounds were coming from the bag, but nothing made sense. The guard left, leaving me alone with Elliot, James, and the mystery hostage.

"What is this?" I demanded, taking a step away from James and towards Elliot.

"I told you, a gift." Elliot tilted his head. "One I think you'll be quite pleased with."

He reached down and ripped the bag off the man's head, revealing a guy who had to be in at least his fifties, although he looked much older. Dark circles rimmed his eyes, wrinkles covering his gaunt face. His shoulder-length sandy blond hair was brittle, clumps missing from his head. The woodsy undertone of his soured apple scent told me he was a Varg. He looked on the verge of death, but it was a face I could never forget, no matter how withered and frail he now looked.

I hadn't seen him in fifteen years when he got off his trial on a technicality.

"You!" I snarled, lunging for the man who killed my mother, my fingers wrapping around his throat to keep him on his knees.

"Wh—who are you?" He looked up, milky blue eyes barely able to focus on me.

"Still into Wolfsbane, I see." I gripped a bit harder, the man choking on air. "Have you stopped selling and are now using?"

His cheeks reddened. "I don't know what you're talking about."

"Allona Mallanis." I made him look me in the eye, his own widening at the mention of her name. "Ring any bells?"

"Um… well…" He shook his head, his pulse racing under my grip. *Good. He should be scared.*

"Remember at your trial, the little thirteen-year-old girl who sat in the front with the rest of the family?" My arm was shaking, and I didn't care that there was an audience. I had been haunted by the potential for this moment for too long. It had arrived, and I was taking advantage.

He gulped, the pressure of it pressing against my palm. "You were the daughter."

"Yes, of the Gamma you murdered in cold blood!" I threw him, his body skittering back a few feet and crumbling. I was weakened, but at least I was stronger than a drug addict. He whined, the scent of urine filling the air. I rolled my eyes. What a wimp.

I looked up to Elliot. "How did you find him?"

"One of the perks of overthrowing the strongholds of Kazola is access to many important people in the government and the underbelly." He walked towards me, steps slow and methodical. "After you told me about him, I knew you deserved to confront him again."

"How is this to help me?" I shook my head. "He got off his trial! There is nothing I can do but let him go."

He pulled out the silver dagger from the holster on his hip, the tip gleaming in the light. Reaching out, he offered it to me. "There is one more thing you can do."

My eyes widened. "No."

"Are you saying you don't want to?" He reached down and grasped my wrist, pulling it towards him palm up so he could place the dagger in my hand and wrap my fingers around it.

I let him do it because I wanted to feel the weight of the weapon. My heart beat violently against my chest, my brow sweating. The temptation of what he was offering swirled within my veins.

He moved to my side, leaning down to whisper in my ear. "You deserve the vengeance you have been deprived of for so long. Don't you want that? This man has walked free in Kazola for fifteen years while your mother has not. Is that fair? Is that the Kazola you want to live in?"

"Are you saying you would create a better one?" I stared at him, my chest heaving deeply with stuttering breaths.

"Criminals will be dealt with properly in my Kazola." He leaned forward. "You wouldn't have had to wait through a whole trial just to have him set free. I would have been able to make that decision right away, and he wouldn't have walked away, I promise you that."

I shook my head, my thoughts too scrambled between my fury at the man in front of me and the vows I made to serve Kazola. Killing this man, no matter how many times I had daydreamed about it in the darkest parts of my mind, was not who I was. I protected life. I did not take it whenever I saw fit. It was not my place to make this choice; it never would be. No matter the heartache and pain he put my family through, taking his life would make me no better than him. And I would not sink that low.

"No." I shook my head, throwing the dagger on the floor and stumbling back. "I will not become who you want me to be. Not when I already know who I am."

I was expecting anger and lashing out. I expected him to punish me, hit me, or do something. Instead, he just looked at me with pity because I would not take the man's life.

"I suppose that's your choice." He reached down, picking the dagger up. However, instead of putting it back in its holster, he grabbed the man by his hair and sliced a clean, meticulous line right across his throat and carotid artery.

I screamed, my hands covering my mouth, shaking. I had seen death, witnessed it, and even doled it out on some dark occasions, but never had it affected me as this did. His body collapsed to the floor, eyes bugged open as he gurgled for breath around the blood already welling from his lips. He began to seize, hands grasping at his gaping throat in hopes of stopping the bleeding, but it was pointless. In only seconds, his body stilled, and his eyes drained of any life.

He was dead.

"How could you?" I whispered.

He wiped his blade off with a cloth from his pocket, moving towards his desk to throw it away. "I will be your darkness until you are strong enough to embrace your own."

I struggled for words, for anything to say to the evil man in front of me. I should have been screaming, fighting him. I should have told him this was not what I wanted, that pointless death and killing was not the way Kazola should be run. Ruthlessness did not equal prosperity, it represented tyranny. But I didn't say any of that, I couldn't.

I was too transfixed on the bright red blood spilling from the gaping wound.

My stomach growled, something within telling me to take, to

finally sate the desperate hunger I had been living with for so long. It didn't matter that he had killed my mother. It didn't matter that he was a criminal or that he was the reason that my family had broken all those years ago.

All I saw was blood. So much fresh, delicious blood spilling from that large artery in his neck. It was bright and beckoning; every drop that fell to the floor wasted.

I was no longer in control, the hunger was. It wasn't me who leaped forward. It wasn't me who threw herself on the body, and it wasn't me who clamped her canines on the dead man's throat and slurped like a glutton.

At least, that was what I had to tell myself because if I thought too hard about it, that I was taking life from the man who stole my mother's, I didn't think I could come back from that.

So, I drank and savored and moaned as I stole as much as I could, not caring that I had an audience. I was greedy and gross, covering myself in the substance I had been craving for many weeks now. My body sang at the first drop and begged me to take as much as I wanted.

Drink. Drink. Drink. More. More. More.

It was all I could do, my only focus. I wanted it to go on forever, or until my belly was finally warm and full.

But that would have been too easy. Too kind.

Instead, it was only seconds if I had to guess, my mind still fogged when long fingers grabbed my hair and yanked me away like a feral animal that needed to be controlled.

I screeched and kicked and fought as that tight grip dragged me away, taking me farther and farther from the body I had been feasting on. Finally, we stopped, Elliot crouching down in front of me, his grip still tight in my hair.

"Oh, bad, bad, Kasha." He tisked, eyes shifted blood red but a smirk on his lips. "You know that's not allowed."

I cried, tears rolling down my cheeks, tangling with the warm, sticky blood smeared along my jaw and up my cheeks. "Please," I begged. "I need more."

His hand moved from my hair to my throat, gripping me tight, my breath struggling to pass through properly. "You know the rules. If you want blood, you take from me. Are you finally willing to give in? Are you finally going to let me take care of you and help you?"

It was stronger this time, the temptation. After getting a sip of blood after so long, my body craved it even more, knowing it wasn't enough.

I clenched my fists, my teeth grinding together as I forced myself to say, "No."

He shook his head. "Stubborn girl, only hurting yourself over stupid pride." He released me with a shove, my body falling backwards. "Take her back to her room."

Arms yanked me up, tugging at my muscles in the wrong way, but I didn't care. I let them push and move me around to their liking. The blood had diminished some of the more intense symptoms, my muscles a bit stronger and my legs no longer shaking, but it wasn't enough. My mind was still foggy and my body still compliant to whoever was stronger than me.

James began walking us towards the door until Elliot stopped us.

"One more thing," Elliot called out, both of us turning to look at him. "You're no longer to leave your room. Lock her in there, James."

Panic settled in my mind and body, breathing no longer even and my memories spiraling to another time I was locked in a room.

White walls. Doctors. Forced space. No escape.

"No, no, no, no, please!" I shook my head, trying to break James's hold, but he was too strong, wrapping his arms around me from behind and clamping my arms to my side. I was stuck in his vice grip. "You can't lock me in! Not again! Not again, please!"

"You broke the rules, so you must be punished." He tilted his head, giving me a warm smile just as all those doctors had in the facility. "It's for your own good, so you can learn. You'll see."

I didn't have words or thoughts or ideas. All I knew was that I couldn't go back into a locked room. I tried to fight, to kick back and force myself out of the hold, but I was just too damn weak. I was at their mercy. I sank into the tight hold, giving up and unable to fight anymore.

It no longer seemed worth it.

CHAPTER 54

Nolan

Three weeks and three days.

We had been in Luspan for a week, working with their Faction to try and find Kasha as quickly as possible.

But that was the problem with Luspan. It was covered in mountain ranges, making traveling across the largest territory on the Isle slow and complicated. Towns were easily hidden, and a lot of private property was sanctioned off. So, unless we had search warrants and evidence to back them up or approval from local authorities to come and search, we couldn't raid them. Which meant even with a Territory to search, the pursuit for Kasha was still moving too slowly for my sanity.

I even tried to reach out to her, to find that mental pathway to her mind to let her know we were close. But I could never find it. She was either too far away or too weakened to be able to have a far enough mental reach to me. I prayed it was the former.

"I just got word from my Gamma." Dornan, Luspan's Alpha, strode through the door to their conference room, a mirror of our own. "Ralaria was a bust." He went to the map we had tacked on the far wall to track our search progression and drew a small X over the town.

I had never been in a Faction with Dornan, but my path had crossed his three years ago when he asked me to consult on the Elliot case when he had been sighted there. It had only been for two months, my heart still freshly bruised from the loss of Cleo.

And now I was back, even more heartbroken over the loss of Kasha.

At least this time I still had hope that I would find her before it was too late.

"Damnit." I clenched my fists, forcing myself not to bang it against the table, my arm quivering under the desperate need to punch out my frustration.

Coming here had been a give-and-take. It wasn't my territory, which meant in the end I didn't have the control I would have liked to lead the search. I needed to rely on Dornan and his team.

But we were closer, I could feel it in my bones. This was the territory Kasha was in. Maybe it was wishful thinking or me just going crazy over trying to find her, but that hum in my chest beckoned me to keep going, keep searching.

Yeah. I was most likely going crazy.

I shook it off, raking my fingers through my hair and breathing deeply a few times before unfurling my fists. I needed to stay focused and calm.

"Next steps?" I asked the group of tired Ibridowyn in the room with me, leaning forward.

"Liv and I are going out with some of the team later today,"

Eden said. "We were able to get in contact with another mining town who is willing to talk to us and let us look around."

I nodded. "Thank you. Grey, Lucas, and I can send out more letters in the meantime. Hopefully, we'll get a few more positive responses."

"Beckett should arrive tomorrow night too," Liv noted.

Beckett and Emric had been switching off every few days so at least one Keturi member remained on our Compound. Emric had left that morning, and knowing Beckett, he would drive all night to get there as quickly as possible.

We were making moves, slow ones, but it kept me moving forward. It kept giving me hope, and I just had to pray that Kasha was still holding out hope too. That she had enough trust and faith in me to keep true to my promise.

It was steps forward. All leading to finding her.

"Alpha Nolan?" A young Omega knocked on the partially open door, a letter clutched to his chest.

"Yes?" I waved them in, trying my best to soften my expression so as to not scare him.

"This just arrived for you via Falcon Mail." He extended the letter towards me, the plain envelope unadorned, with just my first name scribbled across the front in sloppy writing.

I smiled, but inside, my stomach was rolling as I wondered what could be hidden inside. Was Elliot watching us? Was he sending me something to taunt me with? I had seen plenty of handwriting samples of his, and none of them looked even remotely close to this. His penmanship was perfect, sleek, and professional, even when writing a taunting letter about killing others.

This looked rushed, as if the writer barely had five seconds to get it down and sent out. With a deep breath, and the rest of my team's gazes focused on me, I ripped into it, pulling out its contents.

In the end, it was nothing but a square piece of parchment, a few words written across it in the same rough handwriting as the envelope:

"Your heart can be found in the Sanctuary of Guards once past."

"What the…" my voice trailed off, reading it over and over again.

Your heart… my heart…

"Kasha," I breathed out, my finger tightening around the paper. It was sheer will keeping me from ripping it in half. "It's about Kasha." I read the words out loud, tracing them with my fingers.

It was a clue to where we should go.

"What does it mean?" Liv asked. My mind was screaming at me. It was difficult to focus on the words because all I knew was that this would lead me to her.

Find her. Save her. Protect her, my wolf screamed, not caring that we still needed to figure out where the hell this was.

Eden peeked over my shoulder to look. "Nolan, there are coordinates at the bottom."

I gasped. I had been so focused on the words, at the hint that Kasha was close, that I hadn't even noticed the combination of letters and numbers scribbled across the bottom.

"Where is this?" I shoved it at Dornan, his hand already outstretched to look. He walked over to the map, eyes scanning over the large picture.

"Here." He tapped on an area at the northern tip of the territory.

"But that can't be right."

"Why not?" Liv asked, her fingers twisting together in front of her, our nerves setting in, the room filling with an uncontrollable tension.

"That's the old Faction Compound that was sold over five years ago." He shook his head. "It was sold to a mining family who was expanding to the mountain range a mile north."

"Or so they led you to believe," Greyson said, arms crossed tightly against his chest.

"The note said we could find her in a sanctuary of guards once past." Eden pointed to the words. "This has to be it."

"That's where she is," I said, my chest tightening, that bit of hope I had been clinging to cracking through even more. "That's where we go next. That's where we focus."

"Do you think it's another trap?" Greyson asked, speaking the words none of us had wanted to whisper, to bring negativity to such a potent lead.

"Elliot is a direct person. He wouldn't speak in code like this." I took the parchment back. "Plus, he likes to play games. Why give the coordinates? He would want us tripping over the riddle, focused on trying to decode it, not just lead us right to him and Kasha."

"He's also a perfectionist," Eden pointed out. "I don't think he would ever send a letter with such scribbles."

"He's above hiding his identity now, so there would be no need to disguise his handwriting," I said, my soul settling, trusting my gut that I knew following this lead was the right thing to do. "He didn't send this, but someone on the inside did. Maybe even Kasha.

We can't risk not following through, especially if it was her. We have to head out right away."

"We need to wait for the High Faction to approve the search warrant," Dornan said, growls escaping many of our lips at his words. "You know the rules, and this is my territory. What I say goes."

"Dornan…" I took a step towards him, but he stopped me with a raised hand, his eyes softening.

"I am going to put this through right now and push for a quick turnaround," he promised. "I will call them every hour until I have the documents in my hand and then we can head north. We'll get her back."

I let out a shaky breath, nodding at his words. He leaned forward, squeezing my shoulder before rushing out of the room, the paper still clutched in his hand. I looked over at my team, weary hope veiled over their expressions. None of us completely trusted that we weren't walking into a trap, but we had no other choice. Kasha would walk into fire for any of us, and now it was time to do the same for her.

I'm coming for you, sweetheart.

CHAPTER 55

Kasha

Days lost all meaning, my life moving around me inside the confines of the pretty room I had been locked in.

I wanted to stay moving as much as possible. I would collapse in bed, and each time I woke up, it was a different time of day. It took me longer and longer to push myself up and off the mattress. Everything was deteriorating quickly, as if the small taste of blood I had gotten had just fed the hunger more instead of sating it.

It was torture.

I was pacing around my room, touching every surface just to know I was still here, that I was still around things and conscious. Then my fingers went numb, unable to feel the slight brushes of the wooden side table or the stone of the fireplace. So, when I needed to prove to myself I was awake, I held my hands in front of the fire, leaning down and inching closer and closer until I felt the burn of the flames skitter across my skin without actually burning myself. I flinched back, dropping my head gently to the mantle, focusing on the residual sting coating my palms.

Just to make sure I was still alive.

Would this ever stop? Would I survive?

"Little Shadow…" I flipped around, rubbing my eyes at the person lounging on one of my chairs. A familiar face for so long.

"Ollie?" He chuckled in response to my stunned posture.

"Forget about me?" a voice came from the other chair. I turned.

"Caleb!" I went to rush forward, but they both put their hands up as if they didn't want me to come any closer.

I halted. What was going on? Shouldn't we be trying to escape? Why were they in casual clothes?

"Are we leaving?" I looked around the room, searching for anyone.

"Why would we?" Ollie shrugged.

"I'm your sister!" I cried. "You always protect me!"

Caleb leaned back in his chair, shrugging. "But without you, we would no longer have family drama. It would be peaceful."

I took a step back, shaking my head. "No…"

"Father wouldn't need to worry anymore," Ollie said. "Life could go back to the way it was."

Ollie was saying that? It couldn't be right.

"You cause too much pain." Caleb stood, crossing his arms and towering over me.

"You aren't worth it." Ollie mimicked his posture.

I whimpered, covering my eyes and rubbing them again, shaking my head. What was happening?

When I looked up again, they were gone.

I whipped around, looking for any sign they were there. No indent in the chairs as if someone had just been sitting. No lingering scent of my brothers.

It had been a hallucination.

I was reaching the peak of my hunger. It was finally settling in.

I collapsed onto the bed, burying my face in my pillow, punching it, screaming and cursing my brothers' names. They weren't really there, but it didn't stop the slicing pain of the words the illusion had brought me.

"Goddess above, why did it take us so long to see how weak she is?" A light, feminine voice drifted to me from the foot of the bed.

I knew it right away. Eden.

"Can you believe we called her our best friend at one point?"

Liv.

"You're lucky, I've known her since childhood," someone scoffed. "She's more of a burden now than ever."

Lea.

Why were they being so cruel? Was this how they felt?

No, it wasn't real. It was the hunger.

"You aren't real, You aren't here," I chanted into the pillow, refusing to look up to see them. If I ignored them, it would eventually dissipate.

"Are you sure about that?" A deep voice penetrated my chants.

Beckett.

"No." I shook my head. Not Beckett. Why were they all there?

"I always seem to find you when you're at your weakest." He sighed. "Will you ever be strong enough to take care of yourself?"

"I am strong enough," I said, although the pathetically quiet voice that came from me had little effect on the words.

"Then prove it," he challenged. "Look at us."

I didn't want to. I knew it would ruin me since they weren't really there. But that churning of my gut and something in my heart ached to look at their faces. The floodgate of my denial, of my survivor mode pushing them from my mind so I could make it within Elliot's stronghold, flowed into me, begging me to see my friends again. It didn't matter that they weren't real. I needed to see them. Those who had once given me strength and protection. It made no sense, but I was too exhausted to try and figure out why.

I sat up, my feet dangling over the side of the bed as I faced my newest torture.

They were all there, the entire Hierarchy of my Faction and Lea. My friends, my confidants, my partners. Those who I considered family, who stood by me through all. We had fought together, loved each other.

But none of them looked happy to see me. They sneered, judging me, looking at me with disdain. It wasn't them, but it was their faces. It was how I expected them to be when I had tried to take my life so long ago. It was how I expected everyone to treat me.

But they hadn't.

Had they? I could no longer remember what had been reality and what had been my anxious imagination making up false truths.

Why? Why was this torturing me?

"Please, leave me alone," I whispered to them, my stomach sinking.

"I can't believe we ever saw you as a worthy Beta," Lucas spat.

"You don't deserve us as Gammas." Taylor agreed with his brother, both of them rolling their eyes at me.

"Please stop!"

"At least you all didn't have to feed her for years." Emric scowled at me. "I had to give her my blood!"

"Please." I shook my head, my eyes burning, my heart fluttering.

They aren't here, they aren't here, they aren't here…

"Pathetic," Greyson added, a man of few words that always seemed to cut the deepest.

It needed to stop. It all needed to stop.

I closed my eyes, clasping my hands over my ears and huddling my knees to my chest, rocking back and forth and humming. The voices tried to break through, but I just hummed louder until they faded into the background. I opened my eyes, the room empty.

All alone again.

My muscles hurt. My mind was shutting down. It was all too much. The hallucinations, the taunting, the loss and failure that kept replaying over and over in my head. It was too much.

I collapsed on the bed, and as the darkness of sleep found me. I knew if I didn't try to get up, I wouldn't be escaping the bed again.

Yet, I still let sleep take me.

***

"Kasha…"

Someone was luring me from sleep, a deep rumbling voice that was male, but I couldn't figure out who it was.

"Wake up, sleepyhead." It was kind with a hint of laughter, accompanied by a dizzying scent that was familiar, comforting. Spice and citrus.

Nolan. Nolan had come. He had kept his promise.

"No—Nol—" I tried to say his name, to reach out to him, but I could barely open my eyes. When I finally pried them open, he was nowhere to be seen, but the prickling on the back of my neck told me I wasn't alone. Rustling and footsteps. Someone was behind me, near the head of the bed. I tried to twist around, to finally see him, but a gentle hand on my shoulder held me in place.

"You're so weak." He coated me with concern, the words laced with it. "Don't move. It isn't safe until you feed."

"Hungry…" I croaked, my voice weathered and unused for words but overused from screaming and crying. I barely sounded like myself.

"I know, I know." His fingers swept across my forehead, greasy strands of hair plastered to it. "I can help."

His arm appeared in front of me, his wrist exposed and hovering over my lips. My stomach and mind churned, my eyes widening and my focus solely on what was in front of me. This couldn't be real. Somehow, I managed to reach my shaking hand up, brushing it gently against what was in front of me—warm, soft skin. It was here, it was real. There was an offered wrist, blood and sustenance.

I hesitated. I didn't know why. It was Nolan, and he was safety. I should have been taking what I had deprived myself of for too long. Yet, something felt wrong, a twinge in my belly trying to warn me. But the raging voice in my mind told me to ignore it.

To feed, to eat, to strengthen.

So many warring thoughts pulling within me; it was too much.

Why was it wrong?

"Please. You aren't safe to go home unless you feed from me," he encouraged, his wrist hovering over me, although something seemed to be missing from it. Still, all I could focus on was the pressing of the pulse against his thin skin. "I just want to get you back to Seathra, to the Faction. If you eat, I can do that."

It made sense. It was logical, just like Nolan. But why couldn't I see him? Was he alone?

Why was I questioning this? He was trying to save me like he promised. He was taking care of me.

I pursed my lips. Maybe just one taste… just a little…

A whisper grazed across my ear. "Eat, lovely."

I halted, my lips hovering over the pulsing wrist just under my nose.

Lovely? Did Nolan call me that?

It wasn't right. Maybe? Everything was just too jumbled in my head.

"I love you, sweetheart."

That voice, those words. Those were right. Those were the truth.

Sweetheart. I'm his sweetheart.

As for lovely…

My heart hammered as I looked over my shoulder, finally coming face to face with who was actually in the room with me.

I screamed, rolling away, escaping the presence I found myself with. Not the one I had wished was there. Elliot had tricked me.

The spicy scent was still potent in the room, even though I could finally see him.

He tried to touch me again, but I thrashed, unable to stop myself from tumbling from the bed, sheets still tangled around my legs. I cried out at the hard impact, my shoulder radiating with a throbbing pain. I shook my head, using my hands to push myself, but it was no use. There was no strength left there. I just thudded back to the floor.

He sighed, standing up from the bed and picking me up. I tried to fight the hold, but I could either let him place me back in the bed or stay on the floor. I was as good as an infant, unable to hold myself up.

He gently placed me back, looking down at me. I cried, wetness coating my cheeks. "Just leave me alone. Please."

"Let's just hope you are as strong as I believe you to be." His cold fingertips grazed my face one last time before he walked away, my head rolling to look at the wall and not at him. "I will return soon, *Rogthna*. You are ready."

The door closed. His voice faded.

I cried myself back into the darkness.

★★★

The clicking of the door. Footsteps, grunts, and whispered curses.

Someone was there. Were they real or not? Was I so far gone? Was I still asleep?

Too many questions. Too many unknowns. Who was I anymore?

"You need to eat."

I didn't have words to reply, just whines and whimpering cries as I rolled around in the bed, sweat-coated and heavy. Nothing could save me. No one was coming. No one was there to bring me out of that terrible place.

I was alone.

"We don't have time for this!" the voice seethed, the mattress below me compressing from a heavy weight. A tight grip took hold of my chin, forcing me to look up into the bright red eyes of a brutish man. "You need to feed from me. Now."

"Leave me alone, James." That was his name, right? I wasn't being tricked again?

Although, why would James come to me in a hallucination?

"Not until you eat. We don't have time to argue." I tried to pull my head away from his grip, but I was too weak. "Kasha, please, he… he's coming soon, and you need strength for his plan."

He. Elliot.

"Just let him kill me." I shook my head. I hated that I was saying the words because I didn't mean them. I didn't want to die, I wanted to live and explore the future I had been so ready for. But with each day and each moment in that blood-fueled torture, I wasn't sure I could hang on much longer. I wasn't sure I was strong enough to survive.

"He would never do that. Not intentionally." James's round eyes filled with a far-off weariness. "But he does have something planned, and I'm concerned you're too weak to come out of it with your mind intact without some blood. So, please, just let me help you."

His words were cutting through the fog; the desperation, and the pleading, Somehow, it was convincing me in a state of pure agony. He was serious. He was going against Elliot and protecting me. If he was willing to do this, then whatever Elliot had planned, I needed to survive. I needed at least a little strength.

"Why?" I croaked. I knew I should have elaborated, but my head was banging too hard, too focused on the pulsing wrist he was offering.

"Her patients meant everything to her." His words were full of sadness.

He was doing this for Vanessa. For the woman he loved.

"Please." He pushed his wrist almost flush with my lips. "We don't have a lot of time."

I didn't argue anymore, just clamped my sharp teeth into his soft flesh, his free hand going to cradle the back of my neck to help keep it upright.

The flavor assaulted my taste buds, but I could barely focus on it. It didn't matter. All that did was that I was feeding. I was taking strength; I was getting blood. I sucked and slurped, the numbness in my lips starting to tingle back to life and a bit of heat trickling into my clammy hands.

I wished I had counted the seconds or the number of pulls I had taken because, all too soon, he unlatched my jaw from him and was wrapping his wrist in a white cloth before pulling down his sleeve. He stood from the bed, the jostling of the mattress sending a wave of nausea through my entire body, my head spinning.

It wasn't enough. I still couldn't get up.

"Please…" I reached up to him, my fingers shaking. "More."

"I'm sorry." He shook his head, backing away from me slowly. "I can't. If you're strong enough to sit up, he will suspect. This will have to be enough. May the God and Goddess watch over you tonight."

He was gone, and silence welcomed me once again.

CHAPTER 56

Kasha

Time continued without me. Even with the little blood James was able to feed me, I still fell back into darkness, into a fitful sleep, and I had no idea how long passed. Orange rays of sunlight still came through the window. Dusk if I had to guess.

I was still weak, but at least my muscles didn't feel like lead and I could find the mental strength to try to focus on what was the reality around me. Chills ran up my spine because I knew right away… I was no longer alone.

Voices. Shuffling feet. Snapping fingers. Bone-chilling laughter.

"What?" My voice felt broken, and my mind splintered with it as I tried to put together what was going on around me.

"Shh, *Rogthna*. It will be all right." His voice was even more grating than normal, slithering over every inch of my skin. I was desperate to escape. With the little bit of strength the blood had given me, I tried to shuffle away, to escape.

But it was impossible due to the bindings around my legs and arms.

I cried out, struggling within the thick leather straps and cuffs. On any other day, a normal day, I could have ripped myself out of them easily. Only chains would have been enough to hold me and, even then, I knew a few tricks that could help. Now, though, weak strips of leather were enough to keep me in place.

Oh, how I had fallen.

I whimpered, my body shaking, still struggling even though I knew it was useless.

"Oh, don't do that." Elliot moved in front of me, smoothing my greasy hair off my sweaty forehead. "You'll hurt yourself if you struggle too much."

"Just let me go," I pleaded, shaking my head back and forth against the hard surface that cradled my head. It felt familiar, like I had sat in this seat before. I looked down, my body completely laid out on a long leather chair, slightly tilted back so I was in a reclining position.

Why did I know this type of chair? Why was it familiar?

"Is she ready, sir?" an unknown, nasal voice asked. I rolled my head towards it. A lanky man sat to my left, hunched over and fiddling on a small table behind him. I couldn't make out what it was or any striking qualities on this fairly generic man. Or maybe he just looked generic through my blinding hunger.

Dread filled my belly, letting me know that he was not there to help me. He was there to hurt.

"I think so." He stroked my cheek one more time. I noticed he was still in a dress shirt and pants, but the sleeves were rolled up, exposing his forearm that was tightly wrapped in a white bandage.

Did someone hurt him? Had I hurt him and just didn't remember? Goddess, I hoped that was the case. At least if I was going down, I would go down fighting.

He moved to my right side, sitting in a seat and grasping my hand. I kept my grip loose and unwelcoming, but he didn't care; he kept his hold tight.

"This is going to hurt, *Rogthna*." With his other hand, he moved his knuckles up my arm in slow, agonizing strokes. I wanted to vomit in my mouth. "But it will be over soon. Just breathe through it."

"Don't…" I had no words to say, none that would make any difference.

So, I waited, closing my eyes and shivering in the chair for whatever I was about to be dealt…

Burning fire engulfed my arm. It snaked around my elbow and crawled up and down, piercing my flesh and scalding it away. I screamed and tried to flail around, but the bindings were just too strong for my weakened body. I looked at the unknown man bent over my exposed left arm, a sharp object in his hand, gently stroking against my skin.

"No!" I screamed, trying to rip it away, to take myself away from him.

"It's all right. He's helping," Elliot soothed. "Soon, you will no longer need to worry."

"I don't want this," I pleaded to him, my chest fracturing, breaking apart little by little. He was dismantling everything from the outside in. He said he needed me, but how was this going to help?

"But you need it. I can give you strength." His silver-blue eyes pleaded with me as if anything that was coming out of his deranged mouth made sense. "This will help, I promise."

There were no more words to say. Nothing more I could do to protect myself. I had let myself get weak. I had let him into my mind and peek into my soul. He had taken it and twisted it and was trying to ruin it just for himself. Soon, he would succeed. Soon, I would be nothing more than his doll to move and play however he saw fit. I was on the brink, my mind teetering between the reality of what he wanted and all that I left behind.

So, I did the only thing I could. I breathed through the burning, engulfing pain and let what was now my life take over.

No one was coming. No one would save me.

I needed to accept that maybe I was now his. That last shred of hope, the burning ember of a love most likely lost refused to budge, but how long could it hold out? How long until it too drifted into nothingness?

I couldn't do this anymore. I slumped into my seat, the humming of whatever the man was scraping across my skin slowing down before pulling away, cooling wetness drifting over the pain, soothing it.

"You did it," Elliot praised, the words twisting in my mind and bile rising in my throat. "I'm so proud of you."

Scuffling and shouts drifted from behind the door, gaining on us.

James and Ari stumbled in, both in what looked like gray leather armor, and my body winced. James didn't even pay attention to me and Ari, barreling straight for Elliot. "They've breached the gates. It's only a matter of time before they find the manor."

"Leave us," Elliot said, but it must not have been for James or Ari because they didn't budge, although I did hear the door slam behind us. My fuzzy, tunneled vision was slowly sinking away, darkness slithering in, but I focused all my remaining energy to keep myself awake.

"Elliot? Did you hear her?" James shoved his shoulder. "They will be in the house in mere minutes."

"Then let them find it!" Elliot snarled, not moving an inch away from me. "Let them see what I have created and who she belongs to now."

Oh, Goddess, please don't let them be talking about me.

"They're coming!" Ari screamed at him, her bright eyes frantic as she tried to tug Elliot away from me. "Leave her behind!"

"I will not!" Elliot snarled, tugging his arm out of her vice grip.

James pushed into his line of vision. "Elliot, this just seems…"

"This was the plan. It was always the plan." He stalked towards them, eyes wild. "You must trust the God and Goddess. This is their will. Are you questioning what they want?"

James swallowed. "No, but…"

"It certainly sounds that way." Elliot tisked.

"I have always been dedicated to you, Elliot," James argued. Although, I couldn't help but wonder if Elliot had any doubts. I certainly did. "But this… this is a risk!"

"The God and Goddess will see us through." He clasped the back of James's neck, pulling their foreheads together. "We will be reunited soon, my brother. Trust in what is best for Kazola. What is necessary."

"*Chu Fui na Deithe*," James whispered.

"*Chu Fui na Deithe*." Elliot saluted. "Hold them off as long as possible. We won't be able to test my theory today, but I want to say goodbye."

James nodded, my insides curdling because I had no idea what was going on and that was never okay with me, especially when it sounded like I was about to be involved against my will. Again.

Just wonderful.

He turned next to his biggest fan. "Ari, you know your orders. Take your team and prepare for the next phase at the safe house."

"Elliot…" she whispered, eyes pleading.

"You're the only one I can trust with this." He cupped her cheek, my stomach rolling as she looked up to him with unadulterated praise. "I know you won't let me down."

"I promise to do everything you asked." She leaned up on her toes and kissed his cheek, giving me one last signature sneer before heading for the exit.

The door slammed shut. Elliot shuffled across to secure the locks against it before moving back to kneel next to me. The bindings were still holding me down. I was stuck with just him, no one else to protect me.

What would he do?

"Shh, *Rogthna*. It's going to be all right." He cupped the back of my neck, the touch burning. *Wrong. So, so wrong.* "Just know that you must trust me after today. We are meant to find each other once again when the time for us to finally reclaim Kazola is upon us. Just know that I will return for you. I will bring you home."

Someone else had made me this promise. The green-eyed man

who I loved with all my heart. When he said those words, I had been flooded with peace, love, and devotion. When Elliot spoke them, fear jolted through my veins and disgust filled my heart. I wanted him far away. I wanted him to bleed. I wanted to see the life leave his eyes.

I just wanted to get away from him.

But I was too weak. I was stuck. I was his.

An onslaught of noises came to us, echoing through the house and down the halls. Screams. Clashing metal. Splintering wood. Crunching bones. The sounds of only one thing: battle.

He didn't let me go. All he did was soothe and whisper nonsense words into my ear until they finally broke through, the door blowing inward, splintering wood blasting across the space.

I was still hallucinating. I had to be. There was no other explanation for the potent scent of cinnamon citrus that was surrounding me.

CHAPTER 57

Nolan

Three weeks and six days.

That was how long it had taken to make good on my promise to find Kasha.

We rushed into the room we had been fighting the past half an hour to get to, following her scent and the whimpering cries of pain she was emitting through the halls. To our surprise, there were no guards outside or inside the room, only Elliot and Kasha. We had fought past most of his defenses, but I was still shocked he had refused any other sort of protection. I rushed at him, my fist connecting with his cheek, a satisfying crack ringing into the space as he toppled away from Kasha.

"Stay away from her!" I snarled, blocking him from returning to Kasha's side. He would never get close to her again. Her brothers were instantly on him, locking his arms and overpowering him quickly.

"Let me go!" Elliot's voice boomed in the cramped space. "She needs me now! You can't keep us apart."

"You won't get near her ever again if we have anything to say about it," Oliver snarled, he and Caleb dragging Elliot from the room, their grips harsh and punishing.

"Don't worry, *Rogthna*. You'll be okay!" he screamed, but it was muffled as they dragged him out the door, bringing him to the armored cart we had outside to transport him and those we captured to the local garrison for keeping.

"It's okay, Kasha. We've got you," Beckett said, dropping to one side as I turned and kneeled by her as well, trying my best not to cry at the sight in front of me.

She whimpered, gibberish words slurring through her cracked, bleeding lips. Her eyes were hooded, barely able to focus and open. Her black linen shirt and pants were drenched in sweat, her beautiful honey-brown hair greasy and tangled. Her face was sunken in and paler than normal, deep bruises rimming her eyes. A bandage was freshly wrapped around her right forearm, hiding whatever he had done to her.

I reached out, stroking her dirty hair off her forehead. "Shh, sweetheart. We're here now. You're safe."

"Thisss…issnnn't….reaaal!" she wailed, slowly rolling her head back and forth against the headrest of the chair she was strapped to.

"Help me get her out of these damned bindings," I demanded. We needed to get her free right away; she hated being kept down.

We ripped at the bindings, making quick work of them before I reached forward to pull her into my arms. However, she had a different plan, her eyes wildly alert the moment they dropped to the floor. She pushed me away before I could press her into my embrace, falling ungracefully to the floor and scurrying away on her hands and feet to the closest corner she could find.

What was happening? My chest ached, my stomach rolling as I watched her eyes fill rapidly with paranoia and fear.

"You're not here, you're not here, you're not here," she cried, curling herself into a ball and digging her fingers so tightly into her matted hair I was terrified she would rip it out.

"It's me, sweetheart." I inched forward, my hand going out so I could touch her, hold her hand so she could feel the warmth of my palm against hers. That had grounded her from panic attacks in the past; it could help now. "I made you a promise. I wouldn't break that."

The moment my fingertips brushed the back of her hand, her eyes flashed, sharp teeth protruding from her lips before she lashed forward, gripping my hand between them.

"*Futeacha!*" I swore, pulling my hand away, the back of it dripping with blood from the shallow nip.

"She's starving," Beckett whispered from behind me, his voice trembling.

"She needs blood." I reached out, bearing my wrist to her. "Here. Kasha, drink!" I insisted.

She lurched forward to lash at me again, and I barely pulled my arm back in time. "No! Stop trying to trick me!"

"Trick you? No, Kasha. I'm trying to help!" I pleaded with her, but she didn't seem to comprehend a word I said, her head shaking rapidly back and forth, her whole body shaking.

"I can sedate her." Beckett took another step forward. "That way we can get her out of here."

"No!" I threw myself in front of her but still kept my distance so she didn't lash out again.

"Nolan," Beckett said calmly. "It's the only way we can get her the treatment she needs. She's starved, probably been hallucinating for days now. She can't discern what's real and what's imaginary. We have to get her to a clinic. They're the only ones who have the equipment to treat her if we have any hopes of saving her life."

"You can't!" I insisted. She had told me once how much she hated being sedated. It reminded her of her forced hospitalization. "Please, just let me try and talk her down."

Beckett shook his head. "She's too far gone. She doesn't even think we're real, let alone safe. She won't come with us."

I turned back to her, looking at her with every bit of desperation I could, pleading with her to recognize me. "Please, sweetheart. I just want to help."

"Go away! I don't want to be your *Rogthna*! I don't want to be here!" She kicked her legs out, her bare feet slapping against the floor.

Tears threatened to escape my eyes at the words. "I'm not Elliot," I whispered. Even my wildest fears hadn't prepared me for her not to recognize me.

"Yes, you are." She growled. "Stop trying to trick me!"

I turned back to my Faction, their faces collectively reflecting the pain I knew was in their chests watching one of their closest friends struggle with reality.

But they could be nowhere near as agonizing as the ball of pain threatening to eat me alive.

Beckett nodded to our left, my gut twisting at the grave expression on his face. Eden and Greyson came at me, each of them clutching my arms, forcing me to heel to their forceful grips. "No!" I shouted, but they didn't listen, pulling me back so Beckett, Liv, and Taylor could slowly approach Kasha.

"No!" She screeched, kicking and fighting, but her lethargic, weakened movements were too easy for them to overpower. Still, she never stopped fighting, even when Liv and Taylor had her successfully pinned down to the ground between them.

"Stop!" Ollie's voice came from behind. I turned just in time to watch him barrel through the door, but Lucas caught him, throwing him against the nearest wall and pinning him there.

"Beckett is trying to help," Lucas's deep, gravelly voice explained.

"Oh, Little Shadow!" The agony in his voice was potent as he slumped into Lucas's hold.

By the time I turned back around, Beckett was rummaging through the small satchel clipped at his hip. My heart shattered as I forced myself to watch them hold her down, her sharp, desperate cries for release shredding my soul to bits.

"It's for her own good," Eden whispered into my ear, her grip never wavering.

I tried my best to keep telling myself that as Beckett approached, needle in hand. He knelt next to her and gently submerged the thin needle into Kasha's neck.

They released me just in time to catch her slumping body against my chest, curling her against me and picking her up into my arms. And I knew, even before I carried her out of the room, that I would not release her until absolutely necessary.

CHAPTER 58

Nolan

The clinically white room hurt my eyes the longer I forced myself to stay awake, but I refused to get sleep when I was by her bedside. Sometimes, when Ollie or one of the Faction was with me, I allowed myself to get a little, but I couldn't sleep unless I knew someone was watching over her.

We transferred Kasha to the nearest clinic, which also had plenty of physicians who specialized in Ibridowyn care, so she could have the best team possible to work with her and help her get better.

But that was five days ago.

She had woken up a few times but was still too feral to feed, and the physicians forced me out of the room so they could sedate her. They had been feeding her blood slowly through a tube, but she wasn't absorbing it fast enough. They said she had been starved for almost the entire month she was there, and because of that, there was a chance her mental state might never recover.

I refused to believe it. Statistics and studies could only tell you so much. I knew Kasha better than any of the physicians who claimed to know what would happen to her. She was a survivor. A fighter. She would never give up like this or let her life be controlled by the likes of Elliot. She was too damn stubborn for that.

"Please, sweetheart. Please let me help you." I gripped her hand between mine, peppering kisses against her cool knuckles. "When you wake up next, let me feed you so I can take you home."

A part of me hoped her eyes would flutter open, but she just stayed there, lying completely still in the narrow bed. Nurses had cleaned her and redressed her in a thin white nightgown, her hair braided and color returning to her skin because of the nutrients, fluids, and blood they had been giving her.

But it still wasn't enough. Not yet, at least.

The door opening quietly pulled my attention from her. Ollie walked in, Caleb and one of the physicians who had been working on her case right behind them.

"Meela has some things she wants to go over with us," Ollie explained. I stood as the brothers moved beside me. "About some treatment options."

"Should her father be here?" Meela asked, gingerly picking up Kasha's hand to begin checking her pulse.

"No," Ollie gritted out from between clenched teeth. "I am Kasha's medical proxy now, not him."

"Since when?" Caleb's eyes widened, jaw slackened.

"After she was released from the hospital earlier this year. She removed you and Father and named me sole proxy over her medical treatments in case of emergency," he said to his older brother before turning back to the physician. "I don't approve him being a part of this conversation."

"Very well. And her Alpha?" She nodded to me.

"He's her paramour," Ollie said, gripping my shoulder tightly in solidarity. "She would want him here."

She nodded, putting Kasha's hand down and turning to us. "It's been five days with no progress. With the combination of blood lust and whatever he did to her in captivity, her body and her wolf are in fight mode. As we mentioned before, we aren't sure if, in her current state, she would be able to recover from that."

"What do you mean?" Ollie's brow creased in confusion.

"Basically, her wolf is fighting her for dominance, which is making her feral."

My heart sank. Kasha had worked so hard to find harmony with her wolf for so long. Now, only a few weeks later, they were at war again. But instead of disappearing, her wolf was fighting against her instead of with her.

Would my sweetheart ever catch a break?

"So, that's it?" Caleb said. "There's nothing we can do?"

Meela bit her lip. "There is one thing that I believe could cure her of the blood lust that is making her wolf feral."

"What is it?" My voice croaked.

"We could give her the Removal serum," Meela explained. "As a Varg Anwyn, she is not pre-disposed for drinking blood as a necessity. So, if we took that part of her away, she should recover fully."

"No." I shook my head, my heart aching at the idea.

"If she wanted to join the Guard again, go through the mutation process, could she?" Caleb asked, worry creasing his face.

Meela sighed. "No, I'm sorry. Once a Brido goes through the Removal, there is no going back into the Guard. She would have to retire."

I scrubbed my hand across my face before rubbing two fingers against my temples. "What are the chances she could recover without the Removal?"

"With each day that passes, her chances shrink." She looked at the three of us, sympathy glazing her eyes. "Today, we are at a fifty percent chance of recovery. But giving her the serum would bring that up to a ninety percent chance."

My eyes narrowed. "And the other ten percent?"

"That is the fatality rate."

"Fatality?" Ollie shouted. "So, she could die if we put her through the Removal?"

"With the state her body is currently in? Yes."

"So, we have to choose to either risk her life or risk her going feral?" Ollie stepped forward, his hand reaching down to brush against his sister's arm. "Is that correct?"

Meela nodded. "I know this isn't an easy decision, so I will give you some time to think about it. But please, come to me as soon as you do decide."

She clicked the door shut behind her to give us privacy. It felt impossible to stay standing, my legs collapsing back into my chair.

"Ollie?" I watched him walk around the bed, falling into the empty chair over there. "What are you going to do?"

He reached down, grasping Kasha's hand. "I don't want to lose her."

"We aren't left with a choice that doesn't risk it," I said. 'We need to make the choice she would make for herself. We must honor her wishes as best we can."

Ollie nodded before turning to Caleb. "What do you think?"

I turned to look up at him, Caleb still standing a few feet away, a wistful look glazing his gaze as he stared down at his sister. "It isn't my place to give an opinion."

Ollie snorted. "Not like you."

"I need to be better for her. To show her respect, even when she isn't awake." He sighed, running his fingers through his hair. "She doesn't want me to make this choice for her, she wants you, Oliver. And Nolan, I believe she would want you to be a part of the conversation too. But I haven't earned that part of her back yet, so I will leave it to the two of you."

I blinked at him a few times, surprised. He had been hard-headed when we spent time in his territory. Even though they had taken a step towards healing, it wasn't complete yet. Still, this showed he was determined.

"The Removal gives her the highest chance of survival," Ollie said, his words emotionless.

I sat up straighter, my fingers tightening around Kasha's limp ones. "She wouldn't want that! She went through torture to keep her position, and now you just want to take it away from her, without her consent?"

"I can't lose her, Nolan!" Ollie pleaded. "With each hour that passes, she slips away a little bit more. But with that procedure, she has a higher chance of surviving. She can find her way in this world. We will all make sure of it, but we can't do that if she is lost to us forever."

I understood his position. I knew he was trying to not only save her life but the hearts and souls of everyone who loved Kasha.

But she wouldn't want that. She gave up so much for this position, even her story and the truth of what happened to her. She had dedicated everything to this life. I couldn't just take that away from her. I knew in my gut and my heart she would want us to take the risk, believe that she was strong enough to be in that fifty percent recovery rate.

I believed it. Now, I just had to convince her brother of it as well.

"Please," I begged, willing to get on my knees if that was what it came to. "Give me one more chance. Let her wake up one more time and let me try and convince her that we're here to help. To get her to feed."

"I don't know." He narrowed his eyes.

"Please, Oliver." I let all of my pain and desperation leak through my words, showing him just how much I believed this was what his sister would want.

Silent, tense moments passed before he finally sighed, nodding his head. "All right. One more chance. But if you can't get through to her, if you can't get her to feed, then we give the go-ahead for the Removal."

I nodded in agreement, knowing it was the best I was going to get with Ollie's stern, decided words.

One more chance. That was all I needed.

Or at least, I hoped it was.

CHAPTER 59

Kasha

I couldn't make sense of anything, my mind floating and fighting, still trying to figure out what was real and what was a twisted game meant to torture me.

My eyes slowly fluttered open, heavy from what felt like too many hours of sleep. My limbs were weighty, but I rolled my head a bit, taking in my surroundings. White walls, gray, minimal furniture, and I lay in a narrow bed. I twitched my finger, my wrist throbbing from a needle and tube protruding from me. A clinic?

Or one of Elliot's experiment rooms in his lab?

Fight. Flee. Kill.

My wolf didn't like this, but… this place seemed different. Even with the cold, sterile environment, it didn't seem inherently wrong, not like the lab floors did when I explored.

Find safety. Find home. Woods. Trees. Moon.

She was screaming and barraging at me from within, unhappy with my treatment of her these past few weeks, refusing to keep her strong. She wanted control. She wanted to keep us safe. She wanted to take over.

Would that be better? I was so tired, and giving over to her, trusting her, seemed to be the easiest option.

I could slip away and enjoy life in freedom.

But that wasn't right… was it?

No. No, I couldn't. I had people, didn't I? A life? A purpose?

It was slowly coming back to me, but it was muddled, and my wolf was trying hard to drown it out, but I pushed against her, trying to grasp onto my reality, my life.

My home. My sweetness.

"Kasha…" A concerned, cautious voice pulled my gaze to my left, bright forest green eyes reflecting back at me.

Trick! Get away.

Run!

I fled from him, stumbling out of the bed, wires and tubes ripping from my arm and making me bleed, but I didn't care. I needed to get away from whatever new torture he was putting me through.

I didn't get far, collapsing into the corner of the room, pressing myself into it and hoping whoever it was, fake or real, would just leave me alone.

"Sweetheart, please." The hallucination reached for me, but I slapped it away, a feral snarl ripping from my lips before morphing into more whimpers and tears. I could barely register that he didn't disappear. That I felt my hand against his warm skin. "It's me. Nolan."

"No, no, no, no, no…." I pressed my face into my huddled knees, trying to escape back into the darkness that had been my only reprieve over the past few weeks. I wanted them gone. It would only give me false hope again.

"For the love of the Goddess, Kasha. Please. You have to eat." I heard Nolan's voice, but it mixed with the distorted reality I had been living in for endless days. "I just want to help you. I want you to get better."

I couldn't figure out what was real and what was fake. What was in front of me and what had been conjured from the hours of starvation, torture, and brainwashing. Who was in front of me? Were they friend or foe? Was it really Nolan, or was that just my broken heart wishing he was here to protect me?

I cowered away from the touch, curling myself into a ball in the corner of the cold room. I rocked back and forth, my face buried into my legs, my braided hair thumping against my flushed cheek. I didn't want anyone here. I didn't want anyone's help. Why wouldn't they just leave me alone?

Why couldn't Elliot just let me die?

"Kasha." Nolan's voice drifted to me again.

"You aren't real… you aren't real…" I kept repeating those words, pleading and hoping the mirage would go away and my heart would stop playing tricks on me. Weeks had gone by. No one was coming to save me.

No one cared.

At least, that was what I had thought until the voice whispered directly into my mind. *I told you I would find you, Kasha. I'm keeping my promise.*

I pulled my head up with the last of my strength, my vision blurry and unfocused from weeks of refusing blood and torture.

How…

But Elliot could speak within my mind. He was an Ibridowyn.

"I don't…" I looked up, the fake Nolan still in front of me, worry creasing his handsome face. He kneeled, but a good few feet apart, as if he was trying to placate a timid, feral animal.

"Remember when we spent our first night together?" He continued to talk into my mind. *"And I had that panic attack? But you helped me through it. You took care of me and put my mind at ease, even with all that fear brewing within me. It allowed me to move forward, and I told you that Cleo would want me to be happy and that she would love you."*

His words were beautiful, eliciting an incredible memory from not so long ago. Could this be a trick still? But Elliot wouldn't know any of this… right?

"Or when we spent a night together in Ravach?" he continued, feeding me memories, bringing me back to that life I had struggled to regrasp. *"Holding you in my arms, you giving me so much trust to take care of you? To worship you like you deserved. I had never felt such pleasure. It was in that moment that I realized I was lost to you. That I was completely and irrevocably in love. You were my future, and now, I'm fighting for that future. So please, my love, recognize me. Trust me. Let me in."*

Only Nolan would know these special times for the two of us. I never would have told Elliot, even within the deepest of tortures. I would never have given him a piece of Nolan and me and our bond. It was too precious to me. Which meant…

"Nolan?" My voice was hoarse, as if I was dragging my words through sand before releasing them from my lips.

His face fell with relief, hand reaching out to stroke my wet cheek. "Yes, sweetheart. It's me. I'm here, I promise."

I wanted to collapse in his arms, to crawl to him and finally be safe, but my body couldn't find the strength to move. It could barely find it to keep looking at him, but I forced myself to. It was the only thing keeping me awake, knowing he was there.

He shifted his hand away from my cheek, bearing his wrist to me, the pulse jumping strongly against the thin skin. I snarled, his spicy scent sending a wave of dizzying pleasure through my system.

"You're in a clinic in Luspan, sweetheart," he murmured, coming to my side. His arms moved me with ease, placing my back against his chest, my entire form safely protected between his legs. "You're recovering here before I can take you home. But you need to eat first."

I didn't even try to protest, my instincts to survive taking over me as I found a bit of energy to shift my teeth, bite down, and break the tender flesh in front of me. I groaned the minute the sweet, warm liquid brushed against my tongue, my slurps gluttonous and sloppy. The warmth of Nolan's blood began to dribble out of the corners of my lips, my tongue trying to lick and devour every delicious drop.

Nolan's forehead fell against the top of my head. "That's it, sweetheart. Take as much as you need."

I didn't know how long we sat there. How long I began to feel the semblance of strength return to my body. The heaviness in my limbs loosened. A warmth I hadn't felt for weeks began to spread up my clavicle and into my cheeks. The door opened, footsteps barging into the small, cramped room.

"You did it!"

My body jerked at the new voice, the tormentor of my past colliding with my present.

My father was here.

I released Nolan's wrist from my teeth, a whimper escaping my lips as I curled inward into Nolan's chest, burying my face there. I couldn't look at my father, even though I could scent both of my brothers standing by his side. I couldn't see yet another person who tried to take everything from me.

Another person who almost succeeded.

Nolan's arms wrapped around me, pulling me tightly against him, his lips never leaving my hair. The grumble of his words from deep in his chest rumbled against my cheek. "Get out."

"She needs to eat more. Let me…"

A slap echoed off the walls. "Don't you dare touch her!"

My tears came back, streaming down my face and staining Nolan's soft cotton shirt. I couldn't stop shaking. Father's presence loomed behind me, the memories of his betrayals trying to flood back. His lack of trust in my truth, voting against me, calling me a disgrace to our family name…

"Get out, get out, get out, get out," I mumbled into Nolan's shirt, my words full of desperation for yet another round of torture to end.

"Ollie, get him out of here now!" Nolan barked.

"Gladly," I heard him say smugly before the sound of dragging footsteps and loud protests echoed away.

"He's gone, sweetheart," Nolan whispered into my ear, his lips brushing against me. "He's gone. Please eat more."

I clamped back onto his wrist. I knew I should have worried about drinking too much of him, that I should slow down and make sure he was all right. But weeks of starving was catching up to me, my mind focusing on one thing. More blood. More, more, more…

"Nolan, let me take over." Beckett's deep voice approached, his hand brushing against Nolan's wrist and pulling it out of my mouth. I whimpered the second it was gone.

"I'm fine," he argued.

"Nolan." Beckett refused to let go, his grip tight on Nolan's arm. "You don't even have to let go of her, but let her eat some from the rest of us. We can't risk your health. We need to stay focused on hers."

Seconds passed, my body shaking and begging for more blood. I didn't care who from, as long as I got more.

Nolan sighed. "Fine."

Time became irrelevant as my mouth savored the delectable tastes that paraded in front of me. I lost count of how many people; I didn't even try to guess who it was by the taste. All I cared about was getting out of there, getting strong, and feeling safe.

I finally had my fill, my chest heaving, face covered in blood as I collapsed backward, my neck cradled in Nolan's arm. I stared up at him, my gaze finally back in focus. The brows above his forest-green eyes were pinched inward, his lips trembling, staring down at me with the utmost care and love.

I reached upward, my shaking hand cupping his flamed cheek. "I love you."

A chuckle escaped his lips, his face softening as he stroked my hair. "It took you getting kidnapped and held hostage to finally feel comfortable saying it back? Really, Kas?"

I gurgled a laugh. "You know me. I'm never about taking the easy way with things."

He leaned forward, his lips firm against my sweat-drenched forehead as he mumbled, "I love you too."

It was the last thing I heard before I fell back into a darkened oblivion.

CHAPTER 60

Kasha

D ry mouth. Beating heart. Shaking fingers.

Those were the first sensations to finally come through and torture me when my soul floated back to consciousness, but my mind was still a few beats behind.

I groaned, the low light of a lamp sitting next to me burning my eyes as they fluttered open. The sterile white ceilings were an unwelcoming sight, my gaze peeking down to see my body tangled in starch-white sheets. Something stirred next to me, my stomach clenching as it rocked the bed a bit. My hand reached down, feeling something soft tangling between my fingers.

Hair.

I leaned up, a gasp of pain escaping my lips as the two figures that were resting their heads on the sides of my bed startled awake.

"Kasha?" Caleb's eyes blinked open rapidly, and he fell from the chair on my right side, his knees shuffling forward to kneel by my head.

"You're awake!" I turned to my left, not even a little surprised to see Ollie there, purple bruises sitting heavy under his eyes, his hair a tousled mess.

My heart burst, my chest clenching with a need to cry.

I was safe. My brothers were with me, and I was safe.

"How long have I been out?" I sounded like I had swallowed a beach worth of sand. The ache radiating in my throat reminded me I had been screaming and crying a lot the last time I was conscious.

"A day since you woke up last." Ollie's fingers tightened around mine. "Seven since we found you."

Found me. They had rescued me. They and my Faction and…

I tried to bolt up, but my heavy, weakened muscles clenched at the sharp movement, making me cry out.

"Easy there." Ollie gripped my shoulder, guiding me to lie back down.

"Nolan," I said, my gaze flinging around the small, private room that just had my bed, a bedside table, a few pieces of medical equipment, and the chairs my brothers had been occupying while I was asleep. "Where is he?"

Ollie huffed a laugh. "Eden and Greyson pulled him away to eat. He's barely left your side since you've been here."

"He'll be back soon, don't worry." Caleb smoothed back a few tendrils of sweat-soaked hair from my forehead. "He hasn't even left the clinic."

I relaxed a bit more into the cushioned bed. Nolan was there. He had kept his promise and he had found me. He was there and I was safe.

I was safe.

"Here." Caleb kneeled next to me, a plastic cup in his hands, a curved straw a few inches from my lips. I wrapped my lips around it, pulling in a few small sips, the cool water instantly soothing a bit of my raw vocal cords.

"Thank you," I said, a bit more of my normal voice peeking through.

"The physicians also figured you would want some of this upon waking as well," Caleb said, his hands reaching out with something.

My eyes zeroed in on the sealed plastic bags, swirls of deep crimson liquid captured inside.

I snarled, pulse erratic against my neck, stomach growing hollow. I had been so weary and unfocused when I had first woken up. Now, with it right in front of me, I was ravenous, the haze of lust overtaking my body once again.

Blood. I needed blood.

I didn't even wait for them to do the proper thing and pour it into a cup. Instead, I yanked the full bags from Caleb's hands, ripping the pour spout out with my teeth, and downed the cherry-flavored blood that I knew very well as Emric's. Ollie kept his arm banded around my back, making sure I didn't choke on any of it, continuing my greedy rampage of eating, my stomach finally feeling full after three full bags.

"Good." Caleb took a cloth and wiped at my face, smears of red staining the white fabric. "You'll need to eat some real food soon too."

I nodded, and Caleb rearranged the pillows before I relaxed my weight into Ollie's arms as he helped me lie back against them in my narrow bed. Now I was sitting up to face them a bit more.

Ollie looked down at me, glassy eyes threatening to brim over as he leaned down and kissed my forehead. "I missed you, Little Shadow," he whispered before falling back into the chair on my left.

"How long?"

"How long?" Caleb leaned forward in his chair, dragging it forward to be a few inches closer.

"How long was I gone for?" I had lost count once I had fallen into the delirium of the bloodlust.

"Almost a month." Caleb grasped my hand, pressing it against his cheek, his tears pressing into my icy fingers. "We were so scared, baby sister."

"I was too." I opened my palm, wiping away a few more stray droplets on his cheek. "But you all found me."

"Nolan found you," Ollie said, pulling my attention. "We just helped."

My heart swelled, weird giggles rushing from my lips, and my head spinning a bit. I wasn't sure why. Probably shock mixing with whatever meds they had given me to keep me stable. Still, Nolan had kept his promise, just as he always said he would.

My mind was swirling and bending, struggling to focus on anything, warring between the warm fuzzy feelings Nolan was conjuring up and the dark, inky twists of my pain edging back to the forefront to try and poison my mind against the world once again.

I shuddered. I didn't want that anymore.

"Tell me something good," I whispered to them, desperate for anything that would help keep the warm glow that was steadily rising in my chest once again.

"What?" they chorused, brows pulled in just as our mother always did when she was shocked and confused.

"I need some more good. Tell me something that will help me feel better."

Caleb tugged gently on our clasped hands. "Logan's officially been found guilty."

I couldn't help it. No matter how twisted it might have been, I smiled. "You did it? You caught him with the *Marc Gealach*?"

"Found it on him, and the team I had waiting nearby confirmed it all," Caleb said, but his gaze didn't meet mine.

"What is it?" I whispered.

He heaved a heavy sigh. "While we were getting ready to transport him and Cole, we got the call that you had been taken."

My heart sank. I couldn't believe all of that had happened within the same night.

"I started raging, struggling to stay in human form as my wolf tried to take over so we could run and find you. My team had to gang up on me to get me to calm down." He hesitated, the strained look on his face letting me know he was full of shame over what he was about to say.

"Caleb?"

"The bastards used the opportunity to escape." He finally looked up at me, regret in his gaze. "Both he and Cole have been on the run since that night."

He had gotten away. Again. Escaped in the night like the criminal he was. But still, he had been caught with the Crest of

Lunestia by multiple Guard Members. There was no coming back from that.

And even though his presence would still haunt me, lurk in the shadows until the day he was thrown in jail and I was finally safe, I felt the first sliver of peace enter my soul, knowing he was no longer safe. He would be caught, and he would be brought to justice.

It gave me hope. Even in the darkness that threatened to consume me at a moment's notice, I clung to that feeling and buried it deep within for whenever I needed its strength.

Jaded, coarse laughter escaped me. "Then we need to find him, so we can build a new case against him."

"Won't be hard." Caleb traced a circle on the back of my hand with his thumb.

"Oh?"

"His current Beta came forward after we announced to them that he was on the run and a person of interest." Hardness glazed over his silver eyes, Caleb's jaw twitching. "He had done the same to her. We even found forged letters in his office as well."

"Fucking bastard," I spat, my lips curling at the idea that someone else had suffered. A dark, vengeful part of me hoped that those on the High Faction who had voted against me felt insurmountable amounts of guilt. And the logical part of me hoped that this time around, they would do the right thing.

Only time would tell.

"Cole has also been put under investigation and has officially been removed as High Tribune of the Vargs. Seeing as he's on the run, it speaks volumes of his guilt that they were able to pass the motion without him present," Ollie added. "Nice little cherry on top for you."

"Thank the Goddess." I looked up to the ceiling, willing the tears of relief to not roll down my cheeks. After everything I'd been through with Elliot, this one piece of news lifted something off my shoulders, my chest lighter.

It was like I could breathe again.

Tense silence fell, my gaze roaming over to my oldest brother, his face warring with too many emotions for me to decipher. "Caleb?"

"We're taught that saying I'm sorry is how you start earning forgiveness." He snorted again. "But nothing has sounded more pathetic after everything I've done."

"When trust is broken, words are not the way to fix it. Action is," I said, his glassy eyes looking back at me. I was happy to have him there. After everything I went through, his presence was oddly comforting, familiar. Still, I wasn't over everything that had happened. "You said plenty of promises and vows to me over the years and you chose to ruin them all when you refused to believe me."

"You're right." He looked between Ollie and me. "But at least it's a start. Kasha, I am so sorry for everything I did. From not believing you, to being complacent in what you've been forced to go through, to being all around cruel when I didn't know what else to say."

"Thank you." I squirmed. "Those words… they mean more to me than I expected them to." It was true. Something in my soul started to stir and settle properly.

"I'm sorry to you as well, Ollie." Caleb sighed. "I know those words mean nothing after what I've done. You and Kas have no reason to let me back in, to let me try to make right what I did."

"Caleb," Ollie whispered.

Caleb just kept going. "I should have been there. You stayed strong. You took on everything when Kas was hospitalized. You told her we were forcing her to stay there and visited her every week. You sat there and watched as she deteriorated and then fought her way back from the pits of darkness. You supported her when she needed strength. You did that all on your own and that wasn't how it should have been. It should have been both of us. I abandoned you almost as badly as I abandoned Kasha, and neither of you deserved that."

"We were a team, the three of us." Ollie's voice shook, the pain of the past year reflecting in his gaze.

Caleb was silent, his face pale and hardened, eyes flickering with emotions I rarely saw from him. This was a lot for all of us. A place we never expected to be when we were growing up. But there we were, and we needed to do what was best for all three of us.

He pulled in a deep breath, running his hands across his legs before looking back up at us. "Do you think I will ever be worthy of your forgiveness?"

There would always be a hurt, broken part of me living in the memories of the past year and Caleb's part in it. Those would forever be branded on my soul, and the dark part of me was tempted to turn my back on him and let him suffer in pain as he had done to me. But there was a kinder part of me, a loving part of me, that missed him and wanted him back, beckoning me to give him another chance.

Yet, I knew what I needed at that very moment.

"Kasha?" Ollie said, allowing me to take the lead on this.

"I want to forgive you." I had to be honest, my fingers winding at the ends of my braid. "And I am, slowly. I'm not completely there yet, but with all that you did for me, going after Logan like that, you're showing me with your actions that you want to earn my trust back. But still, I'll never be able to forget, so I can't promise that everything will go back to normal."

He nodded solemnly. "You're right. Things can't go back to the way they were a year ago."

My heart broke, my lip trembling. "No, they can't." A tear slipped down my cheek.

"But I wouldn't want them to." He tapped his fingers against his leg as if he was stopping himself from reaching out to me. "A year ago, I was our father's mindless soldier, but I refuse to be that anymore. It's time for us to rebuild our relationship, hopefully into something better."

My heart swelled at the words. It gave me that fleeting feeling of hope again for the first time in too many weeks.

Born by Blood, Bound by Loyalty.

We may not have been there completely yet, but we were closer, and that was enough for me for the moment.

"Thank you, biggest brother, for all that you did for me. For finding your way to the truth." I smiled at him weakly. "I can't wait to watch you become the man you were meant to be."

I was too weak still to lean over and hug him. Instead, I just lifted my hand and grabbed his, tightening our grips together and letting him know I was there. He smiled with misty tears in his eyes at the gesture.

I looked over to my other side. "Oliver?"

Oliver looked down at me with an assessing gaze before looking back at Caleb. "If Kasha is willing to try, then so am I."

Caleb sighed in relief. "Thank you, little brother and sister. I will do everything in my power not to let either of you down again."

Ollie chuckled. "I'm holding you to that."

Even with the relief of Caleb's words, my two brothers were still rigid in their seats. I looked between the two of them, both of them still frowning. "What aren't you telling me?"

"Kasha…" Ollie started.

My fingers fisted inward, my gut clenching. "Tell me. Now, please. I can't take any more secrets."

"All right, Little Shadow," Ollie soothed, running his hand up my bicep. "When we found you, Elliot had been in your room, and you were strapped to a chair."

"What?" My voice cracked around the single word. Vague memories tried to pull through the fog. The ghost of being tied down and a buzzing surrounding me, and Elliot's soothing, vile words.

"We think Elliot experimented on you, Kas," Caleb whispered, the pain in his voice straining against each word.

I bit my lip, my teeth threatening to pull blood from the pressure. I shouldn't have been surprised after what I saw in his labs and the bits of memories I had from my final days in Follanoch, but it didn't stop my stomach from threatening to burst.

"He branded you. With a tattoo on your arm." Ollie's fingers ghosted over a bandage that was firmly wrapped around my forearm, just below my elbow. "We don't know what it is, but it doesn't look… um… normal."

Normal? What did that mean?

"I want to see it." I croaked, tears already threatening to escape, my right hand moving over to try and rip the bandage from my left arm.

"Kasha," Ollie said in warning, his fingers catching my hand before I could pull the cloth off me.

I whipped my head over to look at him. "It's my body and I have a right to see what he did to me!"

His gaze flicked over my head, probably looking at Caleb as they silently communicated. I snarled again, and Ollie's shoulders sagged, a resigned look spreading across his weary face as he released my hand. I pulled away the rest of the bandage, a scream erupting from my lips as I saw the newest design added to my body.

A crest, but not Elliot's or the Onyx Guard. A serpent was twisted around a full moon, its long body circled around the orb and then up the center so the head rested at the top. It was surrounded by a circle of thorn-covered vines, the arching words of Elliot's motto scrawled above it.

My fingers traced it, the redness of the fresh ink still swollen a bit around the edges of the design. I saw what Ollie meant by not normal. The ink took on a reddish, rusty hue instead of the typical inky black that was used by certified artists. What had Elliot put on me? What had he done to me?

I screamed again, not caring that my wails could probably be heard throughout the entire ward. I screamed out all my pain and all of my hurt and everything I had been put through over the past month. I scratched at my arm as if my jagged nails could claw the disgusting tattoo off me. The hard grip of someone separating my arms and holding me close seeped against me, my body hugged protectively between my two big brothers. I sagged into them, too weak and tired to fight against it.

But the crying and the screaming didn't stop. It couldn't.

Elliot may have been arrested, but I would forever be reminded by this brand that, for a time, I had been at his mercy.

CHAPTER 61

Kasha

For three weeks, they kept me in a bed.

They had transferred me back to Seathra after another five days in the clinic once I was stabilized enough to make the journey. I had been forced to lie down in the back of a horse-pulled carriage, Beckett and Nolan never leaving my sides. Once we had arrived back at the Compound, I was swiftly carried up to Nolan's bedroom and tucked in, and monitored until Beckett finally gave the go-ahead that I could start moving and working with the post-arrest dealings. Of course, I was only allowed to do desk work. He had threatened to banish me back to bed if he saw me anywhere near the training building.

I had been begging everyone who came to visit to tell me something, but no one would talk. A pact that they had all taken, said it was best for me to rest, heal, and then as a team, they would catch me up.

It was how I found myself back in the same conference room I knew so well, Nolan close by my side as the rest of my Hierarchy, my brothers, and my father crowded into the room. Not to mention the conference Comm projected on the wall, the rest of the High Faction looking around at us.

Mitchell leaned forward, grabbing everyone's attention. "Well, first we wanted to give all of you a big congratulations…"

"Don't," I bite out, Nolan's hand tightening on my shoulder.

"Excuse me?" Mitchell blinked a few times.

"Let me guess, you wanted to congratulate us on being the Faction to capture Elliot?" I waited for Mitchell's nod of confirmation. "Well, we don't want it."

"Maybe the rest of your team does." Father leaned forward, seated a few chairs away from me. "They did work tirelessly to bring you home."

And what did you do, Father? was what I wanted to say, but I kept those venomous words contained. I didn't have the mental energy to get into that fight.

"We don't want it." Nolan glared at him, my body instinctively leaning into his hold.

"How surprising that you would take your paramour's side."

"None of us want it," Beckett bit from behind me. "Can we move on?"

"Well, I speak for the Varg Anwyn's now." Father kept his voice smooth, but the harsh lines forming on his forehead let me know he was on the brink of losing it. "And I say you deserve the credit."

"You're the new High Tribune of the branch?" I glared at him. My insides swirled; so many conflicting emotions. I had been held hostage, and he had been promoted. Yeah, sounded about right when it came to my father.

He glared right back. "Interim until an official vote can be taken. Your safe return was the top priority."

"Glad to see you used my capture to your benefit, Father."

Silence fell around the room, although, when I glanced at my brothers, I couldn't help but notice them both struggling to hide the smirks desperate to grace their lips. Seemed I wasn't the only one to notice.

Father had refused to leave Luspan and return to the Château until I was better. On the surface, he seemed like the good, concerned parent he needed to be. But I knew the truth, and so did my brothers, since they had kept him far away from me the entire time I was recovering. This was the first time I'd seen him. He was there out of duty, not love or concern. He was there because his daughter was caught in the storm that was the biggest case bust in Kazola history. He couldn't risk being seen in a poor light, especially when he was most likely vying to keep that High Tribune seat.

How utterly predictable of him.

I was done letting him in when he hadn't earned it. It didn't matter that he was my father or that he had raised me. He had proven too many times in my adult life that he wasn't worth it.

So, I just continued to glare at him, my words stunning him into silence. *Good, let him see that I'm no longer willing to earn his love.* It was time for him to earn mine.

"Next steps." I turned back to the screen, focusing on the rest of the High Faction.

"We have begun discussing how his trial will go about." Imogene shuffled some papers in front of her. "He is being held in our highest security facility here in the capitol, but it will take time to pull all the ones we wish to prosecute him on."

"This is a precarious position we are in." I looked at all of them. "Do you not realize that if handled incorrectly, you could make a martyr out of this man."

Imogene cleared her throat. "We are aware…"

"Even worse, he told me that he still plans to reclaim Kazola." I shook my head, my insides quivering. I placed my hand on Nolan's leg, gripping it tightly for strength and grounding. "He whispered those words to me right before being taken by all of you. This could all be a part of his plan."

"What can he do from inside a jail cell?" Jasmine asked. "We have all of his highest-ranking officials as well."

"That you know of," I scoffed. "James and Arielle were only the beginning…"

"Arielle?" Violet said, flicking through a stack of papers in front of her. "We don't have anyone by that name in captivity."

My stomach sank. I barely remembered anything from those final days, but she had been in the room when my Faction had arrived to save me. Unfortunately, I couldn't seem to remember anything that was said between her, Elliot, and James. How had she gotten away?

Even worse, she probably had orders from Elliot to follow through on, and she also had a personal vendetta for the unwanted attention he liked to give to me. Seemed like I had more than one enemy now on the run.

The more the merrier, I suppose.

"Further solidifying my point," I continued. "He had people

all over this country. He couldn't be there, so he set up his own government in each territory. You may have caught the leader, but his generals are still out there, waiting for their dictator to give them the signal to strike."

"You're safe from him now, Beta," Mitchell tried to soothe me.

"Don't patronize me," I spat. "Do not treat me as delicate because of what I went through. I spent all my time there trying to gather as much intel as possible. I saw things, learned things. Use them."

"We're just beginning our discovery in the town…"

"She has a firsthand account." Nolan cut Mitchell off, shaking his head. "She experienced and saw things. Her eyewitness account will give you a better idea of where to focus and also how to make sure you handle this correctly. Listen to her."

I had started to open up to Nolan about everything I saw. Not all of it and only when I had woken up from a nightmare. I didn't keep it in. I let him hold me and rock me through the pain until I was ready to talk. It was very different from the last time I had felt so exposed and vulnerable, but it was the right thing to do. If I had learned anything over the past year, it was that I wasn't alone. I was supported and loved, and that was the greatest weapon I had to fight the battles my mind tried to war on me.

It was my fight, it was my war, but I was not alone. Never again.

"This seems highly inappropriate." Father once again spoke up. Why did he keep blocking this? "She needs…"

"Maybe listen to the woman who was under his thumb for the past month!" Taylor seethed. The control in the room was precarious. By the stunned, tense faces of the High Faction, they all knew it too.

Lucas stood tall next to his twin. "Listening to what she says is best because if anyone knows, it's her."

Silence kept creeping in until Kyler said, "She is correct. We need to listen to her."

"We should send out some Delegates to interview her," Evette suggested.

"My daughter needs rest," Father countered.

"Your daughter can speak for herself," I told him. "Evette is right."

"Then we will send people out as soon as possible." Evette nodded. Although it was through video and could have been to the general room, I knew it was directed right to me, a sign of respect.

"You'll need to send a list of who plans to come so we can approve it," Nolan said. I hid my smile at his demand.

"That's not how this works, Alpha." Imogene frowned. "We will send who we think is best."

"If you don't send that list, you might just find that our gate guards don't let you in." Eden smirked at all of them, her hair no longer a bright red but a dulled pink. She must not have dyed it for the past month.

"Are you threatening us?"

"Of course not." Eden shrugged, although a smirk played on her lips.

"She's just speaking the truth," Greyson said.

My father looked ready to implode and most of the High Faction wasn't far behind. However, Kyler spoke up once again.

"We will get that list over as soon as possible. Now, we need to discuss how we plan to relocate the residents of…"

I tuned them out, leaning my head on Nolan's shoulder and trying to block out the talks about the horrible town I had been in for the past month. I didn't need to hear it. Instead, I let a bit of warmth crawl back into my chest at the strong, united words my team had just spoken for me, supporting me as always.

They had tried to keep control of us all those months ago when we were willing to speak up about Logan. Maybe we were a bit insubordinate, but only when it was necessary to follow through on the oath we took.

We would protect Kazola, even if it meant protecting them from its own government.

I didn't want to admit that Elliot had valid points, but sometimes, he did. He was dangerous and vicious; he was not the leader that Kazola needed. He would bring us to ruin. I knew that with my entire heart and soul. However, he had amassed a following for a reason; because people were unhappy. They felt let down or turned away from the High Faction.

Change was needed, but we could only complete it once the threat of Elliot was behind us. Then, and only then, could we become the country the God and Goddess meant for us to be.

I only hoped that I would be there when it happened. Although I was back home, I had the itching feeling that I was still far from safe.

CHAPTER 62

Kasha

We kept going in circles until I faked being tired and made everyone break for a bit. I wasn't in the mood to listen to the High Faction over and over again or feel my father's stare on me any longer. I didn't care what they had to say.

At that moment, I cared about seeing one more person before going back and hiding in Nolan's house.

With the overflow of some of Elliot's followers taking up our cells, ones that had been caught around Seathra during the investigation to find me, the team had decided to put Vanessa under house arrest in the other spare townhouse. I nodded to the Dairchta guards sitting outside and the few that loitered around the downstairs before walking upstairs. I knocked on the only bedroom door, a whispering voice letting me know I could come in.

"Hi, Vanessa." I walked in, crossing the small bedroom to stand at the foot of the bed.

Like she always had in the cell, she was sitting on it, although this one was much softer and decorated with a simple blue quilt. I looked her over, and already I could tell she had taken advantage of the shower, her raven hair a bit glossier and less greasy. She was wrapped in a simple gray blouse and a pair of linen pants, probably borrowed by someone in the Faction who was around her size. Color had returned to her cheeks and her eyes didn't seem as empty or full of resigned fear.

"It's good to see you, Kasha." She laid a book in her lap gently to save the page she had been reading.

"I'm assuming they told you that, with my return, Elliot has been arrested as well."

She nodded. "I'm so sorry for what happened. How are you?"

"What did they tell you?" I pulled a chair from the small desk and turned it to face Vanessa, settling in, my muscles still weak and shaky.

"Just that you had been held hostage by them for the past month and when they finally tracked you down, they were able to arrest Elliot and a good portion of his main followers." She looked me over. "I'm assuming there was a lot more that happened in between."

I scoffed. "Plenty, but that's not why I'm here to talk to you."

Her eyebrow raised. "Oh?"

"I met James." I leaned back in the chair, wrapping my arms around myself.

Vanessa's chin dropped to her chest, ragged breaths stuttering from her lips. "I don't…"

"You don't have to see him." I shook my head. "I didn't come here to convince you to see him or talk to him."

"Then why?"

"I didn't feel right about having met him and you not knowing," I whispered, my foot tapping against the floor. I was already sick of the reappearance of those stupid ticks. I thought I had been doing better, but Elliot just had to blow that all apart.

I needed a new psycho-physician. Even if I could forgive Vanessa for her place in the torture that had been the past few months, she was too wrapped up in Elliot and his following. I needed someone outside of it.

The only thing that gave me a light of hope flickering in my chest was my realization of this need. That I knew right away that I wanted help. For my own mental health, I would willingly go back to counseling and help myself get better and cope.

That alone showed me how much I had grown, despite everyone trying to keep me down.

I held onto that spark as I looked back up at Vanessa, her gaze wandering to peek outside the window above the bed.

"Thank you," she whispered, her body slumping against the wall behind her.

"He talked about you as well." I didn't feel right keeping anything from her. So much of her life those past years had been looking over her shoulder every day, fearful that someone would track her down. So, I told her everything. How James had been my guard. About our fight and what he admitted. How he still considered her his wife, even though something had sent her running. Something she had seen.

"What did you see that made you run?" I had to ask. I had to know if it was similar to what I had seen in the lab.

"Elliot was crossing lines." She looked over at me, a weak smile appearing on her lips. "He was experimenting on people. He lets only a certain number of the clean drug addicts back out in Kazola to help spread the message or do his bidding. But the rest are manipulated into staying at the lab. To let him experiment and do things to them."

More memories, more flashes. Screams, burn marks, unnecessary surgeries, smiling people saying it was for the greater good.

"I saw them too." I shook my head. "It'll haunt me for the rest of my life."

"He doesn't care about life, only about glory. He's a genius; that is obvious to everyone who meets him. Mixed with his charm and ability to manipulate, it was easy to convince the recovered addicts that they owed him something or that they could use their newfound sobriety to help Kazola and others who were like them. He preyed on their guilt."

A shiver ran up my spine. Those halls had been disgusting. I wondered how many of the past victims had also been experiments gone wrong. Or how many of them had been test subjects for whatever Elliot had done to me and the tattoo he marked me with.

It was a horror I never wanted to experience, but now I had to live with it.

"It's one thing to say you want to help people." Vanessa leaned forward. "But hurting one group of people for the sake of others isn't the way to go about it. It was when I realized Elliot didn't care about helping Kazola. He only cared about proving to the world that they had made a mistake removing his Alchemy license. About getting vengeance against those who said he was dangerous."

"They were right." I shook my head. "And they still aren't taking it seriously."

"Are you worried?"

"It was too easy." I twisted my fingers together. "I'm not sure if it's the trauma or I just know him too well now, but this doesn't feel over."

"Listen to your gut," she said. "The only way this will end is when Elliot is exposed to his army. When they see the truth. Until that day, the unrest won't settle."

"I agree." I nodded. "I understand why you left."

"I hated doing it without James." Her cheek ticked, her fingers going up to rub at her chest. "He was a good man, the most amazing husband I could have ever had. Up until the day I left, he was devoted, honest, and loving. He never hurt me."

"You didn't leave because of him."

"But he wouldn't go with me." A single tear rolled down her blushing cheek. "I knew I had lost him to Elliot, and I had to make a choice. I chose myself and I don't regret it."

"I would have done the same." My heart ached as I admitted it.

If Nolan had insisted on staying like James had, I probably would have left still. It would have broken my heart and made me a shell of a person, but I wouldn't have been able to stay in good conscience.

"He saved my life." I bit my bottom lip, my fingers tracing the horrible tattoo that peeked out from the rolled-up sleeves of my sweater. "I don't know if I would have survived Elliot's experiment if it hadn't been for James."

I looked up, Vanessa's eyes wide and glassy with tears. "But how?"

"He gave me blood, fed me when Elliot had ordered everyone to let me starve unless I fed from him." My stomach revolted, flashes of the needling pain and tight restraints trying to pull me back to only a few days ago. But I pushed through. "He went against Elliot's orders because he knew how close I was to dying."

"Ibridowyns can't die."

"No Ibridowyn has gone through what I have." I shook my head. "I felt on the brink. My heart could have kept beating, but that doesn't constitute living. Those few pulls of blood he let me take from him cut the edge and gave me back my sanity and enough strength to make it through the experiment. He saved me."

Tears finally rolled down her face, her hand flying up to cover the whimper escaping from her lips. "Are you sure?"

"He might not be as lost as you think."

I didn't move any closer as the tears and Vanessa's wailing increased. I didn't know how to console her or give her advice. But she deserved the truth. The part I knew anyways.

And maybe, one day, James would be able to give her the rest of the truth to settle her soul like she deserved.

CHAPTER 63

Nolan

I waited in my living room for Kasha to return, the events of the past two months slamming into me for one final, overwhelming moment. When she was back in my arms, I hadn't cared about anything except helping her get better. But now, after that talk with the High Faction, I realized how close I had been to losing her, to having another love slip away.

The thoughts were too dizzying, too heartbreaking and soul-crushing to completely absorb.

Kasha finally came through the door, walking in as if this was her home, just another normal day returning from work. She had been good the past weeks, allowing us to take care of her with minimal complaint, even if I did see the defiance sparkling in her gaze most of the time. She was no longer classified as starving, color and shape returning to her face, although she still looked tired and moved a bit lethargically. The sweater she had wrapped around her was one of mine, a spark blooming in my chest knowing that my clothes brought her comfort. She could take my whole closet if she wanted just to imprint her scent within them for me to enjoy.

She smiled at me when she spotted me on the couch, her eyes lighting up brightly. "Hi."

It was reminiscent of when she came by and told me she wanted to give us a chance. To give me a chance. It had been such a happy, blissful memory, even when we knew chaos was brewing on the horizon.

A lifetime had gone by since then.

"How are you?" I pushed a glass of water over to her, full and topped with plenty of ice. She gulped half of it down before settling onto the couch next to me.

"I'm… all right. It was good to see her." She relaxed into the cushions, a bit of tension releasing from her muscles.

"We need to decide what to do with her." I slung my arm over the back of the couch, her body instinctively moving closer to my side. I didn't like having any distance between us. Having my hands on her, even in mundane ways, reminded me that she was next to me, not lost anymore.

"I know." She nodded, looking down at her hands.

I knew she was struggling to decide what to do with Vanessa for far longer than she was probably willing to admit. With everything going on, the idea of turning her over to the High Faction seemed wrong to Kasha, even if Vanessa technically had committed treason. Vanessa had helped Kasha a lot, but the High Faction wouldn't care about that. With an impending war, we all knew they would use her as a public example of what would happen if someone tried to betray them.

And although she had been caught in Elliot's snares, she had escaped and tried to help others to make up for it. It was a hard decision to make, even though we all knew where the path would ultimately end for Vanessa.

"I'll get an answer to everyone tomorrow on it," she said, a weak smile forced on her lips.

"Take your time," I whispered, my gaze settling on her, my mind swirling as terrible, dark thoughts started to take over.

You almost lost her. You almost failed her.

You are unworthy of her.

Kasha tilted her head, curling her legs beneath her. "What?"

There was a kind curiosity in her gaze, looking at me like I was the center of her world. And that was all it took for me to fall to my knees in front of her, my eyes brimming with the tears I had been keeping inside for far too long.

"Nolan…" she whispered, leaning forward and reaching out to gently brush her thumb against my flushed cheek. The light, loving touch broke the sobs to wrack through me fully. I collapsed against her, wrapping my arms around her waist, face buried against her belly as I kneeled between her legs.

I held on for dear life, letting all the hurt, pain, and sadness bleed from me. I had been holding it back for far too long, letting it build within me and not letting anyone in. I couldn't. I had been too determined to find her to let my grief and hurt out. I was too scared it would slow me down and keep me from finding her.

"I thought I had lost you, Kasha," I said between chest-heaving sobs. "I thought I would never see you again."

"But I'm back. I'm here." She stroked her fingers through my hair, reminding me I wasn't alone. "You saved me, just as you swore you would."

"I never want to let you go again."

She leaned down, peppering kisses on the top of my head. "I know."

"Promise me," I mumbled into her shirt. "Promise me you'll never leave me."

"Nolan…"

It was unfair in a way to make her promise this. With our job and the life we had sworn ourselves into, it was a promise that would be almost impossible to keep. But I had to ask because I wasn't sure I could leave the house without saying them. My strength was becoming so entangled in her, and my trauma was blooming again. Only this time, I had a second chance to keep her safe, to protect her like I had failed to do too many times already.

"We are a team, Kasha." I finally looked up, so much concern and love reflecting in her beautiful blue eyes. "Please, don't ever put your life in that type of danger again, not without me at least. You don't have to shoulder the burden alone. I want to help."

If I expected her to lean on me, then I had to do the same. We were partners, equals, and I could trust very few people with this side of myself.

But Kasha… she was the one I trusted above all else.

"I promise," she said, pulling me up to kneel tall, so we were face to face, "that I will always try my best in the future to include you. To make sure we're in this together. Even if that means we walk through the fire hand in hand."

"Thank you." I let out a deep breath, my face relaxing.

"Thank you for never giving up on me." She smiled.

"I don't deserve you." I moved my hand to the back of her neck, gripping it tightly to press our foreheads together.

She giggled, that lovely smile of hers blooming on her plush lips. "Funny, I'm always thinking the same of you."

I closed the distance between us, crushing my lips against hers and pouring all of my love into her, showing her just how much I needed her.

I would probably always have a bit of self-doubt in the back of my mind that what we had, I would never earn. But that wasn't how love worked. It wasn't how relationships worked.

We would always have to fight the darkness that had been drilled into us over the years, and we would have to fight new battles that would plague us after what we had just gone through. It was inevitable, but this time, I was not as fearful. I wasn't as beaten down.

We may have been forced together in the beginning, but through it all, we had found our true place in each other's lives.

Together, not apart.

CHAPTER 64

Kasha

"*K asha…*"

The voice whispered in the deepest parts of my mind, poking and probing from places I didn't know existed.

I stirred in bed, drifting in the in-between of sleep and awake, Nolan's grip on me still tight around my waist. Was this voice just my dream?

"Kasha… I know you're there…"

I groaned, rolling away to sit up, rubbing my eyes. I focused within, trying to see if anyone was close by or awake, but all seemed settled on the Compound. I let out a tired yawn, already sick of the nightmares that were going to start taking advantage of my sleeping hours. Still one of the worst parts of this whole healing thing. I threw myself back on the bed, rolling to cuddle into Nolan's warm back, ready to drift off into sleep once again,

"It's me, Rogthna."

That name. That voice.

I screamed without thinking, pushing out the blood-curdling

fear that coursed through my veins, my body skittering away from the bed and into the closest corner.

No, this couldn't be true. It couldn't be him.

"Oh, but it is." I could hear the smirk in his voice even within my mind. I was awake, I was sure of it now. This was really happening. Elliot had really breached my mind.

"Kasha?" Nolan's groggy voice came from the bed, his feet slapping against the floor to cross over and crouch in front of my cowering form.

"No! Stay back!" I put my hands up, and I swear I heard Elliot's melodically cruel laughter singing in my mind.

I focused within, trying to build the strong foundation that kept others from barging into my mind. But when I went to test its power, all seemed normal and closed off from the outside. No one should be able to get into my mind without my permission, not even Nolan, and yet…

"You can't keep me out any longer, lovely. I'm yours now." He laughed, and the grating noise was full of too many promises I wanted to shred and throw back at him. No matter how hard I tried, he was still there, echoing in my mind, forcing me to cower away.

I gripped my still-healing forearm. The tattoo… it had to be a part of this.

But how?

"We will be together again soon and all will be explained, I promise." He blew me a kiss before disappearing, releasing me from the chilling hold.

What did this mean? What was going on? What had he done

to me?

Too many questions, too many voices, too much painful fear coursed through me. So, I did the only thing that would make me feel better.

I screamed into the blackness that my life was about to descend into once again.

End of Book Two

Kasha and Nolan's story continues in...

TETHERED BY FATE

Coming Summer 2024

Acknowledgements

First off, I must thank you and all of the readers who just took the time to read the second part of Kasha and Nolan's story. Were you surprised and excited to see Nolan starting to throw his two cents in? Trust me, so was I! I hope you enjoyed every moment of the book and the characters journeys. I cannot wait to continue on in the final book!

To my family and friends, who stand by me during the crazy times and listen to me rant about my bookish habits. My husband, Nathaniel, my sister, Dr. Liz, my parents, Ellen and Mark, and my besties Meaghan, Chelsea, and Alyson. You all bring a special light to my life every day and your encouragement to follow these dreams of mine will be something I forever cherish.

To my amazing writer friends Brianne, Leah, and Renee. This book would not be the same without you. Thank you for reading my books when I needed advice, hyping me up when I needed motivation, and letting me bounce dozens of ideas off of you as I figured out exactly how Kasha and Nolan's journey was supposed to go. I could not do it without you all!

To my incredible editors, Cassidy and Karen. It is because of both of you that I discovered new sides of myself as a writer. You challenged me and pushed me to be better, and I will forever be grateful for all of your hard work and collaboration on these books. Can't wait for you to see what I have planned for you next. And of course, a huge shoutout to my Beta reader team who helped me complete that final developmental polish. I hope you all loved the final product!

To my cover artist, Jupiter. Your artwork is impeccable and working with you and watching you create such perfect covers for this series has been one of the highlights of publishing these books. Thank you and can't wait to start showing off book three's cover!

To all of you, thank you for making this adventure of mine a bit extra special. Until next time, happy reading!

About the Author

Kathryn Marie is the indie author of the fantasy series, the Kazola Chronicles and the Midnight Duology. She began writing at the young age of thirteen, when she was stuck in bed recovering from spinal surgery. Ever since then, she's loved creating stories and characters for others to enjoy. When she is not at work or busy writing in her home office, Kathryn can be found spending time with her wonderful husband or friends, experimenting with new makeup techniques, or watching reruns of her many beloved TV shows.

Follow Kathryn on social media for updates!

<u>**Website Newsletter:**</u> www.authorkathrynmarie.com
<u>**Instagram:**</u> @author_kathrynmarie
<u>**TikTok:**</u> @author_kathrynmarie
<u>**Facebook:**</u> @authorkathrynmarie

www.ingramcontent.com/pod-product-compliance
Lightning Source LLC
Chambersburg PA
CBHW050842210726
48290CB00004B/1046